Check o___
or to renew
www.birming
www.birmin___

 Birm___

Erin Kaye was born in 1966 in Larne, Co. Antrim, to a Polish American father and an Anglo-Irish mother. She pursued a successful career in finance before giving it all up nine years ago to write. Her previous bestselling novels include *Mothers and Daughters, Choices* and *Second Chances*. She lives in North Berwick on the east coast of Scotland with her husband Mervyn and happily combines writing with raising their two young sons.

CLOSER TO HOME

Kath left Northern Ireland for Boston and established a new life there, with a highly successful career, a condo, and a lovely relationship. Yet her world, and her heart, are suddenly shattered: her man Carl turns out to be married, and then she hears her father has died . . . Kath returns to Ireland and throws herself into restoring her family's fortunes. But then Carl turns up and Kath faces a dilemma — he's left his wife, and has come to try and win her back . . .

Books by Erin Kaye
Published by The House of Ulverscroft:

MOTHERS AND DAUGHTERS
CHOICES
SECOND CHANCES

ERIN KAYE

CLOSER TO HOME

Complete and Unabridged

CHARNWOOD
Leicester

First published in Ireland in 2006

First Charnwood Edition
published 2007

The moral right of the author has been asserted

This novel is entirely a work of fiction.
The names, characters and incidents portrayed in it
are the work of the author's imagination.
Any resemblance to actual persons, living or dead,
events or localities is entirely coincidental.

British Library CIP Data

Kaye, Erin, *1966 –*
   Closer to home.—Large print ed.
   Charnwood library series
   1. Love stories 2. Large type books
   I. Title
   823.9'2 [F]

ISBN 978–1–84617–653–1

Published by
F. A. Thorpe (Publishing)
Anstey, Leicestershire

Set by Words & Graphics Ltd.
Anstey, Leicestershire
Printed and bound in Great Britain by
T. J. International Ltd., Padstow, Cornwall

This book is printed on acid-free paper

For my youngest son,
Liam

1

'I've decided. I'm going to do it.'

Kath O'Connor paused, wondering why the words she wanted to say did not come easily. She stared out the window of the coffee shop while she summoned the courage to formulate the sentence she had thought about so often but never vocalised. Outside, on Boston's chic Newbury Street, the rush-hour traffic crawled by like a caterpillar, its progress hampered and muffled by the falling snow. Already a thick layer carpeted the sidewalk and the road. The dark grey clouds, swollen with snow, had brought with them a premature nightfall.

'Emmy,' she said at last, 'I'm going to ask Carl to marry me.' The fingers on her right hand trembled. Quickly, she replaced the glass teacup on the saucer. The camomile tea glowed amber, like melted butter, in the yellow lights of the coffee shop.

'Oh! I see,' said her best friend, sounding surprised. Then Emmy put her elbows on the table and rested her head on her hands. She regarded Kath thoughtfully from under black arched brows, her wide-open green eyes outlined in soft grey eye pencil. Her cheeks were rosy from the cold, like the bright-cheeked baby Kath had spied that very morning being carried into the nursery at the end of her street. 'Well,' she said finally, 'that is a surprise.'

'You don't think I should, do you?' said Kath and she looked at her hands, folded together on the table. The huge diamond-and-emerald-encrusted band that Carl had given her for Christmas sparkled on the ring finger of her right hand like ice — a painful reminder of the engagement ring she had hoped for but not received.

'No, no, it's not that at all,' said Emmy, concern clouding her pretty face, and she gave her head a little shake.

'What is it, then? Because I sense that you don't think this is a good idea.'

'I just wasn't expecting it, that's all. One minute you're dating the guy, the next you're talking about proposing to him! It just seems like a big leap to me.' She smiled then and went on with more enthusiasm, 'But, seriously, if it's what you want . . . well, then, go for it!'

'Right,' said Kath but Emmy's half-hearted reassurance was not the reaction she'd hoped for. She watched a snowflake splatter on the window, cling for a few seconds, then slither down the glass until it melted into a miniscule rivulet. Her Celtic-pale face, reflected in the glass, was tired-looking, the freckles faded by a winter spent mostly indoors and her red-brown hair darkened by lack of sunlight. She sighed inwardly. What she needed right now was full-hearted support from Emmy, not reservations.

'I know you've never liked Carl — ' she began, trying not to sound piqued.

'No,' said Emmy, interrupting quickly, 'that's

not true. It's just I . . . it's taking a while to get to know him properly. I hardly ever see him because he's away most weekends when I usually see you. I would like to get to know him better, Kath, I really would. I'd like us to be proper friends.'

There was a lull in the conversation during which Kath reflected that she was being over-sensitive. It must be nerves.

Then Emmy said tentatively, 'About Carl . . .'

'Yes?'

'I didn't think you had talked to him about marriage — even in the most general terms . . .'

'Well, no, I haven't — this is why I'm thinking of asking him. I told you before — every time I try to steer the conversation towards it, something happens. The moment never seems right somehow.'

'I see,' said Emmy slowly. 'And have you considered that maybe he's not ready for it, Kath? You've been seeing him for what? Just over a year.'

'Nearly a year and a half,' said Kath defensively.

'Well, whatever. It's not a long time as relationships go.'

'Are you trying to stop me from doing this?'

'No, not at all. I just want you to go cautiously. I don't want to see you get hurt.'

'Emmy,' said Kath, suppressing the irritation that welled up unexpectedly, '*I'm* ready for it. If I wait any longer it'll be too late.'

'Too late for what?' said Emmy, turning her palms upwards to indicate her incomprehension.

3

'You could always move in together like me and Steve. Marriage is only two signatures on a bit of paper. It doesn't *mean* anything.'

'It does to me,' retorted Kath quickly and then she added, her voice softening as she addressed the drinks card in the middle of the table, 'It's not just about marriage, Emmy. I'm going to be forty this year. And you know I want to have children.'

'Ah, I see!' Emmy leaned back in her chair. 'And you're sure that Carl's the man you want to have them with?'

'Of course — I love him,' said Kath, meeting Emmy's gaze, 'and he loves me. I want us to live together, to be a family.'

'Well, in that case, I guess you should ask him,' said Emmy, nodding her head sagely. Then she added, more light-heartedly, 'Hey, don't look so worried!'

'But what if he says no?'

'He won't.'

'How can you be sure?' asked Kath, feeling a little confused. A minute ago Emmy had been worrying about her getting hurt.

'Because he'd be absolutely stark raving mad to say no, that's why! Look at you! You've got the skin of a twenty-year-old, gorgeous chestnut hair without a hint of grey — unlike me,' she said ruefully as she pulled taut a lock of her shoulder-length, unnatural Cher-black hair while her eyes strained to examine it. 'And, you've got the figure of a model. Not to mention a well-paid job as a management consultant. Who wouldn't want you as their wife?'

4

Kath smiled then, aware that her friend was trying to boost her confidence. 'You know, you're a real honey. The very best friend.'

Emmy grinned and said, 'I know. What would you do without me?' Then she glanced at her watch and added, 'God, would you look at the time! Steve'll be wondering where I am.' She peered out the window. 'I suppose I'm going to have to face the Arctic out there sometime.'

'Sometimes this weather gets you down, doesn't it?'

'Oh, the snow can be a pain all right — but it's magical too, isn't it? When did we ever get a white Christmas in Ireland? I think that's one of the best bits about living in Boston. A white Christmas. Most years anyway.'

Emmy slipped into the knitted black cardigan she had draped on the back of her chair and twisted a long, thin red scarf round her neck three times, before tying it in a secure knot under her chin.

'There was one in Ballyfergus when I was a child,' said Kath, remembering fondly. 'The trees in the garden were laden with snow and Dad could hardly get the car out of the drive.'

She watched while Emmy pulled a long, tangerine-coloured, padded duvet of a coat over her neat frame.

'May I ask you something, Emmy?'

'Go ahead.'

'Doesn't it bother you *at all* that you're getting older, and Steve and you aren't making plans to have children?'

Emmy paused and screwed up her face so that

5

her eyebrows nearly met in the middle. It was some moments before she answered.

'To tell you the God's honest truth, I just don't think about it. I'm too busy doing other things, I suppose. And you know, I can't see myself changing smelly nappies and cleaning up sick all day!'

Kath laughed. 'I'm sure it's not like that all the time!'

'Well, rather you than me. Now, when are you planning on asking Carl?'

'Tonight. We're going out to Piattini's — that new Italian on Columbus Avenue.'

'OK,' said Emmy, doing up the last button on her coat. She leaned over, kissed Kath on the cheek and hugged her. 'Good luck. Now phone me first thing in the morning with the good news.'

Outside, Emmy waved goodbye, her mittened hand like a paw in the dim light. With the hood of the coat pulled over her head she looked like an over-sized version of one of the orange traffic cones that accompanied the progress of the 'Big Dig' through the city. Conceived on a phenomenal scale to combat Boston's horrendous traffic problems, it was the biggest construction project ever undertaken in the United States. Kath, like the other city residents, had often bemoaned the impact of the works on her life. But now it was nearing completion and everyone was both relieved and proud of their rejuvenated city. The exuberant civic pride and general optimism of Bostonians was one of the reasons Kath loved it here.

That and her friends and, of course, Carl. She gathered her things together, paid the cheque and headed for the subway station. The snow was falling steadily and she worried briefly if the bad weather would scupper her plans for tonight. After finally working herself up to ask him the 'big question' that would be a complete anti-climax.

Remembering that she wanted to have a full pamper session before going out, Kath quickened her pace to the station, swiped her travel pass in the turnstile and descended on the escalator. During the journey she changed subway lines, swept along at a brisk pace by the flow of commuter traffic, like a leaf carried on the surface of a fast-flowing river.

She thought about the conversation she'd had with Emmy and how, though they came from very different parts of Ireland — Emmy was from Waterford while Kath came from Northern Ireland — they both referred to it as 'home'. Kath was happy with her life in Boston but home for her would always be Highfield House, where she'd grown up and where her mother and father still lived. Was that a peculiarly Irish phenomenon, she wondered, or did all emigrants feel the same?

But she was sure that she would feel differently about living here when she had children and was more fully integrated into a suburban community, where she imagined she and Carl would make their home together. Moving to Ireland, she assumed, was completely out of the question. Even if Kath wanted to, she guessed there was no way Carl would consider it. He thought that the USA was the best country in the world and, peculiarly, seemed to have no desire to see other parts of the planet.

Before she entered her own apartment in a well-maintained brownstone building, Kath knocked on the dark brown door across the hall. She glanced at her watch impatiently while she waited for Mrs Eberstark, a widow who lived alone, to open the door. Kath heard the telltale scraping sound as the little metal flap over the spy-hole was pulled back — she looked at the small glass orb and smiled — then the clink-clink of the safety chain being released and the sound of the lock sliding back.

'Kath, it is you,' said Mrs Eberstark, in her thickly German-accented voice, as she pulled back the creaking door. 'Come in, come in!' She gestured with her right hand for Kath to enter the apartment. Her gnarled left hand gripped the marble head of an elaborately carved ebony walking-stick without which she would have fallen over. Her white hair was swept up elegantly into a tight chignon, a hangover from her days as a ballet dancer. The latter part of her career, until her retirement nearly twenty years ago, had been spent in various administration roles with the Boston Ballet.

'Oh, I can't, Mrs Eberstark,' said Kath without moving. 'I'm going out tonight. But I just wanted to check that you were OK.'

'Ah, you will be seeing Carl, I suppose?'

'Yes. Look, can I get you anything? Milk? Bread?' said Kath, anxious, in spite of her

8

concern for Mrs Eberstark, not to become involved in a lengthy conversation.

'He's a fine man, Kath,' said Mrs Eberstark. She had a soft spot for Carl on account of his Germanic ancestry.

'I know,' replied Kath, smiling in spite of herself.

'But when is he going to make you . . . what do you call it?' She mumbled to herself for some moments and then said with flair, 'A trustworthy woman!'

Kath smiled and supplied, 'I think you mean 'an honest woman'.'

'An honest woman, that's it!' said the old lady with a wicked grin and Kath blushed like a schoolgirl. 'When is he going to make you an honest woman?'

'Well, if you don't need anything . . . ' said Kath, choosing to ignore the question, and took a step backwards.

'I'm perfectly fine, Kath. My daughter called over today, on account of the snow,' said the old lady, a smile still playing round her lips. 'But thank you for your concern.'

'I'll pop over at some point over the weekend then,' said Kath.

'You're a good girl. Now go and have a lovely time with your beau!' she commanded.

Mrs Eberstark was an inspiration, thought Kath, as she let herself into her pristine apartment, checked the post, the answering machine and turned up the heating. Mrs Eberstark lived a lively and independent life in spite of her age and lack of mobility — the years of dancing at professional level had taken their toll on her body. And she was a good friend to Kath, a surrogate grandmother for the ones she'd left behind in Ireland and who were now dead.

Kath put a Norah Jones CD on and turned the volume up loud. Then she chose her clothes for the evening with care — fine wool trousers, black kitten-heeled leather boots and a crimson cashmere sweater — and laid them carefully on the quilted bedspread. She ran a hot, deep bath, poured in her most expensive bath oil, a present from Carl, and poured herself a glass of Vouvray, her favourite, white wine. After replacing the bottle in the fridge, she changed her mind, retrieved it and carried it into the bathroom where she set it, along with the glass, on the corner of the white bath.

She eased herself gratefully into the fragrant, rehabilitating water, her knees emerging wet and glistening above the surface like two small islands.

Kath tried to imagine sharing her home with Carl. She'd become used to living on her own. It would be strange lying in the bath like this, knowing that Carl was pottering around outside the bathroom door. Strange but nice.

She knew very well why she was nervous about asking Carl to marry her. It wasn't that she doubted his answer, rather it was the very act of asking him that caused her disquiet. For Kath had been raised to believe that, when it came to men, a girl should retain an air of mystery and aloofness. Asking a man outright to marry you was brazen — it smacked of desperation. At least that's what her mother would have said. But, Kath reminded herself, her mother's views were moulded by the 1950s Ireland she'd grown up in. This was twenty-first century Boston and a very different place from the insular, backward-looking island her mother had known as a young woman. Nowadays women went after what they wanted as surely as men did. The nagging doubts that had held her in check until now, Kath reminded herself, were nothing more than antiquated notions from a different world and time. And she wasn't going to let her chance of happiness slip by because of them.

Emmy's less than enthusiastic support of her plan was harder to disregard. But it was only natural — she didn't want to see her dearest friend hurt. But Emmy didn't know Carl the way Kath did. She didn't know how much he adored her. She was the centre of his world, he said, and Kath knew it to be true. The only reason Carl hadn't asked her to marry him, she was certain, was that he had no biological clock ticking. He probably hadn't even thought about having children. Men simply weren't as preoccupied with these things as women.

Kath had drunk the first glass of wine more quickly than usual and now she poured herself another. She was going to need a little bit of Dutch courage. For tonight was going to be the most important night of her life.

★　★　★

11

'That's it for tonight, guys,' said Carl Scholtz, throwing his Montblanc pen onto the black-and-white architectural plans on the conference table, where it landed with a slap. 'I think we've done as much as we can on this for now.'

He leaned back in his chair and interlocked his fingers in his thick blond hair. He felt the shirt strain across his back and, glancing down, noticed a little fold of flesh protruding slightly over the belt that encircled his slim waist. Where the hell did that come from? Carl prided himself on keeping in shape — he'd have to increase his visits to the gym. Quickly he sucked his stomach in, unfolded his hands and sat up erect in the chair. The faces round the table were tired and Carl glanced at his watch. It was after six o'clock on a Friday evening.

'I know it's been a tough week for you all,' he said. 'When a client changes the brief this late in a project — well, it can be infuriating. But don't forget that they are always number one. The customer gets what they want no matter how many times we have to rework the plans. That's what the reputation of this firm is built on. That and innovative design. Do you agree?'

There were weary murmurs of assent round the table.

'Good. Now, team, I want you all to go home and have a great weekend and forget all about this. You'd be surprised how great your subconscious mind is at solving problems. You just need to give it the space and time to get on with the job.'

He stood up. Papers were stuffed into folders,

and chairs scraped the parquet floor as people stood up from the table.

'And one last thing,' said Carl.

All movement halted and a hush descended once more.

'You're doing a great job, every one of you. Thanks. I really appreciate it.'

With these few words of encouragement he could see the spirits of the dejected team rise. He wasn't part-owner of Boston's biggest and best architectural practice because of his technical skills. At this level it was all about motivating other talented people to do the work for you, something at which Carl excelled.

Some of these youngsters had proven themselves to be better architects than he. Carl was clever enough to recognise this and harness their talent to his advantage — and theirs. He could never be accused of exploiting anyone — few chose to leave the practice, because there was nowhere better to go. And those who felt they were ready to set up on their own, Carl encouraged and supported. They posed no threat to the predominant position of Scholtz & Vives Architects. The name was a misnomer really — at fifty-eight years old, Joe Vives was semi-retired to a beach-front in the Cape where he spent most of his time fishing. The firm was, in reality, entirely under the day-to-day control of Carl.

Back in his office, after everyone had gone, Carl swivelled round in his leather chair and stared at the city lights below and the gently curving black outline of the semi-frozen Charles

River. Though he could have stayed in the more affordable former office premises on Commonwealth, relocating to this office suite in the Prudential Tower had been a shrewd decision. It conveyed the impression that this firm was going places — a force to be reckoned with. And that confidence had been translated into impressive business results. Who would have thought that the forty-five-year-old son of a factory worker from Wisconsin would have made it this far?

Pulling himself together, Carl realised that he couldn't put off making the phone call any longer. He checked the time and frowned — he was supposed to be meeting Kath in less than two hours. Just enough time to do what he had to, get home, changed and out again. He picked up the handset, held it against his chest for some moments while he composed himself, then speed-dialled.

'Hi, it's me,' he said cheerfully into the phone. 'How are you? And the girls?'

He listened for a while and then said, 'Listen, honey, something's come up.' A pause, then he added, 'I know. I know. You think I like it? There's nothing I can do about it. We've got to get these plans right for Monday or we'll lose the job. I'll be working here till the small hours.' Another pause, then he said with feeling, 'Tell me about it, Lynda! But the buck stops with me and that's the way it is. Listen, I'll be down tomorrow just as soon as I can.' He listened for some seconds more, then said, a little calmer now, 'Yes. Yes. Don't worry. I'll be there in plenty of time for dinner at the Rawsons'. I'll see you then. Give my love to the girls. Love you. Bye.'

Carl put the phone down, his mood heavy now with guilt. His mother had raised him never to tell lies, but that was all he seemed to do these days. But sometimes a white lie was better than the truth, wasn't it? If he told the truth people would get hurt, hearts would be broken. The only person suffering at the moment was himself. The rest of them were blissfully unaware and therefore happy. He was, in reality, protecting them from hurt so painful and deep they had no idea what it could do to you. But he did.

In the early days perhaps he should have walked away, before things had become so complicated. But now he was in too deep — it was too late to wish for what might have been. For how could he stop seeing Kath? He loved her. But he also loved his kids, and he cared for Lynda too. Albeit very different types of love — but each as compelling as the others.

'There's no reason things can't go on like this forever, is there?' he asked himself out loud, but he was shaking his head as he said it, an instinctive answer to his own question.

'Did you want something, Carl?' said a high-pitched female voice and Carl nearly jumped two feet in the air.

'Mandy!' he exclaimed and looked up sharply.

The short, round frame of Mandy Cruz, his secretary-cum-personal-assistant, had appeared in the doorway of the office — he must have left it ajar. She was staring at him, her black eyes like shiny beads in her moonlike face. Her podgy feet were jammed into smart black high heels, so tight her feet must have ached.

'What are you still doing here?' he asked. 'Go on home to the kids, Mandy.'

'They're with their father tonight. He's taking them to the movies with Charlene.'

The intonation with which Mandy delivered this sentence conveyed everything she felt about her husband and his new girlfriend, for whom he'd left her. She hated them both.

'That's nice,' said Carl.

'Hmm,' said Mandy, and she marched right up to the desk. 'I'm sure you don't want to hear this . . .'

She was right. He didn't.

' . . . but you should see the state of her. The short skirts, the low-cut tops. And,' she added triumphantly, 'she smokes! I don't like her around my kids. She's a bad influence.'

Mandy had been with him too long, Carl decided — nearly two years. The success of his elaborate deception depended on the effectiveness of the barricade he had erected between work and his private life. If you kept a secretary like Mandy around too long she became familiar — she got to know too much about you. And she felt the need to tell you more than you wished to know about her.

But Mandy was a good, reliable worker and she desperately needed her job. Still, Carl made a mental note that he'd have to do something — perhaps he could line her up with alternative work somewhere else. He'd have to be careful how he handled it, though

— he didn't want her causing trouble.

'He didn't make his last maintenance payment, you know. Spending all his money on that — that — ' stumbled Mandy — she only just managed to restrain herself from uttering a profanity and finished the sentence with, 'woman.'

Look what telling the truth had done to the Cruz family, thought Carl. In its wake the truth had left a broken home, a bitter, angry wife and three fine-looking boys — Mandy kept a picture of them on her desk — turned overnight into single-parent latchkey kids.

'Anything exciting planned for the weekend, then?' said Mandy, suddenly cheerful, startling Carl out of his reverie.

He stood up, pulled the suit jacket off the chair and shrugged it on, both arms in the sleeves at the same time.

'Oh . . . not much. Just a quiet weekend hanging out with the kids. Dinner at a neighbour's on Saturday night. The usual.'

'Hmm,' said Mandy nodding slowly, without taking her eyes off him. Then she threw a glance in the direction of the window. 'It's been snowing again. You'd better get on the road if you're gonna make it home tonight. You've a long drive ahead of you.'

Carl put his hands in his pants pockets and said, 'Yes, you're right, Mandy. Now you get off home too, will you? And have a great weekend.'

★   ★   ★

17

Outside, the snow was still falling softly and relentlessly. On the sidewalk it was as if someone had unfurled an oversized roll of cotton wool along its length. The snow came over the top of Carl's Italian-tooled shoes and clung to the hem of his fine wool pants legs. He cursed himself for not bringing boots to work this morning, but there was nothing to be done about it now. He pulled the collar of his cashmere coat round his neck, bent his head and walked briskly.

It took only a few minutes to reach the condominium on quiet, tree-lined St Botolph Street, one of the most sought-after locations in Back Bay. Even then the cold had penetrated Carl's thick coat and he could hardly feel his feet. He fumbled for the key, inserted it in the brass lock and let himself into the classic brownstone building where he lived on the second floor. Carl's immediate neighbours were, like himself, businessmen who commuted to the suburbs at the weekends. He never saw them — an arrangement that suited him perfectly.

Inside the high-ceilinged apartment, there were fresh flowers on the mahogany table in the hall and, in the bedroom, five crisply laundered white shirts on the king-sized bed — evidence that the housekeeper had been. At once Carl felt the tensions of the day dissipate. All the rooms were tastefully decorated in shades of coffee and cream with subtle touches of gold and burgundy in the curtains, sofas and cushions. Lynda, with her keen eye for these things, had overseen the entire décor and no expense had been spared.

At the outset, the plan had been for Lynda

and the kids to come to the city for the occasional weekend and during the holidays, when Carl couldn't always take time off work. But, over time, those visits had become less frequent as the impracticalities of driving two under-fives all the way from the Berkshires became all too apparent.

Lynda's life now revolved around the small, friendly community in Williamstown where they'd bought a family home. This was where horse-loving Lynda had grown up, where her parents still lived and where she insisted she wanted to raise her family. She had not set foot in this apartment for nine months. They'd not needed the three bedrooms after all.

Carl took a long hot shower, dried himself with a cream towel and wrapped it round his waist. He went into the master bedroom, selected a shirt, a round-necked navy cashmere jumper and slacks from the wardrobe. He dressed quickly, grabbed a beer from the fridge in the kitchen and went through to the study where he checked his personal emails. Then he stuffed his sodden shoes with scrunched-up newspaper and left them to dry out, propped up either side of the cast-iron radiator in the kitchen.

At eight fifteen, he called a cab, donned his coat and rode the short distance to the restaurant where he'd arranged to meet Kath.

In the cab, he remembered a newspaper article he'd read about the late President of France. For decades he'd kept the existence of his mistress and their love-child a secret from the nation and,

Carl assumed, his other, legitimate family. Such arrangements, it seemed, were not unusual nor were they reviled in France. But here in the USA, Carl knew that what he was doing would attract nothing but hatred and condemnation.

And there was one vital distinction between the situations of Mitterand and Carl — a fact not lost on Carl: Kath O'Connor had absolutely no idea that she was his mistress.

2

In her nervousness, Kath had left the apartment too early and, when the cab pulled up outside Piattini's Wine Bar on Commonwealth Avenue, it was only ten minutes past eight. She paid the driver and stood uncertainly on the sidewalk outside the restaurant's floor-to-ceiling windows. She peered inside — the lighting was dim and the restaurant half-full. After only a few minutes' waiting, the bitter cold forced Kath to seek shelter in the restaurant. She pushed open the door and went in, where she was shown to a shiny copper-topped table set for two.

'What would you like to drink?' said the young black-haired waiter who looked Italian but spoke with a southern Irish, maybe Cork, accent. He was dressed in black trousers and a black shirt. He held a notepad and, as he spoke, took a pencil from behind his right ear.

'Oh, just a glass of white wine for the time being, thanks,' she said, glancing anxiously beyond him at the door. The novelty of striking up a conversation with every Irish person she came across in Boston had long worn off. And it was unlikely that he would detect Kath's roots in her voice in this kind of limited formal exchange. Never strong to begin with, her accent had become Americanised over the years — her speech was much less rapid now and she'd acquired a whole new dictionary of American

21

terms. Chips were 'fries', holidays were 'vacations', aubergines were 'eggplants', trousers were 'pants'.

'We have twenty-seven wines by the glass,' said the waiter with pride and it took a few minutes of consultation for Kath to settle on a 2001 Pinot Grigio.

While she waited for the drink to arrive, she looked round the room. The restaurant was on a big scale — there must have been seating for a hundred and thirty diners. And it wasn't just the number of covers that made it seem large — the room had a very tall vaulted ceiling painted grey-black — to make it seem lower, Kath presumed. The ceiling appeared to be supported by stone-coloured pillars dotted about the room and the floor was clothed with grey slate tiles. The blackwood chairs were upholstered in light brown leather and the walls were an earthy beige colour. Kath was glad she had a table against the wall. The tables in the middle looked lost somehow in this great ocean of a room.

The drink arrived with a little card explaining the wine's vintage. '*Fresh aromas of pears that lead to a refreshing taste of ripe Granny Smith apples and a crisp finish,*' she read. She smelled and tasted the wine and tried very hard to discern these flavours. She must be a complete Philistine, she thought, for while the wine was good, these subtleties were entirely lost on her.

Then the door to the restaurant opened. Kath recognised Carl's tall, athletic figure and her heart gave a little leap.

A waiter took his coat and he came over to the

table, rubbing his hands together briskly. He leaned over and gave her a kiss on the lips which lasted a few seconds longer than protocol demanded. It was little things like this that made Kath so sure that he loved her.

Carl ordered a gin and tonic and then sat down opposite her. 'I'm sorry I'm late. I hope you haven't been waiting long,' he said, his blue-grey eyes the colour of winter sky.

'Mmm,' mumbled Kath through a mouthful of wine, shaking her head, 'you're not late. I was early. Here, look at this — ' She handed Carl the wine card.

He squinted in the dim light to read it.

'Cute, eh?' she asked and he smiled.

'Yeah.' He threw the card on the table, took her hands in his and said, 'Well, how was your day?'

As she started to tell him, a couple came in and sat at a table near them. The woman placed a baby car seat on the floor — inside was a scrunched-up, fast-asleep newborn dressed in blue.

'Oh, look, isn't that sweet?' said Kath spontaneously. 'He's so tiny!'

Carl turned his head to look. 'Yeah,' he said thoughtfully, nodded slowly and turned his attention back to Kath.

'Having kids doesn't seem to stop people doing anything these days,' she said, observing Carl's reaction as she spoke. 'That baby can only be days old and look at the mother out enjoying herself. It's great, isn't it?'

'Well,' he said and he paused as if considering

what to say next, 'they can be a lot of damn hard work too. It's not all fun and games.'

'How would you know?' said Kath and she burst out laughing.

'Well, I hear guys in the office talking, you know,' he replied, a touch defensively. 'Sleepless nights, crotchety wives,' he continued and leaned across the table, holding the menu up as a shield while he hissed, in a stage whisper, 'no sex!'

She laughed conspiratorially and said, 'Ssh! They'll hear you.'

He opened the menu and, changing subject, asked brightly, 'Shall we decide what to eat?'

She glanced over the contents quickly. 'What's this — Cold Piattini, Hot Piattini? What's a 'piattini'?'

'It means 'small bites'. Instead of ordering a starter and a main course, you can have lots of little dishes instead.'

'Oh, that sounds like fun! Some of these sound delicious. Let's have those.'

'Sure,' he said and they set about choosing a selection.

'Hey, what's with these tables?' said Kath, once the food was ordered. 'It's like eating off a bar table.'

'What sort of bars do you frequent?' he said wryly.

'These remind me of the beaten copper tables we used to have in pubs back home in the eighties. And they were horrible then too.'

'Do you know,' he said, rolling the stem of his wineglass between his fingers, 'that everything here has been handmade by local artisans using natural materials? Look at those mirrors.'

'Mmm, they're lovely.'

'The owner,' he continued in an almost reverent tone, 'Josephine Oliviero, is said to have taken her inspiration from her aunt's kitchen in southern Italy. Not, I think, a spit and sawdust pub in darkest Ireland.' He smiled then, his eyes dancing mischievously beneath raised eyebrows.

'Now you're making fun of me,' said Kath, pretending to be hurt. 'Anyway, I'll have you know that we don't have sawdust on the floors of our pubs in Ireland. We have proper floors just like everywhere else.'

'I'll take your word for it.'

She took a sip of wine and scrutinised him over the top of the glass. He seemed relaxed, at ease. It was time she moved the conversation in the direction she wished it to go.

'You know what?' she said and set the glass on the table. 'You should come with me to Ireland for a holiday. My family would love to meet you.'

He coughed and broke eye contact in order to rearrange the cutlery around his place setting. 'Yeah — well — maybe,' he said and then added, 'You know it's hard for me to get away. I don't like to be too far away from the States with my mom's condition.'

'But it's only a five-hour flight away! You could be back home within twenty-four hours if you had to.'

'Ireland's on the other side of the world,' he said, making eye contact with her again.

'You can fly direct into Dublin,' she mused, ignoring his last remark. 'We could go this summer!' She was becoming excited by the prospect. 'That's the best time to see Ireland. It's too wet and miserable the rest of the year! What do you say?'

'I don't know if I could take the time off work,' he said lamely, shaking his head slowly.

'You don't want to. That's it, isn't it?' she said, failing to keep the coolness, born of disappointment, out of her voice.

'I'd love to meet your family one day, Kath. I really would. And I'd love to see Ireland.' He placed his hand over hers and squeezed it gently. 'But you can't rush these things.'

A chill ran down Kath's spine but she ignored it. She mustn't lose her nerve now. Like she had done dozens of times before tonight. She pressed on, trying to keep the conversation focused on the issues that would lead naturally to the subject of marriage.

'Are you heading off in the morning, then?' she asked brightly.

'Yep. I'll fly back Monday morning.'

'How's your mom keeping?'

'She's doing all right.'

Carl's mother had suffered a stroke shortly after they'd met. From what he had told her it sounded as though she'd not made a great deal of progress since then and she was still hospitalised. Carl made the grueling six-hour journey to Wisconsin nearly every weekend to see her — a loyalty and devotion so unusual in work-busy, fast-paced American life that it aroused great admiration in Kath. Here was a man with the capacity for a great deal of love.

26

'Better? Worse?' persisted Kath, who could never understand Carl's reluctance to talk about his family.

'I dunno. Much the same, I guess.'

'And how's your dad coping?'

'He gets by. He has to.'

'Your sister still comes over every day?'

'Yeah, that's right,' he said shortly and he glanced around the room at the other diners.

'If you don't want to talk about it, that's OK. I understand. It must be upsetting.'

Carl shrugged and just then the waiter arrived with more wine. They watched in silence while he topped up their glasses, then withdrew.

'I know it's difficult with things being the way they are,' she continued, aware that she was treading on what had always been very private territory for Carl, 'but I would . . . well, I'd like to meet your parents. Some day.'

Carl stared at her, his blue-grey eyes wide open, his expression unreadable.

'What's wrong, Carl? Have I said something to upset you?'

'No, no,' he said, hastily shaking his head, and then he spotted their waiter, laden with plates, coming towards the table. 'Ah, here comes the food!' he cried with what sounded very much like relief.

They spent the next forty-five minutes sampling the wondrous variety of dishes laid before them. Dreamy herb polenta with wild mushrooms; marinated white anchovies curled inside thinly sliced cucumbers and topped with tomatoes in vinaigrette; gnocchi, tiny and whisper-light, sauced with chunky tomatoes and sprinkled with parmesan; braised calamari with olives and capers.

While they ate and exchanged small talk, Carl seemed himself again — happy, loving, relaxed. Had she imagined his peculiar reaction earlier? When they'd first met, she'd quickly learnt that Carl was essentially a very private person when it came to certain matters. But you didn't keep secrets from your spouse. Once they were married, things would be different.

'Carl, this is delicious!' She licked the tips of her fingers, after devouring a piece of shrimp-topped bruschetta. 'How did you find this place?'

'There's one on Newbury Street. We went there for dinner once, don't you remember?'

'Nope. Must've been before my time. I hope so anyway!'

But Carl didn't smile. He looked slightly embarrassed.

'I'm only joking, Carl,' she added and he smiled then, a fleeting crease of the laughter lines around his mouth.

'Well, I heard they'd just opened this place and I thought it'd be worth a try.'

'Well, what a good choice! I'm absolutely full up.' She patted her tummy. 'I couldn't eat another thing.'

They ordered coffee and Carl held her right hand in his, palm upwards, and slowly kissed the soft fleshy pads at the base of her fingers, one after the other. This action, intimate and loving, was intensely erotic. Then he held her hand away from his face a little and squinted in the dull light, examining it.

'What?' said Kath, giggling. 'What is it?'

'Did you know that I know how to read palms?'

'Don't be silly! Since when?'

'A man has to have his secrets. Wait a minute. Let me have a closer look. You see the way your palm is long and your fingers are long too?'

'Yes.'

'That means you're imaginative, emotional and sensitive.'

'Mmm . . . that sounds like me. I mean the person I'd like to be.'

'It is you. Now, let me see . . . what have we here . . . that's interesting. D'you see that line there?' He traced a crease across her palm with his little finger.

'Yeah.'

'That's your fate line. You see the way it's broken there. That represents major changes in your life.'

'You mean changes to come or changes that've been already?' said Kath, her interest quickening.

'I'm not sure. It's not an exact science.'

'That's fascinating, Carl,' she said, staring at grooves and ridges on her hand that she'd never before noticed. Here they ran parallel, there they intersected — like roads on a map. 'Where did you learn how to do this?'

'Oh, it's just something I picked up. You know,' he said vaguely and shrugged his shoulders.

'No, I don't,' she persisted gently. 'Tell me. Please.'

Carl considered this for a moment and then said, rather reluctantly, 'All right. It was my mother. She used to go to a palmist every month. She made me go along with her. What she was hoping to hear, I'll never know.'

'That wasn't so painful, was it?' she asked, teasing, and then returning to the subject of the palm-reading said, 'Tell me something else.'

'OK, let's see. Relax your hand. That's it. Do you see the way your little finger stands apart from the ring finger?'

'Yes . . . '

'That means you're independent. Or it could mean you're in a relationship you don't want to be in.'

'That is definitely not true. I love you. Tell me something else.'

'I love you too,' said Carl and he smiled broadly, exposing his magazine-bright teeth. 'OK,' he said, serious again, 'let me have a closer look.'

He peered at Kath's palm, frowned and shook his head.

'What?' she said excitedly.

'It says here that you don't want to be alone tonight.'

'Does it indeed? Well, what are you going to do about that?'

'Your place or mine?'

'Yours,' she said quickly. He much preferred staying at her place though she couldn't understand why — he had a much nicer, more spacious apartment.

He hesitated momentarily, then nodded his agreement.

'One last question,' she said, reluctant to end the intimacy of the palm-reading.

'OK. What?'

'Where's my marriage line?'

'Your marriage line? Oh, that's those lines here at the base of your little finger.'

'Well, what can you see?'

Carl folded the fingers of Kath's hand over her palm, the jewels in her ring sparkling like stars. 'I can't remember that,' he said quietly and then smiled at her. 'Come on,' he said then, his voice husky with desire, 'let's go.'

In the cab on the way home, Kath snuggled up to Carl and he put his arm around her shoulder, protecting her. She loved the bigness of him, the way he made her feel small and feminine, though at five feet seven inches tall she could never be described as petite. She loved the roughness of his overcoat against her cheek and the way his possessive fingers gripped her upper arm.

Inside Carl's front door, Kath kicked off her boots and her stockinged feet sank into the yellow-gold carpet. Carl's home had always impressed her. Not for the obvious reasons — because it was in one of Boston's most desirable areas or because it must have cost well over a million dollars — but because it wasn't at all like the bachelor pad she'd expected. The sumptuous fabrics, carefully chosen antiques and subtle colour-scheme all suggested a highly developed feminine side to this macho man's man.

'Carl, I've been meaning to ask you — did you design this place yourself?'

'What do you mean?'

'The décor. The colour scheme. Or did you have an interior designer do it? You did, didn't you?'

'Why?'

'It's just not what I expected of a man living on his own.'

'It's not? Well, I might have had some help,' he said vaguely.

'Who was it? I'll have to get their number off you. My place could do with a make-over and I don't know where to start — '

'Never mind that now,' mumbled Carl and he helped her off with her coat. He kissed her right shoulder, starting at the top of her arm and working his way up — slowly, sensuously — to the base of her neck. She turned to face him and ran her fingers through his short blond hair, loving the way it bristled at the nape of his strong neck. She kissed him on the cleft in his chin that she thought made him look like Michael Douglas, and then on his full lips.

He led her into the bedroom. They undressed each other slowly and made love unhurriedly on the bed. Their lovemaking was wordless, instinctive — the kind of deeply satisfying sex that only people who are very familiar with each other can experience.

When he came at last, after Kath, Carl put his face in her hair and wept.

'It's OK, baby,' she said softly, 'it's OK.'

He was quiet for a few moments and then said, his voice rusty with emotion, 'I love you, Kath O'Connor. I love you.'

'I love you too, Carl.'

She lay completely motionless, her heart pounding in her chest, the weight of Carl's tanned, fit body weighing down on her. She knew that this was the moment. This was what she had been waiting for, not just tonight, but all her life.

'Carl,' she said.

He rolled off her and, with his face on the pillow just inches from her own, he stroked her cheek with the back of his hand.

'What?' he said and smiled at her, his eyes moist and full of love.

'Carl,' she said again and paused.

He continued to stroke her face but his eyes clouded with concern.

She mustn't spoil the moment. She must do it now. Before she lost her nerve.

'Carl,' she said for the third time, 'will you marry me?'

The rhythmic movement of Carl's hand on her cheek stopped momentarily. Less than two seconds later it recommenced, but she could feel a tension in his touch that hadn't been there before. She watched his Adam's apple bob in his throat as he swallowed and she knew what his answer would be. She felt the happiness leach out of her like a slowly deflating balloon.

She turned her face to the ceiling and closed her eyes to stop the tears coming. She inhaled deeply to regulate her erratic breathing. She did not want to cry. She did not want to make a fool of herself. Now she would have to endure his platitudes and pretend that it didn't matter. That it didn't hurt.

'Kath, Kath,' he said softly, 'look at me.'

He grasped her chin gently, but quite firmly, in his big hand and turned her face to his. Kath blinked and opened her eyes, praying that the soft bedroom lights would disguise the pain in them.

'Don't look at me like that,' he said.

'You don't love me the way I love you, Carl.'

'I do. Oh, Kath, I love you more than life itself!'

'Then why can't you say 'yes'?'

It was Carl's turn this time to roll on his back, face to the ceiling. He laid his forearm across his eyes and sighed deeply.

'I can't marry you, Kath. I simply can't. I want to but I can't.'

'Why not?' she said quietly, but he did not answer.

They lay there in silence for what seemed like minutes though it could only have been seconds. Humiliation, closely followed by anger, welled up inside Kath, filling the place where her joy had been until it consumed her entirely.

'I think I'm going to go now,' she said suddenly, and she slid out of bed, reached for her clothes and began to dress.

Carl sat up, covered his face with his hands and dragged them downwards, distorting his features. 'Don't be like this, Kath. Please.'

'I'm not being like anything, Carl,' she said, pulling her red jumper over her head. 'I just need to be alone. I need to think.'

'You don't understand.'

She pulled on her trousers, zipped them and said, 'What don't I understand?'

But all Carl did was shake his head and issue what sounded like a tutting sound.

'Can you call me a cab, please?' she said. 'Or shall I do it myself?'

She insisted on waiting downstairs in the entrance foyer for the cab to arrive. By the time it did, she was shaking but not because of the cold. She got in the cab and looked up — she could see Carl's silhouette at a second-floor window, looking down. It was only when the driver pulled away from the building that she started to cry.

'You OK, honey?' said the kindly cab driver.

Kath shook her head, bit her lip and watched the city streets fly by.

'You too good for him, honey,' said the driver, in a strange eastern accent. 'Don't worry. You find good man to take care of you. One that don't make you cry.'

But Kath lowered her head on her chest and sobbed all the more. No man would ever come close to Carl Scholtz. He was the only man she had ever loved. The only man, she was quite sure, that she was capable of loving.

The cab dropped her outside her brownstone and she climbed the steps wearily. Inside she took a shower, suddenly desperate to wash away all reminders of Carl. Inexplicably, for the first time in her life, she felt cheap. She made herself a mug of tea and sat in bed and tried to analyse all that had passed between them.

What did he mean when he said that he wanted to marry her but he couldn't? Had he been married before and not told her? Maybe, though he was separated, he wasn't divorced. Well, that could easily be put right. Or perhaps it was to do with religion. She knew he'd been raised a Calvinist — she was a Catholic. Was that it? Neither of them were regular churchgoers, but if it was a problem for Carl, why, she would convert. The only other reason she could possibly think of was that he really didn't love her enough but she knew deep down that this was not true. He adored her, just as she adored him.

The mistake she'd made was that she'd surprised him. She could see that clearly now. Emmy had been right. He wasn't ready for marriage just yet. Maybe he was afraid of marriage — lots of people had a problem making a commitment. But with her love, she would help him overcome whatever it was that was holding him back. She was sure of it. And so thinking, she fell asleep with the empty mug cradled in her hands, exhausted by the emotional rollercoaster of the last few hours.

3

'Marry me,' whispered David O'Connor. He watched Simone Boyd open her peat-brown eyes and blink in the grey misty light of an Irish winter morning. He kissed her lightly on the tip of her little turned-up nose and she stared at him, consciousness slowly taking hold. They were lying in bed in the ranger's cottage they shared on Glenburn Estate, just outside Ballyfergus.

He ran his fingers through her thick hair, red-brown as the bracken that carpeted the floor of the forest in autumn. Tendrils of it spread out on the pillow, dark against white, like the winter skeleton of a tree against the rain-heavy sky.

'Marry me, Simone,' he said again. In spite of the magnitude of the question, David was so sure of her answer that he couldn't help but grin. She was so pretty, so pure in body and in spirit. Simone required no artifice to look lovely — unlike David's former partner Viv, whose attractiveness depended entirely on her ash-blonde highlights, spray-on tan and gym-toned body. The contrast between the two women couldn't have been more startling.

The corners of Simone's mouth curled up slowly into a wide, open smile, revealing a fine set of teeth marred only by two front incisors that overlapped slightly, giving her a slightly goofy, but loveable, appearance.

'Yes,' she said. 'I thought you'd never ask.' She held out her arms to embrace him and he lay against her warm skin.

'I can't believe how lucky I am,' he said into the fragrant heat of her neck. 'I never thought I would find love like this. I never thought I would get a second chance. What do you see in me, Simone? You could have any man you want. What are you doing with a man on the wrong side of forty, with a bald head and a beer belly?'

'I don't see you like that at all,' said Simone seriously. 'I like the age you are. And I like your bald head,' she wrinkled her nose up with pleasure as she rubbed the smooth dome of his head, 'I think it makes you look sexy. I like the way your face and arms are always weather-beaten. And if we're talking beer bellies,' she added, laughing as she pinched the doughy flesh of his midriff, 'I think I could give you some competition.'

He grabbed a handful of flesh on either side of her generous waist and said, 'Mmm . . . I see what you mean.'

'Don't you be so cheeky,' she retorted but she was laughing at herself as much as anything, a quality that David adored in her.

'We'll have to tell Murray!' she said suddenly and she glanced at the clock on the bedside table. 'He'll be awake by now.' Then she added anxiously, 'Do you think he'll be pleased?'

Murray was David's five-year-old son from his ill-fated relationship with Viv. He came to stay every alternate weekend and, in David's opinion, Simone was a better mother to the child than Viv was. Even at a time as momentous as this, her first thought was of the boy. But, then, Simone was a midwife and loved children.

Downstairs, in their dressing-gowns, they found Murray playing on the GameCube that David had bought him for Christmas. He was sitting cross-legged in front of the TV screen, his feet bare, a fleecy dressing-gown hanging open over his skinny frame. Coarse brown hair stuck up in spikes all over his head.

'You'll catch your death sitting there. The heating's not on,' said Simone, going over to him and clasping one of his little feet in her hand. 'I was right — his feet are freezing, David!'

Murray went on playing the game, oblivious to their presence.

'Don't fuss so,' said David but Simone had already left the room.

She was back in seconds with a pair of blue Spiderman slippers. She jammed them onto the child's feet, amid moans of protest while he wriggled to keep his eye on the screen and his hands on the controls. The movement activated red flashing lights embedded in the fabric of the slippers — they twinkled, unnoticed by Murray, for a few seconds before going out.

'Come on, son, time for breakfast,' said David.

'No,' said Murray evenly, without taking his eyes off the screen.

David waited for a few seconds then said, 'Come on, Murray. You can play with it later.'

'No,' said Murray, louder this time.

'Please, son. Don't make me get cross with you!' David was irritated already by the child's defiance. He decided to switch the television screen off.

'No. No. No! *No!*' said Murray, his voice rising an octave with each step his father took towards the television.

David stopped and said sharply, 'Now, if you're going to make a fuss like this, I'll not let you play with it for the rest of the day.'

'Just let me finish this game!' yelled Murray.

David shook his head. Murray threw the hand-held controller to the floor and grabbed his father's leg to prevent him getting any closer to the television.

'Murray!' shouted David, in frustration. Why couldn't the child do what he asked him? Everything was a constant battle, from brushing his teeth to getting him to eat anything other than chips and chicken nuggets. 'I'm sorry I ever got you that blasted thing!' He yanked his leg free of Murray's grasp, then hit the button on the television. The screen went blank.

Simone came over then and shook her head vigorously at David to indicate her disapproval of the way he'd handled the incident. She knelt on the floor and scooped the now sobbing Murray into her arms.

'Your daddy's right, pet. You can't play with that silly old thing all the time, can you now? You'll get square eyes.'

'I hate you! *I hate you!*' shouted Murray at his father, straining in Simone's arms like a toddler in a tantrum. His face was raspberry red and the muscles on the side of his neck stood out like chicken tendons.

'Now, now, now,' said Simone calmly, 'settle down, Murray. You don't hate your daddy. You should never say that.'

Murray collapsed into her embrace, his sobs muffled by her bosom. She rocked him gently, murmuring words of comfort like a prayer. David left the room feeling inadequate, as usual.

In the kitchen he flicked on the heating, put bowls and spoons on the table and got the boxes of breakfast cereal out of the cupboard. When it came to fathering Murray he just couldn't seem to get it right. He didn't have the knack Simone had for getting the child to do what he asked him. Sometimes it seemed like his entire relationship with Murray consisted of one confrontation after another. He knew he had a quick temper — but only Murray knew how to flick the switch so effectively.

David thought of the relationship he had with his own father, Brendan, and hoped that he and Murray would have a better one. He'd fallen out with his father over the hotel. Brendan wanted him to take over the family business — David wanted to become a forest ranger. At least they were speaking now, but David knew that his father had never forgiven him for choosing the life he had here over the Sallagh Braes Hotel.

He heard sniffing behind him and turned around. Murray was standing in front of him, his shoulders hunched, looking at the floor. Simone was behind him, one of her hands resting on each of the boy's shoulders.

'Go on then,' she urged gently and gave the boy an almost imperceptible nudge forward.

Murray mumbled something.

'A bit louder, Murray,' said Simone in a kind, but firm, voice. 'Your daddy can't hear you.'

'I'm sorry, Daddy,' said Murray and he raised his red-rimmed eyes to look at his father. His long eyelashes were clumped together with tears and his big brown eyes, the same as his father's, made him look like a soulful puppy.

David flushed with shame. 'I'm sorry too, son.' He ruffled the boy's hair and said, 'Friends again?'

Murray nodded.

David sighed. 'I hate it when we argue, Murray. I — I just wish you'd do what I ask you sometimes. It would make life so much nicer for all of us.'

'Would you love me then?' said Murray in a small voice.

David gasped and fell to his knees. He pulled Murray to him, enfolding him in a tight, fierce embrace. 'But I do love you, Murray! No matter what you do. I've always loved you and nothing you do will ever stop me loving you.'

He felt the tension go out of the little body and he was filled with remorse. He kissed Murray's winter-pale cheek and hugged him again and again until the child returned the embrace. When he eventually released him the little boy's face was calm, a small, cautious smile on his bright red lips.

'Come on, son. Let's get you some breakfast.' He scooped the boy up in his arms and deposited him on a stool by the breakfast bar. 'Now what are you having? No, don't tell me. I can guess. The ones with the most sugar in them.'

'That's right,' said Murray giggling and David poured him a massive bowl of chocolate-covered puffed rice cereal. David added milk and a spoon and Murray was soon munching away happily.

'It's OK,' whispered Simone when she sat beside David at the table. She placed a comforting hand on his shoulder and said, 'I know how hard it is sometimes.'

After a few minutes' silence, broken only by the clink of metal spoons against china, she nudged David under the table with her knee. When he looked at her she nodded at Murray.

'This is the mountain,' said Murray to himself, referring to the puffed rice he had scraped into a mound at one side of his bowl.

'Go on then,' said Simone quietly to David.

'And this is the lake,' said Murray, sticking his finger into the coffee-coloured milk at the bottom of the bowl. He shoved it in his mouth, pulled it out with a 'pop' and said, 'Delicious.'

'Don't put your fingers in your food, or in your mouth, Murray,' said Simone with quiet authority.

Murray shifted in his chair, the only indication that he had heard the reprimand.

Simone smiled encouragingly at David and waited.

'Murray?' said David.

'Mmm . . . ' said the boy distractedly.

'Simone and I have something to tell you.'

Without lifting his head, Murray's searching gaze darted quickly to his father's face, then

Simone's. He rubbed his lips with the pad of his left thumb, an indication that he was stressed. But whatever he saw in their faces reassured him, for the fear in his eyes soon abated. He reached into the cereal box and extracted a single dry grain of puffed rice.

'Simone and I are going to get married,' said David.

'And this is the boat!' Murray set the grain of rice carefully on the lake of milk where it floated, motionless.

David looked at Simone, frustrated by Murray's reaction, or rather lack of it. But Simone only raised her eyebrows and smiled indulgently at the child.

'Murray,' she said gently, 'did you hear what Daddy said?'

'Uh huh,' said Murray, as he navigated the rice boat around the chocolate lake with the tip of his spoon.

'Do you know what it means?' persisted Simone.

Murray frowned and put the spoon down on the table. He pursed his lips, thought for a few moments and then said, confidently, looking from one to the other, 'It means that I'll have two mummies.'

David and Simone burst out laughing at the same time. Murray joined them a few seconds later, his laughter hollow and uncertain.

'I'm right, I'm right,' he said, nodding his head. 'Amn't I? That's what it means, doesn't it?'

'That's right, son,' said David. 'That's exactly what it means.' And, when they'd finally stopped laughing, he asked, 'How do you feel about Simone becoming your second mummy?'

'It's OK,' said Murray and he picked up the spoon, shoved the mountain into the lake and ate it.

'What did you think of Murray's reaction to us getting married?' David asked Simone some time later, when they were all dressed and taking a walk in the forest. The air was mild and damp and the path underfoot, though little used by visitors this time of year, was sticky with mud. Murray was ahead of them, darting in and out of the trees.

Glenburn was a plantation forest established in the early eighteenth century by the owners of Glenburn Castle. Amongst the native oak and ash were introduced species like sweet chestnut, larch and Norway maple. The castle was still in private hands but the forest was now managed by the Forestry Service — David's employer.

Simone's reply was muffled by the pale green scarf wound round her neck and over her mouth. 'Normal, I suppose. In real terms it'll make little or no difference to his life. We'll go on living here and he'll keep on coming to stay.'

'Hmm . . . I guess you're right.'

She turned look at him then. 'What did you expect from him?'

'I don't know. He just seemed . . . well, he seems a bit disconnected sometimes. He was more concerned with what was going on in his cereal bowl this morning than what we were telling him.'

'That's because kids live in a parallel world a

lot of the time, David. At that particular point in time, that *was* the most important thing to him. It doesn't mean he didn't take in what you were telling him. He'll ask us plenty of questions, believe me — but only when he's ready.'

They walked on in silence for a few minutes more. Then David stopped, looked at his watch and said, 'I'd better be getting back. Viv'll be here in ten minutes. Look, I've been thinking, Simone. I'd better tell her about our plans before Murray does. He's bound to blurt it out and then she'll be furious with me for not telling her first. Why don't you take Murray down to river and throw some sticks in the water. It's running nice and fast this time of year. He'll love it. Give me fifteen minutes or so, will you?'

'Of course. Good luck!'

'I'll need it,' he replied, kissing her quickly on the lips. 'You know what she's like.'

By the time he got back to the cottage, Viv's bright red Seat was parked outside and she was sitting behind the steering wheel, stony-faced.

'What're you doing sitting there?' he said good-naturedly, as he opened the driver's door and leaned in to speak to her. 'Sure you know the door's never locked. Come on in and get a heat.'

Viv got out of the car, pulled the edges of her long black cardigan across her low-cut top and shivered. The cardigan had furry stuff at the cuffs and collar but it was thin and loosely knit — it couldn't have afforded much protection against the elements. She was always half-dressed; she never wore suitable attire for the

46

weather or the time of year.

'Where's Murray?'

'Down by the river with Simone.'

'I haven't got all day, David,' she said irritably, tucking a stray lock of bleached hair behind her ear. 'We're supposed to be going to my mum's for Sunday lunch.'

'They'll be along in a minute. Look, why don't you come inside and wait? I've got something to tell you.'

Her interest aroused, she glanced sharply at him. Then, without further comment, she picked her way across the gravel in her high-heeled beige suede boots. In the porch, David removed his mud-encrusted wellies and padded into the lounge with his trousers tucked into chunky hiking socks. He thought momentarily of untucking them because that is what Viv would have told him to do in the past, and then he remembered that he no longer had to try and please her.

'Well?' she said, standing in the middle of the lounge on the faded Turkish rug with her arms folded across her chest as though it was as cold inside as out.

'Have a seat,' said David.

'No, thanks,' she said evenly. 'I won't be stopping long.'

David scratched the top of his head and said, 'Well, the thing is . . . Simone and I have decided to get married. I thought you'd like to know.'

'Oh,' she said with a little start, and her arms dropped to her sides. He waited and she stared at him, her eyes flickering like a computer screen

47

while she processed the news.

'I thought you'd prefer to hear it from me rather than second-hand,' he offered to fill the silence.

'Yes. I see. Have you told Murray?'

'We told him this morning.'

'And how did he take it?'

'OK. He seemed . . . well, unmoved by it. As Simone says, it probably doesn't mean much to — '

'I don't know about that,' she said, cutting him off in mid-sentence. 'He's a very sensitive little boy.'

'Well, he seems happy enough about it to me,' he replied, sensing that this conversation, like all the others, was about to degenerate into a bickering match. He resolved not to rise to the bait.

'When's the Big Day then?' she said, her voice heavy with sarcasm and her blue eyes flashing like emergency lights.

'I don't know. We haven't talked about it yet.'

She nodded slowly, refolded her arms across her chest and said, 'You *will* be sure to look after Murray's interests, won't you?'

'What on earth does that mean?'

'He *is* your son after all . . . '

'I don't need you to tell me that,' he snapped and then, as the realisation hit him, he added slowly, 'Oh, wait a minute. I see . . . I see where this is going. You're worried about his mainte- nance payments, aren't you?'

'All I'm saying is that you have a responsibility towards that boy,' she said, averting her gaze, 'and I don't want you going and forgetting it.'

David had opened his mouth to reply when Simone came in with Murray.

Viv's face broke into a huge smile when she saw her son — he ran to her and she hugged him tightly.

'Hello, Viv,' said Simone cheerfully, unwinding the scarf from round her neck, 'Lovely day out there.'

'Hello,' replied Viv coldly, and then she focused all her attention on Murray.

They said their goodbyes and Viv steered Murray outside and into the car, ignoring David and Simone.

As soon as the car had driven off and they were back inside, Simone said to David, 'Well, I can guess how that went.'

He sighed. 'All she's worried about is her bloody maintenance payments. Money-grabbing little — ' The phone rang then and he slapped his brow with the flat of his hand. 'What now?'

'I'll get it,' said Simone quickly. She picked up the handset and spoke quietly for a few seconds, her brow furrowed with concentration. Then she held the phone out to David and said in a voice little more than a whisper, 'It's your mum, David, and she's terribly upset. I can hardly make out what she's saying.'

David put a hand on the receiver but before she released it into his grasp, Simone said, warning him, 'David, I think that something terrible has happened.'

4

Less than fifteen miles away David's sister, Bridget McVey, stood in her immaculate designer kitchen with a red gingham apron wrapped around her curvaceous waist. She was putting the finishing touches to a cake for her youngest child, Charmaine, who was having her fourth birthday party the next day.

On the black granite counter were six small plastic bowls of jelly beans, each one containing a different shade of pink, from cerise to shell. She'd had to order them on the Internet, along with bags of ready-to-roll pink icing, after Laura, who was eight, convinced Charmaine that her birthday wouldn't be complete without Nigella Lawson's Barbie cake. Bridget cast a withering glance at the *How to Be a Domestic Goddess* cookbook on the shelf and cursed the authoress.

It was all very well if you lived in the city and could go swanning off to Selfridges to pick out *just* the right shade of pink jelly bean. But for people like Bridget who lived, let's face it, out in the sticks, it was a different story. Even getting hold of real parmesan cheese was a challenge, never mind the dozen or so other exotic ingredients Nigella couldn't seem to live without.

Bridget rolled out the bubble-gum-pink icing and carefully cut out a skirt for the Barbie doll cake, using the cake tin as a template.

Charmaine's fourth birthday marked a huge milestone in Bridget's life. In the autumn, the child would start school and Bridget would, at last, be free. For the past ten years, living the domestic idyll in her fabulous converted farmstead, she'd felt as though she'd been treading water.

Sometimes she found it hard to believe that, pre-children, she'd worked in the busy offices of *Ulster Tatler*, that she'd been at the cutting edge of fashion, never went to bed before twelve and partied every night of her life like it was about to end. And then she'd fallen in love with the handsome, successful Ned, fell pregnant and allowed herself to be persuaded that a life of domesticity was what she'd wanted.

And it was — to begin with at least. When she'd held her first child, Alex, in her arms, Bridget wanted nothing in the world more than to care for the infant exclusively. No one else could do the job as ably as she and she guarded him with a fierce possessiveness.

After Laura arrived and then Charmaine, four years later, Bridget had been too exhausted and busy to notice that her brain had slowed down, that she wasn't getting the intellectual stimulation she once had. And then later she noticed that, if she listened to herself hard enough, all she seemed to talk about was her children, the pros and cons of this one's and that one's cleaner and where to buy the freshest flowers.

Once she horrified herself when she realised she didn't know who the Chancellor of the Exchequer was, and worse, she didn't really care.

The entire family dressed in Boden clothes — the mail-order catalogue of choice for staid, middle-class families — and she bought all her underwear in Marks and Spencer. She was slipping inexorably into premature middle age.

But it was not too late to reverse the trend, she told herself with nervous determination. She slapped warm apricot jam onto the Barbie doll's chest and lower back — a real doll, stuffed into the middle of a conical cake — and dreamed of what she might do with the rest of her life.

Maybe she could go back into magazine publishing — she still had some contacts in the industry. She could revamp her image — ditch all those fuddy-duddy clothes, lose a stone or two and resurrect her sense of fashion. She'd dye her dull brown hair blonde again and get it cut in the latest style. She could even change the colour of her hazel-grey eyes with coloured contact lenses. In short, she could re-invent herself.

In planning all this, one thing was very clear to Bridget — the new future she envisaged for herself depended entirely on one crucial factor. She must not, under any circumstances, have another child. She'd dedicated ten years of her life to her offspring and, though she loved them dearly, enough was enough.

Ned came into the kitchen rubbing his rounded stomach. He was still a handsome, if slightly overweight, man, with a wide dimpled smile, even temper and lively green eyes. He came over to where Bridget was working, picked up a jelly bean and popped it into his mouth.

'When's dinner?' he said. 'I'm starving.'

'Will you leave those alone, please, Ned,' she snapped. 'Didn't I tell you I had to send away for them? If I don't have enough — '

'Jesus, will you listen to yourself, Bridget,' interrupted Ned. 'It's only a bloody jelly bean.'

She was about to retort that this was her domain — she didn't go into his office picking and poking round his work papers. But he wouldn't understand. She pressed a little pink corset cut out of pink icing onto Barbie's torso and was surprised by the professional result.

'Dinner's in the oven. It's a casserole and baked potatoes. It should be ready . . . let's see . . . ' she said pleasantly, glancing at the digital clock display on the Gaggenau oven, 'in about an hour.'

She applied the rest of the pink icing to the cake and set about sticking the jelly beans onto Barbie's dress.

'Charmaine's going to love that,' said Ned.

'She is, isn't she?' Bridget dipped the last sweet in warm water and stuck it to the full skirt of Barbie's ball gown. She stood back, wiped her hands on a damp cloth and admired the result. If any of her former colleagues could see her now, she thought, how they'd laugh. Making a picture-perfect birthday cake was her greatest achievement these days.

'Can't believe our baby's going to be four,' mused Ned, running his thick fingers through his thinning but still full head of mid-brown hair. 'I don't want her to grow up, do you?'

She looked at Ned, his face filled with pleasure

at the homeliness of the scene. He loved the world she had created within the walls of this stunning home. He was a good, hard-working, family-oriented man and she knew she should be grateful for that. How could she tell him that the life she led here in this beautiful home, with their three adorable children, was killing her?

She'd tried to explain to him before how she felt but he didn't hear it — didn't *want* to hear it. Once she'd actually been offered a part-time job — working in a friend's coffee shop — and he managed to talk her out of it. But this time, she thought with uncertain resolve, she was going to stick to her guns.

'Ned,' she said cautiously, 'where are the children?'

'The girls are in the den engrossed in *Sleeping Beauty* and Alex is up in his room, probably surfing the Web for porn sites.'

'Ned!'

'Only joking,' he said grinning, munching on a black grape he had picked from the bunch in the fruit bowl. 'He's playing some computer game.'

'Come over here and sit down a minute,' she said, untying her apron and laying it on the work surface. She'd been through this conversation with Ned a hundred times in her head. It was now or never.

'OK,' said Ned uncertainly.

He followed her to the bay window on the other side of the large room where two comfortable sofas, arranged at a forty-five degree angle to each other, faced a huge floor-length window. This looked out onto the garden and the gently undulating countryside beyond, but today the fields were empty of livestock and a mist rolling in off the sea restricted the view.

Bridget perched on the edge of one sofa Ned sat down heavily on the other. He flung both arms across the back of the couch and said, 'What?'

'Ned, I've been thinking about us. About the future and what I might do when Charmaine starts school.'

'What do you mean 'do'?'

She coughed and said, 'I was thinking of going back to work.'

'Right,' he said thoughtfully, rubbing his chin as though checking for bristles. Bridget held her breath until he said, 'Do you think you'll have time what with running the house and all?'

'I'll have from nine to three every day, except Fridays,' she said defensively. 'It should be possible to fit in a part-time job.'

'Finding something to fit in with those hours could be a problem,' he said doubtfully, 'especially round here.'

'Maybe.'

'And there's the holidays to think about too. The kids get a lot of time off school — '

'We'll jump that hurdle when we get to it,' said Bridget, more sharply than she'd intended.

'Hey, don't get shirty with me! I'm only pointing out the pitfalls. Anyway, we've been over all this before, Bridget. I thought we'd agreed that it wasn't really . . . ' he paused, searching for the right word, '*practical* for you to go out to work.'

'I know, but that was last year. Charmaine starts school in the autumn and I don't want to sit round here all day in an empty house. But look,' she said briskly, anxious not to be deflected from her agenda, 'whatever I decide to do, there's something we need to sort out first.'

'What's that?'

'Contraception.'

'I don't follow.'

'We don't want to have any more children, do we? You always said that three was enough. And we've never really found a satisfactory form of birth control. The coil was making me bleed too heavily, condoms cause too much irritation and none of the other methods are reliable enough.'

'I said I wanted only three children before the insurance business was established. We're very comfortable now, Bridget, and I've provided well for the future. You don't need to be worrying about going back to work.'

'Ned,' said Bridget, the tension rising in her as he failed to grasp what she was trying to tell him. 'I want you to have a vasectomy.'

'Hey, steady on!'

Instinctively, he folded his hands across his lap, a gesture that seemed slightly ludicrous to Bridget. If she hadn't been so serious about the whole matter, she'd have burst out laughing.

'That's a bit OTT, 'n't it?'

'No, not at all,' said Bridget airily.

'Listen, love, it's not a problem if we had an accident,' he said earnestly. He was by this stage sitting on the edge of the sofa. 'I mean you're only thirty-seven. Another child wouldn't be a disaster. We can well afford it and there's plenty of room in this house.'

'Don't you see, Ned, it's not about money?' snapped Bridget, and she felt the muscles in her jaw tighten as she fought to remain calm and rational. 'It's about me,' she said evenly. 'It's about me having a life outside these four walls.'

'What are you talking about? Sure you're never done running here and there. To the health club, having coffee with your mates, shopping, nipping over to your mum's.'

'Filling time, Ned. Keeping myself busy.'

'You mean you're not happy. Is that what you're telling me?' he said sadly. His head slumped into his shoulders and he looked crestfallen.

Bridget wrung her hands together and said carefully, 'I am happy, Ned. I have been happy here raising the children. But I want something different now. I want a career. I want to be out there earning my own money, making a difference.'

'But you're making a difference at home, Bridget. You're doing a job I could never do as well.'

'I'll still do that job at home, Ned. I'm not asking you to do it.'

'But things won't be the same, Bridget. You know they won't.'

There was silence then for some minutes while Bridget tried to figure out what to say next. Ned was right — things at home wouldn't be as comfortable for him, or the children, if she went out to work. And the only way it could work was if they all pulled their weight a bit more around the house. But, she thought miserably, without Ned's support it would be nearly impossible to fulfil her plans.

'I'm not having a vasectomy,' said Ned with finality. 'If you feel that strongly about it, why can't you get sterilised?'

'Because sterilising a woman is a much more invasive, complicated surgical procedure than a simple vasectomy,' she explained evenly.

'Depends on who's having the operation,' he said grimly.

'But that's just not fair, Ned,' she said frustration. 'I've had two children normally — you've seen what that entailed — and one Caesarean. Don't you think it's your turn to do your bit?'

Ned had just drawn breath to reply when Alex burst into the room with a navy and maroon rugby shirt in his arms.

'Mum,' he said, throwing the garment at his mother, rather than into her arms as he'd probably intended, 'can you iron this?'

'Please' would be nice,' said Bridget, picking the shirt off the floor, where it had slid from her knees.

'Whatever,' he replied cheekily and Bridget shot a look of annoyance at Ned, expecting him to intervene and chastise Alex for his rudeness. But Ned had picked up the remote control for the TV and was staring at the screen.

'Dad's taking me over to Davie's this afternoon. I need it for then,' said Alex and with that he plonked down on the sofa in front of the

58

TV beside his father.

Bridget stood up, looked at the shirt in her hands, at Ned and then at Alex. She felt invisible. She walked into the large utility room where an ironing board and iron were permanently set up. Simmering with anger she roughly ironed the shirt, deliberately not giving the task the attention she normally did. When she noticed that one button was missing, she resisted the urge to pull out her sewing box and mend it. She switched off and unplugged the iron.

'I'm fed up being general bloody dogsbody,' she said miserably aloud to herself as tears welled up in her eyes. 'I'm sick of being everyone's doormat.'

And the worst of it was that she knew it was her own fault. She didn't have the confidence to stand up to Ned, just the way she'd never had the confidence to stand up to her overbearing father, Brendan.

As a child she'd been terrified of him — his booming voice, his indifference to her mediocre achievements, the way he chided her for slouching and talking too quietly. She did love him but it was a love always tinged with fear. Kath, on the other hand, one year older than Bridget, was his favourite. Pretty, intelligent and dynamic, she could always, even as a child, win him round with a winning smile or quick-witted retort.

To this day, in her sister's company, Bridget felt dull, boring and unattractive. All her life she had struggled not to hate Kath — it was easier

59

now that she lived on the other side of the Atlantic. But Brendan's legacy to Bridget was the lack of confidence and self-esteem that had plagued her all her life. She couldn't even stand up to her own children. She feared that they would stop loving her if she didn't do everything for them. And yet she hated her life of domestic tedium.

Just then the phone rang. She wiped the tears from her eyes with the tips of her forefingers so as not to disturb her make-up, sniffed and went through to the kitchen. Ned was still sprawled on the sofa, showing absolutely no sign of rousing himself to answer the phone. His hands were folded behind his head, the remote control still held in one as though he was afraid someone might come in and change channels on him.

'Can you get that, love?' he shouted, without taking his eyes off the TV screen.

Bridget picked up the receiver.

When, a few minutes later, all that could be said was said and the call was finished she put the phone back in the base unit. Then she folded her arms around herself and slid quietly onto the elm-wood floor. And this is where Ned found her some five minutes later sobbing soundlessly into her tearstained hands.

5

When the phone rang the next morning at ten thirty, waking Kath, her first thought was of Carl. She remembered, with a sinking heart, what had happened last night and that he would be halfway on his way to Wisconsin by now. It must be Emmy on the phone, she thought and groaned. She'd be wanting to hear all the gory details of last night and Kath wasn't sure she was up to it.

Last night she'd had no problem finding plausible explanations for Carl's behaviour — she wasn't sure that Emmy would be as credulous. She decided to let the call trip to the answering machine but when it did, instead of leaving her usual cheery '*Hi, it's me. Call me!*' message, Emmy hung up. Within seconds the phone rang again, and again Emmy hung up when the call tripped to the answering machine.

If she rings again, I'll have to answer it, thought Kath crossly, sitting up in bed and rubbing the sleep out of her eyes. What is wrong with her this morning?

When the phone started to shrill again, Kath picked it up after two rings and said sleepily, 'Hey, what's up with you? You woke me up.'

'Pardon?' said a woman's unfamiliar voice.

'I'm sorry,' said Kath, shaking off her sleepy stupor. 'Who's calling, please?'

'Is that Miss Kath O'Connor?' said a clear East Coast accent.

'Who's calling, please?'

'Can you confirm that I'm speaking to Miss Kath O'Connor?' said the woman's voice — too persistent, too icy to be a salesperson.

Kath sat up and swung her legs over the side of the bed. Her naked shoulders made her feel vulnerable so she wriggled into a dressing-gown.

'Yes, this is she,' said Kath using phraseology to match the woman's formal tone. She held the handset under her chin while she tied the cord on her dressing-gown. 'But if this is a sales call,' she added, deliberately adopting a tone of annoyance, 'I'd ask you to hang up immediately.'

'This is no sales call,' said the voice on the line and a feeling of dread descended on Kath. There was something supercilious about the woman's tone of voice, a knowing quality that made her feel as though she was being watched. She glanced out the window but there was nothing there, only grey sky. She told herself not to be so silly. She stood up to lend her voice more authority — a trick she had learned in work.

'Who is this?' she said, trying to keep the unease out of her voice.

There was a pause, during which she could hear the woman breathing down the phone.

Then the strange voice said very clearly, 'My name is Lynda Scholtz. Mrs Lynda Scholtz.'

'Mrs Scholtz!' said Kath in surprise. What on earth was Carl's mother doing phoning her? She didn't sound like a bed-ridden invalid — her voice was strong and young, somehow. And there was a definite coldness about it. Had she phoned to warn Kath off her son? Maybe this was the reason why Carl couldn't marry her. He had an overbearing mother who dominated him.

'Is everything OK, Mrs Scholtz?' she said carefully. Then, suddenly fearing for Carl's safety, she asked, 'Is it Carl? Is he alright?'

The woman gave a hollow laugh. 'I should think so. He's on his way here right now. I'm expecting him for luncheon.'

The woman was talking as if she was in her kitchen, not in a nursing home. This was getting stranger and stranger. Maybe she wasn't ill at all. Maybe Carl had made the story up to keep his mother away from her. Or keep her away from his mother.

Kath prepared to square up to her.

'So soon?' she said, to fill the silence. 'I thought he had to change at Chicago?'

There was a long pause and then Mrs Scholtz laughed, this time a genuine throaty chuckle, but something told Kath it was at her expense.

'You think,' Mrs Scholtz said at last, 'that I'm his mother, don't you?'

'Why, yes,' said Kath stupidly.

Mrs Scholtz laughed again and said, 'Miss O'Connor, I am Carl's wife.'

Kath's heart sank. Her original instinct had been right. Carl had been married before. Why didn't he tell her? And, more importantly, what did this woman want?

'And you're divorced?' she ventured.

'No, we're not.'

'You're separated then?' she said warily.

63

'You don't seem to understand the situation, Miss O'Connor. Contrary to what he might have told you, my husband and I are very much together.'

'I don't believe you,' whispered Kath as she pulled the dressing-gown tight round her neck with her right hand.

'We have a house in Williamstown,' continued Lynda Scholtz as though Kath had not spoken, 'in the Berkshires — where he lives at the weekend with the children and me. We bought the condo in Boston purely to avoid Carl having to commute during the week.'

'Children,' whispered Kath and her image of Carl, her future husband, slowly crumbled into dust. She sat down heavily on the edge of the bed, her legs unable to support her any longer.

'That's right. Jasmine's five and Daisy's two. He never mentioned them?'

'No,' said Kath, gripping the receiver with both hands like a lifeline, her voice little more than a whisper.

There was another pause and then Lynda Scholtz said, this time in a softer voice, 'You really didn't know about us, did you?'

'No,' said Kath, again barely managing to form the words with her lips.

'Well, I'll give you credit for one thing. At least you didn't know you were dating a married man. I feel sorry for you, I really do.' Then she added, with no hint of malice or glee, 'Carl's led you right up the garden path, hasn't he?'

Tears rolled down Kath's face and she was silent.

'How long have you been seeing him?' Lynda

Scholtz asked gently.

Kath opened her mouth to answer, compelled now to confess her unwitting part in Carl's adultery. But the words would not come. She tried again.

'Eighteen months,' she croaked.

'That long! What a bastard!'

'And you . . . you didn't know about me?' Kath managed to ask, between deep breaths.

'Not until very recently,' said Lynda Scholtz and then she paused, before changing tack, her voice all businesslike again, 'Kath — may I call you Kath?'

'Mmm,' mumbled Kath, unable now to form any coherent words.

'Kath, the reason for my call today was to ask you to stop seeing my — '

'There's no need,' said Kath, suddenly finding her voice and her dignity, 'I won't be seeing Carl again. Believe me, if I'd known he was married, I never would have . . . ' She broke down in tears then and could not continue.

'OK then,' said Mrs Scholtz, her voice a mixture of relief and satisfaction. 'Thank you. And I am sorry for what he's done to you, Kath. I truly am.'

The phone went dead then and Kath sat and listened to the dull monotonous tone for several minutes before hanging up. She looked at the handset curiously, amazed that such a simple instrument of communication could have wrecked her life in just a few moments.

Carl — the man she loved, the man she had wanted to marry, the man who was going to give her the children she craved — did not exist. He might as well be dead. She wished he was. For knowing that he was out there, living the life she wanted for herself with another woman and her children, was more than she could bear.

Kath fell to her knees and screamed, a long anguished howl, like a wolf. Then she ran from room to room in her apartment, picturing Carl in every seat, seeing his outline behind the shower screen, seeing him standing in the kitchen chopping onions, the tears streaming down his cheeks. He was everywhere, he was all around her, he was inside her and she hated him. She found herself back in the bedroom, panting between sobs, overwhelmed by fatigue.

She crawled back into bed and hugged a pillow tight, while wave after wave of pain radiated from her chest to every extremity of her body. She thought momentarily that she was dying — that her heart was giving out. But then the pain lessened to be replaced with a curious, unfeeling numbness.

Her brain scanned through millions of images of the times she'd spent with Carl. What did he tell his wife when they went on holiday that time to South Carolina? 'Another boring conference, darling'? And that ludicrous story about his mother's illness. How could she have been such a fool as to have believed that nonsense about flying down to Wisconsin every weekend?

She remembered how he'd left her alone in Boston over the Christmas holidays while he 'did his duty by his parents'. Now she knew where he had really been — cosied up in the Berkshires enjoying a family Christmas. As for the condo, his wife had been responsible for the décor, not an interior decorator. Slowly, she began to realise that she didn't know Carl Scholtz at all. Virtually everything he had told her about himself, or allowed her to believe by his omission, was a falsehood.

But the worst part, the very worst part of all, was what he'd done to her. He'd turned her into his mistress, one step up from a whore. Yes, it was terrible what he'd done to his wife, but everything about the conversation with Lynda Scholtz — from her choice of words to her tone of voice — told Kath that she was no victim. She sounded like a woman who was not only well able to deal with Carl's adultery, but possibly had had to deal with it before. But Carl had taken the pure, untainted love Kath had offered him and turned it into something dirty and cheap and wicked. And for that she could never forgive him.

When the phone rang again at one o'clock, Kath ripped the flex from the phone socket and threw the machine across the room. It smashed against the mirror on the wall above her dresser, and she watched as her face fell from the wall in a thousand pieces.

She lay in bed all day Saturday, ignoring the sound of Mrs Eberstark calling for her at the door, and all through the long, cold night that followed, remembering what her life had been like before the call. Imagining Carl with his wife and children. Wishing that she'd never answered the phone.

And then, in the early hours of Sunday morning a thought took hold and Kath was surprised it had taken so long to dawn on her. She lay peacefully while a relative calmness descended on her troubled mind.

What if someone was out to hurt Carl or her? She could think of no one from her past who would do such a terrible thing, but what about him? He was reluctant to talk about his family and his past. And maybe he had good reason. It could be a jilted lover or a jealous former wife with a vendetta against him.

All those things Lynda Scholtz had told her could be complete fabrication. Lynda Scholtz might not even exist! The woman on the phone could even have been Carl's mother, determined to break up their relationship — it was possible, wasn't it?

Kath sat up in bed and looked at the remains of the smashed phone on the floor, guilt flushing through her at the readiness with which she'd condemned Carl. She should have known he wasn't capable of such a terrible deception. And she wouldn't be able to retrieve the woman's number from the broken phone now. There was only one way to find out what the hell this was all about. She would have to ask Carl.

Her thoughts were interrupted by the sound of the doorbell, followed by Emmy's voice calling her name through the letterbox. She hauled herself from the bed, weak with exhaustion. The bedside clock told her it had just gone ten o'clock. She'd not eaten nor drunk since yesterday morning. As she stumbled past the mirror in the hall, she caught a glimpse of a pale, haggard face that she did not recognise at first as her own. She stopped and peered in the glass. The face of the woman staring back was blotched and her eyes were red and swollen. But in spite of her battered appearance she was not yet defeated. There was still hope in her eyes.

'Jesus Christ! What the hell's happened to you?' cried Emmy when Kath opened the door to her. 'You look terrible.'

'I'm alright,' mumbled Kath.

'Well, you don't look alright to me. Are you ill? What's wrong, Kath?'

'I'm fine really.'

'I've been trying to call you. What's wrong with your phone? I thought maybe you and Carl had gone off on an impromptu dirty weekend to celebrate.' Kath winced at these words but Emmy, not noticing, went on, 'And then I couldn't get you on your mobile. I started to worry.'

Kath went into the kitchen, filled a glass with water from the tap and drank it without pausing for breath.

'Kath,' said Emmy, who had followed her, 'if you're not ill, will you please tell me what on earth is going on?'

'I think you'd better sit down, Emmy. You're not going to believe this.'

She related the events of Friday night, as well as a line-by-line account of the telephone call the next morning.

'Oh my God,' said Emmy. She put her hands over her mouth and shook her head. 'Kath, I am so sorry!' She got up and put her arms around Kath where she sat on a kitchen chair. 'What a complete liar! A complete and absolute bastard! I always knew there was something shifty about him. I just knew he wasn't everything he appeared to be. But this — this is awful! It's worse than anything I could've imagined.'

'No, hold on a minute, Emmy,' said Kath and she pulled away from her friend's embrace and looked her in the eye, blinking back tears. 'That's exactly what I thought at first. But I've had time to think things through, and you know what?'

Emmy shook her head.

'This woman could've been anyone. She said she was Carl's wife but how do I know that?'

Emmy looked at Kath sadly and said, 'Oh, Kath, if only that were true . . . '

'But she could be a jealous ex-lover or even an estranged wife, couldn't she, trying to get back at Carl? It could even have been his mother, trying to split us up.'

'Oh, Kath,' said Emmy shaking her head, and she was about to go on but Kath silenced her by putting a finger to her own lips.

'Don't say it. Until I know for sure, Emmy,' she said firmly. 'I'm not going to condemn Carl. And I don't want you to either.'

'OK,' said Emmy slowly and then added, 'But how are you going to find out the truth?'

'Why, I'm going to ask Carl, of course. And I'll know if he's lying to me.'

6

It was late on Sunday night when Carl got back to St Botolph Street. Lynda had arranged for the family to go over to her parents for Sunday lunch — a fact she'd conveniently forgotten to tell him about — and of course he couldn't get out of it. He'd spent the afternoon being bored to tears by Lynda's father, Ted, who'd been drafted into the US Army in the 1950s and posted in the Philippines. Carl nodded politely and laughed in all the right places at stories he'd heard a hundred times before. Inside he was simmering with anger at Lynda — he'd wanted to spend the day alone with Jas and Daisy.

He'd only just taken off his coat and shoes when the buzzer on the door went. He answered it cautiously — he wasn't expecting anyone and it was well past ten o'clock. So he was surprised when Kath's voice came through the intercom. He pressed the button to open the main door to the building and, a few seconds later, she was in his apartment.

'Hello, babe,' he said, his pleasure at seeing her diminished only slightly by the unscheduled nature of her call. He planted a kiss on her cold cheek and said, 'What're you doing out at this time of night? You should've called to let me know you were coming.'

'I need to talk to you, Carl,' she said simply and she walked past him in the hall, her face impassive.

71

'Well, of course,' he said uncertainly and he followed her into the lounge. He noticed that she did not ask after his mother as she usually did on his return from a weekend away. He sat on one of the sofas, rested his right foot on his left knee and tried to look relaxed. But Kath remained standing.

'I'd rather sit in there,' she said, indicating with a nod of her head the dining room that lay beyond the glazed double doors at the end of the room.

Carl cocked his head a little in surprise but uttered no protest as he rose from the sofa and followed her into the next room.

'What's wrong, Kath?' he asked but she did not reply. He thought with concern of her family so far away in Ireland. 'Is someone in your family ill, Kath? Or worse?'

'No, no,' she said absentmindedly, her voice full of sadness. 'Nothing like that. Here, sit down there.'

She indicated a carver at the head of the mahogany table and he sat down. Then she sat in the chair to his left so that they were at right angles to each other.

He noticed that beneath her carefully applied make-up her eyes were bloodshot and swollen. 'Have you been crying, Kath?' he said and reached out to touch her cheek.

She withdrew sharply.

'Jesus, Kath, will you tell me what the hell is wrong?'

'I plan to,' she said coolly and Carl's heartbeat quickened as though he was on the running machine at the gym. 'Turn round a little,' she instructed, 'so that I can look at you. That's right. Come closer.' She took both his hands in hers and leaned in so that their faces were only a ruler-length apart. Her expression was stony, hard, like he'd never seen it before. It did not suit her soft features.

He shifted in the chair uneasily. 'What has happened, Kath?' he said and coughed, breaking eye contact with her. He tried to think what calamity could have induced such a change in her and was immediately filled with fear.

'Look at me. Please, Carl,' she said and she stared deep into his eyes with a penetrating gaze.

He felt her grip increase in pressure and realised then that her hands were shaking.

She blinked rapidly as though she was trying to hold back tears.

'I got a phone call yesterday morning, Carl,' she began, her voice high and thin. 'It was a woman calling herself Lynda Scholtz.'

Now his heart battered against the walls of his chest and he took several deep breaths. He tried to maintain a calm exterior but the muscles in his left eye twitched uncontrollably. This was the moment he had dreaded for so long. The moment he had hoped and prayed would never come. He said nothing. He waited for her to go on while his brain searched desperately for a plausible explanation.

'She said, Carl — ' Kath's voice broke then. She paused briefly, composed herself and went on, 'She said that she was your wife and that you have two children with her.'

That bitch, thought Carl. His eyes darted quickly to the left, then the right, but Kath held her gaze, forcing him to make eye contact with her again. Lynda had acted normally all weekend. Why had she not told him what she'd done?

'She said that you lived in the Berkshires, Carl, and that that's where you go every weekend.'

There was a pause then that seemed to last forever and all Carl felt was fear and panic. He bit his bottom lip and knew that he could not, must not, lose her. He knew that he should have laughed as soon as Kath said he had a wife and kids. He could have dissipated the tension immediately by brushing off the accusations as lightly as he brushed dust off his sleeve. But he'd been frozen with fear. And now the moment had passed.

Kath's eyes narrowed slightly and her black pupils contracted.

'Kath,' he said, in a light-hearted tone that sounded false even to him, 'I've never heard such rubbish in my life! Me married? Kids? Hey, you've got the wrong guy!'

She stared at him, and he knew by the misery and the grief etched on her face that she did not believe him. She knew he was lying.

She let go of his hands then and stood up without a word. Then she said, very quietly, 'All I want you to do is tell me the truth, Carl. I can find out, you know. Williamstown — that was the place she named. It can't be that big, can it? It wouldn't take much effort to track her down.'

She was right. They were listed in the phone

book, for Pete's sake! One call would lead her to Lynda. There was nothing for it now but to admit the truth and hope and pray that he could, by some miracle, persuade her to understand. If she loved him as much as he loved her, she would find it in her heart to forgive him.

He sighed deeply, glanced down at his hands now clenched together on the table to stop them trembling, raised his head to look at her again and said, 'It is true.'

Her hands shot up to her face and she whimpered like a puppy. She moved backwards away from him, knocking over a vase on the sideboard. It smashed on the parquet flooring but she did not seem to hear it. Her eyes were fixed on him in horror. He rose from his chair and, as he approached her, she ran out of the room.

'Kath, please! Let me explain. You don't understand,' he cried and he chased her into the hall.

She pulled the door open, swung round and shouted, 'I hate you, Carl Scholtz! I hate you! How could you have done this to me?' She paused, seemingly oblivious to the tears flowing down her cheeks, and then resumed, her voice full of steely anger, 'You said you loved me. You lying shit! Here, take this! I don't want it. I don't want to ever see you again.'

She worked at her left hand for a few seconds and then threw something at his face. It was hard and hit him just above the eye, nipping like a bee-sting. He tried to hold her in his arms, but she screamed and pushed him off.

'Get your hands off me! Don't you ever touch me again!' Her voice was breathless and full of hate.

Someone opened a door on the landing above, no doubt disturbed by the noise. Carl let her go and she disappeared down the stairs. He knew that there was no point in running after her. He heard the door on the landing above close with a soft click.

Carl closed the door and spied the ring he'd bought her for Christmas on the floor. He picked it up and examined it. A small lump formed in his throat and he swallowed. The ring had cost him a small fortune. He'd had it made specially for her in platinum — chosen the emerald and the diamonds himself. How he'd wished with all his heart that it could have been an engagement ring! It represented everything he thought about Kath — perfection, beauty and purity.

And now she hated him. A tear crept out of the corner of his right eye and he brushed it away angrily. He sniffed and gasped for air and stopped himself from crying. He got up and went into the lounge and sat on the edge of the sofa and twirled the ring round and round his little finger. He should have known that he would be found out one day.

But how did Lynda find out about Kath? He'd been so careful to separate his two lives and he'd been successful for so long. Then he remembered the conversation he'd had with Mandy on Friday night and knew immediately that she'd shopped him. Damn! He should've followed his instincts and got rid of her a long time ago.

Bitter and vengeful, Mandy probably couldn't wait to expose his duplicity. He could imagine the smug smile on her fat, round face as she called his wife. The pleasure she would take in his undoing — her revenge against all men for the wrong done to her. And who could blame her? On the face of it, what he'd done was unforgivable.

He saw now that he'd been living in a fantasy world — he had thought he could have his cake and eat it. But that didn't happen in real life and now he would be forced to choose between Kath and his family. For he was quite sure that Kath would never accept the status quo — not now that she understood what it was. And he didn't think that he could live without her. How did he ever get himself into such a mess?

Carl buried his face in his hands.

7

On Monday morning, Kath arrived at work on time, walked quietly to her desk and tried to carry on as though nothing had changed. Her work seemed pointless now — without Carl her entire life was pointless. The Boston that she'd loved so much now seemed noisy, dirty, squalid. Just another faceless city full of strangers with their sordid little secrets. People who weren't at all what they appeared to be. People like Carl.

She got a coffee from the machine and sat down heavily at her desk, her legs weak with exhaustion from lack of food and sleep. She shouldn't really have come to work — she wasn't capable of doing anything constructive — but she couldn't bear to be in the apartment all day. It was best to keep her mind and body active, otherwise the pain was too much to bear.

She noticed that the light on her answering machine was flashing — an angry bright orange wink. She wondered who could have left messages over the weekend. Surely not Carl? She glanced over her shoulder to ensure that no one in the open-plan office could overhear, then pressed the play button. She held her breath and listened. But the call wasn't from Carl.

'*Kath, it's me. David,*' said the voice. Kath's shoulders relaxed and she took a sip of coffee to moisten her parched lips. '*I can't get you at home or on your mobile. Look, can you call me as soon as you get this message? It's important.*

Kath detected a strained note in his voice. He didn't phone her often — they weren't that brilliant at keeping in touch with each other — and never at work. She frowned, put down the coffee cup and waited to hear the next message.

'Kath, I left a message earlier,' said David's voice again, but this time he sounded worried. *'I should have said. This is . . . it's . . . it's urgent. Call me.'*

Had something happened to Murray? Or Simone? Kath's heartbeat quickened. She strained to hear the last message on the machine. There were muffled noises in the background and, this time, the anguish in David's voice was laid bare.

'Kath, you have to call home. Day or night. Just call, will you?'

Something terrible had happened, that much was certain. Kath glanced at the clock on the wall. It was early afternoon in Ireland. She found David's number on her BlackBerry, and dialled. It tripped to his answer machine. She hung up, found her mother's number and dialled again.

It was David who answered.

'Thank God you've phoned, Kath! We've been trying to get you since yesterday afternoon. Where have you been?'

'Never mind that now. What's happened, David?' she said in a voice much calmer than she felt. 'Tell me what's happened.'

There was a long pause on the line and she was about to speak again when he beat her to it, sounding close to tears.

'Oh, Kerr,' he said, using her pet name from childhood, and she steeled herself, knowing that she was about to hear some awful news, 'it's Dad . . . ' His voice trailed off.

Kath froze and waited.

'It's Dad, Kath. He's dead.'

★   ★   ★

For the next twenty-four hours Kath had little time to grieve. Her first instinct was to phone Carl and then she remembered that she could no longer rely on him. So she phoned Emmy instead and she immediately took control. She collected Kath from work in a taxi, took her back to her apartment and checked her passport was up-to-date. Then she booked the earliest available flight out of Boston, got her sterling notes from the bank and helped her pack.

Kath phoned David to advise him of her travel arrangements — she would be flying with Virgin Atlantic direct to London early on Tuesday morning, then on to Belfast International Airport with British Airways. David agreed to pick her up from the airport. 'Under the circumstances Mum's holding up well,' David said, and Kath longed to be home. By the time she arrived in Ireland her father would have been dead for two days. The powerlessness of her situation, so far away from the people she loved and cared for, left her tense with frustration.

Once Emmy was satisfied that all the necessary arrangements were in place she took Kath and her suitcase over to the apartment she

80

shared with Steve where they smothered her in kindness. They coaxed her to eat, gave her a large whiskey and put her to bed early in the spare room.

But Kath lay wide awake into the small hours thinking of the last time she'd seen her father — he'd visited Boston only last summer with her mother. He'd seemed in rude health then and there had been no reports of ill health from home since then. David had been uncertain about the cause of death — it had been 'very sudden' and they were awaiting further information. It must have been a heart attack or a stroke, she concluded. What else could have carried him away so suddenly without any warning? Maybe she should be grateful, she thought, that he had gone quickly — that he hadn't suffered.

It wasn't until the Boeing 747 started to taxi down the runway at JFK Airport that Kath felt the first salty tears run down her cheeks and into her mouth. The shock of the news, on top of Carl's betrayal, had frozen her inside. Only now was she starting to melt.

She turned her face to the small glass window and watched as the plane took off, circled over Hudson Bay and was soon engulfed in low, dense grey clouds. How different her emotions were now compared to what they'd been when she'd arrived here all those years ago at the tender age of twenty-two!

Fresh out of university, there were few work opportunities in her native Northern Ireland and the prospect of going back home to Ballyfergus to wait out the recession filled her with dread.

Matt Doherty, her boyfriend of two years, had asked her to marry him and she'd said no. She was shocked to learn of the depth of his feelings for her — feelings that she could not reciprocate. And then she felt guilty for having gone out with him so long — 'leading him on' her mother had called it. She couldn't walk down the High Street without bumping into a friend or relative of his, none of whom looked kindly on her for breaking his heart.

So, when she discovered that she'd won a post-graduate year's paid work experience with a management consultancy in Boston, she jumped at the chance. She'd arrived in the city awestruck, excited and optimistic — and she'd never looked back. But look at me now, she thought bitterly. Her life was in tatters — the only man she could ever love was married to someone else and her beloved father was dead. At least Matt had found happiness — he'd married and had a clutchful of kids.

Kath rummaged in her bag for a packet of hankies and wiped her tear-stained face. She found the gifts Mrs Eberstark had pressed on her as she was leaving the building: the old lady's favourite *stroop*, or syrup, waffles and a box of chocolate-covered marzipan.

Poor Mrs Eberstark — she'd taken the news of Carl's betrayal so badly that Kath was sorry she'd told the old dear. Naturally Mrs Eberstark felt sorry for Kath with her love life in shreds and the tragic news about her father. But she grieved also for the shattered trust that she and

Kath had shared by believing in someone like Carl Scholtz.

The plane reached cruising altitude, the seat-belt signs were switched off and the interior lights switched on. Kath shut her eyes and her thoughts turned to home. She remembered the long, carefree summers of her childhood idled away in the grounds of the family hotel, the Sallagh Braes. She remembered how she and her siblings fought for turns on the rope swing hanging from the old chestnut tree and made a den in an unused shed at the back of the hotel.

Her head was filled with the smell of the heat shimmering on the crazy-paved patio and the heavy perfume of the blown lilies on the table in the dark reception hall. She associated her father with the hotel, rather than home, because that was where he spent so much of his time. She remembered his mahogany-lined office behind the reception desk, reeking of tobacco, where he kept Fisherman's Friends in the drawer beside his pipe.

She recalled how she sat on her father's knee and he fed her boiled lemon sweets. He called her his 'bonnie, blue-eyed girl' and this always confused her because her eyes were grey. If there was anywhere in the world, Kath thought, where she could heal her bruised and broken heart, it was there.

Kath sighed and saw that she'd been too busy — no, she corrected herself, too wrapped up with Carl — over the past eighteen months to visit home as much as she should have. It had been a year since her last visit and the guilt crept over her like a chill. She'd wasted all that time with Carl when she should have paid attention to her family. Now she would never see her father again . . .

'Can I offer you a drink?' said a woman's voice and Kath opened her eyes. The air hostess proffered a doll's-house-sized cup on a small plastic tray and Kath shook her head.

And how would Mum cope without Dad? They didn't have the kind of marriage where they lived in each other's pockets, but there was true and deep affection between them.

Would her mother stay on in Highfield House, the beautiful Georgian home she'd lived in all her married life? As for the hotel, the assistant manager was more than capable of running the business until it could be sold.

But Kath knew how much her father, Brendan, loved that hotel. And her mother too — it had belonged to Kath's maternal grandparents, and they had only one daughter, Fiona. On her marriage to Brendan, he had taken over the running of the business and Fiona had attended to matters at home. Even when her family were grown, Fiona never became actively involved in the day-to-day running of the hotel. It seemed so incredibly old-fashioned now, but that was how things were done back then. In the world Fiona came from, your wife only worked if she had to.

It would break Mum's heart to sell the hotel but David and Bridget weren't interested in it. Kath's heart beat rapidly in her chest and she sat upright in her seat. What if she took over the running of the hotel? It would mean making her life in Ballyfergus but what was waiting for her back in Boston? Nothing but crushed dreams and empty promises.

For her the city would always be tarnished with hateful memories of the pain Carl had caused. She never wanted to see him again as long as she lived. And how could she walk the familiar streets and sit in the cafés where they'd once been so happy together? Yes, this was what her father would've wanted, Kath was sure of it. And it would be her eulogy to him. A tribute to the very best father in the world.

8

'The house seems so empty without Brendan,' said sixty-five-year-old Fiona O'Connor. 'I can't believe he's really gone.'

Willie Ross, their solicitor and long-time friend, nodded comfortingly. Spread out on her elegant dining table in front of them both were the contents of Willie's briefcase. The casement clock, a wedding present from her parents, tick-tocked in the corner of the room — otherwise the house was deathly silent.

'You know,' she went on, ignoring the papers strewn across the polished wooden surface, 'I used to quite like it when he went away on business to those conferences. Sometimes it was nice just having the place to myself for a night or two, watching the soaps on TV and not having to bother making a proper meal. And now I feel so guilty because this time he won't be coming back . . . ' She bit her lip to stop her voice from breaking.

'You mustn't beat yourself up, Fiona. Everyone has regrets when they lose a loved one. Your Brendan was quite a man, wasn't he?' said Willie, and he nodded his head slowly, remembering, not expecting an answer. 'People used to say you could hear him coming before you saw him. He could light up a room just by standing in it.'

Fiona smiled thinly at Willie's characterisation of her dead husband — but his clichés were accurate all the same. Brendan had been larger than life in many ways. Through the dining-room window her gaze fell on the wet grey roofs of the Sallagh Braes Hotel, which lay only a few hundred yards down the hill from Highfield House. She could not look at it without thinking of Brendan.

'I'm just going to miss him so much,' she said and the tears welled up.

'I know, Fiona,' said Willie gently. 'We're all going to miss him. But I know you'll feel it the most.'

How would she carry on without him? She missed the way he filled the house as soon as he stepped through the front door, the way he shouted her name until she appeared, the way he regaled her with anecdotes of the day's activities at the hotel. She missed his smile and his good nature and, most of all, the companionship they'd shared. She dreaded the future without him.

She spied the bare branches of the ancient chestnut tree in the grounds of the hotel and her heart ached. She pictured the black-painted wrought-iron bench encircling the thick trunk — the bench where, all those years ago, Brendan had asked her to marry him. How could he . . . No, she told herself, she wouldn't think about it now. It was too painful.

'Ahem,' said Willie, clearing his throat, and she realised that he had asked her something.

'Sorry, Willie, what did you say?'

'I was just wondering where the others are? You shouldn't be here on your own.'

'It's only for a little while. David's gone to get Brendan's sisters from the airport and Bridget's gone home to make supper for her family.'

The truth was that she'd been glad of the peace to be alone with her thoughts. For all she'd thought about since Sunday was why. Why? Why? Why? But she had found no answers yet.

'Fiona, are you alright?' said Willie gently. 'We don't have to do this right now if you're not up to it?'

Holding back tears, she touched her greying hair to check it was still neatly restrained in a tidy bun and, with the flat of her right hand, she smoothed her tweed skirt over her knees. It wouldn't be right to let her appearance slip, she thought, even at a time like this.

'No, Willie, I'm alright. Really. Let's — let's just get it over and done with. Now what were you trying to tell me?' She squinted her eyes slightly as she prepared to concentrate. Then she folded her hands to stop them shaking, nodded and listened very carefully.

'I don't know how much you know about the hotel,' said Willie and he paused, waiting for some response from her.

'Well, you know I wasn't involved in the day-to-day running of the business,' she said matter-of-factly. 'Why, is there something I should know?'

'But you did know that things were — difficult, didn't you?' he persisted, as though willing her to understand something that he wasn't articulating.

'The hotel trade's always been a difficult one,

88

Willie,' she said, having no idea what he was alluding to. 'There's nothing new in that.'

He blinked at her for a few moments and said, 'I'm afraid I have some bad news for you, Fiona. Some very bad news.'

Her heartbeat quickened and she noticed with rising panic that he rubbed his hands together, as though washing them under a running tap. He only did this when he was extremely anxious. What on earth was he about to tell her?

'It's taken a long time for matters to — to deteriorate this far,' he said, and beads of sweat appeared on his bald patch.

'What matters?' said Fiona, trying to make sense of what he'd just said.

'The truth is that the hotel hasn't been profitable for years.'

She said, making no attempt to disguise the irritation in her voice, 'Willie, I have no idea what you're talking about.' Brendan had just died. Why was Willie wittering on about hotel profits? Hadn't she more important things to worry about, like arranging the funeral?

'Fiona, I'm trying to tell you that you are in very serious financial difficulties.'

She tried to absorb this statement and blinked at him, still uncomprehending.

'What exactly do you mean?' she said slowly.

'I mean that you . . . that Brendan has left you with no money. No money at all. The hotel's in the red and there's no prospect of trading out of these difficulties.'

'But, Willie,' said Fiona and a smile sprang involuntarily to her lips, 'my family have always had money. We own the hotel and this house. They must be worth something. How can I be — be penniless, like you say?'

'I'm telling you, Fiona,' he said and sighed deeply. He rubbed the palms of his hands over his bald patch as though smoothing down the hairs that once grew there. 'Listen, it's — it's complicated. Let me explain.'

'Alright,' she said stiffly, assenting mainly out of politeness. But she'd never known Willie to talk nonsense before . . .

Fear crowbarred its way quietly into her heart.

'Brendan kept the hotel going these last few years by borrowing money from the bank. And when that ran out — well, he borrowed some more. Look at the last four years' annual accounts,' said Willie and he eagerly pushed four sheets under Fiona's nose, as though the paper could deliver the terrible news so he wouldn't have to.

She blinked hard but the figures on the pages in front of her were indecipherable. She could not make sense of them and then she realised why — her vision was blurred by exhaustion and unshed tears.

When she said nothing, he coughed and went on. 'See here,' he said, pointing to a base-line figure on one of the pages with the point of his slim silver pen. Fiona noticed that his hand was shaking. 'By the end of 2000 the hotel was fully mortgaged. The bank refused to lend him any more.'

'Fully mortgaged?' she said, her head

befuddled by Willie's talk of annual accounts and mortgages.

'That's right. It means that the bank had loaned him as much as they thought was safely covered by their security over the hotel.'

'But that was nearly five years ago. How did he keep the business going . . . ' Her voice trailed off. Then she took several deep breaths as an unwelcome comprehension crept over her. Surely Brendan wouldn't have risked the one thing, second only to her family, that she held most dear? He wouldn't have done that, not without telling her. Not without discussing it. 'So,' she said carefully, 'where did the money come from to keep the hotel afloat for the last five years?'

'Ahem,' said Willie and he rested the elbows of his dark grey suit on the table. He looked down, rubbed the bridge of his nose with a crooked forefinger and looked up at Fiona again. 'This,' he said at last, with a gravity that chilled Fiona to the bone, 'is where we come to the difficult bit.'

Suddenly Fiona remembered signing a legal document some years ago. It was to do with tax, Brendan had told her vaguely. Something about it being financially prudent if the house was in his name . . . She stared at Willie, her heart gripped with dread, and waited for him to go on.

'He borrowed money using the house as security, Fiona. By the end of 2003 the business was haemorrhaging cash. And then in 2004 the roof needed replacing. You remember?' She nodded dumbly and he went on, 'And the same year The Marine Hotel opened their new function suite which took away a lot of the wedding business . . . ' He paused, took off his silver-framed glasses and rubbed his eyes.

Fiona struggled to make sense of what all this meant in relation to the house. 'If Brendan put the house up as security for the hotel's debt . . . ' she began uncertainly.

'That means that the bank can repossess the house to repay those debts,' said Willie, answering her implied question.

'But that's — that's not likely to happen, is it?' she said and she held her breath.

Willie laid the silver pen down on the papers in front of him and said in a voice so quiet Fiona had to strain to hear him, 'I found out this morning that the bank called in the debt weeks ago, Fiona. They served repossession papers on Brendan for the hotel — and this house — on Friday afternoon.'

Fiona gasped loudly and covered her mouth with her hands. Poor, poor, darling Brendan! Why didn't he tell her? Why did he carry this terrible burden all by himself? It would've driven anyone to despair. If only he'd confided in her. They could have got through it — somehow.

'Brendan didn't actually borrow that much against the house, considering its value, but with accrued interest and a forced sale of the hotel . . . well, I don't think there's going to be much left. In the end, you know, he owed nearly one and a half million.'

Fiona held onto the arms of the chair and gritted her teeth. Her whole body convulsed with grief and horror. That was a fortune! How could they possibly owe so much money? It was inconceivable. And how could she not have noticed what was going on?

It was her fault. She'd been too selfish, too absorbed in her own life and petty concerns to notice that the business, and Brendan, were falling apart. Even now, looking back, she couldn't remember any major change in his behaviour to indicate that anything was gravely amiss. He'd been quiet and withdrawn for a few weeks, that was all. She sobbed quietly for a few moments and then composed herself.

'But the house, Willie,' she whispered. 'This is my home.'

'I'm sorry, Fiona, truly I am. But unless you can find some way to repay the debts immediately, the bank is going ahead with the repossession of the hotel and the house. The hotel will have to stop trading immediately. I've spoken to the staff.'

'Thank you,' said Fiona, her reply more the result of innate good manners than any genuine appreciation. 'You know there isn't any money, Willie. Not enough to meet this level of debt. But wait! What about the insurance policies. Won't they pay out?'

Willie shook his head sadly. 'Not when it's . . . not under these circumstances. No.'

If only she'd known what desperate straits they were in, she could have done something to help. If only Brendan had confided in her!

'Why didn't you tell me, Willie?' she said, suddenly full of bitterness. 'I thought you were my friend. And Brendan's.'

Willie sighed again, hung his head and rubbed his forehead with his right hand. 'Brendan was a sole trader. I had no authorisation to discuss his business with you. And anyway, he told me that you'd agreed to put the house up as collateral. I thought you knew — I thought you must have known. I never imagined that he would keep all this a secret from you. Look, I've spoken to the bank and persuaded them to give you a few weeks. Out of respect for Brendan. But after that, Fiona . . . ' His voice trailed off.

'I'm out on the street,' she said flatly, finishing the sentence for him.

There was a long silence between them then which Willie eventually broke, his tone now less the accountant and more the friend.

'I feel terrible being the harbinger of this awful news, Fiona. I tried to talk to Brendan, I really did. I saw the way things were going but he wouldn't listen. He just stuck his head in the sand, hoping it would all blow over. Hoping some miracle would come along and make everything right again.' He stopped, cleared his throat and continued, his voice now creaking with emotion, 'I wish now that I'd done more to help him. But I never thought it would come to this. He never gave any indication that he was so desperate. If only I'd known . . . I've lost a good friend and to tell you the truth I feel responsible. And I always will.'

When she gave him no response, Willie quietly collected his papers, leaving a few sheets on the table, and put them carefully into his briefcase. The metal catch snapped shut like a gunshot in

94

the silence. Then he stood up and walked over to the chair where Fiona sat, stunned, staring out the window at the hateful chestnut tree. She didn't even have the right to fell it now — it belonged to the bank. Willie placed a long brown envelope on the table in front of her.

'There's just the small matter of the will, Fiona. It's pretty straightforward. He left everything to you.'

'For what it's worth,' she said ironically.

'Well, I'll leave it here anyway. There's something you should . . . well, I think you should read it, that's all. I am so very sorry, Fiona, I really am.' He placed what Fiona imagined he thought was a comforting hand on her shoulder. It felt like a dead weight. 'I don't like leaving you here on your own like this. Can I call anyone? Bridget?'

'No,' she said, her voice faint but commanding. 'David will be back shortly.'

He walked to the panelled door.

'There is one thing you can do for me,' said Fiona.

He paused with his hand on the door handle. 'Anything,' he said.

'The police will need to know about these — these financial circumstances.'

'I've already talked to them. I don't think they'll be bothering you again.'

★ ★ ★

Fiona listened with relief to the creak of Willie's footsteps in the hall and the dull thud of the

95

front door as he closed it gently behind him. Then she allowed her gaze to fall on the chestnut tree again and she was consumed with emotion, chiefly guilt.

She had failed Brendan. If she had been a better wife, a better soulmate, he would have told her what was wrong and between them they would have found a way to put things right. But she knew she could be harsh and critical — she did not suffer fools gladly. And she knew that this was why Brendan had not confided in her. He could not bear to be the object of her scorn and derision. And that was exactly how she would have reacted had he told her the truth. If anyone was to blame for what had happened, it was she.

Earlier all she wanted was to understand why. Now she had the answer to the question that had haunted her since Sunday — but it brought no peace of mind, only despair. Now she understood why he had done it, why he had taken the rope and . . .

'Why our tree, Brendan?' she asked aloud. It had been special to her — to both of them — and now her happy memories were destroyed forever. Why couldn't he have left her those at least?

She closed her eyes and the tears rolled unbidden down her cheeks. She saw him throw the blue nylon rope over one of the strong lower branches of the chestnut tree. She saw him fashion a makeshift noose — how would he have known what to do? — and put it round his neck, like a medal on a ribbon. She imagined him

96

standing on the wobbly little stool from the hotel kitchen. She pictured him kicking it over with his heels as he jumped — and she cried out.

She buried her face in her hands and wondered what his last thoughts were. Did he think of her? Did he, at the very last moment of life — when it was too late — change his mind?

She could not imagine how utterly alone he must have felt. She could not even begin to understand the darkness that had led him to this point. She still could not believe that he had chosen death over financial ruin. All she knew was that she was responsible and she would never forgive herself.

Fiona sat on until her heartbeat had regulated and the sickening feeling in her stomach receded. Then she looked at the clock — it told her that David would be due back from the airport soon with Brendan's sisters, Patricia and Theresa.

She took a tissue from the pocket of her skirt and wiped the tears from her face. She reminded herself that she still had her dignity, if nothing else. And dignity, her mother had taught her, was not something you were given, or something that could be taken away from you. It came from inside, drawn from the unlimited reservoir of your character.

And this is where Fiona knew she must get her strength from now on. All the outward signs of status that she had taken for granted — the house, the hotel, the money — were gone. She was stripped of everything but her core qualities as a human being.

She thought of her children and knew that she must be strong for them. The news of the family ruin would have to wait until tomorrow, when Kath arrived. For Kath did not yet know the truth about her father's death and Fiona would have to tell her first, before tackling the thorny issue of money.

Steeling herself, Fiona got up and went through to the kitchen to make tea and put out a plate of biscuits in preparation for her visitors. Her hand shook when she held the kettle under the running tap and, through sheer willpower, she forced it to stop. They said bad things came in threes. First Brendan had committed suicide and now the family were ruined. Surely things couldn't get any worse?

9

'Oh, God,' said Kath as soon as she saw David at Belfast International Airport. The combination of grief, pent-up anxiety over the last few days and sheer exhaustion took its toll — she burst into tears.

He took her in his arms and hugged her fiercely and, for a moment, it felt like her dad's arms around her. The tears came even more freely. They stood like that for some moments, amid the hustle and bustle of the airport, until Kath's sobbing had eased and David gently released her from his grasp.

'It's all right, Kath. You're going to be all right,' he said and she sniffed and nodded and searched in her bag for a hankie. When she'd wiped her eyes and calmed down a bit, she took her first proper look at the brother she hadn't seen for nearly a year.

'David,' she exclaimed, 'you look terrible. Are you feeling all right?'

'I'm fine,' he shrugged. 'It's been . . . a difficult few days.'

'Of course,' she said, 'and I'm so sorry that I couldn't get here any earlier. I tried to get a flight out on Monday but they were all booked up and then Aer Lingus phoned me back and said that — '

'Kath, it doesn't matter,' he said gently, cutting her off in mid-sentence. 'The important thing is that you're here now. Mum's desperate to see you. Now let's get these things in the car and get you home.'

As they made their way out of the arrivals hall, Kath stuck close to David, finding his physical presence a source of strength and comfort — she'd forgotten how much he looked like her dad. Briefly he told her the events of the last few days — how the funeral was booked for early next week and how relatives were already starting to congregate.

'And how is Mum?' said Kath.

'Devastated.'

'It was such a shock. I — I can't believe he's dead, David.'

'Neither can I. I wish now that I'd — ' He stopped abruptly.

'That you'd what?' said Kath softly.

'That I'd made up with him. After the fall out over the hotel, we never really made it up. Not properly.'

'But I thought you were speaking to each other.'

'Well, we were. On the face of it, everything appeared normal. But we never discussed the hotel and my decision not to come into the business. There was a coolness there. I don't think Dad ever forgave me for disappointing him.'

'It was unfair of him to expect you to do it,' said Kath quietly, and she flushed with shame for speaking ill of the dead.

They emerged from the airport terminal into a dull, overcast day — Kath felt beads of cold mist settle on her face and the dampness seep into her bones. She shivered.

'Nearly there,' said David and he pointed out the mud-splattered green Land Rover in the car park. He loaded her suitcase into the boot, ditched the luggage trolley by the kerb and they got in the car.

David exited the car park and pulled safely onto the main road. The sides of the road were trimmed with dirty grey snow and a fine misty rain landed soundlessly on the windscreen.

'So what exactly happened, David? Was it a heart attack?' she asked, once they had been driving for a few moments.

He turned the heating controls in the car up full and said slowly, 'No, we don't think so.'

'What then?'

He checked the wing mirror and ran a hand over his ruddy face, from forehead to chin. The skin on the palm of his hand was so roughened it made a sound like sandpaper. He looked like he hadn't slept in days.

'The doctors aren't quite sure.'

'But what else could it have been?'

Silence. David indicated and overtook the car in front.

'There'll need to be an autopsy, won't there?' she persisted.

'I suppose so. I hadn't thought about that.'

Perhaps David was more upset than she'd realised, she thought. Or perhaps his reticence about their father's death was due to nothing more than sheer exhaustion.

The car sped on through the rain for a few

minutes. The only sound breaking the silence between them was the squeak of the wipers on the windscreen. Then Kath asked cautiously, 'So where exactly did — did it happen? Was anyone with him?'

David cleared his throat and replied, 'In the garden of the hotel. John Routledge found him but by then he was . . . he was already dead.'

'Poor John,' said Kath and she blinked back tears. And poor Dad, dying alone with no one he loved beside him. She prayed it had been a painless, instantaneous death. 'But where exactly was he at the time? I mean what was he doing out in the garden at this time of year?' she said, trying to piece together her father's last moments.

David rubbed his face with his right hand again like he was trying to keep himself awake. They approached a roundabout and he came too close to the car in front — he braked hard.

'Kath,' he said gently, 'we've lots to talk about but Mum wants to tell you herself. Why don't you wait until we get home?'

'OK,' said Kath softly and they drove the rest of the way home more or less in silence. If David was acting a little strangely it was only to be expected, she told herself. So she swallowed the questions that sprang to her lips and watched the familiar landscape fly by instead. As they began their gentle descent into Ballyfergus, in spite of her grief, she found her soul uplifted.

Once they were through the town and driving north on the Antrim Coast Road, she strained eagerly to take in the view. Completed over one hundred and sixty years ago, just before the outbreak of the devastating Irish Famine, the fifty-mile stretch of road was one of the most scenic in all of the British Isles. It never failed to take Kath's breath away, even now, immersed as she was in grief.

A triumph of Victorian engineering over nature, the road hugged the contours of the coast — a breathtaking vista of towering cliffs interspersed with rolling green glens, waterfalls and pretty villages, like Ballygalley and Glenarm, with their sandy beaches and picturesque little harbours. Its construction involved pioneering techniques such as blasting complete headlands and using the debris as sea defences to protect the road from erosion. For most of its length the road ran right beside the sea, just above high water mark. Driving north towards Highfield House, the sea and the grey hulk of Scotland were visible on the right.

After some ten minutes they reached the familiar road sign, now a bit battered and worn by winter storms and sea spray. 'The Sallagh Braes Hotel', it said. The hotel had been named by Kath's grandparents after the dramatic rounded cliff called the Sallagh Braes, a notable landmark and viewpoint, at nearby Carncastle. David pulled into the entrance, framed by two stone pillars, and began the ascent up the tarmacked road. They drove past the turn off to the hotel, hidden from view by a wall of trees, and continued on up the narrow road that led to Highfield House.

David stopped the car in front of the

103

handsome Georgian façade and Kath's stomach churned with emotion. Then the front door burst open and Fiona appeared on the top step, her arms folded across her chest and her face creased with concern. Kath jumped out of the car and mounted the steps two at a time.

'Kath! Kath! You're here at last,' cried her mother and they embraced on the top step. Since the age of fourteen Kath had towered over her mother by some four inches but, height apart, they had always been equals physically. Now, for the first time, Kath noticed a change in her mother — she seemed smaller, frailer, diminished somehow from the last time they'd seen each other.

When they eventually pulled apart Kath saw that difference clearly — Fiona was suddenly prematurely aged. The crow's feet wrinkles around her eyes were pronounced, her hair was much greyer now than before and her once proud shoulders slightly stooped.

'Oh, Mum,' said Kath, fighting to hold back tears, 'I'm so sorry about Dad. I can't believe he's gone. I'm going to miss him so much.'

'I know, love. It's been such a terrible shock for all of us,' said Fiona and suddenly she started to cry, a low pitiful moan. For a few seconds Kath stood rooted to the spot — she had never seen her mother cry like this and it unnerved her deeply. Mum was her rock, but right now she needed Kath to be the strong one.

After a few seconds' hesitancy, she said, 'Please don't cry, Mum,' and rubbed her mother's right shoulder as though the physical contact could obliterate the pain. 'Come on, it's going to be all right. I'm here now.'

After a few moments, no longer, Fiona regained her composure. She brushed the tears from her face with two quick swipes of her hand and blinked. 'I'm sorry,' she said.

'There's no need to be,' replied Kath softly.

David brushed past them, laden with Kath's bags, and said, trying to inject some light-heartedness into the situation, 'Are you two going to stand there all day gabbing? Here, get the door for me, Kath, will you?'

'Come on inside, love,' said Fiona. 'You must be famished. I'll get you a wee cup of tea and something to eat.'

Kath allowed herself to be guided into the cosy kitchen with, at its heart, the faithful chipped cream Aga, while David took her things upstairs. She sat at the oak table and touched the scratches and scrapes on its worn surface with the tips of her fingers. Each one was a memory of childhood — of the meals taken here, cakes and biscuits baked and, later, the long hours spent toiling over homework.

David came in and said, 'I'll need to get off now, Mum. I've got to clear that small patch of young rhododendron bushes I noticed beside the river.'

'But why? They have the most beautiful flowers,' said Kath.

'*Rhododendron ponticum* is also very invasive. If I don't keep them under control they'll take over the entire forest and kill just about everything else in it! I'll see you later tonight.'

He kissed Fiona, gave Kath a big bear hug and then left.

'I've made up the bed in your old room,' said Fiona, taking things out of the fridge. 'It's been redecorated since the last time you were here so it's nice and fresh.'

Fiona — seeming more her old self now — made tea and rustled up a sandwich of wheaten bread, cheese and homemade pickle. It was the best thing Kath had eaten in days.

'Where's Bridget?' she said, between hungry mouthfuls.

'She's coming over later with the children and Ned. And Aunt Pat and Aunt Theresa will be coming too. They're staying with your cousin Mary.'

Kath forced herself to suppress the little ball of resentment that formed in her stomach. Much as she loved her aunts, she wanted to have time with her close family alone — time to catch up and reminisce and grieve. But her aunts were her father's sisters, she reminded herself, and they would feel his loss as much as she. They too would need space and time in the bosom of the family to mourn his passing.

After she'd eaten, Fiona said, 'Why don't you go on up to your room and unpack, Kath? I'll be up in a minute to help you, once I've cleared these things away.'

Kath did as she was told. Upstairs, she was surprised to find her old room painted white with a pale blue gingham cover on the bed and matching curtains framing the window. There were splashes of red in the blanket folded at the foot of the bed and the cushion on the chair. The bright, modern scheme reminded her a little of New England — she liked it.

She looked out the window at the view of the slope dropping away from the house, the grey roof of the hotel and, beyond, the dark blue choppy water of the North Channel. She was so glad to be here, safe in what she thought must be the most beautiful place in the world. She wondered that she'd ever left.

The creak of the door announced Fiona's arrival. She came in and shut it carefully behind her.

'I like the room, Mum. Did you get the idea for it when you were over in Boston?'

When her mother did not answer, Kath looked closely at her face. Her expression was grim and there was something strangely laboured about her movements as she walked across to the bed.

'What is it?' said Kath.

Fiona sat down on the checked duvet cover and patted the space on the bed beside her.

'Kathleen,' she said, using her daughter's full name and setting off alarm bells inside Kath's head. She only called her 'Kathleen' when she was cross with her or wanted to indicate that she had something very serious to say. 'Will you come and sit down here a minute?'

If the worst hadn't already happened, Kath would've thought that her mother was steeling herself to deliver some awful news. She sat down gingerly on the edge of the bed facing her mother and waited.

Fiona stared at her wordlessly for a few

107

seconds, her green eyes like wet glass, and then she said, 'Kath, there's something I have to tell you about your father. About the nature of his death.'

Kath took short, shallow breaths and her heartbeat quickened. She *knew* David had been acting strangely. What on earth was this all about? Did Dad have a terminal disease he hadn't told anyone about — like cancer? Or had his death been caused by an accident and not natural causes as she'd assumed? Even more ominously, was there something suspicious about his death?

'Kath,' said Fiona sadly, 'I really don't know how to tell you this . . . '

'What, Mum?' said Kath as the fear inside her grew.

'Your father — ' began Fiona and two tears rolled down her cheeks. She brushed them away angrily, swallowed and cleared her throat.

'Tell me,' said Kath, every muscle in her body tight with dread.

Fiona looked her straight in the eye and said, her voice quivering with emotion, 'Your father took his own life.'

Kath watched her mother's face closely as the words sank in. Daddy killed himself? It wasn't an accident, or a heart attack? He *chose* to die? No, she didn't believe it. This could not be true of the loud, gregarious man she had known who loved and lived life to the full. She looked at the checked pattern on the bedspread and then back at her mother's face.

'Mum,' she said quietly, shaking her head,

'Daddy wouldn't have done that. He wouldn't have left us like that. He loved us. There must be some mistake.'

'No, Kath. I'm sorry, love, but it's true.'

Kath swallowed and stared. 'Tell me what happened,' she said in an emotionless voice that sounded like it came from somewhere outside of her. Inside she was falling apart.

Fiona took an audible, deep breath, before going on in a low, unsteady voice. 'He hanged himself from the chestnut tree in the garden of the hotel after attending Mass on Sunday. I thought it was strange when he said he was going — as you know, he never went to church . . . ' She was lost in her own thoughts for a few seconds and then resumed her story. 'John Routledge, the assistant manager at the hotel, found his body only minutes after he passed away, they reckon. He cut him down — but of course it was too late.' She paused then and her face was etched with misery. 'I wouldn't have told you, Kath, or the others, but well, you know what Ballyfergus is like. You can't keep a thing like this a secret for long. I would have spared you the pain if I could.'

Tears began to stream down Kath's cheeks. 'But why, Mum?' she managed to say, between sobs. 'Why would Dad do such a terrible thing?'

Fiona looked at her hands, locked together in a white embrace, and said, 'He never left a note or confided in me, Kath. That's what makes it so hard to bear.'

'Poor Dad!' cried Kath and she put her hands to her face and sobbed uncontrollably. 'How could he do this to me — to us? How could he do this without saying goodbye?'

'I don't know, love,' said Fiona quietly and she put her arms around Kath and held her tight.

After she had calmed a little, Kath asked her mother to tell her the full facts about her father's death and she listened carefully, her head swimming with exhaustion and shock.

Then Fiona went downstairs, came back with a sleeping tablet and a glass of water which she gave to Kath and put her to bed fully clothed. Kath crawled in under the covers, feeling like a child again, and eventually fell into a fitful doze, full of weird images and strange sounds, none of which made any sense at all.

★   ★   ★

Fiona had only just closed the door to Kath's bedroom, and leaned her back against it, when the doorbell rang. She wiped a tear from her cheek and prayed it wasn't more mourners to offer their condolences and home baking. People had been awfully kind and she was truly grateful for their concern. But it was unbearable listening to the same awkward platitudes and repeating Brendan's tragic story over and over again.

The doorbell rang again, this time a little louder and a little longer. She couldn't possibly ignore it — that would be inexcusable rudeness. So she went downstairs, took a few seconds to compose herself and opened the front door. She was relieved to find John Routledge, assistant manager from the hotel, on her doorstep, rather

110

than a well-meaning distant relative or neighbour who would expect to be invited in for the obligatory cup of tea. His hands were shoved deep into his trouser pockets and he had no coat on, in spite of the leaden sky that promised rain.

'Mrs O'Connor,' he said and he paused, shuffled his feet and looked at the stone step, 'I'm — I'm sorry about Mr O'Connor. All of us are. All of us down at the hotel. It's a terrible thing, so it is, and we just wanted you to know that we're really sorry for your loss.'

At thirty-three years old, John stood six feet tall with a head of thick, straight reddish-brown hair, a lightly freckled face and broad shoulders. He had been, Fiona remembered, a favourite of Brendan's.

'Thank you, John,' she said blinking hard. 'That's very kind of you.' Not trusting herself to cope with a conversation without breaking down, she added, 'It's very good of you to call. I really do appreciate it. Now I — I must get on.'

She started to shut the door but, instead of turning and walking away, John stood where he was, with his hands still deep in his trouser pockets.

'What is it?' she said wearily, her brain slowly shutting down with the stress of recent events.

'I — I wanted to speak to you on behalf of some of the staff. Not for myself, you understand.'

'What about?' said Fiona and she screwed up her eyes as a migraine slowly began to take hold.

'Well, they haven't had any wages for nearly two weeks and some of them are a bit desperate,'

111

said John, meeting her gaze with pained sea-green eyes.

'Oh,' said Fiona and she stood at the threshold for a few moments, dumbfounded. 'I think you'd better come in, John,' she said at last.

He followed her into the lounge where she sat down on a sofa because her legs would no longer support her. She regarded John for a few moments and then decided that he deserved nothing less than the complete and honest truth. She took a deep breath and began.

'I don't know how much Brendan told you about our financial circumstances,' she said and John shook his head gently. She tried to be more direct. 'Well, the truth is that we're . . . I'm . . . ruined. The hotel and the house. Everything is gone.'

'What? What d'you mean 'gone'?' said John, confusion clouding his face.

'The bank is about to repossess the hotel and the house. There's nothing left, John. I have nothing with which to pay staff wages. Oh, my God,' she cried and put her hands up to her face, the shame was so hard to bear, 'I'm so sorry!'

'No, I'm sorry, Mrs O'Connor. I'm sorry I came. I'd — I'd no idea. I knew Brendan had cash-flow problems but — but I'd no idea things were so bad. When Mr Ross said the hotel would be closing until things were sorted out, I thought he meant just until after the funeral. Until you decided what to do with the hotel. I didn't realise . . . '

His voice trailed off and Fiona was surprised to hear real emotion in his voice. He must have been fond of Brendan.

Then he composed himself, stood up and said, 'I'm sorry for bothering you, Mrs O'Connor. I'll go now.'

'No!' cried Fiona and she leapt to her feet. 'I can't send you away with nothing. I can't have the staff not getting paid.' She searched frantically round the room and her eyes came to rest on the valuable antique clock on the mantelpiece. She stumbled over to it.

'Here,' she cried, wrenching the lump of black marble from its position above the fire. It was very heavy and she struggled to hold it in both arms. 'Take this, John, and sell it. It must be worth something. Go on! Go on! Here!'

He stepped back from her then with a look of horror and pity on his face.

'No,' he said and shook his head. 'No, Mrs O'Connor. You keep that. You don't have to do this. I can't take your clock. Here, give it to me.'

Then he came forward again and gently eased the clock out of her grip. Effortlessly he replaced it on the mantelpiece.

'But I feel so responsible, John,' said Fiona, shaking her head. 'If my father were alive today he'd be mortified.'

'I think, Mrs O'Connor, that you've lost enough already. And,' he said, nodding at the clock, 'you're going to need what you have left for the future. I'll let myself out.'

And with that, he walked to the door, opened it and turned round.

'I am so very sorry,' he said in a broken voice

and then he was gone. The door clicked shut behind him.

Fiona sat down abruptly on the sofa because her legs were shaking so much she thought they might give way. How could Brendan bring this shame on the family? How could he leave her with this mess to sort out? She couldn't have the family name marred by gossip and scandal. And she couldn't live with herself, knowing that creditors and staff were out of pocket — not while she had any resources to her name. She would have to find a way to repay them, whatever the cost to her personally.

She thought of John and felt sorry for him, having to come up here to beg for staff wages. She imagined that the confrontation had been as unpleasant for him as it had been for her. And yet he had been nothing but kind and understanding — now she understood why Brendan had been so fond of him.

She glanced at the clock. She knew what she had to do and there was no time to lose. She picked up the phone and dialled Willie Ross's office.

10

'That's them here now,' said Kath, some six hours later, and Fiona's heart sank. Not at the prospect of seeing her youngest daughter and her family, but because their arrival meant she was one step closer to having to divulge the family's ruin. She arranged a serene expression on her face and followed Kath into the spacious hall, full of the sound of people who hadn't seen each other for over a year greeting each other.

'Look how big you've grown,' said Kath, who seemed restored to near normal by her nap. She held Alex's face in her hands and the child squirmed with embarrassment. Not having children of her own, Kath didn't understand nine-year-old boys very well, thought Fiona. A slapping of palms — a 'high five' Alex called it, whatever that meant — would've been much more to his liking.

Kath moved on to greet Laura who stood shyly by her mother's side, with her thumb in her mouth.

'Auntie Kath! Auntie Kath! Look how much I've grown,' interrupted Charmaine in her high-pitched voice. Unlike her brother, she was desperate for her aunt's attention — she stood on her tiptoes and everyone laughed.

'Charmaine!' scolded Bridget. 'Don't be such a show-off! And will you stop shouting, for heaven's sake. And Laura, take your thumb out of your mouth — you're not a baby!' Then, turning to her sister with a strained smile, she said, 'Kath, it's good to see you.'

She put the casserole dish she held in her arms down on the floor and briefly embraced her sister. Ned, hampered by the large cardboard box he held, gave Kath a peck on the cheek.

'Where do you want this?' said Ned to Fiona, indicating the box in his arms.

'Take it into the kitchen,' instructed Bridget, before Fiona could speak. 'And you lot,' she said to the children, 'go into the small lounge and watch TV until this is ready.'

The children obeyed.

Bridget picked up the casserole dish and said, 'It's nothing fancy, Mum — just beef casserole, salad and some crusty bread.'

'Oh, Bridget, it's perfect. Thank you for bringing it. I couldn't have coped.'

'Of course you couldn't, Mum. Nobody expects you to,' said Bridget and she led the charge into the kitchen.

Fiona smiled inwardly — Bridget might be a bit of a bossy-boots, but at a time like this she was exactly what was needed.

Ned deposited his box on the kitchen table and wandered into the hall to see what the children were up to. Bridget put the casserole dish in the hottest part of the Aga and said, 'Half an hour should do it — it's still slightly warm.'

Fiona carved the floury white loaves into rough chunks with a bread knife while Kath and Bridget exchanged chitchat about the children and Kath's journey. She'd let everyone eat in

116

peace, she decided, and tell them afterwards.

'Mum, are we eating in the dining room?' said Kath, pulling knives and forks out of the cutlery drawer.

'I suppose so,' said Fiona, suddenly grateful for the everyday diversion of serving a meal. 'There isn't room for everyone in here,' she said, glancing at the oak table.

'I'll set the table then,' said Kath, depositing the cutlery on the tray with a loud crash. Then she loaded the tray with glasses, place mats and paper napkins and left the room.

As soon as she had gone, Bridget asked, 'Did you tell her about Dad?'

'I did,' said Fiona, piling bread into a basket and still preoccupied with the next challenge ahead of her.

'And? How did she take it?' said Bridget, peeling the cling film off the green-filled glass salad bowl.

'Well, she was very, very upset. She didn't believe me at first, until I told her exactly what had happened. I think what upset her most was the fact that your dad didn't say goodbye. If he'd only left a note or something it would . . . well, it would have made things easier for all of us.' Fiona realised with a jolt that she was angry with Brendan. 'Anyway, I'm glad I told her face to face.'

'Kath always did get special treatment, didn't she?' said Bridget quietly and Fiona shot her daughter a censorious glance. Bridget had a breezy, defiant smile on her face — an attempt to take the sting out of what she had just said.

117

'Bridget,' said Fiona sharply, 'that's not true.'

'Well, how come you told me and David over the phone then?' said Bridget evenly, the smile slipping a little.

'I . . . I wasn't thinking straight. With hindsight, it was a bit thoughtless, yes. But I couldn't tell Kath when she was on the other side of the world, with no one to comfort her, now could I?'

'She has Carl.'

'It's not the same as family,' said Fiona, wondering why Bridget always thought she was hard done by.

Bridget put the salad bowl on the kitchen table, opened the fridge and took out a bottle of salad dressing. She shook it liberally on the lettuce leaves, then tossed them with her bare hands.

'I wonder why he didn't come with her?' she said.

'I expect he couldn't get the time off work. Anyway, it's not exactly the best time to introduce him to the family, is it? Now,' Fiona glanced at the kitchen clock, 'when's David coming over?'

'Any minute now. And he's bringing Simone.'

'Good. I like Simone — she's a very sensible girl. You know, I don't know how he ever got mixed up with that Viv.'

'You really don't like her, do you?' said Bridget, washing her hands under a hot running tap.

Fiona put the bread knife down on the breadboard and dusted the flour off her hands. 'I used to, but since she and David split up she's shown her true colours. She's nothing but a money-grabbing little witch. You know she hasn't so much as telephoned to offer her condolences. When I think of everything we did for her — '

The doorbell went and Bridget said, 'That'll be them now. Let's put the bread and salad on the table, shall we? We can sit down to eat straightaway.'

At the dinner table, everyone was acutely aware of the empty chair at the head of the table. For the sake of the children, the adults tried to act as normal but the conversation was desultory. Nobody ate much.

'Kath,' said Bridget, watching her sister push the food round her plate, 'don't you like it?'

'Oh, it's delicious. I'm just not that hungry.'

'You should watch out, Kath. You're very thin, you know.'

'Am I?'

'You're not on a diet, are you?'

'No. I just look after myself, that's all. And I go to the gym.'

'Granny,' said Charmaine, just as Fiona was about to tell Bridget to stop picking on Kath, 'can I see Granddad now?'

Fiona stared at her granddaughter and the tears welled up. She blinked rapidly, trying desperately to hold them back. She could not speak. The others round the table looked at each other.

It was Simone who spoke first. 'Your granddaddy's gone to heaven, Charmaine,' she said gently, in a matter-of-fact way. 'You won't be seeing him again.'

'Not ever?'

'Well, yes, you will one day — but not for a long time. When you go to heaven he'll be waiting there for you.'

'Will he play with me?'

'Yes, and he'll be just the way he was the last time you saw him.'

Fiona quickly dabbed at her eyes with a napkin and smiled as reassuringly as she could at Charmaine.

'OK,' said the child after a long pause and Fiona was able to breathe again.

Ned coughed and said, 'We'll need to be getting back now. The kids have school in the morning.'

There were mumblings of protest from Alex and Laura.

'You're sending them?' said Kath, sounding surprised.

'Children need routine, Kath,' said Bridget. 'They've had two days off already and the funeral isn't until next week. There's no point in keeping them off any longer. It's unsettling them.'

Steeling herself, Fiona decided that she could postpone the inevitable no longer. She cleared her throat and said, 'Ned.'

'Yes?'

'Could you do me a favour?'

'Of course,' he said graciously.

'Could you take the children home and give Simone a lift on your way?'

'Sure . . . ' said Ned and he looked from

Bridget to David, both of whom raised their eyebrows and shook their heads slightly, indicating that this request was as much of a surprise to them as it was to him.

'I need to have a chat with my children,' offered Fiona. 'We have some . . . some matters to discuss.'

'Surely Ned is family, Mum. And Simone — ' began Bridget in protest but Fiona interrupted.

'This is a family matter, Bridget,' she said firmly. 'There are private things that I need to discuss with you and your brother and sister.'

Ned and Simone must have detected the determination in her voice as, to Fiona's relief, they collected their things and the children, and, without further ado, they left.

★   ★   ★

'Mum, what's all the secrecy about?' said Kath, following Fiona into the library along with the others and deciding that her mother was acting really weird.

'I'm not being secretive,' retorted Fiona. 'Believe me, what I'm about to tell you isn't going to be a secret round Ballyfergus for long.'

'So why send Ned and Simone home?'

'Just bear with me, will you?' said Fiona and the exasperation in her voice silenced Kath.

They all shuffled through the door and sat around the room like the cast in the final 'unveiling' scene in a murder mystery. Bridget and David shared the small chestnut leather sofa, leaving Kath the leather easy chair. She

121

perched on it gingerly, mindful that it used to be her father's favourite seat in the house. Fiona stood facing them, leaning against the edge of the solid oak desk, as though for support. She looked utterly exhausted — and yet determined.

'I'm very sorry,' she said steadily. 'I have some — some unpleasant news to share with you.'

Kath's stomach churned with anxiety — she could not even begin to guess what would come next.

'I have to tell you the reason why your father took his life.'

11

No one made a sound. The room was silent except for the sound of the rain against the window. Everything, even time, seemed to stop.

Kath froze, held her breath and waited for Fiona to go on.

'I met with Willie Ross yesterday morning,' Fiona began and she went on to relate everything that had passed between her and the solicitor.

Kath and her siblings sat in utter silence as she spoke.

David was the first to break the silence. 'But how . . . ?' He shook his head. 'I don't believe it.'

'I didn't either,' said Fiona firmly, 'but I assure you it's true. I've seen the figures for myself.'

Bridget blinked and said, with a nervous laugh, 'But this can't be right. There must be something we can do!'

'I'm afraid not, Bridget. I've been through all the options with Willie and there's no way out. We're going to lose the hotel and this house.'

Kath said nothing and stared at her mother's resolute face, as she tried to take in the implications of what she'd just heard. How could they be ruined? This house and the hotel had been in the family for over eighty years. It belonged to the O'Connor's; it was part of the fabric of their being. But the longer she stared at her mother's implacable expression, the more

123

she knew it to be true. Kath thought of her dream on the plane when she'd fantasised about taking over the hotel. Was that dream to be cruelly shattered, in the same way her dream of a future with Carl had been?

She glanced at David and a terrible thought flashed through her mind. If he had gone into the business with Brendan — if he had been there to help him, as Brendan had so clearly wanted — perhaps this might never have happened. She banished the unjust thought from her mind as quickly as it arose — it wasn't fair to blame David. She'd followed her own path in life — why shouldn't he enjoy the same privilege?

'So the hotel and the house had already passed into the possession of the bank on Friday, two days before Dad died?' said Bridget, the vertical furrow in her brow deep with concentration.

'That's right,' said Fiona. 'I'm only here on their sufferance. They've agreed to let me stay in the house for a few weeks. To give me time, I suppose, to find somewhere to live and to clear out the house.'

'And to avoid bad press,' said David bitterly.

'What d'you mean?' asked Bridget.

'Well, can you imagine the headlines?' said David. '*Newly Bereaved Widow Evicted from Family Home by Bank.*'

Bridget nodded slowly and there was a short silence.

'You're very quiet, Kath,' observed Fiona and Kath stared at her dumbly.

Sometimes, she thought to herself, you have to fight for what you want. The way she saw it, she

124

had two options. She could either sit and do nothing and let fate decide what happened next. Or fight for what she wanted . . .

'I'm just trying to make sense of it all,' she said. She was a wealthy woman, on paper anyway. Her family had no idea what her apartment in downtown Boston was worth — or the fact that for years she'd been investing shrewdly in the stock market.

'But the bank,' said Bridget, continuing on where the conversation had left off, 'they can't throw you out of the house just like that.'

Kath realised that she'd only the vaguest notion what the hotel was worth. But if she liquidated all her assets, and maybe borrowed a bit, surely she wouldn't be far off the mark?

'I'm afraid they can,' said David, in response to Bridget's question. 'Dad had reached the end of the line.'

'Poor Dad,' whispered Kath, only half listening to the conversation around her. This, then, was the reason Dad killed himself. Because of money. It was pathetic and tragic. What a terrible, pointless waste of life! The anger welled up inside her.

'Poor Mum!' said Bridget, suddenly angry. 'Look at the mess he's left her in — left all of us in. He just — opted out. And now Mum's got to pick up the pieces.'

'Bridget!' cried Kath, springing to her feet. 'How dare you talk about Dad like that!' She could not bear to hear her father criticised, even though there was an element of truth in what Bridget said.

Fiona, Kath noticed, lowered her gaze to the dark blue carpet and did not leap to Brendan's defence. Then she spoke — but not to stand up for her dead husband.

'Girls,' she said, 'please. Arguing isn't going to help matters. Now, will you sit down, Kath?'

Kath sat down abruptly, bit her lip and glared at Bridget. She'd been in her sister's company for less than two hours and already they were at each other's throats — just like old times. Bridget was always trying to tell her what to do. After a few moments of awkward silence David spoke again, changing the subject.

'What will you do with the contents of the house, Mum?'

'You're not going to have to sell them, Mum, are you?' chimed in Bridget, aghast.

'What else can I do, love?' said Fiona and she closed her eyes. 'I have to keep reminding myself that they're only material things. I keep telling myself that they don't matter.'

'But they do matter!' said Bridget with feeling. 'What about the things that belonged to Gran and Granddad McIntosh. You can't just — just sell them.'

There was no way her resources would stretch to buying the house as well, thought Kath sadly. The hotel must be her first priority. But one day she'd get the house back too . . .

'Do you think I like it any more than you do, Bridget?' Fiona said sternly and then her voice softened. Her gaze roamed around the room and she said, 'Don't make this any harder for me than it has to be. I thought that I — your father

126

and I — would retire in this house. You know,' she said and laughed feebly, 'I'd even planned, one day, to die here.'

'Oh, Mum!' uttered Kath instinctively, but her voice was choked with compassion — she could say no more.

Then Fiona closed her eyes again and her body which had been rigid with tension suddenly went limp.

'Mum!' cried David, already on his feet. 'Are you all right?'

Kath stood up too, but it was David who caught Fiona just as she started to fall, her legs giving way underneath her.

'Yes, I'm fine,' she mumbled in a woozy voice. 'I just need to sit down a minute. This is all . . . it's all a bit much.'

David helped her into the chair behind the desk and Kath poured her a drink of water from a carafe. Fiona put the glass to her lips with an unsteady hand, and drank it all. Then she set the glass down carefully on a coaster.

'I'm fine now, thank you,' she said.

'Maybe we should get a doctor,' said Bridget and she placed her hand briefly on her mother's brow. 'Mmm . . . you don't seem to have a temperature.'

'Oh, stop fussing!' said Fiona, swatting at her daughter's hand like it was a bothersome fly. 'I'm fine. Really I am.'

'Do you think we should call the doctor?' said Bridget to David, ignoring her mother's protestations. 'It could be something serious.'

'She seems all right to me, Bridget,' said Kath

quietly, thinking that her mother had never looked so alert — or so irritated.

Then David said in a loud, clear voice, 'Are you sure you're OK, Mum?'

'Oh, for heaven's sake!' she replied in a withering tone. 'Will you stop shouting at me, David? I'm not deaf. And Bridget, if I need a doctor, I'll let you know. Now will you please sit down, all of you. I haven't finished yet. I've more to tell you.'

Kath glanced nervously at the others as they all took their seats again. Good God, she thought, what on earth was her mother going to say next? She didn't think she could take much more of this. First there was Carl, then the terrible news of her dad's death followed by the family's financial ruin. What could possibly be next?

'I've been thinking about everything and I'm not completely without resources,' began Fiona.

Kath's spirits rose. There was a silver lining to this black cloud after all.

'I have a fair wee bit of money put by in my name,' continued Fiona, her tone more upbeat than before. 'Your Granddad McIntosh, being a prudent Scot, insisted on the occasion of my marriage that I keep some money by for myself, in my name. He called it my 'rainy day insurance'. Poor Dad, God bless him.' She paused. 'I'm glad he's not around to see this day.'

Maybe Mum would be able to stay in the house after all, thought Kath. Her nest egg might just be enough to meet the loan secured against

128

the house, not of course that she was responsible for it. Dad had run the business as a sole trader and the debts he incurred were his and his alone. But, if she repaid the debt, surely the bank would let her stay here . . .

'I meant for the money to go to the three of you on my death. But now . . . well, it's got to be put to practical use,' said Fiona.

'Good,' said Kath with relief. Her mother was more astute than she'd realised.

'Willie Ross gave me this list of creditors,' went on Fiona, picking up a piece of paper from the table.

Kath took a deep breath. What did creditors have to do with this? It was only the bank debt she needed to worry about.

'And I'm going to pay them all off,' announced Fiona and Kath's heart sank once more.

'No!' she said but Fiona went on, ignoring her.

'There are one or two large debts to be met,' she said, running her forefinger down the list and peering at the names there, 'but a lot of the suppliers had stopped extending credit because they weren't getting paid. And of course there's the staff wages to be paid, up until last night — '

'But Mum, you don't understand!' Kath almost shouted. 'You don't have to do this!' Her mother obviously didn't understand how these things worked. 'Dad was trading under his name,' she explained patiently. 'You're not legally responsible for his debts. Businesses fold all the time. People lose money.'

Fiona visibly bristled and said evenly, 'I know

I'm not legally responsible, Kath, but I feel morally responsible. And no one's going to lose money if I can help it. We have our family reputation to think of and people's livelihoods are at stake.' She waved a hand vaguely in the direction of the hotel further down the hill. 'There are youngsters down the road there who haven't been paid for two weeks. I can't do anything about the money owed to the bank — it's too much — but I'll make sure no one else loses a penny. I want to be able to walk down the High Street in Ballyfergus with my head held high.'

'How much are you talking about, Mum?' said David gently, while Kath flushed with shame, humbled by her mother's integrity in the face of near destitution.

'Willie reckons it's just shy of £40,000.'

'Mum!' said Bridget. 'You need that money for yourself.'

'I'll have enough left over to buy a one-bedroomed flat. That's all I need. And your father set up a small pension fund for me. I'll get by.'

'But, Mum . . . ' began Kath and her voice trailed away. She knew there was no dissuading her mother. Then, suddenly, it became clear to Kath — her mother could not sleep easy in her bed at night unless she took this course of action.

As if confirming Kath's thoughts, Fiona said, 'There's no point in arguing with me over this. I've already decided. I phoned Willie Ross and the bank this afternoon and told them what I planned to do. Now,' she went on, without giving them a chance to comment further, 'there's the small matter of your father's will.' She picked up an unopened brown envelope that had been lying on the table unnoticed and held it up for all of them to see. 'Apparently he left everything to me. You're welcome to read it, if you wish, but it's meaningless now.' Her voice was full of bitterness. 'There's nothing left.'

She threw the envelope on the desk but no one made any move to take it.

David coughed, looked at his sisters and said, 'Whatever you want to do, Mum, we'll support you. Won't we?'

Kath, along with Bridget, nodded dumbly.

'All you have to do is tell us what you need,' said David.

'Well,' she sighed and traced her eyebrows with the middle finger on each hand, 'once this period of grace with the bank runs out, I'll need somewhere to stay.'

'Oh, it goes without saying, Mum, you'll come and stay with us,' said Bridget firmly, and then she hesitated. 'Unless, of course, you'd rather stay with David . . . I don't mind really.'

'You're very welcome, Mum,' said David. 'Of course, I don't have the room or the facilities that Bridget has — '

'That's very kind of you both,' said Fiona, interrupting. 'If you don't mind I'll stay with Bridget, David. You're out at work all day and I'd like to have company until I get used . . . get used to being on my own.'

'And you too, of course, Kath,' said Bridget,

131

turning to her sister, 'unless you've gone back to the States by then.'

'Actually,' said Kath, and she paused and looked about the room at the expectant faces. There was something about her mother's righteous stand that inspired her, that lifted her emotionally onto another plane. She examined her own conscience and realised that she too had to follow her heart.

'I don't think I will be going back to Boston,' she heard herself say. 'Not for good anyway.'

Everyone stared at her in astonishment and Bridget said, 'But why not?'

Kath sighed and looked at Fiona, whose tired face was puckered with concern. 'It's partly because of Carl. I didn't want to burden you with this right now, Mum. You've enough to worry about at the moment . . . '

'What is it, love?' said Fiona.

'Well . . . to cut a long story short, we've broken up.'

'Ah,' said Fiona, and she placed a closed fist on her left breast as though it hurt there.

'I'm so sorry, Kath,' said David.

'But you two got on so well!' said Bridget.

'What on earth happened?' asked Fiona.

Kath took a deep breath and began. She put on a brave front to hide her true feelings but every now and then her voice creaked with emotion, betraying her internal turmoil. When she'd finished relating her sorry tale, Fiona got up and came over to her.

'I'm so sorry, love,' she said as she hugged her and kissed her on the crown of her head. 'I thought Carl was a decent man — but it just shows you how we can all be taken in.'

'What a bastard!' said David with feeling. 'If I ever set eyes on him, I'll bloody well kill him.'

Bridget said, 'And after finding out about you, his wife takes him back! I can't believe it.'

'Well, never mind that now,' said Kath brightly, sniffing to hold back tears. She couldn't bear to dwell on the subject of Carl any longer. It simply reduced her to a blubbering wreck. 'I'd have told you about him eventually. But that's the main reason I don't want to go back to Boston.'

'But where will you go?' said Bridget with an incongruously bright smile.

'Why, I'll stay right here. In Ballyfergus.'

'Oh,' said Bridget and she was so shocked the smile fell from her face.

David uttered sounds of surprise and Fiona said, 'I never thought I'd live to see the day! You couldn't wait to get out of Ballyfergus.'

'Well, things change. You see things — and places — differently as you get older.'

'But what will you do here, Kath?' said David. 'There aren't any management consultancies in Ballyfergus, you know.'

'I'll tell you what I'm going to do,' she said and tried to quell the thumping of her heart against the wall of her chest. 'I'm going to buy the Sallagh Braes Hotel and run it.'

Fiona gasped, Bridget laughed nervously and David said, 'What the hell are you talking about?'

'I'm going to get it back for you, Mum,' said

133

Kath. A shiver of excitement, of possibility, ran down her spine, followed quickly by regret. If only Dad had confided in his family, they would have rallied round. They would have found the resources between them to bail out the business.

'But how, Kath?' asked a bewildered Bridget.

'Like I said, I'm going to buy it back from the bank.'

'But where would you get that kind of money from, Kath?' said David.

'Once I sell my apartment and my share portfolio I should have quite a little nest egg. I've earned a fair bit over the years.'

'You're mad, Kath,' said David. 'Even if you could buy it, what do you know about running a hotel?'

'No more than you, I guess. But I'm a fast learner. And if I could get some of the staff to stay on — like that assistant manager, what's his name?'

'John Routledge,' supplied Fiona.

'If I could get him and a few other key staff to stay, I think I could pull it off.' Kath sounded a lot more convincing than she felt. Her years in business had taught her how to talk up a venture — she just wasn't so sure she could deliver on this one.

'What makes you think you can run a profitable business where Dad failed?' challenged David.

'Naturally I'd have to look at the figures to see how they stack up — but I think there's room for three hotels in Ballyfergus,' she said, referring to The Marine and Ballygally Castle Hotel, 'especially with tourism opening up again.'

'But Mum said the hotel hadn't made a profit in years,' persisted Bridget. 'Look, I know you're a management consultant and all, and you're used to going into businesses and turning them around. But Northern Ireland isn't Boston,' she continued in a slightly patronising tone. 'Things are different here.'

'You do realise you could lose everything, Kath?' said David. 'I don't want to put you off or anything, but you could be throwing good money after bad.'

'Assuming you get the hotel in the first place,' said Bridget knowingly.

Ignoring their negative comments, which unsettled her more than she would admit even to herself, Kath turned to Fiona. 'What do you think, Mum? How would you feel about it? I wouldn't do it if you'd rather see the back of the hotel.'

'You think I'd rather see the hotel taken over by strangers?' said Fiona. 'Not on your life.' She paused then and stared hard at Kath. 'You want to know what I think?' She smiled slowly — the first smile Kath had seen on her mother's lips since she'd arrived home. 'I think that this is exactly what your father would've wanted.'

12

Brendan O'Connor was buried in Greenhill Cemetery on the Cairncastle Road, in the Protestant section of the graveyard where he and Fiona had purchased a plot beside her long-deceased parents. Kath wondered how the staunch Unionist residents of this place would welcome the arrival of a Catholic, albeit a very lapsed one, and allowed herself a thin, brief smile.

As they stood beside the graveside shivering in the cold, Kath shut her eyes. She did not want to see her father's coffin lowered into the grave. And she tried to filter out the rattle of the dry earth as her mother threw a handful on the solid poplar coffin. Inside her head she said her goodbyes to her father and walked away from the grave, across the grass, without looking back.

She remembered the last funeral she attended here — that of her grandmother — nearly twenty years ago. Then the cemetery had been half-full; now there were few unused plots remaining. This bleak landscape with its regimented rows of manicured graves, dissected by grey-gravelled paths, chilled her to the bone. She pulled her coat up round her neck and hurried to the waiting car, got in and waited for the rest of the family.

It was only when the limousine pulled away from the kerbside and began its sleek, steady progress out of Ballyfergus that Kath felt any release from the tension that had been building up all day. The worst part was over; the funeral reception back at Highfield House, full of relatives and friends, would be much more tolerable. In spite of their now straitened circumstances, Fiona had been adamant that Brendan should be seen off in style and caterers had been contracted to provide the food and drink for the reception. All the family had to do was endure.

They drove past the modern Catholic church, on a bleak, windswept site at the top of Greenhill. It was ringed by an ugly green security fence — the type used to enclose factories, industrial yards and the like — with three fierce prongs on the top of each metal paling. There was no planting around the church to soften the hard, brutal architecture — apart from closely clipped grass.

Kath remembered that her father had attended Mass there on the morning of the day he died. What had he hoped to find? Had he sought divine guidance? Solace? Did he look for hope and find none among the burning candles and the incense? Or, with his mind already made up, had he simply sought forgiveness for the sin he was about to commit?

Kath let out a little whimper of anguish and buried her face in her black cashmere scarf. David, who was seated next to her, put his arm around her shoulder and gave her a gentle squeeze. She remembered the last time Carl had done that — in the taxi on the way home from

Piattini's. How she longed for him to hold her again — and how she hated him for making it impossible.

Highfield House, like the church, was packed, a physical reminder of the extent and breadth of Brendan's contacts and of the high regard in which he was held. People squeezed into the generously sized public rooms on the ground floor, clogged up the kitchen until the caterers could hardly do their job and littered the stairs and hallway. Kath moved amongst them, grateful for the diversion the full house would provide for the next few hours.

If people were whispering about the suicide and what had driven Brendan to it, they showed no outward sign — everywhere she was met with genuine compassion and grief. It didn't take long for the alcohol to lubricate people's tongues and slough off inhibitions and soon the house was full of animated chatter and even subdued bursts of laughter.

If Dad were watching he'd want to be down here in the thick of the party, thought Kath. His death had been so unnecessary, and that made it so much harder to bear. If he had died naturally she would have been able to accept it, she was sure. But this, she thought bitterly, was such a cruel waste of life. She imagined what must have gone through her father's mind before he died. He must have been suffering from despair totally beyond her comprehension. He must have been partly deranged.

'Kath,' said a deep voice behind her in the drawing room, and she jumped so that the drink in her hand nearly slopped over the side of the glass.

'Careful with that,' came the voice again and Kath turned round to find a man of approximately her age and height standing before her. He looked uncomfortable in the dark suit and black tie, his face, like David's, tanned from an outdoor life. His well-built frame strained the shoulders of the suit and his strong, work-roughened fingers clutched the small beer glass awkwardly. He looked out of place inside the house, as though it contained him too much for comfort.

'It's me, Kath,' he said and she realised then that she had been staring at him for some seconds.

She smiled, cocked her head to one side and tried to place him amongst the many friends and relatives of the family.

'Mike Mulholland,' he added, sensing her confusion, and he held out a hand.

'Mike!' she said warmly, suddenly recognising her childhood friend, and she grasped his hand.

His grip was firm and dry and he held her hand for a few seconds before letting it go.

The Mulhollands owned extensive farmland abutting on the grounds of the Sallagh Braes Hotel. The farm buildings were less than half a mile from the hotel and, as children, the O'Connors and the Mulhollands had all played together.

He smiled then, a little shyly, and his face was suddenly handsome, lit by two rows of strong, white teeth. She noticed that his eyelids drooped slightly with the weight of the longest black eyelashes she'd ever seen on a man.

'I — I didn't recognise you. You've — you've changed.' She thought of the last time she'd seen him, the summer before she'd gone to the States. He'd been skinnier then and had worn his dark greasy hair in a long, shaggy style, following his return home from university. It was shorter now but still thick and dark. The acne that had plagued him as a young man was completely gone, leaving only the faintest telltale marks on his cheeks.

'So have you,' he said and she blushed under his intense scrutiny. Then he glanced away, as though aware that he was staring, shifted his weight from one foot to the other and said, 'I'm sorry about your dad, Kath. He was a fine man and I'd a lot of time for him. He'll be missed very much.'

Kath swallowed back tears and said, 'He always had time for you, Mike — and your dad. I was sorry to hear that he'd passed away. How long is it now?'

'Oh, nearly seven years,' he said with a little upward tilt of his strong chin. He paused, looked round the room and added, 'You know, at the time it seemed like life would never get back to normal. The pain was terrible and I was full of regrets and 'what ifs?'. But that's the way it is when you lose someone you love suddenly. It's just such a shock. You never forget but life goes on somehow and, in time, the pain diminishes. And you, well, you learn to live with it. Well, that's how it was with me,' he finished abruptly, and he stared at his shoes as though suddenly embarrassed.

Kath, touched by his openness, brushed him lightly on the sleeve of his jacket with her hand. 'Thank you for sharing that. It . . . it helps.'

He raised his eyes again and smiled.

There was a short silence then and Kath, not trusting herself to keep her composure, cleared her throat and said brightly, 'We used to have great fun playing together when we were kids, didn't we? D'you remember the time we all built that bridge over the brook and it collapsed, and Bridget fell in wearing her best Sunday dress and got completely soaked?'

'I do,' he said and laughed. 'And do you remember the time the cows escaped into the grounds of the hotel and trampled all the flowerbeds? Your dad was furious!'

It was Kath's time to laugh now. 'He had us all out replanting them the next day.' She sighed. 'Those were great days.' There was a brief silence between them and then she said, 'It all seems so long ago, Mike. What happened that we lost touch?'

He gave his broad shoulders an almost imperceptible shrug. 'We grew up,' he said simply and smiled at her.

She felt her cheeks warm under his gaze and, changing the subject, said, 'I believe you've taken over the farm?'

'Yeah, it's funny how things turn out. As the eldest, John was in line to take it on, but he never showed any interest in farming. When I returned from uni and Dad's health started to fail, it just

141

seemed the natural thing to do.'

'But didn't you ever want to do something different? Didn't you ever wonder what was beyond Ballyfergus?' said Kath earnestly, curious to find out what made Mike tick.

'Oh, yes. That's why I went over to Leeds to study. But four years away, studying and travelling, gives you a different perspective. And when Dad offered me the farm, I realised that was what I wanted.' He paused then and regarded her keenly before going on. 'It sounds a bit romanticised but I think it was — it *is* my destiny. It's in my blood. Mulhollands have been farming this land for over a hundred and fifty years. And there's nothing in the world I'd rather do.'

'Mum mentioned that you'd expanded the business,' said Kath, a little unsettled by his intensity.

'Yeah, I've opened two butcher's shops — one in Ballyfergus and one in Ballymena — as well as a wholesaler's. It seemed like a natural extension of the livestock farming business . . . '

Kath watched him as he spoke on about the farm, mesmerised by his animation and enthusiasm — and his quiet confidence. She thought of the pie-in-the-sky plans she had for the hotel and her shaky confidence all but evaporated.

'So, when do you go back to the States, Kath?' he said, interrupting her thoughts.

'Ah, good question,' she replied and paused, deciding whether or not to confide in him. Emboldened by the white wine she'd drunk, she opted for the latter, took a deep breath and went on. 'It's not common knowledge yet,' she said, bowing her head and leaning a little closer to him, 'so please keep it to yourself for the time being.'

'I will,' he said firmly.

'You do know the — the circumstances we — er — we find ourselves in?'

'There are rumours floating about.'

'Well, whatever you've heard it's probably true,' she said glibly, not wanting to discuss the miserable details of her family's ruin. He nodded almost imperceptibly and she went on, 'Well, I'm thinking of buying the hotel and re-opening it.'

'I see.'

'At least that's what I told Mum and the others. And now I'm having second thoughts, but I've raised their hopes and I don't want to dash them. Especially Mum's. The hotel means a lot to her.'

'It belonged to her parents, didn't it?'

'That's right.'

'It's a big undertaking all right,' said Mike.

Kath waited for him to go on, expecting him to express an opinion as to the possible success, or more likely failure, of the venture. But he said nothing.

'Well,' she said prompting him, 'what do you think? Do you think I should?'

He thought for a few moments before answering her. 'There are a lot of people round here who held your father in high esteem, including myself. If you reopen the hotel, you won't be without help or goodwill. Especially

143

after what your mother's doing to see the creditors right.'

God, thought Kath, news does travel fast in Ballyfergus. She'd forgotten about that aspect of life in small-town Ireland.

'And I can't tell you what you should and should not do, Kath. But,' he lowered his voice an octave or two, 'I could, if you want, tell you what I'd *like* you to do.'

Was this a chat-up line? No, she was reading too much into a straightforward conversation.

'What . . . what would you like me to — '

'Kath!' came her sister's voice, breaking her concentration.

She glanced at Bridget's approaching figure, then looked back at Mike, her mouth open in mid-sentence.

'Hello, Mike,' said Bridget pleasantly as she came up to them, and then turning to Kath said, 'Aunt Agnes and Uncle Ron have to leave now. They've a long drive ahead of them back to Enniskillen. You'd better come and say goodbye. Excuse us, please, Mike.' She steered Kath firmly out of the room into the hall.

It was only then that Kath remembered that Mike and Bridget had dated each other for a time in their early twenties, when she was in the States. The relationship had, she remembered, fizzled out after a few months.

As soon as she'd said goodbye to her aunt and uncle, Kath returned to the drawing room, hoping to resume the conversation with Mike. But he was talking animatedly with a group of farmers in the corner of the room. Mike's recent words were still ringing in her ears.

She would not be alone if she undertook this adventure. She realised that there was no time to lose regarding the hotel. She'd have to move fast if she was to secure a deal with the bank, liquidate her assets and get the hotel open for the summer season. She was sure she did not want to leave Ireland for good just yet.

She wandered into the hallway where she spotted John Routledge standing with a group of hotel staff, looking uncomfortable.

'John,' she said, going up to him, 'how are you?'

He offered her his condolences and they talked briefly about Brendan. She was moved to see how affected he was by her father's death, though it came as no surprise to her — her father had been one of those people loved by everyone.

'Listen, John,' she said, checking that no one could overhear them, 'I wondered if I might have a chat with you about the hotel. I'm very sorry that you've lost your job as a result of this — this tragedy.'

'Oh, don't worry about me — I'll get another one,' he said bravely, with more conviction than Kath imagined he felt. There were few jobs in the hotel trade in Ballyfergus — he'd probably have to move to Belfast for similar work.

'In a way, that's what I wanted to talk to you about, John.'

'What do you mean?'

'Well, about the hotel. I was just wondering

145

what you thought of the way the hotel was being run latterly?'

'Brendan was a good employer, Kath. He was fair with all the staff,' said John loyally.

'That's not really what I mean.'

'I hope you're not asking me to speak ill of — '

'Oh, John, I wouldn't do that. That's not what I meant. I was just wondering if you had any ideas for how the business might have been . . . *improved*.'

'What does it matter now? The hotel's closed.'

'Well, that might not be the case for much longer,' she said and he looked at her through narrow, cautious green eyes. She took a deep breath and went on. 'If I can get the finance together and the price is right, I'm thinking of buying the hotel and re-opening it.'

'Oh, could you do that?' he said, and his features came alive with interest.

'Why not? The bank'll be looking for a quick sale. Now the doors are closed, it's worth nothing as a going concern. And the longer a property like that sits on the market, the more it depreciates. But I need to know that the business can be made to work. I've had a look at the books and I can see, on paper, how the outgoings outstripped income. But what I need to understand from you, John, is what exactly was going on behind those figures.'

John looked nervously about the room, coughed and then his eyes came to rest on Kath. 'Well . . . ' he said reluctantly.

'Go on,' urged Kath.

'I think that Brendan found it hard to — to

146

innovate. He was running the hotel the same way it had always been run for the past twenty years. But people expect a — a higher standard of service these days. Towards the end, nearly all of our business was coming from cheap tour operators' bus parties — and they demand a high discount, which cuts into profits. A hotel like the Sallagh Braes needs to attract regular local custom all year round. Functions like weddings, birthday, Christmas and anniversary parties, hen nights — that sort of thing. And people just wanting a good meal out on a Saturday night as well.'

'And do you have ideas as to how to attract that sort of business?' said Kath, her interest in John quickening. With his knowledge of the Sallagh Braes Hotel and the industry in general he was, she realised, crucial to her chances of success.

'Oh yes,' said John. 'I learnt a lot at college and I like to keep up to date with what's going on in the industry but Brendan . . . well, as I said, he was a bit conservative.'

'I haven't had a chance to inspect the hotel yet,' said Kath. She had wanted to, but respect for her father and her mother's feelings had kept her away so far. 'What sort of a state is it in?'

'The building has been well-maintained and there's not much wrong with the furnishings and fittings. It could do with a lick of paint, I suppose, to freshen it up, but nothing major.'

'Come with me a minute,' said Kath, and she led the way up the stairs. She was amazed that Brendan had been able to hold onto someone as bright and capable as John for so long. It was a pity he hadn't given John more of a free reign though, she thought with heavy regret — he might have been able to save the hotel from failure. She took John into the empty sitting room on the first floor and closed the door behind them.

'Have a seat, John, please,' she said, 'and tell me all about it.'

They talked for over half an hour, during which time Kath secured his agreement to come and work for her as assistant manager — if her plans came to fruition. They were just about finished when Fiona opened the door.

'Oh, there you are,' she said, scowling slightly. 'What are you two talking about?'

'The hotel.'

'Oh, I see,' she said, her expression softening as though she'd half expected another answer. 'Kath, people are starting to leave now. Could you come downstairs, please?'

Kath excused herself to John and followed her mother onto the landing.

'Mum,' she whispered, 'you just ignored John Routledge!'

'Did I?' she replied absentmindedly.

'Oh, never mind. It doesn't matter,' said Kath, thinking that the strain of the day was all too much for Fiona — her normally impeccable manners were starting to falter.

Kath linked arms with her mother and they walked down the broad flight of stairs together to face their guests.

Mike Mulholland was waiting with his mother

148

in the hallway. Gladys Mulholland was a slim, good-looking woman who had always seemed a little too glamorous for a farmer's wife. Her blonde hair, which, as a child, Kath had thought natural, was expertly highlighted and she wore a smartly tailored grey coat, unbuttoned, over expensive-looking clothes. On her feet were low-heeled black patent court shoes and draped around her neck, resplendent against the black clothing, was a thick solid gold guard-chain.

But then the Mulhollands weren't ordinary farmers — they were extensive landowners and Mr Mulholland had always employed a farm manager to oversee his holdings. But, in spite of their considerable wealth and standing in the community, it had not gone to Gladys's head. She was kind-hearted and sincere — Kath had always been fond of her.

'Goodbye, Fiona,' said Gladys and she placed a light kiss on Fiona's cheek. 'And you remember that we're only up the road. You just let us know if you need anything. Anything at all. Mike's usually around. And I'm truly sorry for your loss.'

'Thank you,' said Fiona, and her voice sounded hollow. She didn't look at Gladys Mulholland but at the boldly patterned wallpaper behind her head.

Kath felt a sudden rush of protectiveness towards her little mother.

'Now, Kath,' said Gladys, 'you will come up to the house and see us before you go, won't you?'

'I will,' promised Kath. She glanced at Mike's inscrutable face and blushed — she had not

149

corrected Gladys's assumption that she was returning to Boston. Her plans were not yet advanced enough for general publication.

'I hope it's not so long until your next visit,' said Gladys kindly, but Kath winced, taking the innocent comment as a rebuke for her past neglect of her parents.

Guilt, she thought, was like a magnet, drawing hurtful inferences from everyday remarks. It would help if she could blame Carl, but she knew it wasn't his fault. She had been more than happy to revolve her life around his orbit. She would not make the same mistake again.

'Goodbye, Kath.' Mike leaned forward unexpectedly and kissed her softly on the cheek. As he did so, he whispered in her ear. 'Good luck!' Then he was gone.

13

The next morning Kath woke late with a terrible hangover and immediately thought of Brendan, then Carl. Desolation settled on her like fine mist. Determined to shake it off, she showered, went downstairs and breakfasted.

She found her mother working in the study with Willie Ross. They were sorting out payments to the creditors and Fiona said that they did not need her assistance. She seemed fully recovered from the trance-like state she'd been in the night before.

Outside it was a still, perfect winter's day — a rare clear blue sky, bright sunshine and frosted landscape. Kath put on a warm coat, hat and green wellington boots and walked the short distance down the stone-walled track to the hotel. The ground underfoot was hard, the mud frozen into many little ruts by the passage of vehicles on their way home from Highfield House last night. The air was still and her breath formed white puffs of steam which disappeared in seconds.

The landscape in front sloped away steeply to the sea, some quarter of a mile or so away. The view was spectacular — the sun sparkled off the gently rippling waves and burnished the entire hillside. In the afternoon it would steal westwards and this side of the hill would slowly be engulfed in shadow. In the presence of such awesome natural beauty, the misery that had accompanied Kath since her father's death abated. A set of keys to the hotel, which Fiona had not yet handed over to the bank, burned in her pocket.

As she walked down the tarmacked single-lane road to the hotel, her heartbeat quickened with fear and anticipation. What would she find? What was she hoping to find? The first thing that caught her attention was the old chestnut tree — she walked over to it and put her bare palm on the trunk.

The rough bark was freezing cold, like it was dead. The branches were shorn of leaves and she searched the lower limbs for evidence of the tragedy that had taken place here — rope burn perhaps, or a broken branch. But there was none — the tree stood, solid and enduring, where it had stood for the last two hundred years.

Fiona wanted to cut it down — and who could blame her — but Kath felt differently. She detected her father's presence here and it was not in any way disturbing. She liked to believe that, in death, he had found the peace he could not find in life. She would like to put a plaque on the trunk to commemorate him. It would, she decided, be a fitting, living memorial to him. She would have to persuade her mother to her point of view.

The Sallagh Braes Hotel had a pleasing late-Victorian façade which cleverly concealed the rather ugly, but functional, 1980s extension adjoining the property at the back. Kath took a deep breath and walked purposefully across the lawn towards the hotel. She noticed that the garden was strewn with autumn leaves and there were dead weeds in the flowerbeds. She approached the bright red front door quickly, mindful that she was in fact trespassing, and noted with alarm the smashed skylight above the door.

Had it been like that for some time? John had said that the building was well maintained, so was it the recent work of teenage vandals? In this fairly isolated spot, she thought this improbable. It was more likely the handiwork of a disgruntled creditor.

She inserted the key in the lock, turned it and looked over her shoulder before entering — a foolish gesture, she realised. Who else would be creeping round the hotel on a Tuesday morning in late January? Still, once the door was shut and locked behind her she felt more comfortable.

The shards of glass from the skylight crunched underfoot, confirming her suspicion that the breakage was very recent. The half-glazed inner door, with clear sheets of glass in the panels on either side, was shut but not locked. And it was dark — the only light came from narrow stained-glass panels down either side of the front door and the skylight.

She fumbled for the light switch and turned it on but it was dead. Then she remembered that the electricity would most likely have been turned off and the gas too. No doubt the utility companies were amongst the many creditors on the list Fiona and Willie were examining right now.

Soon, Kath's eyes accustomed to the gloom and she ventured further. In the absence of any heating the inside of the hotel was as cold as the outside and she worried about burst pipes. Something would have to be done about that as a matter of urgency.

She had never been in the hotel when it was entirely unoccupied — the utter silence was unnerving and, though she knew that she would meet no one here, her heart pounded in her chest.

She walked nervously through the public rooms, examining every detail with a keen eye. The woodwork was well painted, the window frames showed no sign of flaking paint or decay and, she remembered, the hotel had been rewired within the last twenty years. The dining tables and chairs, the sofas, coffee and side tables in the lounge were all in good condition, if not entirely to her taste. The tables in the dining room were laid for breakfast with crisp white linen and good quality stainless-steel cutlery, as though guests were expected any minute. Obviously Brendan's problem hadn't been spending money — it was making it. The hotel was in good shape.

On the downside, the hotel had last had a proper make-over fifteen years ago. Kath tried not to judge it too harshly through eyes accustomed to a sophisticated urban environment. But even by Ballyfergus's less demanding standards, it was desperately dated.

Everywhere it was decorated in a rich and ostentatious style. From the swags-and-tails window-dressing in the dining room to the gaudy floral curtains and the richly patterned carpet in the lounge, the place was an excess of style. Kath knelt on the floor in the lounge and worked at the carpet until she loosened a corner. Then she tugged it free of the carpet rails and, pulling up the foam underlay, examined the floorboards underneath. They were thick planks of solid oak, well-protected by carpet over the years. Stripped and polished, they would be beautiful.

Lifting the set of master keys from behind the reception desk, Kath continued her foray into the bedrooms. The ones in the old house were decorated in similar fashion to the rest of the hotel. The ones in the newer annex were more simply, and therefore more tastefully, done out.

She would not have the resources to extend her renovation beyond the public rooms. The bedrooms would have to stay as they were. Back in the main house the kitchen too withstood close scrutiny — it was clean and functional. It would, she estimated, take no more than four, maybe six, weeks to revamp the hotel. Little structural work was required, saving time and expense, but money would have to be spent bringing the décor into the twenty-first century.

In the wood-panelled office behind the reception desk, Kath stood in front of her father's tidy desk and stared at his well-worn leather chair. She looked at the open door, half-expecting him to come sauntering into the room. She walked carefully round to the other side of the desk and opened the top left-hand side drawer where he used to keep his pipe.

She let out a little gasp — the pipe and a small pouch of tobacco were there alongside a crumpled, empty packet of Fisherman's Friends. The sweet peaty smell of the tobacco filled her nostrils and she was transported back to a time when this room was the centre of her world. This was her father's domain and a place of sanctuary where she was always welcomed, always safe, never criticised or reprimanded. 'My sweet Kathleen' he used to call her and even as a child she knew that he spoiled and indulged her. She closed her eyes and remembered how much he loved her.

'I miss you, Dad,' she whispered as tears spilt down her cheeks and her voice sounded like a foghorn in the stillness.

'Who the hell are you?' said a deep, indignant voice, scaring the living daylights out of her.

'Aahh!' she screamed.

She swivelled round abruptly and immediately felt like a fool. In the doorway stood a man in a light grey suit, white shirt and yellow spotted tie. He wore a black wool coat, unbuttoned over the suit. In his hand was a black briefcase and he wore silver, square-framed glasses. He was slim with brown hair and he was staring at Kath crossly.

She quickly wiped away the tears on her face.

'I'm Kath O'Connor,' she said when she'd pulled herself together, and a little of the wind went out of her would-be assailant's sails.

'I see,' he said slowly. 'You must be Brendan's daughter.' When she offered him no confirmation or denial of this statement, he went on, 'Well, you really shouldn't be here, you know. You are aware that the hotel has been repossessed by the bank?'

'You have me at a disadvantage,' said Kath, ignoring his question and thinking that he looked every inch the bank manager. Stiff, formal, squeaky clean.

'I'm sorry,' he said, stepped forward two paces and offered her his hand. 'I'm the manager of the bank.'

She looked at his clean, well-manicured fingers, then at his face and hated him for who he was — the architect of her father's downfall.

When she did not take his hand immediately, it dropped to his side and he regarded her calmly for a few seconds. Leaving the introductions aside he said, bluntly, as though he could read her mind, 'I suppose you blame me for what happened to Brendan?'

His perceptiveness, bordering on telepathy, unnerved her. She did not expect it from a banker. She looked at the floor and refused to speak, feeling like a stubborn child. Of course she blamed him — the bank had foreclosed on her beloved father, forcing him to take the only way out he could. To be fair, this man was only a front for the faceless bureaucrats at Head Office, but it helped to be able to blame someone.

'I was very fond of your father,' he said, 'and I am very, very sorry for your loss. It must be a terrible time for all of you.'

'You,' she said with real venom, 'have no idea.'

He regarded her thoughtfully for a few

moments, seemingly unperturbed by her caustic remark. 'Miss O'Connor,' he said evenly, 'your father was an intelligent man. He entered into a contract with the bank and he fully understood the implications of that contract. I supported him as far as I could, but in the end — '

'I thought you said you were fond of my father?' snapped Kath, riled by his apparent lack of emotion. 'Why did you call in the debt so suddenly?'

'The debt wasn't called in suddenly, as you put it,' he said quickly, and the muscles in his jaw-line tensed. 'All the formal procedures were followed. I counselled your father on many occasions that the business was running into trouble. I tried to help him as best I could. In the end, the decision was taken out of my — '

'I know, I know. Head Office made the decision. And it had nothing to do with you.'

'I protected him as far as I could. I extended the loan well beyond my level of authorisation which got me into serious hot water. When Head Office got involved, I knew there could only be one outcome. And there was nothing I could do to stop it.'

'Well, as far as I'm concerned, you have blood on your hands. My father's blood,' she snapped before she could stop herself.

'That,' he said, 'is totally out of order.' He took his glasses off and stared her out, his bright blue eyes flashing with rage. Without the glasses he looked younger, in his mid to late-forties.

Kath held his gaze, defiant.

'Retract that at once,' he demanded and they

glared at each other.

Kath listened to the sound of his shallow breath in the silence and knew that she had overstepped the mark. 'OK, maybe it was a bit over the top,' she said feebly and looked at the floor.

There was a long silence then, the tension between them like electricity. The only sound was the distant scraping and banging sounds of someone at work out in the reception area.

She knew that she was judging the bank manager harshly — and unfairly. If what he said about exceeding his lending limit was true, he had put his job on the line for her father. And, she reminded herself, if she wanted to negotiate over the hotel, this was the person she would have to deal with.

'I'm very upset by my father's death, as you can imagine,' she offered by way of an apology, meeting his gaze again. 'You must forgive me.'

Ho nodded and said in a conciliatory tone, 'Kath . . . may I call you Kath?' All the hardness was gone from his eyes.

She nodded her assent.

'What *are* you doing here?'

'I'm . . . I'm collecting some of my father's things.' To prove her point she reached into the drawer and withdrew the pipe and tobacco. 'See,' she said, holding them up for his inspection.

He nodded slowly.

'What brings you out here?' said Kath.

'The locksmith was coming out to change the locks and I wanted to have a look around.'

'But the bank repossessed the hotel last

Friday. You're a bit slow in getting around to changing locks, aren't you?'

He grinned then as though what she'd said amused him and the smile transformed his face. 'Yes, you're quite right. It was an oversight. It should've been done before now.'

The bank manager was an enigma. He had a hardness about him, a steeliness that she knew she possessed also. It came from having to operate in the real world of business — where failures were more common than successes and sometimes tough decisions had to be made. But there was also a warmth to him and his concern for her father appeared genuine. This chance meeting was an opportunity in disguise, she realised — a chance for her to sound out the bank's strategy with regard to disposal of the hotel.

The bank manager turned around and took a step towards the door.

'Did you see the broken skylight above the front door?' she blurted out and he stopped and glanced over his shoulder at her.

'It's hard to miss,' he said and then walked out of the room.

She followed him into the reception area. 'Must've been a disgruntled creditor.'

'Could've been,' he replied absentmindedly, poking through the things behind the reception desk. The locksmith hammered noisily at the front door, trying to remove the old lock. 'Or just teenagers messing about.'

'Once word gets round that the hotel's empty it'll attract all sorts of vandals and nosy parkers,' persisted Kath, watching his reaction to her words keenly. 'It'll be hard to keep an eye on the place unless you have a full-time security guard onsite.'

'I couldn't justify that expense,' he replied as she expected.

'You'll be wanting to get rid of it pretty quickly, I should imagine.'

He looked at her then, cocked his head to one side and said, 'Maybe.'

'Has anyone shown any interest?' she asked casually.

He paused before answering and said slowly, 'No. It's still very early days. Why? Do you know someone who might be interested?'

'Hmm. Maybe,' she said vaguely.

He set his briefcase on the floor and buttoned his coat against the penetrating cold. 'Well, aren't you going to tell me who it is? I can't stand the suspense.'

Kath looked at her mud-caked wellingtons and wished that she'd worn something more — more business-like. 'Actually,' she said, pulling herself up to her full height so that her eyes were level with his chin, 'It's me.'

'Really?' he said, and he paused on the third button. Then he resumed his task and said, 'I didn't know you had a background in hotel management. Brendan said you worked in finance, was it? In the States somewhere.'

'Management consultancy. And it is — was — Boston. I've had experience working in the sector and of course first-hand experience working here too.' She was suddenly annoyed with herself. Why did she sound like she was trying to convince him of her credentials? Maybe, she thought, it was because she wasn't sure of them herself.

'I see. And you have the — the resources to fund the purchase?'

'I think I can pull the finance together.'

'Do you know how much we're talking about?'

'Do you?' she retorted, disguising the fact that her information on this subject was a bit shaky.

'I haven't had the valuation report yet but I think we're looking at a little shy of a million. Even with the hotel closed.'

Kath swallowed and tried to look like this had not come as a shock. If she cashed in all her assets she would still be well short of this target.

As though sensing her surprise he said, 'Property values in Northern Ireland have rocketed recently — they've gone up by nearly fifty per cent in the last three years. And, even though this is commercial property rather than residential, I still think it'll be worth a fair bit. It could be attractive to a developer interested in turning it into flats.'

'Flats?' said Kath with horror. 'I don't think so. I mean, who would want to live out here in a flat? It's a great location for a hotel, with the scenery and all, but it's not very convenient for Ballyfergus, now is it?'

'You'd be surprised. This whole stretch along the coast is considered very desirable. And it's only a ten-minute drive into town.'

Flats, thought Kath, over my dead body. She would find the money somehow. She would beg, borrow and steal if she had to.

'I don't mean to be harsh,' he said, 'but what makes you think that you can make a go of the hotel?'

'When my father couldn't,' she added, articulating what she knew he was thinking, but was too polite to say.

'Well, yes,' he admitted. 'It's not easy making a place like this pay.'

'The Marine Hotel manages it.'

'Yes, well — '

'So there's no reason why this hotel can't be profitable too. I want to attract more overseas visitors using the web. Do you know the hotel doesn't even have its own website? Another thing I need to do is diversify — the restaurant needs to stay open all year. We need a really good chef so that it becomes the first choice for locals eating out. And something's got to be done about the décor.' She surveyed the patterned wallpaper behind the reception desk. 'It's just too dated. It needs to be comfortable and friendly but sleek and modern too . . . ' She stopped then, suddenly aware that she was getting carried away.

'You've obviously given this a lot of thought,' he said, 'and I very much hope that you get the chance to put your ideas into practice.'

'Well, I'll be in touch just as soon as I'm in a position to put in an offer. I take it the bank would be willing to consider one from me, in spite of my connection to Brendan?'

He shrugged his shoulders and raised his eyebrows over the rim of his glasses. 'There's absolutely no reason why not.'

'Right. I'll be off then,' she said and then remembered that his arrival had distracted her from her purpose. 'If you don't mind I need something else from the office.'

She went back into her father's office, headed straight for a filing cabinet which was, as she knew it would be, unlocked. She removed a file from the front of the drawer and quickly glanced at the contents.

'What's that?' said his voice behind her. 'I really don't think . . . '

'Yes, just as I thought,' said Kath. 'It's the list of customer bookings over the next few months with all the contact details.'

'How did you know?'

'Old habits die hard. Once the electricity's back on, you'll find exactly the same information on the PC,' she said, nodding at the blank-screened computer on the desk. 'But Dad never did trust computers — he printed a paper copy of everything.' She remembered the good-natured arguments she'd had with him when she discovered this eccentricity.

'What on earth do you want it for?' he asked.

'Someone's got to contact these poor people, haven't they, and tell them what's happened? Look, there are some bookings in here already for the summer.' She stopped her perusal of the document and looked up at him, 'Unless of course you fancy doing it?'

'No, no, just you carry on,' he said, retreating from the room.

She smiled to herself. If her plans came to

164

fruition she wouldn't be cancelling many of these bookings — she would be honouring the ones from May onwards when, all being well, she would be proprietress of the Sallagh Braes Hotel.

She strode purposefully out into the lobby again with the file in her hand. 'It was good to talk to you,' she said, 'And I'm sorry for being rude earlier.'

'That's OK,' he said, more graciously than she felt she deserved.

She walked to the door and stopped a few paces from the workman kneeling on the floor. He was wearing blue overalls over a thick Aran-knit jumper and a woollen-knit hat — his face was ruddy with the cold. She turned around.

'You never did tell me your name,' she said to the bank manager.

'I'm Frank. Frank Morrison.'

'You will do something about the heating, won't you, Frank? If a pipe freezes and bursts, the place'll be a mess. And I don't want to have all that to clean up when I take charge.'

And with that she strode out into the sunshine and walked away from the hotel with as confident and bold a stride as she could muster in the clumsy wellington boots.

14

Kath was astounded by her own audacity in acting as though her ownership of the hotel was as good as secured. She had wanted to demonstrate to Frank Morrison that she was a confident, serious businesswoman — she hoped she'd convinced him for she was going to need his help to realise her plans for the hotel.

She retraced her steps back up the track but, instead of turning off at Highfield House, she continued along the lane to the Mulhollands' farm. Her breath came in short gasps now and the blood pulsed quickly through her veins, warming her. She unbuttoned her coat and tramped past the new, sprawling white bungalow that had been the Mulhollands' home now for two years.

She was disappointed to find no cars outside the house and no signs of life within — she realised that she'd hoped to bump into Mike. She stood and looked around her, not sure what to do next. The white bungalow stood out against the muted greens, greys and browns like a discarded milk carton in a grass verge. No doubt, with double glazing and central heating, it was warm and comfortable but Kath thought it blighted the landscape. In contrast, the older stone farm buildings scattered around it looked like they were part of the natural landscape — well weathered over many decades, they blended with their surroundings.

She set off along the track again and soon came to the old family farmhouse. Checking that there was no one about, she peered through one of the downstairs windows. She could see into the front parlour or best room, which she remembered from when she was a child. Some of furniture was the same but most of the ornaments on the dresser and pictures on the wall were gone.

She thought it a pity that the Mulhollands had eschewed this pretty two-storey farmhouse building in favour of the modern monstrosity further down the hill. She wondered who lived here now? Mike perhaps? Or maybe it was let out to holidaymakers in the summer. It deserved better than that.

'Hello,' said a man's voice and Kath nearly jumped three feet in the air.

'Oh! You scared the life out of — ' she blurted out and then saw that it was Mike. He was wearing outdoor clothes and muddy boots and two young black-and-white collies frolicked at his feet. Her heartbeat quickened. She was embarrassed to be caught snooping.

One of the dogs jumped up on her, and she recoiled, not used to animals. It left big muddy paw prints on her coat but Mike seemed not to notice.

'Down, Tess,' he said sternly to the dog and then to Kath, 'She's just saying hello.'

'Oh, that's OK,' said Kath, wondering if the mud would come off the coat.

Mike's gaze fell on the farmhouse.

167

'I hope you don't mind,' she said quickly. 'I was just having a look at the old house. You've looked after it.'

'Aye. I rent it out to holidaymakers in the summer. Not much call for it at this time of year though.'

'It seems a shame for it to be lying empty.'

'I'd love to see it lived in but we're a bit out of the way here.' He paused. 'Do you want to see inside it?'

'Oh, no. I wouldn't want to put you to any trouble.'

'It's no trouble,' he said and set off down the track before she could say another word. He returned in a few minutes with the key to the house, opened the front door and let her in.

'It's cold,' she said, standing in the hall. They walked through to the large homely kitchen at the back of the house and she said, 'Why did you give it up?'

'It was Mum's idea. She wanted something all on one level with central heating and all the mod cons. Personally, I prefer this.'

'Mike?'

'Yes?'

'You know the way I'm hoping to buy the hotel?'

'Uh, huh.'

'If it works out, I'll need somewhere to stay.'

'I see.'

'And I was wondering if . . . no, forget it.'

'What?'

'Nothing.'

'No, really. Please go on.'

168

'Well, I was just thinking it would be nice to rent this house — it's so close to the hotel and everything. But . . . '

'What?'

'It was just a thought. Never mind. I probably couldn't afford it. Forget it!' She walked back into the hall.

He followed her, caught her gently by the arm and she froze.

'You can have it for £200 a month.'

'But that seems awfully cheap to me. Wouldn't you get a lot more from holiday rentals?'

He let her arm go and her flesh, beneath the thick fabric of the coat, tingled.

'As I say, we don't get much business out this way. You'd be doing me a favour in a way. I'd rather see the house lived in and loved than lying like this.'

'Oh, Mike, I do love it. I'd take good care of it. I promise you.'

'Well, then that's it settled. If things work out with the hotel, we'll be neighbours.'

'I'd like that.'

'So would I, Kath,' he replied and stared at her with those intense eyes of his. 'The place is yours for as long as you need it.'

She was mesmerised for a few seconds, then, suddenly self-conscious, she broke eye contact with him and said, 'I'd better be getting on.' She walked quickly outside, hoping he hadn't noticed her red face. What was it about him that made her feel like a giddy fourteen-year-old?

'Where are you off to now?' he asked.

'Up there,' she said and indicated, with a wide

sweep of her arm, the rocky crest of the hill.

'There's nowhere better on a day like this. The views are . . . well, they're just out of this world, aren't they?'

'Yes, they are.'

'Enjoy it,' he said and set off down the track without looking back, the frisky dogs yapping at his heels.

Kath watched his broad, stocky figure recede and thought that he seemed so much at home here, so much the master of this beautiful place. It seemed almost a part of him and him a part of it. He rounded the corner of the white house, glanced back once, and disappeared out of sight.

★ ★ ★

After a long walk to the top of the hill and back Kath headed back home to Highfield House, physically exhausted but with her spirits restored. It was nearly lunchtime by the time she walked through the front door. Upstairs she found Fiona alone in the bedroom she had shared with Brendan. There was no sign of Willie.

'Mum,' she cried when she saw the opened suitcases on the bed, 'what on earth are you doing?'

Fiona, who was rummaging in the opened wardrobe, walked to the bed with some clothes in her arms. She threw them down and began to fold them quickly and put them in the suitcase.

'I'm packing,' she said simply, went over to the chest of drawers between the windows and

170

scooped the contents of the top drawer into the same suitcase.

'I can see that, Mum. But where are you going?'

Fiona stood up straight, rested the palms of her hands momentarily on the small of her back, as though it was sore, and said, 'I've decided to leave before I'm thrown out. I've spoken to Bridget and she says we're more than welcome. She's got the guest suite all ready for us. You'd better get your things packed, Kath. Ned's coming over with the Range Rover to help as soon as he gets home from work.'

'But Mum, don't you think this is all a bit . . . rushed?'

'Of course it's a bit rushed,' she said irritably. 'It's all been a rush since your father died. I haven't had a minute to think. But I'll tell you one thing. I'm not going to sit around here waiting for the bank to serve an eviction notice on me.' She sighed, closed the suitcase gently and added, without the slightest hint of irony, 'That nice man from the bank was up here this morning while you were out. He talked about Brendan and asked after you and David and Bridget and, well, he finally got to the point. The bank wants us out by next Monday.'

'Frank Morrison called here?'

'That's right. Straight after you went out.' Fiona was examining the contents of a wash bag. 'I felt sorry for him.'

'You felt sorry for him? Why?' Kath was incredulous.

'He and your father were quite good friends,

171

you know. And I could see it was very difficult for him having to come up here and tell me the bad news.'

'I'm sure it was breaking his heart.'

'Don't be so cynical, Kath. The poor fella's only doing his job.'

'I don't understand you, Mum,' said Kath tetchily. 'You're the one that's lost your husband, your home and your parents' hotel. You've just used the best part of your life savings to pay off half of Ballyfergus and you're spending your time fretting about other people!'

Fiona looked at Kath and her face hardened. Her wide-set brown eyes, that had once been her main claim to beauty, glinted like sun off steel. 'What do you want me to do, Kath? Sit in a corner and weep all day? Would that make you feel better? Well, I'll tell you something. It wouldn't change a thing and I'm not going to wallow in self-pity. What's done is done. Your grandmother always said that whenever misfortune befalls you, it's helpful to focus on other people. It puts your own problems into perspective.'

Fiona threw her wash bag into the suitcase and Kath, feeling suitably admonished, did not say anything. She watched her mother, her expression grim, pack clothes and shoes into the second suitcase on the bed. The fine lines on her face seemed to have deepened over the last week and her always-tidy hair was a mess.

'Here, Mum. Your hair's falling down at the back. Let me fix it.'

Obediently her mother sat on the stool in front

172

of the dressing table and Kath undid the clasp, brushed the hair into a pony-tail and then twisted it up into a neat bun, securing it with pins. The hairstyle was terribly old-fashioned and made her mother appear much older then her sixty-five years — but now wasn't the time to berate her sense of style.

She remembered when Fiona's hair was thick and dark — now it was thin and mostly grey. Kath found the physical act of touching her mother's head strangely disconcerting. Though they kissed each other on the cheek and hugged, they weren't a particularly demonstrative family. Kath realised how rarely she cared for her mother in this hands-on sense. The caring had always been one-sided with Kath the recipient — the nature of all mother-child relationships?

Sitting on the stool, her mother's shoulders were slightly rounded and she appeared smaller than Kath remembered her — she was a poignant, heart-wrenching combination of strength and frailty and vulnerability.

'There. All done,' said Kath brightly. Then she laid the brush on the dressing table and turned away quickly so that her mother could not see the sadness in her face.

Fiona returned to her task of fitting clothes in the suitcase and Kath sat quietly on the bed. Her mother was truly an incredible woman. And she was right — there was a lot to be said for having a stiff upper lip in the face of such misfortune. There was nothing else for it but to soldier on.

After a few moments had passed she said, 'Mum?'

'What, love?' said Fiona, sounding tired.

'You did love Dad, didn't you?'

Fiona stopped what she was doing and stared at her daughter. 'Of course I did. What a strange question.'

'I'm sorry, Mum. It's just that . . . well, you don't seem all that — distraught, if you don't mind me saying so.'

Fiona sighed deeply and said, 'Oh, I'm distraught all right. I'm more than distraught.' She closed the second suitcase and sat down heavily on the bed beside Kath. 'In fact, I'm so angry with your father I could scream. I can't believe he has left me with — with this mess to sort out.'

'Mum. How can you say such awful things about Dad when he's — he's not here any more?'

'It's no more than the truth, Kath. If he was here right now, I'd give him a piece of my mind. I'm so angry with him I've almost no room for grief. How could he do this to me? How could he keep so much from me — his own wife?' Her face twisted with anger. 'And I can't believe I was so — so blind to what was really going on.'

'Don't say any more — please!' cried Kath, jumping up from the bed and covering her ears with her hands. 'I can't bear to hear you talk about Dad like that!'

'If you knew the half of it,' repeated Fiona, shaking her head.

'What are you talking about?' said Kath and there was a deathly silence.

Fiona stared at Kath. Then she dropped her

head and mumbled, 'Oh, never mind. It doesn't matter.' And then she said, more distinctly, 'But next time if you don't want to hear the truth, don't ask. Now, go and get your things packed, will you?'

'Mum, what are you keeping from me? Is it something about Dad?'

'No, of course not, don't be silly,' said Fiona. She held her left arm up to the light and squinted at the watch on her wrist. 'Now hurry up — we don't want to keep Ned waiting.' Fiona avoided further eye contact by busying herself with the catches on the suitcases.

Whatever it was that was bothering her, Fiona obviously wasn't going to share it. And though curiosity was killing her, Kath knew better than to pursue it any further.

So, changing the subject, she asked, 'What about all your other things — like the ornaments and furniture and all the kitchen equipment?'

'David's organised a container for later in the week. I have to decide what I'm taking with me and it's to be put into storage until I get a place of my own.'

'And is the rest going to auction?'

'That's right. Clancy's, the auctioneers, will be clearing the house out on Saturday. It'll all go under the hammer the week after.' She tilted her chin upwards in defiance against the terrible blow fate had dealt them.

Fiona threw the keys to the house on the bed with a clinking sound and they both stared at them. There were three long, old-fashioned keys for the front door and two more modern, shinier ones for the Yale lock on the back door. Attached to the set of keys by a tarnished silver-coloured chain was a heart-shaped, red-enamelled fob — it had hung from her mother's key-ring as long as Kath could remember.

'I've put all the keys on the one key-ring,' said Fiona. 'The ones for the French doors are hanging in the key box in the kitchen. Can you take them, Kath? I don't think I can bear to look at them.'

Kath nodded, slipped the keys into her pocket and looked gloomily about the familiar room. In just a few days' time the citizens of Ballyfergus would be poring over the remains of the O'Connells' life here in this house. And she hated the thought.

15

Bridget's guest suite consisted of two bedrooms and a bathroom in an annexe to the main house.

Fiona entered her bedroom in Bridget's in trepidation.

'Is everything OK for you?' said her daughter, standing by the door with a big smile on her face, like the proprietress of a B&B. She went over to the window and placed her hand on the radiator under the net curtains. 'Good. The heat's coming through now.' She removed her hand from the hot metal and rubbed it against the other one, as though transferring the warmth from one hand to the other. 'The room'll be nice and cosy in a little while.'

Fiona looked around the comfortable room, at the vase of pale pink roses on the bedside table, the newly purchased magazines arranged neatly on the shelf underneath and the fluffy dark blue towels on the bed.

'It's lovely, Bridget. Everything's just lovely,' she said, hiding her misery as best she could.

'Well, supper will be ready in twenty minutes, Mum. I'll leave you to get settled.'

Bridget went out, closing the door behind her, and Fiona stood by the double bed, with her hands clasped together. Her daughter had done everything she could to make her welcome, yet it still felt like a room in a hotel. It lacked the character of Highfield House — the high ceilings, the fireplaces in nearly every room, the cornicing and the single glazed windows with their imperfect glass.

Fiona wasn't used to living in a house like this. In truth she found her daughter's immaculate home with its triple glazing, under-floor heating and no-clutter policy sterile and cold. On the bright side, at least the house was big enough to afford her some privacy, even if it was only behind her bedroom door. Still, it wouldn't be for long, she told herself — she'd get a place of her own soon. She would visit the estate agent's first thing in the morning.

At the supper table, Bridget was cheerful and bright and Ned was the perfect host. The table was laid with white linen and Bridget's best cutlery and she served a three-course meal.

'This is delicious, Bridget,' said Fiona and she watched while Ned topped up her glass with red wine. 'Do you have wine every night?'

'No, not as a matter of course,' said Bridget.

'You don't have to have it on our account,' said Fiona. 'We could be here for a while. It would be best if you just carried on as normal. And me and Kath will fit in round you.'

'It's only a glass of wine,' said Bridget shortly.

'Do you usually lay the table like this on a midweek night?' said Fiona and Bridget glared at her without answering. 'Look, all I'm saying is that you don't need to put yourself out, love. You're just making extra work for yourself and it'll be stressful enough with us living here. I don't want a fuss.'

Bridget looked angry and Fiona realised with

regret that she had hurt her feelings. But it had to be said — Bridget wasn't the most relaxed of individuals and two extra people in the house would be enough work without creating more.

Ned broke the tension by changing the subject. 'Well, Kath,' he said, 'I believe you're thinking of buying the hotel. Are you serious?'

'Absolutely.'

'How far have you got with your plans?'

'Well, I've found out that the bank wants nearly a million for it.'

Everyone around the table, including the children, gasped.

'Never!' said Bridget and Kath nodded solemnly, indicating that it was indeed true.

'A million quid, Dad, did you hear that?' said Alex. 'That's like, awesome!'

'That's the most money in the world!' cried five-year-old Charmaine.

Fiona looked at the half-eaten apple-pie on her plate and entirely lost her appetite. She'd no idea her parents' hotel was worth so much. How could Brendan lose a hotel worth nearly a million pounds? She told herself that it was only money, but she felt sick to the stomach. She had so hoped that Kath would be able to buy the hotel — she couldn't bear the idea of it falling into someone else's hands. But Kath didn't have that kind of resources — none of them had.

'Where on earth are you going to get the money from?' said Bridget.

'I'm planning on liquidating all my assets,' replied Kath and Fiona's hopes rose a little.

'And they're worth that much?' said Ned.

'Not quite,' said Kath calmly. 'I made a few calls today. I've instructed my broker to sell all my stocks and shares. He's to come back with an exact figure. And I've instructed the realtor to put my condo on the market. Apparently there's a waiting list of people wanting to buy in my area of the South Side. She reckons it'll be snapped up.'

'What's a realtor?' said Fiona, bamboozled by Kath's quickfire delivery of information.

'Estate agent,' provided Kath. 'I bought the apartment ten years ago — the realtor reckons I'll clear $700,000 or so after paying off my mortgage.'

Fiona stared at her daughter in admiration and realised that she was deadly serious. If anyone could get the hotel back it was Kath. She was so focused, single-minded and capable. She only hoped that she had more business sense than her father.

'That's about £400,000,' observed Ned, 'but it still leaves you well short of the purchase price.'

'I made a lot of money working in the States, Ned. And I saved a lot — don't forget that I've only had myself to look after these past seventeen years. I worked with these guys who were real hot shots in finance. They used to invest on the stock market and I followed their lead. Where they invested I invested. It was a gambling in a way but it's paid off. My portfolio of shares is worth about £300,000.'

'Can I leave the table please?' interrupted Alex, bored now by the conversation.

'Yes, you may,' said Bridget and Alex's little

sisters chimed in with the same request. Once the children had left the table, Kath continued where she'd left off.

'I can't see the bank getting a million for the hotel. I think if I went in with an offer and it was the only one on the table, I might get it for less. Maybe £850,000 or £900,000.'

'It would've been worth a lot more as a going concern,' observed Ned.

'Yes, it would,' agreed Kath.

'But even if the bank is prepared to accept your offer, you still don't have enough, love,' pointed out Fiona. 'And it's terribly risky putting all your hard-earned money into this. You could lose everything.' The last thing she wanted to see was Kath throwing good money after bad. Much as Fiona wanted the hotel back in the family, she didn't want it at the expense of Kath's entire life savings.

Kath played nervously with the teaspoon in the sugar bowl. A shower of sugar spilled onto the tablecloth. She set the spoon down on the table.

'I know that,' she said. 'And you're right. I don't have enough money. I reckon I'm going to need another £200,000 or so to buy the hotel and spruce it up a bit. So,' said Kath, turning her keen gaze on Bridget and Ned, 'that's where you two come in.'

Ned glanced at Bridget, who raised her eyebrows in surprise and laughed a little nervously.

'Kath, we'd love to help, we really would,' said Ned, 'but we don't have that kind of cash lying

181

about, do we, Bridget?'

Bridget shook her head slowly.

'I'm not asking you to lend me the money, Ned. I think the bank'll lend me it but, without a track record, I reckon they're going to want a guarantor.'

Ned leaned back in his chair and crossed his arms across his chest. 'You're asking a lot, Kath. You're asking me to put my own family's security at risk. If you default on the loan, I'll have to cough up the money to repay the debt.'

'I understand your concern,' said Kath, 'but that's not going to happen. And I'm not doing this for myself, Ned — I'm doing this for the family. For Mum and for my nieces and nephews. That hotel belongs to the O'Connors and this is the only chance we have of getting it back. There's no one else I can turn to.'

Ned whistled through his teeth — a sharp intake of air.

Kath said hurriedly, 'I'm not asking you for an answer right now. All I'm asking is that you give it some thought.'

Fiona held her breath. Ned looked glumly at the faces round the table and, under the tablecloth, Fiona crossed her fingers.

'All right,' said Ned, glancing at Bridget. 'Give us a few days and we'll let you know our decision.'

★   ★   ★

'What are you doing, Mum?' came Bridget's voice from behind Fiona's back, and she bristled.

182

'Just putting in a load of wash,' said Fiona brightly, turning round to face her and trying to disguise her irritation. She felt like she couldn't do anything in her daughter's house without her breathing down her neck. Only yesterday she tried to help with the dinner but Bridget practically told her to get out of her way. She was fed up treading on eggshells all the time.

'But I wanted to get this lot on,' said Bridget tersely, indicating the full laundry basket in her arms. 'Alex needs his uniform for school tomorrow.' When Fiona said nothing she sighed. 'Never mind,' she said, but clearly didn't mean it and, instead of leaving Fiona to it, she stood and watched as she fiddled with the controls on the machine.

Fiona tried to ignore her but she could feel the tension in the little room. Over the past two days she'd come to realise just how controlling her daughter was. She had a strict routine for running her house and she did not like anyone interfering with it.

'You know, you don't need to do that, Mum. I'd prefer — I mean, it would be better if you left the laundry to me.'

'There, got it,' said Fiona, standing up. 'Where's the powder? Ah, there it is . . . ' She lifted the box of powder off the counter.

'You've got whites mixed in with coloureds . . . '

Fiona set the box down on the counter with a dull thud. 'All right, I'll separate them out,' she said, casting what she hoped was a withering glance at Bridget. She bent down and tugged the

183

clothes out of the machine onto the terracotta-tiled floor.

'But then you'll only have two half loads and it's wasteful to run the machine when it's only half full.'

'Bridget, why don't you just tell me what you want me to do?' said Fiona, standing up straight.

'Look, why don't you leave the washing to me,' said Bridget with a big, tense smile — the one she used for dim-witted shop assistants and the like. 'Just put it in the basket with our laundry and I'll take care of it.'

'Fine, if that's what you want,' said Fiona and she walked out of the kitchen, through the lounge and down to her bedroom.

She closed the door behind her and sat in the wicker chair in the corner of the room and reflected on the last few days. Her premature move here had been ill-judged. She should have stayed at Highfield House until the end. Here she wasn't even allowed to do her own laundry.

The problem with Bridget was that she didn't believe that anyone could do anything as well as she could herself. So she ended up doing everything herself and acting like a martyr in the process. She strove for perfection in everything to the point of obsession. Perhaps she needed something else, other than running the perfect home, to occupy her mind. Because right now she was driving Fiona mad. She made Fiona feel as though she was in the way all the time. She made her feel old — and useless. The sooner she got out of this house the better.

Going back to Highfield House was out of the

184

question. Leaving it once had been bad enough; she did not want to endure that a second time. On top of the chest of drawers were the sets of particulars that she had collected from the estate agent's in Ballyfergus. She set them on her lap and sighed.

None of them appealed to her — they were all a terrible disappointment compared to Highfield House. Poky little terraced houses in the worst part of town and characterless flats in modern red-and-yellow brick buildings that all looked the same. She dropped them on the floor and rubbed her tired eyes. But her days of living in Georgian splendour were over, she reminded herself, and she was going to have to get used to it. She picked the bundle of papers up, put on her glasses and began to read.

Half an hour had passed when Kath popped her head through the door.

'David's here with Murray,' she said and then, noticing the papers on Fiona's lap, asked, 'Have you seen anything you like?'

'Anything I like?' repeated Fiona, looking at Kath over the top of her glasses. 'No, I wouldn't go so far as to say that. But all these properties are within my price range. I'm sure one of them will do.' She knew she sounded like a sour old woman but she couldn't help herself.

Kath came into the room and pushed the door closed behind her.

'I know that none of them will be a patch on home, Mum. But we'll all help you to make the best of it, wherever you end up.'

'Thanks, love. That's sweet of you,' Fiona said,

the rancour dissolving. 'But what about you? You need to get somewhere to stay too. You can't stay here with Bridget forever. You know you're more than welcome in my place, when I get it, but it could be a bit cramped.' She leafed through the schedule on top of the pile in her lap — a nicely decorated, but very small, flat. 'Most of these have only one bedroom . . . '

'Thanks but I think I'll get a place of my own.'

'Oh, are you thinking of buying somewhere?'

'I won't have the money for that. I'll have to rent but don't worry — I think I've something sorted.'

'Oh,' said Fiona, her interest quickening. 'Where?'

'The old Mulholland farmhouse. I saw Mike up there a few days ago and he showed me around the place. It's hardly changed from when we were kids. If my plans all work out, you could come and stay with me.'

'Thanks. But I don't think so. I'm going to have to get used to living on my own,' said Fiona, her words sounding a lot braver than she felt. 'But if you don't mind me asking, Kath, how can you afford to rent it? Wouldn't it make more sense to stay in the hotel?'

'I'd rather not and the farmhouse is only £200.'

'A week?'

'No, a month.'

'You must've made a mistake, Kath.'

Her daughter frowned, looked puzzled for a few seconds and then said, 'No, Mum, I'm quite sure he said £200 a month. He said it was mine as long as I needed it.'

Fiona regarded Kath thoughtfully. 'Have you ever considered that Mike Mulholland might be after you?'

'After me?' repeated Kath, as though the thought had never crossed her mind. 'Don't be ridiculous. What on earth makes you say that?'

'Because that house rents out for £300 a week in low season, and nearly £600 a week in July and August.'

'No! You're joking.'

'I'm not joking, Kath.'

'Why on earth would Mike give it to me for such a ludicrously low rent?'

'Well, if you don't think he's after you, then you'll have to work out the answer to that question yourself,' said Fiona, peeling off her glasses and throwing the documents on the bed. 'Now, come on. David and Murray will be wondering where we are.'

Fiona was glad David had come. Much as she loved her daughters she had a soft spot for him — she thought it was because he was her only son. Or maybe it was because he was more accepting of her than her daughters — he was certainly less critical than them. Even as a child he'd adored her in a way his sisters never did and the relationship between them was much stronger because of it.

Bridget's cream-and-white lounge looked like one of the rooms on the front cover of the *Homes and Gardens* magazines that were arranged in a fan on the coffee table. Beside them was a tall, slender glass vase full of white lilies, opened to perfection. The room looked like it was never used.

As soon as Fiona entered the room, David embraced her warmly.

Murray stood on the other side of the room staring at her knowingly. His hair stuck out at all angles and she resisted the urge to march over and comb it down with a wet comb. It wasn't the boy's fault, though — his hair grew in a clockwise direction from not one, but two, crowns on his head, making it impossible to style. Still, the very sight of him annoyed Fiona. She wondered if Murray knew what she thought about him? Could he read her mind?

'Hello, Murray,' she said brightly but the boy, as usual, did not acknowledge her. Fiona blamed it on his mother — Viv was common as muck and her ill manners were rubbing off on her son.

Fiona pursed her lips to indicate her disapproval and David said quickly, 'Aren't you going to say hello to Gran, Murray? Go on. Give her a big hug and a kiss.'

'Hello, Gran,' he mumbled in that insolent way Viv had about her, and Fiona forced herself to smile at the child. He remained where he was, his feet planted firmly in the deep pile of Bridget's expensive pale-green rug. Fiona noticed that Bridget had made the child take off his shoes. What was a house for if it couldn't be lived in? she thought. Her house may have been grand but it was always a home first.

David, Bridget and Kath were talking about the arrangements to clear Highfield House. But

Fiona hardly heard a word they said.

She did try to love Murray, she really did, but it did not come easily. What was it about a child that you could take one look at them and instantly dislike them? Was it the way his eyes crossed slightly giving him a sly look? Or the way he hardly talked, keeping his thoughts and emotions to himself? Was it the way he sniggered behind his hand in a way that made you think he was laughing at you? Or was it simply because he was dull and slow?

Whatever, she couldn't seem to get on his wavelength no matter how hard she tried. When she attempted to engage him in conversation, he would turn away without a word and resume playing his computer game or watching TV. She didn't know how to handle a child so secretive and introverted. Bridget's children were the opposite — bright, inquisitive and vivacious — just like her own children had been.

'Mr Clancy said to put Post-its on everything you want to keep, Mum,' said David. 'Then he'll know what's to go into storage and what's for auction.'

'That sounds like a good idea,' said Kath.

Murray had a toy aeroplane made of wood in his hand and now ran round the room holding it up above his head, making loud engine noises. He threw it in the air and the plane hit the glass patio doors with a thud and crashed noisily on the pale wood floorboards.

'Murray, will you stop playing with that in here!' said David.

'Why don't you go and sit with the others in

189

the playroom?' suggested Bridget in a soft voice, her tight smile betraying her irritation. 'They're watching *Shrek 2*.'

Murray picked up the plane and ran quickly to his father's side. 'No. Don't want to,' he said and glared at his aunt from under a deeply furrowed brow.

Fiona felt like giving him a good slap.

'Well, you need to be careful if you're playing in here,' said David evenly. Then, turning his attention to the adults in the room, he said, 'We'll all come over and help Mum sort it out, won't we?' and the others voiced their agreement.

How could Fiona decide what parts of her life to keep and what parts to throw away? She didn't want to throw any of it away. She wanted to stay in Highfield House, surrounded by all her beautiful possessions. She would never feel at home anywhere else. It was going to be too painful and Fiona wasn't sure she could bear it. So she tuned out the sound of the others, while they talked about what had to be done, and thought about Murray instead.

She blamed Rosemary McGarel, the pharmacist's wife and an old schoolfriend, for planting the first malicious seed of doubt. One afternoon in the car, on their way back from a bridge game, Rosemary told Fiona what she said half of Ballyfergus knew.

'That Viv Watson is quite a little raver, you know. I heard that the baby she's carrying could belong to one of a number of men.' Her eyes were bright with the passion that a juicy piece of gossip can inspire in middle-aged women.

Fiona, in the passenger seat, had calmly looked out the car window while her insides contorted with shock. It was true that when Viv announced she was pregnant with David's baby they were not seeing each other — they'd broken up a month or two beforehand. But now they were living together again.

'Who told you that?' she said, remembering with despondency the joy on David's face when he'd told her he was going to be a father.

'People like to chat when they're waiting for their prescriptions. I wouldn't have said anything, Fiona, but I've heard it from a number of sources. I thought . . . well, I thought you should know.'

Fiona dithered over what to do. At the time she thought Viv was a nice girl — she hadn't yet revealed her true nature — and David was very fond of her. By the time Fiona had drummed up the courage to tell David, he was utterly besotted with the idea of becoming a father and there was talk of an engagement. Fiona weighed the importance of telling David the truth (if it *was* the truth) against her son's happiness. His welfare won — she decided to put the rumour firmly out of her mind.

And there it would have stayed had things not changed so dramatically. Now, Viv was history, David and Simone were a couple and Murray lived with his mother. David only saw the boy every other weekend and when he did, by all reports, he found him difficult and rude. And now that David and Viv were no longer together it rankled with Fiona that David could be supporting another man's child.

The thing about a seed is that if you water it and give it light and air, well, it keeps on growing. Where other people claimed to see a family resemblance, Fiona saw the features of another, anonymous man imprinted on Murray's face. At every family gathering where harmony reigned, Murray could be guaranteed to cause trouble — the cuckoo in the O'Connor nest. And so it was that Fiona came to believe, partly because she wanted to, and partly because the evidence before her seemed so irrefutable, that Murray was not David's son.

'Careful,' said Bridget, as Murray sent the toy plane off on another flight round the lounge.

'I told you,' snapped David, as the plane came to rest in the unused fireplace throwing up a little puff of grey dust. 'Don't throw that plane in here. If you want to throw it, go play in the playroom or outside.'

Murray retrieved the plane but did not leave the room. He skulked in a corner behind the sofa until the adults were engaged in conversation once more. Then he stood up and took aim once more with the plane. His eyes locked with Fiona's — she shook her head vigorously at him and mouthed, quite clearly, 'No'

His sharp little eyes glinted in defiance and he launched the plane with all his might towards her like a missile. It collided with the lilies in the vase — the slim tube of glass wobbled for a second or two, then the weight of the plane sent it toppling over. Fiona saw what was about to happen, and reached out to catch it, but she was too late.

The vase hit the glass-topped coffee table with a loud crash. A thin white crack, like a chalk mark, appeared on the glass.

'No!' shrieked Kath, jumping to her feet.

Water sloshed over the glossy magazines, ruining them, then onto the rug. The force of the fall ejected the flowers from the vase and they, along with a good cupful of cold water, landed on Fiona's lap.

She leapt up and the flowers tumbled to the floor. But it was too late — her beautiful cream-coloured Marina slacks were spotted with bright saffron-coloured stains from the lily pollen. They would never come out. She'd bought the trousers only three weeks ago, at Fulton's just outside Coleraine. They'd cost her a small fortune and she knew that she would never be able to afford such a pair of lovely trousers again. Tears of sorrow and rage pricked her eyes.

Murray giggled. Fiona's head snapped round to find him standing behind the sofa, his hand over his mouth and his eyes crinkled up with laughter.

'Look what you've done!' she cried. 'You stupid child!'

'Oh, my beautiful coffee table!' gasped Bridget. Her face was pale.

'If you'd left the room when you were told this wouldn't have happened!' roared Fiona, her hands shaking with rage. 'Look! Look what you've done! You've smashed your Aunt

193

Bridget's table. And look at my beautiful trousers. They're ruined. You stupid, stupid child!'

'OK, Mum,' said David coming up behind Murray and resting his hands on his shoulders. 'That's enough.'

'That is one naughty little boy,' said Fiona, lowering her tone but her voice was dripping with menace. 'He never does what he's told. And I can't stand disobedient children.'

'Mum,' said David, 'don't talk to your grandson like that.'

Rage welled up inside Fiona. She wanted to wipe that impudent smile off Murray's face.

'That,' cried Fiona, and she paused — fury fought with her good judgement — and won. The words sprang from her lips before she could stop them. 'That,' she repeated, 'is no grandson of mine!'

The room went utterly silent and Murray stared at her with those blank, puppy-like eyes of his. Fiona blinked defiantly at her children. Bridget and Kath looked up wordlessly from where they were kneeling on the floor, trying to repair the damage caused by the water. David stood, open-mouthed, his chest rising and falling quickly and Fiona could see his grasp on the boy's shoulders tighten. Suddenly, her anger abated as quickly as it had arisen. Panic and regret engulfed her.

'What did you say, Mum?' said David quietly, his voice full of hurt.

'I was angry. Look, you saw what he did,' she said quickly, breathlessly, pointing at the flowers strewn on the floor and the smashed coffee-table. 'This never would have happened if he'd done what you asked him. If he'd done what he was told for a change instead of — '

'You didn't mean it though, did you?' interrupted David and Fiona bit her lip.

'Murray,' commanded David, 'leave the room.' And for once the child did as he was told.

'I want you to take that back,' said David, as soon as Murray was out of earshot, 'and say you're sorry to Murray.'

Fiona stared at David while her mind raced. She had no proof of Murray's paternity. If she told David what she suspected, he might not believe her. And if he did believe her, he would despise her for telling him. Either way — he would hate her and she could not bear that. She had no choice but to retract — not unless she wanted to open up the entire can of worms right here and now.

'I'm sorry,' she said carefully. 'I take back what I said.' This was not the same, in Fiona's mind, as saying that she did not mean it and therefore it was not a lie. Not exactly. 'But I'm not apologising to Murray. It's he who should be apologising to me — and to Bridget.'

'He will apologise — in a minute. I'll go and get him now,' said David. His expression was still grave but, to her relief, he sounded placated.

He left the room and Fiona collapsed on the sofa.

'Why did you say that, Mum?' said Kath, who had risen from the floor with a sodden towel in her hand.

'I was — I'm not myself,' she mumbled. 'Everything's getting to me. It's all just too much. I overreacted, that's all.'

'But to say he's not your grandson, Mum. Can you imagine how hurtful that is?'

'I know, I know. I said I was sorry. It's just that Murray's so unlike the O'Connors. He is, isn't he, Bridget? He's nothing like any of your children.'

'Well, he has a different mother. Of course he's going to be different.'

'Exactly. I think he's got more of his mother's genes than he has of his father's.'

'And that's why you dislike him?' said Kath.

'I don't — ' began Fiona and blushed.

But before she could finish the lie, Murray was propelled into the room by his father.

Churlish apologies were extracted from him, but he did not appear in the least bit remorseful. If anything, he seemed to sense that something momentous had just occurred and that, somehow, he had gained the upper hand.

When David and Murray left, Fiona retreated to the privacy of her bedroom. She looked at her reflection in the mirror and swore, not for the first time in her life, that she was going to keep her big mouth shut in future. She was a great believer in telling people what she thought but, she reminded herself, sometimes that wasn't the best option. Some things were best left unsaid — and some things, like the content of Brendan's will, were best kept secret. If David believed Murray was his child — if he *wanted* to believe that — then who was she to destroy that illusion?

16

If she had the power to make dreams come true, thought Kath, she would be with Carl right now, living the life she had lived only a few weeks ago. Except of course there would be no Lynda and no children waiting in the wings . . .

'Well, has he phoned yet?' said Bridget and she set a cup down on the table beside Kath.

'Carl?' said Kath, realising as soon as she said it that this was not what Bridget meant.

'No, silly. The bank manager.'

'No,' said Kath, glancing at the phone on the table beside her. 'Not yet.'

She pictured two little girls dressed in pink fairy outfits, their faces animated with delight like little pixies. She could never break up a home — happy or otherwise — and the thought that she might have been close to doing so made her feel sick. She reminded herself that she was completely innocent of any wrongdoing — but still the shame lingered like the smell of burnt toast.

'Thanks for the coffee,' she said, aware that her sister was staring at her.

Bridget opened her mouth to speak, paused and then pressed on. 'Do you still think about Carl a lot?'

'Every day,' sighed Kath. 'You know, part of me really, really hates him for what he's done and yet another part of me still loves him.'

'Part of you always will,' said Bridget wistfully. 'That will never change. But,' she said, with a little shake of her head as though clearing her thoughts, 'the important thing is that he loves you, doesn't he?'

'Yes, for all his faults, I think he does.'

'If he loves you he's not going to let you go easily. What would you do if he said that he would leave his wife and kids for you? Would you take him back?'

'I . . . I don't know. I desperately want things to be the way they were before. But I know that's not possible. You see, I don't think that I can ever trust him again. It's the lies, Bridget. I don't think I can forgive him for those. Even if he was free.'

'You might change your mind if you saw him again.'

Kath tried to imagine how she would feel if Carl was here right now pleading with her to go back to him. Bridget was right — it would be hard to resist him. 'I don't know,' she said lamely.

'You know that if you get the hotel, Kath, your future will be here. You won't have the option of going back to Boston.'

'I know that,' said Kath quietly and a surge of panic momentarily silenced her. Was she doing the right thing? 'But I also know that I can't let the hotel go. I can't stand back and watch while someone else takes it over, or worse, turns it into flats. And I really appreciate the support you and Ned have given me. Without your guarantee the bank would never have agreed to loan me the extra money I need.'

'Well, it's in everyone's interests that you make a go of this, Kath. Yours, ours and Mum's.'

Put like that, it all sounded too daunting, too overwhelming, and Kath wondered if, this time, she'd overestimated her ability. She'd taken risks before — in her job and with her investments — but this time she was gambling not only with her own life, but with Bridget and Ned's. And by raising her mother's hopes regarding the hotel, hers too. But she couldn't show any self-doubt to Bridget — not after she and her husband had agreed to guarantee her bank loan and, in doing so, put their own welfare at risk.

'What did you make of what Mum said to Murray the other day, about him not being her grandson?' said Bridget, rousing Kath from her worrying thoughts. This was the first time the sisters had been alone together since the incident.

'A slip of the tongue?' said Kath, who had not read too much into it. 'I don't think she meant it literally. Though David was terribly upset.'

'Mmm . . . ' said Bridget and paused in that way of hers that invited further probing.

'You think there was more to it than that?' obliged Kath.

'I just think it was a very . . . definite thing to say. Why not just say 'that boy annoys me' or 'he makes me mad'? To say a child isn't your grandson, well, it's like disowning him. It sounded to me like the expression of a conscious thought.'

'So you think,' said Kath slowly, 'that Mum

199

thinks that David might not be Murray's dad?'

'I've really no idea. Mum won't talk to me about it.'

'Me neither. But I can't believe that to be true. I mean we'd just *know*, wouldn't we?'

Just then the phone rang and the two women looked at each other. Kath snatched up the receiver, put it to her ear and said, 'Kath O'Connor.'

'Hi, it's Frank Morrison,' said the voice on the line and Kath's stomach lurched. In that split second, while he paused for breath, she panicked. If he said her offer had been accepted, was she really ready to take this challenge on? What if the hotel was a white elephant? What if she couldn't make it work?

'Look, Kath. I'm afraid I'm not in a position to accept your offer.'

Disappointment enveloped her. She realised then that owning and running the hotel was what she truly wanted. More than anything right now.

'Another party has registered their interest,' he went on, 'and naturally we need to ensure that we obtain the best price possible in a sale.'

'Another party,' repeated Kath dully. In the face of competition she couldn't increase her offer. She was stretching herself as it was. 'Who is it?'

'I'm afraid that I'm not in a position to divulge that information.'

'Well, what happens now?'

'We wait to see if they want to make an offer.'

'How long? How long do you wait?'

'They need to have a detailed survey done and

200

see if the figures stack up for them. But no more than a week or two, I should think.' He paused then and added, as though he could read her thoughts, 'I'm sorry, Kath. I know you really wanted it.'

'Thanks,' she said dully. 'thanks for letting me know,' and she hung up.

Fiona came into the room then and Kath told her and Bridget what Frank Morrison had said.

'I'll tell you who'll know,' said Fiona. 'Willie Ross. There's not a thing goes on in this town that he doesn't know about. Here, give me the phone. I'll call him. I think it's the very least he can do for us.'

After she had spoken to Willie, she turned to face her daughters.

'Apparently it's the McCormicks. Willie says that they're interested in developing the hotel into luxury apartments. Can you imagine?'

McCormick Limited was a national building firm, based in Ballyfergus, headed up by the aging Noel McCormick, the driving force behind the business. The company was involved in all aspects of the trade and now, it seemed, the redevelopment of old hotels.

'I thought McCormick Limited were builders,' said Bridget, voicing Kath's thoughts. 'You know, big office blocks and schools — that sort of thing. I didn't know they were into property development.'

'Noel McCormick's into anything that makes money,' said Fiona dryly. 'But it's not him that's behind this.' She looked pointedly at Kath. 'It's Matt Doherty.'

'Oh,' said Kath abruptly. 'He works for McCormick Limited now?'

'He does and more than that. He's married to one of Noel McCormick's daughters.'

'Why didn't you tell me?' said Kath.

Fiona shrugged. 'It never came up in the conversation. It didn't seem important — at the time.'

'It's important now,' said Kath, thinking hard.

'Why's that?' asked Bridget.

'Because he hated me for breaking up with him. Maybe he still does. I wonder if this is his way of trying to get back at me.'

'Oh, Kath,' said Bridget dismissively, 'don't you think that you're reading far too much into this? He might not even know that you're interested in the hotel.'

'Well, there's only one way to find out,' said Kath and the other two women looked at her. 'I can't afford to pay a single penny more than I've offered. If he's going to outbid me, I might as well know about it now as sit around for another two weeks. I'm going to see him.'

★   ★   ★

Kath drove her mother's car, a lovely three-year-old Jaguar saloon, over to the McCormick Limited offices. The car had been paid for in cash — at least Fiona wouldn't suffer the indignity of it being repossessed. Kath's hands were shaking and she gripped the steering wheel fiercely until her palms were damp with sweat.

What tack should she take with Matt? Should

she approach him as an old friend? Or keep the meeting businesslike and professional? That would really depend on his reaction to her turning up at his door after all these years. She resolved to take the former approach but if Matt didn't want to be all pally-wally, she'd just have to follow his lead.

She parked the car outside the modern three-storey office block — all steel and tinted black glass. She looked at the blank sheets of glass and asked herself what exactly she hoped to get out of this meeting? She realised she was here to persuade Matt Doherty not to make an offer for the hotel. And that, she had to admit, was a very tall order. She took a deep breath and got out of the car.

'Mr Doherty is engaged at the moment,' said the stern-faced, middle-aged secretary on the third floor.

Kath gave her a friendly smile. 'If you tell him it's Kath O'Connor, I'm sure he'll see me.'

The secretary flashed Kath a bright but insincere smile, asked her to take a seat and Kath sat down and tried to stop her knees from knocking together.

'He'll be with you in a minute,' said the secretary when she came back a few moments later. She went back to pounding the keyboard of her computer without so much as another glance at Kath. Her hair, Kath noticed, was a peculiar shade of auburn that did not complement her sallow skin. An offer of a cup of coffee, Kath thought, would've made her feel so much more welcome.

Nearly twenty minutes had passed and Kath was about to approach the secretary again when Matt Doherty appeared before her. But she didn't recognise him at first. He'd put on weight and, though far from being obese, it was enough to transform his features. But when he smiled she saw that it was him and she stood up immediately.

'Kath! It's good to see you. It's been a long time. You've been in the States, haven't you?' He pumped her hand warmly.

'That's right,' mumbled Kath, both taken aback by, and pleased with, his amiable welcome.

Matt said, over his shoulder, to the secretary, 'Can you bring us in some coffee, please? Thank you.'

He took Kath by the elbow and ushered her into his office, a medium-sized room furnished with an oak conference table and, in the corner of the room, a desk and a large brown leather chair. Several pot plants dotted the otherwise dull room with colour.

He pulled out chairs at the table and indicated for her to sit down. Kath took off her coat and put it over the back of an empty chair. Encouraged by his friendly approach, she found her nerve again and asked after his parents and siblings. They exchanged brief information about what everyone was up to and then Matt said, 'I'm sorry about your father.'

'Thank you. It was a terrible shock.'

Just then the secretary entered the room carrying a stainless-steel tray. She set it on the table, left the room and Matt busied himself serving the coffee.

When they both had a cup in front of them Kath said, 'I hear you're married now with — how many children is it?'

'Three.'

'That's nice,' said Kath and there was an awkward pause between them, during which she hoped Matt would provide some small talk about his family. But he did not.

'You seem to have done well for yourself?' she went on, hoping to appeal to his ego which, she remembered, had always been a little overblown.

'Yes,' he said, bringing the tips of the fingers on each hand together carefully. 'Noel McCormick retires next year and then I'll be chief executive.'

'You *have* done well,' said Kath.

'I've a good wife behind me,' he observed and then said, a little coolly she thought, 'So, when do you go back to the States?'

'I'm not sure I am going back,' she said carefully, with both hands circled round the hot cup of coffee, watching him closely. 'I don't know if you'd heard, but I'm hoping to buy the hotel.'

'I see,' he said and put his cup down in the saucer, but she could not tell by his demeanour whether or not this information was a surprise to him. 'Is that why you've come to see me?'

'Well, I heard that you're thinking of making a bid for it.'

'I might be,' he said and his expression was as inscrutable as his reply. She waited and he said,

205

'So what exactly is it you want from me, Kath?'

She swallowed and decided that there was no option but to plunge in at the deep end. What had she to lose? Only her dignity. 'I — I was hoping to persuade you not to bid for the hotel. I've scraped together everything I can to buy it but I can't afford a penny more. It would mean so much to my mother, and the rest of the family, if we got it back. You know we've lost the house, don't you?'

'Oh, Kath,' he said and laughed cruelly, 'these decisions can't be made on emotive terms. If the development of the Sallagh Braes looks like a viable proposition — one we can make a decent profit on — then we'll put in an offer.'

'Since when did McCormick Limited get into redevelopments? I thought you only did new builds?'

'It's a new sideline I'm developing.'

'And the Sallagh Braes would be your first project?'

'That's right.'

It was as she suspected. She found it impossible to believe that his interest in the hotel was purely business. Why decide to go into this now? And why the Sallagh Braes? There were plenty of other development opportunities out there.

'But I thought . . . I just thought . . . because we were old friends that you might recon-sider — '

'We weren't friends, Kath. We were lovers,' he said shortly and the corners of his blue eyes twitched angrily.

She saw then that it had been a mistake to come here. His cheery front was nothing more than a mask for his true feelings. He did hate her and he was going to make her pay for the wrong she'd done him. The hotel meant everything to Kath's family and nothing to the McCormicks — but that wouldn't stop Matt. It was only now, having been rejected herself by Carl, that she understood how painful her refusal to marry him must have been. The silence between them hung heavy with his unvoiced anger and recriminations.

'I'm sorry, Matt,' she said quietly. 'I'm sorry that I couldn't love you back.'

'That's in the past,' he said dismissively and sniffed. 'It's got nothing to do with today,' and she knew that he was lying. 'Whatever decision I — we make regarding the Sallagh Braes, it'll be based on facts and figures and nothing else.'

There was nothing left for her to do but get out as quickly and gracefully as she could manage. She stood up. 'Well, thank you for your time,' she said evenly. 'You've certainly put me in the picture.'

He stood and strode to the door. Leaning on the door handle, he said: 'You know, my mother always used to say, 'What's meant for you won't go past you', Kath.'

He opened the door and she brushed past him.

'I'll bear that in mind, Matt,' she said and she walked away without so much as a glance behind her.

Sometimes you have to know when you're

beaten was what he really meant, she thought, as she made her way out of the building and back to the car. She paused with the car keys in her hand and looked back at the sightless tinted windows. Little spots of rain dotted the smooth, unblemished glass. She guessed that he was watching her now, pleased with his little act of revenge.

Well, she'd show him. She wasn't beaten yet. And there was no way she was going to let him obliterate her father's memory from the hotel.

Kath got in the car and drove straight into town to see Frank Morrison. Dark clouds had gathered overhead and soon the spots of rain turned to a downpour. No wonder Ireland was so green, with all this rain — though not today. The sides of the road were black with mud and the landscape, so pretty and lush in the summer months, was barren and bleak.

She must persuade Frank to put a closing date on the hotel and to accept sealed bids. The situation must not be allowed to become a bidding war, for she knew she could not compete on those terms. She parked in the car park behind the supermarket, pulled her coat around her and got out of the car. She ducked through a set of automatic doors and made her way through Ballyfergus's only shopping mall. The name was a misnomer really — she smiled when she thought of the huge shopping malls in the States, some as big as small towns.

This was little more than a dingy corridor with a handful of shops that led onto Broadway, the old market square in the middle of town. Once through the mall, she rounded the corner onto the High Street and into the rain. Then she came to the bank building where Frank Morrison worked. She paused, took a deep breath, prayed he would be in and went inside.

The inside of the building was transformed since she had last seen it many years ago. The high security shield behind which the cashiers used to sit, with their desk-bound colleagues slaving away behind them, was gone. It had been replaced with an assortment of open-plan seating and 'pods' dotted about the floor, behind which members of staff were bashing away on their computer keyboards or answering phones.

The effect was somewhat disconcerting as, at first glance, it was not obvious whom to approach with her simple request to see the bank manager. She imagined the intention had been to make the place more customer-friendly but, strangely, the atmosphere was little changed from earlier days — it still felt hushed and reverential.

A slim, smartly dressed girl in her early twenties approached Kath with a broad smile. Kath thought she vaguely recognised her, but could not place her — a situation all too common in Ballyfergus where nearly everybody was related to somebody you knew. She asked Kath to wait while she telephoned upstairs to see if the bank manager was free.

It seemed like an age until she came back. 'He can see you now,' she said, and Kath suddenly became aware that she must look like a drowned rat. She touched her hair, wet from the rain, and cursed herself for not freshening up. But it was too late now to do anything about it. She put on her brightest smile and followed the girl into the lift which took them to the next floor.

Frank's office was a high-ceilinged room with big glass windows that looked out onto the street below. It had not yet been modernised like the main banking hall — the furniture was dated and a bit worse for wear.

'Hi, Kath,' he said when he saw her and she immediately relaxed.

There was something so unthreatening about him. He was open and honest in a way that Matt Doherty could never be. She noticed, for the first time, that there was no wedding band on his finger.

'I've been to see Matt Doherty,' she said, before Frank had a chance to ask why she was here. Then she felt faintly silly blurting out this piece of news without preamble.

'I see,' he said slowly. 'You don't waste much time, do you? Here, let me take your coat. And take a seat. Now, tell me what he had to say for himself.'

She sat down, almost giddy with excitement, or was it nerves? 'It looks like he's going to put in a bid for the hotel.'

'Did he actually say that?'

Kath thought hard for a moment. 'He said that he might be, not that he would. He said that any decision would be based purely on facts and figures.'

'As I said, he'd have to be convinced that he could make money out of it,' Frank summarised,

210

'before he'd put in an offer.'

'I guess so,' she said and paused. 'Frank, is there any way he would know how much I offered for the hotel?'

'No. The only person who knows that, at the moment, is me.'

'Right.' There was still hope then, thought Kath. If she could persuade Frank to her way of thinking.

'What?' he said and she realised that she had been staring at him.

She took a deep breath and said, 'I know you and Dad had a lot of time for each other. You were . . . friends, weren't you?'

'Yes, we were.'

'And I know that you felt bad about the mess Dad got himself in. I know that it had nothing to do with you,' she added hastily.

He looked sadly at a spot on the carpet. 'I'm sorry I didn't do more to help him.'

Kath felt a little stab of shame at the way she was about to try and exploit his common decency. But she had to get the hotel back.

'Well, now's your chance to make it up to him, Frank. Sort of.'

His face jerked up to meet her steady gaze, which belied the anguish she felt underneath.

'You know Dad would've hated the hotel to fall out of the family, don't you?'

He nodded cautiously, giving her the courage to go on, his cobalt-blue eyes trained on her like darts.

'I can't compete against McCormick Limited, not if Matt Doherty really wants the hotel.'

'But what can I do about that?'

'I'm asking you to set a closing date, Frank. Highest offer on the day wins. No negotiation.' He opened his mouth to respond but Kath held her hand up and continued talking, 'I know it's asking a lot. And I don't want you to give me an answer just now. All I'm asking is that you think about it. I might not get the hotel even then — but at least it'd give me a chance. I'm sure this is what Dad would've wanted.'

He swallowed the words that had sprung to his lips and regarded her with a spear-like intensity for some moments while she held her breath. He sighed, looked down at the backs of his hands, looked out the window and then back at Kath. He ran his right hand through his thick brown hair. His good-looking face was contorted with unease and she was full of guilt.

'You know you're asking a lot?' he said.

She nodded and exhaled slowly.

'If I do this and Head Office find out, I could lose my job.'

'I'm sure you're too valuable to them for that.'

He inhaled air through his white teeth.

'If you do this for us, Frank — for me and Mum and the rest of the family — I swear that I'll never ask you for another favour as long as I live.'

★ ★ ★

That night at supper Ned produced a copy of the local weekly paper, *The Ballyfergus Times*. It was folded open at the property section.

'Here,' he said, handing the creased paper to Fiona and glancing sheepishly at Bridget. 'I don't suppose you'll have seen that yet.'

Fiona squinted at the page — short-sighted without her reading glasses — and Kath said, 'What is it?'

But Fiona did not say anything and her face betrayed little emotion, apart from the way she set her lips in a tight, straight line, indicating that something had displeased her. After a few moments, she set the paper down gently beside her plate and continued eating.

Kath picked up the paper and searched the page quickly. She spotted the advert, which took up nearly a quarter of the page, immediately. *Auction of Listed Grade II House*, it said, above a picture of Highfield House.

'What is it?' said Alex. 'What are you reading? Oh, look! There's Gran and Grandad's house!' He pointed at the picture.

'What's it doing in the paper?' said Laura.

Kath swallowed the bubble of emotion that rose in her throat. 'It's an advert for Gran's house,' she said evenly.

'What's an advert?' said Charmaine.

'It means that the house is going to be sold,' said Kath.

'But why does Gran want to sell her house? We love it.'

'Well,' said Bridget brightly, suddenly joining the conversation, 'it's a bit big for Gran, now that she's on her own, isn't it? So she's going to find somewhere smaller in town. Somewhere that's a bit handier for the shops and things. Isn't that right, Mum?'

Ignoring the question, and the children, Fiona looked round the room at the adults. 'Well, we all knew it was coming,' she said stoically. 'But it's still a bit of a shock.'

And Kath found that she could not speak for the tears threatening to choke her words.

She knew she'd done the right thing in going after the hotel first. Highfield House would be safe from the likes of Matt Doherty and his redevelopment plans. True, the house would fall into the hands of strangers, but she would get it back one day, she told herself. But still it hurt.

In bed that night she allowed hot tears to seep silently into the pillow. She wept not for the house — it was only bricks and mortar, she told herself — but for the father of her childhood. He'd seemed so big and strong and so capable, she believed that he could carry the world on his shoulders. And of course in the final analysis he could not, no more than any mortal man.

Guilt tugged at her conscience — if she'd been a better daughter, visited more, kept in touch more, maybe never left in the first place, might she have prevented his death? She thought of her mother lying in the room next door and she wondered if similar thoughts haunted her too about her own actions. But she would never ask her for the very act of asking would be interpreted as an inference that she *should* feel responsible. Which, of course, was not fair. Fiona was no more responsible than Kath. But it was hard making your conscience believe that.

17

'Goodbye, David,' said Kath, standing at the entrance to the departures lounge at the airport. A tear crept out of her eye and she brushed it away, feeling foolish.

'Now, now. It's not for long, Kath,' he said and he patted her shoulder. 'You'll be back before you know it.'

He couldn't know that her tears weren't for what she was leaving behind, but for the painful memories she would have to face on the other side of the Atlantic.

'When I think of everything that's happened over the past few weeks,' she said, 'it's a bit overwhelming. If someone had told me a few weeks ago that I was about to lose Carl, lose Dad, sell up my entire worldly possessions and move home and country, I'd never have believed it.'

'And yet here you are doing just that,' said David thoughtfully. 'You know, you are taking on a lot, Kath. It's bound to be stressful.'

'I still can't get over that Matt Doherty — showing all that interest in the hotel and then not even putting an offer in on the closing date.'

David shrugged. 'He mustn't have thought he'd make enough of a profit out of it.'

'Mmm. Perhaps you're right.'

'You don't sound convinced.'

'Well, I'm not. I think he only pretended to be

interested to get back at me.'

'Get back at you?'

'Yes, for dumping him when I was twenty.'

'Phew! That's quite a statement, Kath. I mean that happened nearly twenty years ago. You don't really think that he was out to get you after all this time?'

'You think I'm a bit paranoid, don't you?'

'I do, a bit. I'm sure the guy's got a lot more important things to worry about.' He paused. 'Did you hear that? Your flight's just been called. Here, give me a hug.'

They embraced briefly and Kath said, 'I'll give you a ring when I arrive and I'll see you in a week's time.'

When the plane took off she strained to catch a glimpse of the murky landscape below and her stomach lurched, not with nausea but with longing. She did not want to leave this place; she did not want to go back to Boston, not even for this short visit.

She realised quite suddenly that Ballyfergus was where she belonged — the place where she had been raised, the place that was in her blood and where she would now spend the foreseeable future. Maybe even the rest of her life. When she was younger and thirsted for the great, wide world beyond Ballyfergus, such a notion would've filled her with horror. Now, the prospect of being among her own people — people whom she could trust implicitly — brought nothing but comfort. She closed her eyes and her mind was less troubled than it had been for weeks.

Her life was set on a different course to the one she had followed for the past seventeen years. A little shiver of excitement, or was it apprehension, made her open her eyes. She'd entered into a legally binding contract to buy the Sallagh Braes. She'd agreed a sale for her apartment and told her boss, Doug Rucker, she wouldn't be coming back to work. He'd told her that the door would always be open for her — a generous gesture considering that she'd left without giving due notice.

So far so good, but there was no room for complacency, she reminded herself. In a few short weeks she would be the owner of a hotel, but she still had to refurbish it, staff it, attract customers and make it profitable. She'd never undertaken anything so challenging in her life.

But somehow, now that the uncertainty of the last few weeks was over, a relative calmness had descended on her. She closed her eyes again and fell into a deep, restful sleep.

★   ★   ★

Emmy and Steven were waiting for her in the award-winning international arrivals hall, which she eventually reached after walking what felt like five miles from the aircraft. Logan International Airport, in spite of the billions poured into modernising it over the past decade, was still a daunting place to be, purely because of its size. She'd read somewhere that nearly twenty-five million people passed through it every year.

Emmy ran to meet Kath, flung her arms around her neck and hugged her.

'How are you?' she said and Kath smiled.

'A bit tired. But all the better for seeing you. It's good to see you guys!'

Once Emmy had let her go, Steve gave Kath a big bear-hug.

She kissed Steve on the cheek and said, 'Thanks for picking me up.'

'No sweat,' said Steve and took control of her luggage trolley, navigating it through the pedestrian walkway to the car park. Emmy and Kath followed, linking arms.

'So,' said Emmy, the welcoming smile faded from her face, 'how was the funeral?'

'Awful.'

'I can imagine.'

'People were very kind. But it was . . . it was the worst day of my life.'

'I'm sorry,' said Emmy and she waited for a few moments before asking, 'And what happened about the hotel? The last time I spoke to you, you'd put in an offer and were waiting to hear.'

'I got it, Emmy. I only found out for sure a couple of days ago.'

'So that's it then. You're definitely going back for good?'

'Yes, I am,' said Kath and she stopped, causing an obstruction in the flow of pedestrians. 'But I'm going to miss you and Steve.'

'I don't want you to go,' said Emmy, sounding childlike, and Kath embraced her while weary travellers of all shapes and colours flowed around them.

When they pulled apart, Emmy wiped tears from her face with the tips of her fingers. She had a ring on nearly every finger and the chains around her neck jangled like bells. She smiled and said, 'I'm sorry. I didn't mean to go all soppy on you.'

'I don't mind. I like it. It means you care,' said Kath and the two women laughed.

'Will you two hurry up?' shouted Steve, who was now waiting for them a hundred yards or so along the walkway.

'Just coming,' shouted Emmy.

They linked arms again and Kath said, 'I'm going to miss you terribly, Emmy, but I know that this is the right thing for me. It's hard to explain.' She sighed deeply. 'I don't want to sound all mystical and New Age but . . . '

'Go on.'

'I think that going back to Ireland and running the hotel is my — my destiny. It's as though everything that's happened has led me to this point. Everything that happened with Carl has propelled me away from my life here.'

'I wondered when you were going to get to him,' said Emmy darkly.

'Why? What's he been up to? Have you seen him?'

'I've not seen him but he's phoned me quite a few times since you left. He's been a bit of a pest really. He kept trying to persuade me to give him your contact number in Ireland.'

'Thanks. Thanks for not doing that,' said Kath and instinctively she pulled the collar of her jacket round her neck with her right hand. 'I couldn't have dealt with him — not on top of everything else.'

'Well, you might have to deal with him now you're here.'

'What do you mean?'

'Well, he seemed quite determined to get you back. He kept telling me what a fool he'd been and how much he loves you. In the end I had to tell him I wasn't an agony aunt.'

Kath smiled at her friend's witticism and inside her heartbeat quickened. 'He said that?' she asked and, in spite of her resolve to freeze him out of her heart, she found she still cared. His love was there then for the taking — all she had to do was let him back into her life. It would be so easy to let herself love him again, to forgive. But could she ever forget? She feared that his duplicity would haunt her for the rest of her life.

'You're not thinking of taking him back, are you?' said Emmy and those trademark arched eyebrows of hers were raised high in alarm.

Kath smiled and shook her head, not able right at this moment to give an authoritative verbal answer. They'd reached the car park now and the blast of bitterly cold air at the end of the tunnel was the first real sensory reminder that she was back in Boston. Some sort of building work was underway — notices said that the car park (or 'garage' as the Americans confusingly called it) was being extended. Boston, it seemed, was a city under permanent construction.

'You know, I've so much to tell you, Emmy, I

really don't know where to start.'

Steve stopped at a machine to pay the parking ticket and Kath, letting go of Emmy's arm, hopped from one foot to the other in an effort to ward off the cold.

'Well, let's start with the facts,' said Emmy. 'Is the sale of the apartment definitely going through?'

'Absolutely. That's the main reason I'm here really. I've got loads of other stuff to do as well — close bank accounts and sort out work and everything. But the main thing is to sign the papers for the sale and clear out the apartment.'

'Right. I'll help you do that and once everything's ready for shipping, you must come and stay with us.'

'Thanks, Emmy. Did the crates arrive from the shipping company?'

'Yes. Steve went over to the apartment and let the guys in. They left them in the hall.'

'Great. Thanks, Steve.'

'No worries,' he said.

'How long are you staying?' asked Emmy.

'I've a flight booked for next Thursday.'

'Less than a week,' said Emmy with a frown. 'Well, then,' her face broke into a grin, 'we've a lot of partying to squeeze in. We'd better get started as soon as we get home. Now, tell me, will you live in the hotel, once it's up and running?'

'I could, I suppose — there are a couple of garret rooms on the top floor — but I don't fancy it much. I'm going to rent a house.'

'Where?'

'This farmer — that makes him sound awfully old, doesn't it? He's a young guy — well, our age.'

'Is he married?'

'Noooo,' said Kath dragging out the vowel sound and casting Emmy a withering glance.

'Only asking. Sorry, go on.'

'Well, his farm is just up the road from the hotel and he has an empty farmhouse that he lets out in the summer. That's where I'm going to stay.'

'Where does he live then?'

'In a big bungalow built a few years ago, a stone's throw from the original farmhouse.'

'So what's he like?'

'Nice. And very kind. He lost his father too, you know. About seven years ago. He seemed to really understand what I was going through.'

'What does he look like?'

'Hard to describe really. He's not handsome in a conventional sense but he's very . . . well, attractive. You know the way I think Tommy Lee Jones is really sexy?'

'Yes. He's the one in *Men in Black* who's old enough to be your father and has pockmarked skin.'

'You make him sound horrible.'

'And?' said Emmy, her hands held out, palms upturned.

'Stop making fun of me!' said Kath, trying and failing to suppress a giggle. 'I'll have you know a lot of women think he's sexy — in a rough, macho kind of way,' she added lamely. 'And, well, there's something of that look about Mike

Mulholland too. He exudes sex appeal.'

'He sounds a bit creepy. Pockmarked skin and a ladykiller.'

'No, no, he's not like that. He's very down to earth — I don't think he sees himself like that at all. He's just a really nice person.'

'Mmm,' said Emmy, nodding her head sagely. 'I'd very much like to meet this Mike Mulholland.'

'Don't look at me like that, Emmy,' said Kath, entirely serious now. 'After what I've been through with Carl, I don't think I'll ever look at another man again.'

★ ★ ★

Two days before she was due to return to Ireland, Kath and Emmy made their way by subway over to Kath's apartment for the last time. There had been no recent falls of snow and what was left from before was shovelled into ugly grey-black mounds on the edge of the sidewalks. But it was still bitterly cold and Kath was glad she'd remembered to bring her woollen hat and thermal gloves back with her from Ireland.

Inside her apartment it was warm and they soon shed their outdoor things. Sturdy orange plastic crates from the shipping company littered the hall, most already packed and labelled.

'Where do you want me to start today?' said Emmy.

'How about in here?' said Kath and she led Emmy down the short hall into the lounge. She looked around her lovely home and felt a twinge

223

of regret. 'I love this flat, you know. But it's only bricks and mortar, isn't it?'

'You'll feel just as at home once you're settled in that farmhouse of yours,' said Emmy reassuringly. 'Now what do you want me to do?'

'Let's see. There's just those shelves left to clear. How about packing everything on them into one of those orange boxes? And I'll finish off in the bedroom.'

'What about the TV and DVD player?'

'There's no point in taking them back to Ireland, sure there's not?' said Kath and she hesitated only for a second before adding, 'Why don't you and Steve take them? You're always saying you want a flat screen.'

'I couldn't do that, Kath. They cost a fortune.'

'I insist. I won't take no for an answer.'

'Well, if you're sure.'

'I am.'

'That's really good of you. Thanks,' said Emmy, with a broad smile. 'Now what are you going to do with the furniture?'

'It's all included in the sale of the apartment. Listen, would you be OK in here for a few minutes? I want to pop over and see Mrs Eberstark. She wasn't at home the last time I called over.'

'Sure, take as long as you like,' said Emmy as she pulled an armful of paperbacks off the shelf.

★ ★ ★

As soon as Mrs Eberstark opened the door to Kath, her face broke into a wrinkled smile and

224

she hobbled forward a few steps and embraced her.

'Kath, my dear, how good it is to see you! Come in! Come in!'

'It's good to see you too. How have you been?' said Kath, who had been worrying that, without her daily visits to check on her, some calamity had befallen the old lady.

'I'm fine. My leg is playing up again. But what can you do? It's old age, that's all.'

'But otherwise you're well?'

'Yes, perfectly well, my dear.'

With her lopsided gait she led Kath into her bright lounge, which was the mirror image of Kath's in shape and size. Otherwise it came from a different world. Whereas Kath's was a homage to minimalism, this room was decorated in the traditional way with ornate pieces of antique furniture, lavish silk drapes on the windows and silver-framed photographs on almost every surface.

Mrs Eberstark sat down and said, 'Now, tell me all about your trip to Ireland. How is your poor mother?'

Kath sat down on the sofa beside her old friend and related the main events of the last few weeks. Mrs Eberstark listened attentively with her head cocked slightly to one side — to favour the ear with which she could hear most clearly.

When Kath had finished she said, 'I am so very sorry about your father. Such a waste of life. It is a terrible tragedy.' She sighed deeply, looked at the top of her walking-stick and then back at Kath. 'But,' she said, in a stronger, clearer voice, 'as for the rest — it is only money.' She paused, blinked her watery eyes several times and went on. 'I never told you this but I was raised in a very wealthy home in Berlin. My father owned shops all across the city. We had housemaids, a nanny and a butler. I never made a bed or cooked my own food until I came to this country.'

'Why did you come here?'

'My parents were very — what do you call it — astute. They saw the way things were going in Germany for Jews like us. They got the entire family out just before the outbreak of the war. It cost them, though — the Germans wouldn't let them sell any of the shops or take any money or valuables with them. They took it all. We arrived here with little more than the clothes we stood up in.'

'I'm so sorry,' said Kath, remembering the fate of Jews across Europe during the war. It put her misfortunes in context.

'But we were so lucky!' said Mrs Eberstark suddenly. 'We were all alive and we made a good life here in America. After a few years my father bought a watch shop with his brother in the South End — my nephew still owns it. Of course, we were never as wealthy as we had been, but we managed. We were free and we were safe. Do you know what the experience taught me?'

'What?'

'That nothing is as important as family. And nothing matters less than money and possessions.'

Kath nodded slowly, as she tried to apply the

old lady's wisdom to her situation. For years Kath had undervalued the importance of her family — only now was she beginning to realise how much they meant to her. Carl's betrayal had made her realise how important it was to be amongst people you could rely on, who would never harm you or wish you ill.

'Now,' said Mrs Eberstark, interrupting her thoughts, 'what will you do next?'

'You know the apartment's been sold?'

'Ah, yes. I saw the sign — and someone came and took it down last week.'

'I've decided to go back to Ireland. I'm going to buy the hotel and run it.' She paused, looked at Mrs Eberstark's implacable expression and added, 'You must think I'm mad.'

'No, not at all. It will be a very big change for you. But I don't think you're crazy,' she said with a little smile and Kath's mood lightened.

'I'll miss you very much, you know,' she said, feeling suddenly tearful.

'And I will miss you too, Kath.' Mrs Eberstark was quiet for a few moments and then she said, 'Is it because of that Carl that you are leaving?'

'Yes,' said Kath, with a sniff. 'No. Not really. He's part of it of course, but it's more than that. I don't want to live here any more and I suppose I feel like that because of Carl. But when I was in Ireland I realised that I wanted to go back there to live. I feel that is where I belong.'

'You will always be an outsider here. Just like me, Kath. And, you are a very lucky girl having the chance to go back to your homeland. That is where you should go. I'm sure of it. And don't worry about me,' said Mrs Eberstark, as though she could read Kath's thoughts.

'But I do,' she replied quickly.

'There's no need. I think I will move in with my daughter soon.' She looked out the window with her rheumy eyes. 'I can't manage with these knees like this for much longer,' she added, and she rubbed her swollen right knee. 'She'll take good care of me.'

'I'll write.'

'I expect you to,' the old lady said with an impish grin and Kath couldn't help but smile back.

'*Viel Glück!*' said Mrs Eberstark suddenly and she leaned forward and kissed Kath with her dry, feathery lips twice on both cheeks.

★   ★   ★

'I'm back!' shouted Kath as soon as she stepped inside her own place, feeling curiously uplifted by the chat with her old neighbour.

Emmy appeared immediately at the end of the hall and ran towards Kath. Her face was screwed up in an angry frown and she gesticulated furiously in the direction of the lounge.

'What's the matter?' asked Kath.

'It's him!' she hissed in a loud stage whisper. 'He's here! I didn't mean to let him in, but he wouldn't take no for an answer.'

'Who?' said Kath, fearing the worst.

'Carl, of course,' said Emmy and Kath put her hands over her mouth and realised that she was not ready to see him.

228

He appeared then at the end of the hall, dressed in his winter coat, and Kath simply stood and stared at him. He was as handsome as ever, but thinner and paler than the last time she'd seen him.

'Carl,' she said at last, and blood rushed to her head making her feel dizzy. Her heart pounded so fast she put a hand on her breast to steady it.

'It's good to see you, Kath,' he replied, his arms hanging in a strangely useless fashion by his sides. His voice sounded hoarse.

The three of them stood there for a few moments in awkward silence and then Emmy said, 'I've just remembered. I have to pop out to the convenience store.'

'You don't have to go on account of me,' said Carl, sounding as though he meant the complete opposite.

'No, no, it's fine. I was just about to nip out for — for a couple of doughnuts. And you're all out of milk, Kath. Do you want me to get some?' She thrust her face into Kath's, her eyes opened wide like saucers.

Kath nodded. Emmy quickly shrugged on her orange coat without buttoning it and brushed past her.

'I'll wait downstairs,' she whispered as she passed. 'Just shout if you need me.' She gave Kath's hand a tight squeeze, and went out the door.

'Shall we go in here?' said Carl and Kath followed him into the lounge. They stood in the middle of the room, a few feet apart.

'How are you?' he said.

229

'Fine,' said Kath, so nervous that she could not regard him steadily. Her gaze flitted around the room like a trapped butterfly.

'I've missed you, Kath. And I'm really sorry about your father — Emmy told me. It must have been terrible.'

Kath accepted his condolences with a shrug. She did not want to talk about her father because she knew she would break down. Tears would render her weak and vulnerable. And she knew that she had to be strong to resist Carl.

'Emmy tells me that you've sold the apartment,' he said, looking at the half-filled crates on the floor.

'That's right,' she said and swallowed. 'I'm going home.'

'Home?' he said, snapping his head round abruptly to stare at her. 'You don't mean Ireland?'

She nodded, not trusting herself to speak. He ran a hand through his thatch of blond hair, an indication that he was shaken. His physical presence was such a painful reminder of the love they'd once shared. She longed for him to hold her and stroke her hair like he used to and tell her that he loved her. She stared at the floor.

'Please, Kath, don't go,' he said. 'I've — I've done a lot of thinking while you were away. And I've realised what a fool I've been. I know that I love you. Truly and deeply and I will never love another woman like this as long as I live.'

She closed her eyes and let his words wash over her, mesmerised, soothed, entranced. She longed for him to make love to her, to erase the

230

pain and misery of the last few weeks. All she had to do was take a few steps, hold out her arms and he would be hers again.

She took one tiny step forward and opened her eyes. But he could never truly be hers. Not while he was married. Her fantasy could never be realised — Carl had seen to that. He only wanted her as his whore.

'In case you've forgotten,' she said coldly and she clenched her fists into tight balls, willing her love for him to turn to hate, 'you have a wife and two children.'

'I'll get a divorce,' he said abruptly.

Kath's palms began to sweat. She stared at him now, her attention fully focused on his face.

'You'd — you'd do that for me?' she said, unballing her fists and rubbing the flats of her hands on her trousers. If Carl was divorced he would be free to marry again. She could have him and the children that she wanted. She could have that house in the suburbs — her dream could come true.

'Yes,' he said, 'I'd do anything to get you back.'

Something inside Kath baulked. 'Anything?' she said, her voice a whisper and he nodded.

Then she remembered the thing he had done to her — all the lies and the cruel deceit. He would do anything, in fact he would do whatever it took, including lying and cheating, to get what he wanted. After all, he'd done it before.

And what about his wife and children? Where did they figure in all this? He couldn't just offload them like excess baggage. She thought about her telephone conversation with the steely

Lynda, who sounded like she had every intention of staying in her marriage.

'But what about Lynda?'

'What about her?'

'Have you spoken to her about this?'

'Not yet.'

'How do you know she'll give you a divorce? Maybe she still loves you. She might want to try and make the marriage work.'

'I won't let her stand in my way,' he said abruptly. Then, in a softer voice, he said, 'Why are we talking about her anyway?' and took a step towards her. He lowered his voice again and added, 'We should be talking about us, Kath. About our future. The life we can have together. The life we both want.'

He held out his right hand, arm outstretched. She looked at it and recoiled.

'But what about your children?'

He dropped his arm, hung his head and sighed. 'I know, I know. I've thought about nothing else these last weeks. And I see now that I can't stay with Lynda. I can't stay married to a woman I don't love just to give them a stable home.'

'And that's why you cheated on your wife and lied to me — because of the children?' said Kath, astounded.

'Yes. I wanted so much to protect them from the pain I . . . from the trauma of a broken home. But I realise now that having a stable home means more than having two parents sharing the same house at weekends. It means having parents who love each other and want to be together all the time. Not two people, like Lynda and me, who lead entirely separate lives. If we were divorced I'd see hardly any less of them than I do now. Look, I never meant to hurt you, Kath. I wanted to tell you the truth but, the longer I left it, the more difficult it became until, in the end, it was impossible. I knew you wouldn't want to have anything to do with me if you found out. And I was right, wasn't I?'

'If only you'd just told me when we first met. If only you'd been honest,' said Kath as her incredulity gave way to a reluctant understanding. 'We could've found some way to work through it. You could have got a divorce. We could've made a life together.'

'But we still can! It's not too late, Kath,' he said earnestly. 'We can put the past behind us and start over.'

'But I know what you're capable of, Carl. And I don't think I can ever trust you again.'

'I made a mistake, Kath. The biggest mistake of my life.' He moved closer and placed a hand on her sleeve. 'Don't make me suffer for it forever. Please find it in your heart to forgive me.'

Kath looked at the floor and then back at his face. There were tears in his eyes and the hand on her arm trembled.

'I can't, Carl,' she said quietly, with a slow shake of her head.

'I know you love me, Kath. And in spite of it all, I'm a good person. Please forgive me.'

'No, Carl, no,' she said, holding back tears. Gently she withdrew her arm and his hand slid off her sleeve. 'I'm sorry. Maybe in time I'll feel differently, but right now I simply can't.' She took a few seconds to compose herself and then said firmly, 'I'm going to Ireland. My mind's made up.'

'There's nothing I can say to make you change your mind?' he said and she shook her head.

He stared at her for what seemed like a very long time and then he said, 'Goodbye, Kath.' He leaned forward and kissed her softly on the cheek. His kiss felt cold and lifeless.

She watched his back as he went out of the room and put her hand up to her cheek where he'd kissed her. She listened to the sound of the door to the apartment opening, and then suddenly she ran after him and stopped abruptly at the doorway. He was halfway down the flight of stairs.

'Carl!' she said and he stopped and looked up at her through the black-painted metal balustrade. 'You did something that no one has ever done to me before. You broke my heart.' And then she closed the door.

18

Carl made his way wearily back to his apartment on St Botolph Street. The meeting with Kath had drained him of all energy — he felt wasted, ill. On the subway he sat zombie-like and reflected on their meeting. She loved him still, he was sure of it, but he had wounded her deeply. She no longer trusted him and how could he blame her? He saw now that he had a lot of work ahead of him to win that trust back. Seeing Kath had only confirmed what he already knew. He loved her more than he would ever love any woman and he must have her back.

He'd done little over the last three weeks but anguish over what to do, frustrated by Emmy's refusal to give him Kath's contact details. He'd hardly eaten or slept and his presence at work had been little more than for appearance's sake. Thank God he had a crack team behind him who were well capable of getting on with the job without him.

Now, he knew, the time for action had come. Kath required tangible evidence of his love and devotion to her. Saying he was going to get divorced wasn't the same as actually doing it. It was time to face up to Lynda.

Carl sighed heavily, his breath a puff of white steam, trudged the last few hundred yards to his apartment and climbed the steps slowly. He fumbled for the key, forgetting which pocket he'd put it in, finally found it, stuffed it in the lock and shoved the door open. As for this madness about Kath going back to Ireland, it was nothing more than bravado — a dramatic gesture to demonstrate her anger at him.

Once inside his own apartment Carl lay down on the sofa, still wearing his shoes and overcoat, and covered his eyes with his right forearm. He felt ancient, weary to the bone.

All was not lost, he told himself — he refused to believe it. He would never believe it. He would divorce Lynda and he would give Kath what she wanted. Marriage. What he wanted too. A second chance at the happiness that, for some reason, had eluded him and Lynda.

Lynda. He thought of her with dread. She had never once mentioned the telephone call she'd made to Kath — the call that in a few short minutes had destroyed his happiness. If she had wanted a divorce then she had a perfectly valid, indisputable reason for demanding one — his adultery. And yet she had not breathed a word to him.

The last two weekends he'd been home she had behaved as though everything was perfectly normal. And he had also, too shaken by the break-up with Kath to know what to do. Nothing, it seemed, in Lynda's world had changed. But his world was turned upside down. She would fight the divorce, he was sure of it. She did not like to lose.

He thought of Jasmine and Daisy, their clear, trusting little faces and their high-pitched voices, sweet as honey, and tears rolled out of the corners of his eyes. He was not, he told himself, choosing between them and Kath. They would always be his little darlings. He would always love them and he would always be their father. His pain came from the realisation that he had failed to give them what he had once craved most — a stable childhood. He knew how much it hurt for your father to walk out on you.

But thinking of his daughters would, he knew, weaken his resolve. And right now he was too exhausted to think any more. Carl rolled off the sofa onto his knees, stood up, shed his coat and shoes and went through to the bedroom where he crawled into bed. The sheets were clean and fragrant and he pressed his face into the pillow and thought of Kath. He closed his eyes and saw her heart-shaped face framed by rich brown hair. He relived the smell of her as he'd leant forward to kiss her and the touch of his lips on her cold, smooth cheek. And, comforted by these thoughts, he fell into a deep sleep.

He woke up in the darkness a long time later, confused and disoriented. His mouth tasted foul — he hadn't brushed his teeth since the morning before — and he craved a drink of water. He fumbled for the bedside light switch, turned it on and lay back on the bed, blinking. Sleep had brought with it a renewed resolve. He would go and see Lynda today.

He glanced at the clock — it was nearly seven o'clock in the morning. There was no point in rushing up to Williamstown immediately. Midweek, Lynda followed a breathless, action-packed schedule consisting of dozens of activities including daily school and nursery-runs, horse-riding, visits to friends, ballet lessons and drama classes for Jasmine, playgroup and water-confidence classes for Daisy. Carl had no idea on any given day where they'd be — it was best to wait until after five when they'd be guaranteed to be home.

He got up, showered, shaved, dressed, rummaged in the kitchen for a breakfast of cereal, milk and toast and left for work. There was no need to pack a bag for he kept duplicates of everything he needed in both homes.

At work he grabbed a coffee and settled down in his office to deal with the backlog of mail that he'd allowed to pile up. Now that his mind was made up, his head was clear and he found that he was able to focus for the first time in weeks. He spoke with a couple of key accounts and checked that all the major projects were on schedule.

At two o'clock he stood in front of Mandy's desk, with his coat on and his briefcase in his hand and said, with a tight smile, 'I'm taking a couple of days off.'

'Oh,' she said, and her hand fluttered at the base of her double chin, evidently unsettled by this unscheduled change to his routine. 'But what about the meeting this afternoon with McIntosh Portman? They're expecting you to be there.'

'Terence can take care of that,' he replied, swallowing the rancour he felt towards her. 'Tell him to call me on my cell phone if there's a problem,' he added as evenly as he could, 'but as far as everyone else is concerned I'm uncontactable. Goodbye, Mandy.'

Carl went straight to the lock-up near his apartment, for which he paid a ridiculous annual rental, got into his new Mercedes SL and set off on the long journey out of Boston. Once out of the city centre the traffic moved freely and he soon found himself cruising at a comfortable sixty miles per hour on the Mass Pike, which was, thankfully, free of snow.

He tried to relax into the seat and focus on the hum of the engine and the sound of the tyres on the asphalt. But his hands were so clammy with sweat that he had to wipe them continuously on his trouser leg. He turned the car heating down and wished he'd taken off his overcoat. It had started to sleet. He turned on the radio, hoping to find some distraction from his thoughts, but could not concentrate on the blaring music.

Why was he so nervous? None of what he had to say to Lynda would come as much of a surprise, surely? Now that she knew about Kath she couldn't expect the status quo to continue. She couldn't expect them to carry on as though nothing had happened. And what would he tell the children? How could he explain what he was about to do in terms that they could understand?

He thought of his father and wondered if this was how he felt the night he'd walked out on Carl and his mother, Petra. Somehow he doubted it. Gunter Scholtz was a violent, unpredictable man given to bouts of depression and binge-drinking.

Carl was nine years old and remembered every

detail of that day as though it was yesterday. What he and his mother had eaten for supper that night — cold ham and home-made potato salad — the sound of children playing in the street outside their rented Cape Cod-style home and the oppressive, humid heat that made his hair stick to his forehead with sweat.

Later he and his mother sat on the rickety veranda overlooking the overgrown patch of garden, trying to catch a little of the breeze that wafted across the city from Lake Michigan.

Carl listened for the asthmatic chug of his father's beat-up Cadillac and picked peeling brown paint off the porch handrail. His stomach slowly tightened into a knot.

When Gunter eventually did appear it was evident from his glazed expression and slurred speech that he had been drinking, though Carl had seen him much worse.

'Have you been drinking?' challenged Petra.

Carl closed his eyes and willed his mother to stop — why did she always say and do the same things when his dad came in drunk? The things that were guaranteed to start a fight in which she always came off worst?

'And what's it to you?' came the predictable, growled reply.

'Well,' she said savagely, folding her stick-like arms across her flowery blouse, 'don't expect to come home in that state and find a meal waiting for you. Your supper's in the trash.'

This wasn't true and was said only to incense him. Carl opened his eyes and held his breath and waited for the slap of his father's hand on

240

his mother's cheek. But tonight something was different, for his father ignored her taunts and went straight into the bedroom.

'And where do you think you're going?' she demanded, following him as far as the doorway and leaning against the door-jamb with her arms still folded across her flat chest.

'I'm leaving.'

'No, you're not.'

'Watch me,' he said as he hurriedly packed a bag.

'You're going to that whore, aren't you?' spat Petra but her words bounced off him like the soft balls Carl used to practise baseball indoors in the winter.

Gunter left without saying another word. And, surprisingly, the whole thing passed without as much as a smack between the husband and wife — Petra was just as capable of physical violence as her husband. He never said a thing to his son. He never even looked at him. Carl knew then that his father did not love him.

'He'll be back,' Petra said confidently, as they watched the car's taillights flicker down the street.

But she was wrong. He never did come back and it was a full three years before Carl saw him again, filling up his car with gas at the station on 17th. And even then he'd looked straight through his son, not recognising him.

Gunter Scholtz might not have been much of a father but Carl still missed him — if not the man himself then the idea of a father. He recalled with longing the few times his father had taken him fishing and the equally rare occasions when he'd taken him to see the Milwaukee Brewers at County Stadium. Gunter was passionate about baseball. When Carl was seven-and-a-half they'd even gone out West on a road trip together, to the place where Carl's paternal grandparents had once farmed. At the end of a dirt track Gunter had shown Carl the derelict two-storey farmhouse that had once been his home, his eyes inexplicably moist with emotion.

'All this land should've been mine,' he'd said.

Carl stared in awe at the vast rippling field of wheat, the same colour as his hair, that stretched out as far as the eye could see in every direction.

'I hate those suitcase farmers,' said Gunter and he'd spat in the dust. 'They don't give a shit for the land. It's all about money, money, money.'

Carl blinked in the hot August sun and tried to imagine what it would be like to grow up on this farm, a country boy, and the idea entranced him. He tasted the dust on his lips and dreamed about having all these acres and acres of land to himself, to roam freely. Imagine this as your backyard instead of the grotty wire-fenced enclosure back home that his mother called a garden. He turned his gaze to his father, shielding his eyes from the sun with his forearm, and wondered — if the farm had still been his would he have been a different, better person?

In the years that followed Carl often told himself, and his mother, that they were better off without him. But he never believed it.

Now Carl brushed the tears from his eyes and squinted as he tried to concentrate on the road ahead. The knowledge that his father did not love him had left him with an underlying sense of worthlessness. He had spent his entire life trying to prove him wrong. That was why he'd worked so hard to be successful and why he surrounded himself with the trappings of wealth. The most important people in all of this, he reminded himself, were his daughters. It was vital that they did not feel the same sense of abandonment as he had done.

19

It was pitch dark by the time he reached the black electronic gates at the bottom of the private road that led to Brook House, the home he and Lynda had bought with such high hopes for a happy future. He entered the drive, the gates closed smoothly behind him and he drove slowly up the road, his heart pounding in his chest. In the garage he parked beside Lynda's SUV — a luxurious black Range Rover — and got out of the car.

Outside, the cold hit him like a slap in the face and painful darts of icy sleet, borne on a high wind, speared the skin on his face. He pulled the edges of his unbuttoned coat around his tall frame and hurried towards the door into the kitchen. Outside he paused, bracing himself to face Lynda and to keep his emotions under check when he saw the girls.

He opened the unlocked door and stepped inside. The wind howled behind him, swirled briefly into the room and he closed the door behind him quickly. The girls were sitting at the kitchen table amid pots of paint and coloured paper, glitter and glue. Their faces registered shock when they saw him, the pair of round-ended scissors in Jasmine's hand motionless in the air. On the floor by his feet was a tangle of bags and boots and discarded sweaters.

Lynda was standing by the cooker, her taut,

hard bottom encased in a pair of tight cream riding jodhpurs and her blonde hair scraped into a loose ponytail. She wore a tight-fitting long-sleeved white T-shirt. Her sinewy body no longer evoked a physical response in Carl, though he guessed many men found her attractive. She was talking into the phone tucked under her chin and stirring something in a pot on the stove at the same time. The room smelt of onions and garlic.

'Daddy!' cried Jasmine and she leapt from her seat at the table and ran to him. She threw her arms around his legs and he picked her up and swung her thin, warm body into the air. Her grey flannel skirt, part of her private school uniform, rode up to her waist and she wrapped her legs, clad in red woollen tights, around his body. Carl blinked to hold back the tears that threatened to cascade down his cheeks. How he loved his children! How he wished his marriage had turned out differently!

'Oh,' said Lynda into the receiver without smiling, as her eyes locked with Carl's, 'Carl's just walked through the door. Can I call you tomorrow, Rosie?' She paused and listened and he looked away.

'Daddy!' squealed Daisy in her baby voice and, one-armed, he hoisted her feather-light frame into the air. He kissed both girls on the nose and then lowered them to the floor.

'Hey, you two are killing me! You've gotten so big I can hardly lift you,' he said, lying, and they giggled with delight at his gentle teasing.

'OK,' said Lynda, grimacing into the phone,

245

'I'll pick Emily up from ballet and bring her home for tea. You can come and collect her at, say, six? OK. Bye now. Bye.'

'We're making birthday cards for Grandma D,' said Jasmine and she pulled Carl over to the table to show him her handiwork. She'd drawn a picture of her grandma on the front of a folded piece of pink card and glued bits of feather and ribbon on for her hair.

Lynda wiped her hands on a cloth hanging from her waist and came over to the table. 'This is a surprise,' she said with a stiff smile, planting a dry, perfunctory kiss on his cheek that left Carl cold. This act of intimacy had, over the years, become a habit, devoid of real emotion. 'You should've phoned to let me know you were coming.'

'Why are you home, Daddy? It's not the weekend, is it?' said Jasmine.

'No, but I missed my girls so much I just had to come home to see you!'

'Will you have something to eat?' said Lynda, clearing the things from the table.

'If there's enough. But don't go to any trouble.'

'It's no trouble,' said Lynda briskly, laying out cutlery on the table at breakneck speed. 'You've time to change if you want.'

When they were seated at the table eating, Carl said, 'This is delicious, Lynda. Thank you.' But he had little appetite and he did little more than push the food around his plate.

'Spaghetti Bollo-knees is my favourite,' announced

Jasmine, and Lynda smiled indulgently, her periwinkle blue eyes shining.

She was, Carl reflected sadly, a good mother.

'Me too,' said Daisy excitedly. Her face and the front of her pink jumper were splattered with tomato sauce. Carl smiled at her and his heart lurched with love. He swallowed and briefly closed his eyes.

'Seriously, Carl, why are you home midweek?' said Lynda quietly when Jasmine was fully occupied instructing Daisy how to suck a single worm of spaghetti through pursed lips.

'I told you,' he said brightly. 'I wanted to see my girls.'

His daughters looked at him and their faces shone with happiness.

Lynda continued to regard him with a fixed stare and he said, 'I do need to talk to you, Lynda. But not now. After the girls are in bed.'

'OK,' she said and immediately struck up a conversation with Jasmine about her forthcoming ballet performance.

After the meal was finished, he said, 'Who wants me to do their bath?'

'Oh, Jasmine has to do her homework first,' said Lynda.

'Hasn't she done it already?' said Carl glancing at the clock on the wall. It was already past seven.

'Don't you remember? She has ballet on a Wednesday and she's just started the most wonderful pottery class.'

'Pottery class!' said Carl incredulously. 'Pottery classes for a five-year-old!'

247

Jasmine yawned and put her head down on the table, her eyes rolling in her head.

'Look at her. She's exhausted. Don't you think she's doing too much, Lynda? You said that you would cut back. She hardly spends any time at home, just chilling.'

'What do you know about raising children?' said Lynda shortly. 'You're never here.'

'That isn't fair, Lynda. You chose to live up here, not me.'

'I did lots of activities when I was Jasmine's age and it never did me any harm,' continued Lynda as though he'd not spoken.

Carl opened his mouth to retort but bit his lip instead and said nothing. After their divorce, he would have little say in the girls' day-to-day routine. They would not share every weekend and all the holidays with him as they did now. The daily phone bulletins from Lynda would stop. Her relatives would rally round and enclose her and the children in the bosom of their tight-knit family. He would become a stranger to his own children. Just as his father was a stranger to him. Sorrow engulfed him and he vowed not to let this happen.

He realised Lynda was staring at him. He thought of Kath and the moment of panic subsided. Divorcing Lynda, he reminded himself, was the only way he could be with Kath. He did not hate Lynda but he did not love her as he loved Kath. Kath he could not live without. He could not stay in this marriage any longer.

'Right,' he said, standing up too quickly, and his head swam with dizziness. He steadied himself by holding onto the edge of the table and the moment of light-headedness passed. 'I'll take Daisy on up to bed, shall I? And you can do Jasmine's homework with her.'

An hour or so later he tucked Jasmine into bed and kissed her goodnight. He descended the stairs filled with fear and padded quietly in stocking feet across the Brazilian cherry floor into the kitchen. Lynda was loading the dishwasher and when he came close she stood up and looked at him. The door to the dishwasher was still open and dirty dishes were stacked on the drainer.

She said, 'So what is it you want to talk to me about?'

'Come over here, Lynda,' he said gently, 'and sit by the fire.'

She obeyed, crossing the vast kitchen with her back as stiff as a poker and her head erect. She sat down in one of the comfortable armchairs on either side of the log fire that burned a few feet off the ground in an open stone fireplace.

Whiskers the cat jumped into her arms and she stroked her long grey fur absentmindedly. Carl's heart pounded in his chest so hard he was sure it must be visible beneath his fine cashmere sweater. He clasped his hands together to stop them shaking.

'I want a divorce,' he said and Lynda looked at her hands, without interrupting their gentle caress of Whiskers.

'I see,' was all she said.

'You know about Kath, Lynda, don't you?' he said and abruptly her hand stopped moving.

Even in the red glow from the fire he could see her face colour. The logs spat and hissed in the silence that followed.

'So you know about the phone call then?' she said at last.

'Yes. And you've known about Kath for three whole weeks, Lynda,' he said, nodding slowly. 'Why didn't you say anything to me?'

'Why didn't you? You're the one who's having the affair, Carl, not me,' she said bitterly and gently pushed the cat, protesting, to the floor.

She laced her long fingers together across her lap and Carl was struck by her physical resemblance to his own mother. They shared the same thin bony frame and sharp features. He'd never noticed it before. Suddenly he felt sorry for Lynda.

'I know. And I'm sorry about that.'

'About the affair? Or about not telling me?' she asked evenly.

'Both,' said Carl and sighed. 'I'm sorry, Lynda. This must come as a bit of a blow.'

'Not as much as you might think,' said Lynda. 'I've been waiting for it. Ever since I found out about you and her.'

'It was Mandy who told you, wasn't it?' said Carl.

'Does it matter who told me?'

'I suppose not,' said Carl despondently and he stared at the fire. 'But that scheming cow is going to get what she deserves,' he went on, his passion aroused at the thought of how he was betrayed. 'The first thing I'm going to do when I get back is sack her.'

'Don't blame poor old Mandy, Carl. You would have been found out some other way. You don't really believe that you could have carried on forever, do you?'

Carl squirmed uncomfortably in his seat, loath to admit that that was exactly what he'd hoped to do.

'I can't believe that you've been seeing her for a year and a half!' said Lynda when he gave her no reply. 'A week, maybe even a month — that I could understand. Forgive even. But how could you lie for so long? How could you keep up such a deception, not only with me but with her? The poor woman sounded absolutely devastated. You had no right to do that to me or her. And we were sleeping together until very recently . . . ' She shuddered, then put her hands to her face and Carl was consumed with shame.

'I said I'm sorry, Lynda. I can't . . . I can't explain to you why I started it. But once I did, it was easier to keep up the pretence than to face the truth. The longer it went on the harder it was to face up to what I was doing. I'm not proud of — '

'Did you always use condoms?' she said suddenly, as though the thought had just occurred to her.

'Yes.'

'That's something at least.'

'Lynda, I — '

'So you love her,' she said, cutting him off mid-sentence.

'Yes.'

There was a long pause during which Lynda

eyed him angrily. Then her body seemed to relax and she said softly, 'Why did this happen to us, Carl? When did it happen? You loved me once, didn't you? We were happy once, weren't we?'

Carl blinked, remembering an easy, comfortable relationship that fitted like a pair of worn-in slippers — not the grand passion he shared with Kath. But he would not deny her this crumb of comfort, if that was what she wanted. 'Yes, we were. I was. But maybe living apart after Jas was born wasn't such a good idea. I guess I was lonely, going home to an empty apartment every night.'

'And I wasn't?' demanded Lynda, aggression returning to her voice.

'It's not the same, Lynda. You were here with the girls and your family on the doorstep.'

'Don't make it sound like a picnic, Carl. It's not easy bringing up two children single-handedly five days out of seven. And when you do turn up at the weekends all you want to do is have fun and games. It's me that puts in all the hard work with the girls.'

'I know that,' said Carl conciliatorily. 'I think you've done a wonderful job with them. And I appreciate it.'

'Obviously not enough,' said Lynda quickly.

'This has got nothing to do with the children, Lynda. It's to do with us.'

'The children have everything to do with it,' she snapped. 'They're the reason we bought this place. They're the reason I gave up my job in the city. That transition hasn't been easy for me. Do you know, if I hadn't stopped working, I'd have been a partner by now? And we probably wouldn't be having this conversation.'

'I know. You were the best lawyer in the firm,' agreed Carl, acknowledging his wife's talent.

'If I remember correctly, you wanted me to give up work more than I did.'

'Well, we didn't need the money, and I didn't like the idea of my kids being brought up by strangers. There's nothing wrong with that.' He didn't add that he'd liked being protector and provider — it made him feel like he was a good husband and father. 'Anyway, I don't remember you putting up much of a fight.'

'They'll be seeing a lot more of strangers if we divorce,' she said darkly, ignoring his last comment. 'I'll go back to work.'

'But you won't have to, Lynda,' said Carl, imagining his daughters, confused and unhappy, dumped in day-care from dawn to dusk. 'I'll make sure you're well taken care of.'

'Taken care of? Like a sick or elderly relative?' she snapped, her voice shrill.

'I didn't mean it like that. I just meant that I'll be fair. You won't have to work.'

'I'll damn well do as I please!' cried Lynda, suddenly animated. 'I gave up everything for you, Carl Scholtz. And this is how you repay me. Well, don't think for one minute that you're getting away with it!'

Carl winced. He'd been right. She would not readily agree to a divorce.

Suddenly, Lynda's brow furrowed with concentration. 'She won't have you back until you divorce me, will she? That's it, isn't it?' she cried.

'Otherwise you'd never have asked.'

'Come on, Lynda,' he said, and this time it was his turn to ignore her question. 'What's the point in contesting the divorce? It just makes the whole thing more painful for everyone.'

Lynda laughed hollowly and said, 'Oh, don't look so worried, Carl. You'll get your divorce. Eventually. But you're going to have to wait. I'll make sure it crawls through the courts. I can make the proceedings last years.'

'Come on. Face facts, Lynda. Our marriage is over. You can't win. I'm not coming back.'

'Do you think my idea of winning is to have you back? Did you really think I'd take you back after what you've done?' she said incredulously, pointing at her chest with the tips of her manicured fingers. 'No, I've had lots of time to think over the last few weeks. Kath O'Connor, God help her, is welcome to you. I wouldn't have you back if you were the last man on earth.'

Carl stood up, put his hands in his pockets and stood awkwardly for a few moments in front of the fire. 'I'm sorry that you feel so embittered. I thought that we could come to some sort of — of amicable agreement.'

'You really are something . . . ' began Lynda and then her voice trailed off. She shook her head and laughed falsely. 'Just go, Carl, will you. There's nothing more to be said.'

'Right,' he replied, relieved that this interview was coming to a close. 'I'll sleep in the guest wing tonight.'

'The bed in the first room on your right is made up.'

'OK.'

'What time do you plan to leave in the morning?'

'I thought I'd stay a couple of days so we can — you know — talk things over.' But even as he said it he realised this was not going to happen.

'Talk things over,' repeated Lynda slowly and the corners of her mouth turned up into a grotesque smile. 'No, I don't think so. The only talking we're going to do in future will be through our lawyers.'

'Oh, Lynda, Don't be like this. Please . . . '

'I want you out of here first thing in the morning,' she said, as calm as still water. 'This is my house.'

Paid for with my money, thought Carl. But in truth he didn't begrudge Lynda the house. He felt that she had earned it. He knew how much she loved it here — he would not take that away from her. And he wanted the children to remain here so that, in spite of the divorce, they would have the stability of a familiar environment.

Suddenly Lynda got up from the chair, pulled the chain-mail fireguard across the fire and said, 'You know, when we married you swore that you would never do to your own children what your father did on you . . . '

'Don't, Lynda, that's not fair,' he said, the mention of his father bringing raw emotions to the surface.

' . . . and here you are doing exactly the same thing. Leaving your wife and family. I hope you feel good about that.'

'You know that's not fair!' he shouted, his

255

temper rising for the first time tonight. 'There is no comparison between my father and me. I love my daughters and I will continue to be a good father to them!'

Lynda walked to the kitchen door and switched out the lights, in preparation for going upstairs. Soon Carl was left standing in a pool of red light from the fire, the stream of yellow light from the hall failing to reach the side of the room where he stood.

'Oh, so you think you're a good father, do you?' she said, her voice heavy with sarcasm, and he imagined her sneering in the darkness. 'Don't kid yourself, Carl. Eighty per cent of the time you're not here. The kids are so used to it that they hardly notice you gone. They've learnt how to cope without you.'

'That's a mean thing to say, Lynda, and it's not true,' said Carl, the anger swelling up inside him, and he balled his hands into tight, damp fists. 'Those girls love me. And when we're divorced, I plan to see them every bit as much as I do now.'

'I'll see you in court about that one, Carl,' she retorted, and then she walked out of the room leaving Carl panting with rage.

20

That night Carl lay in bed and stared at the ceiling and could not sleep. The storm that had battered the house earlier had subsided and now, in the early hours of the morning, the sky was clear. Moonlight streamed through the open curtains and a bitter frost descended. Outside, the fir trees close to the house glittered in the moonlight. Carl pulled the down-filled comforter round his neck and wished he'd got in the car and gone straight back to Boston last night.

In a few hours he would have to endure Lynda's icy reception and pretend, in front of the girls, that nothing was wrong. Coming from a family where everyone wore their hearts on their sleeve, and thought nothing of airing adult grievances in front of a child, Carl believed firmly that the girls should be shielded from the truth for as long as possible. He shuddered when he recalled Lynda's parting comment about seeing him in court over access to the girls. That was the one card she held over him — and he would fight her to the last over them.

Carl attributed Lynda's intransigence to her fury. Perhaps, when her anger had subsided a little and she had time to think things over, she would behave more rationally. He reminded himself that his objective was to secure a divorce as quickly as possible. If he made her a very generous offer — much more than the courts were likely to award her — perhaps she might agree to file jointly for divorce. That way the whole thing could be wrapped up in a matter of months rather than years. Yes, he'd give her time to calm down and then present her with his proposal.

But, meantime, what would he tell Kath? If he told her the truth — that Lynda had threatened to contest it — would she be prepared to wait? No, he couldn't take that chance. He must make her believe that he would be free soon. And it was only a white lie — after all the lies that had gone before, what was one more? Once he and Kath were married he promised himself that the lying would stop. Once all this was over, he would be a new and better man.

At last he dozed off and woke at dawn — he realised immediately that Lynda was right. There was nothing more to be gained from staying here any longer. What mattered now was getting back to Boston and telling Kath his good news — that he would soon be free to marry her. He would beg for her forgiveness and she would take him back. He was sure of it. She had been this close to taking him back that day in her apartment — he could feel it.

He showered and dressed quickly — there was no time to lose — and emerged into the kitchen to find the girls sitting at the table fully dressed, eating breakfast.

'Daddy, will you play rough and tumble with us after breakfast?' said Jasmine.

'You won't have time, Jas,' said Lynda, who was by the fridge hurriedly stuffing sandwiches and fruit into a pink tin lunch box. 'We have to leave for school in a few minutes. Daisy, hurry up and drink that smoothie. You're not going anywhere until it's all finished.'

Daisy pulled a face and emitted whines of protest but she did what her mother instructed.

'Daddy, will you play with me when I get home from school?' said Jasmine.

Carl glanced at Lynda, who pulled on a thick padded coat and picked up the car keys from the counter without so much as giving him a glance. She pointed the remote control for the garage doors through the kitchen window and pressed a button.

'I won't be here when you get home, honey. I've got to get back to work.'

'Oh, Dad!' wailed Jasmine.

'Come on, girls. Chop, chop! Time to go!' said Lynda and she bundled both the girls into their outdoor things.

Carl gave them a brief hug and a kiss and Lynda steered them out into the crisp, cold morning acting as though Carl wasn't there. He watched her Range Rover emerge from the garage. The doors closed slowly behind it and the big vehicle disappeared down the drive, emitting a jet of white steam from the exhaust.

Carl locked up the house without bothering to stop for breakfast, got in his car and drove impatiently back to Boston, speeding on the Mass Pike and praying that he wouldn't be caught. Exhaustion threatened to catch up with him — he had to stop and buy a strong coffee before continuing on his way.

Once back in Boston, he drove straight to Kath's apartment, rushed upstairs and banged on the door.

'Kath!' he shouted. 'Kath, it's me, Carl! Let me in! I have to talk to you.'

He banged the door with his closed fists and waited, panting breathlessly. But there was no answer. She must be at Emmy's, he decided, and turned with the intention of descending the stairs.

'Carl?' said an old lady's voice and he froze.

He looked up and found Mrs Eberstark standing in her doorway right in front of him, regarding him with a pinched look on her face.

'Do you mind? I am trying to rest,' she said with dignity. 'If you don't leave I will call the police.'

'No!' said Carl, just managing to stop himself from shouting. He lowered his voice and added, 'Please, you must help me, Mrs Eberstark.'

'How can you ask for my help after what you've done to Kath?'

'I need to know where she is. I need to talk to her.'

'She is not here,' said the old woman flatly.

'I can see that,' replied Carl. 'But where is she? Is she at Emmy's.'

'She was.'

'Right,' he said and added, for some reason anxious to retain the old lady's goodwill, 'I'm sorry if I startled you, Mrs Eberstark. But I must go now.'

He took the first three steps in one stride but her voice halted any further progress.

'She's not there now.'

He stopped on the fourth step and stared up at her as beads of sweat oiled his forehead. 'Where is she then?'

'You are too late, Carl. She's gone back to Nordirland.'

He leaned against the wall and closed his eyes.

'She does not want you, Carl. She does not love you any more. And you are not worthy of her.'

Carl opened his eyes and glared at the wrinkled face looking down on him with such distain. 'You are wrong. She does love me. And I will get her back.'

'*Nein*, I don't think so,' said Mrs Eberstark. She threw him a filthy look and closed the door to her apartment without another word.

Carl slid down the wall and sat on the step, physically exhausted but full of anger. Who was she to judge whether he was worthy or not? And she was wrong about Kath. She still loved him, he was sure of it.

But now what would he do? How would he find her? Emmy wouldn't divulge Kath's phone number in Ireland — he had no way of contacting her. She probably wouldn't talk to him on the phone anyway.

He had no choice — he would go there and track her down. He would find her and bring her back. Such a grand gesture would surely melt any hardness in her heart and make her realise how much he loved her. Ireland was a small country — half the size of Wisconsin, his home state. It wouldn't be that difficult to find her, surely?

What was the name of that place she came from? Bally-something. Ballyfergus. That was it. And the name of the hotel her father owned — what was it? He couldn't pronounce it the way Kath did, with that guttural sound at the back of her throat. But it was something like 'Sallack-Brays'.

Carl stood up and looked down at his crumpled clothing from the day before. He ran a hand across his fevered brow and realised that he needed time to pull himself together. He couldn't go over there looking like this. He needed rest and he needed to compose himself. He needed to have all his wits about him if he was to persuade her to come back. On a practical note, he'd have to get a passport — Carl had never felt the need, nor the desire, to travel outside the United States.

Also, more importantly, he had been seriously neglecting the business. If he was going to pay Lynda off with a vast part of his wealth then it was important that he kept on top of the business. Though he knew Kath cared little for material things, they would still need the income from the business to support them in the future.

Full of renewed purpose, Carl left the building and returned to his apartment where the very first thing he did was sit down in front of the computer. He keyed in 'Ballyfergus,' clicked on a website thrown up by the search engine and started to read . . .

21

On the day that Highfield House went up for auction at Wilsons' Mallusk Auction Complex, just outside Belfast, Kath moved into the Mulhollands' farmhouse.

She cleaned the house from top to bottom — it had not been lived in over the winter — removing all the dust and spiders' webs. She laid a fire in the sitting room for later and then unpacked the few belongings that she had brought back with her from the States, along with the linen and crockery that her mother had salvaged for her from the family home.

Downstairs she arranged the crockery in the kitchen cupboards, which already contained the basic bits and pieces required for holiday living. Through the kitchen window she caught a glimpse of the bright yellow Renault Clio hatchback she'd purchased the week before and smiled. It represented freedom and her new life. She'd bought the second-hand car at a local auction — with David's help. It had been several years since Kath had owned one and she loved the bright little machine with its under-powered engine and black plastic interior.

Upstairs, she made up the double bed in the biggest of the three bedrooms on the top storey and placed a photograph of her mother and father, taken in Boston a few years previously, on the bedside table.

263

She pulled a small snapshot of herself and Carl, taken at her last birthday, from the bottom of suitcase and stared at it. She did not want to forget Carl — she couldn't even if she'd tried. She wanted to remember the happy times they'd shared. You could not love someone and then cut them out of your life as though they'd never existed.

It had been several weeks since she'd last seen Carl and she'd had time to come to terms with the fact that he was no longer in her life. She knew he loved her and she yearned for him. But she could not find it in herself to forgive him. She would have to learn to forget him, she told herself.

'It's me,' came her mother's voice from downstairs and Kath froze. Fiona had no time for Carl Scholtz after what he'd done. 'Where are you?'

'Up here,' called Kath and quickly she shoved the picture in the bottom of her underwear drawer. 'Just coming.'

'I've bought you a house-warming present,' said Fiona as she met Kath at the bottom of the stairs.

'Oh, Mum, you shouldn't have!'

'Oh, it's just a token,' said Fiona, thrusting a bunch of yellow daffodils into Kath's hand. 'Our days of buying expensive presents are over,' she added matter-of-factly.

'Oh, Mum, they're beautiful. Here, I'll put them in this.'

She peeked inside a sage-green tin jug that sat on the table in the hall and carried it and the flowers into the kitchen.

'This old place is holding up well,' observed Fiona, following her daughter. 'It's just as I remembered it. I haven't been in here since Gladys moved out.'

'Yes, it's great, isn't it?'

'It'll be cold in the winter, mind.'

'No more than Highfield House and there are two storage heaters, don't forget.' She arranged the flowers in the jug and set them with a flourish in the middle of the kitchen table. 'They're lovely, aren't they?'

'Speaking of Highfield House . . . '

Kath steadied herself by holding onto the side of the table. 'Did it sell?' she said, searching her mother's inscrutable face.

Fiona nodded. 'Willie just phoned me,' she said glumly.

'And?'

'It went for £410,000.'

'Is that all? Someone's got an absolute bargain!' said Kath, full of bitterness that she hadn't been able to save it. She went and stood by the window and stared out at the blustery spring day.

'I know. If your father were alive . . . ' began Fiona and then she stopped. 'Well,' she said with a sniff, and her voice started to break, 'what's the point in wishing?'

Kath went over to her mother, put her arms around her and buried her face in her wiry hair. It smelled of tangerines. Kath closed her eyes and made a silent vow. *I will get Highfield House back. I will. I don't care how long it takes but I will, one day, get it back. For all of us.*

'Are you alright?' said Fiona, gently extricating herself from her daughter's embrace. She put her hands to her face, briefly, and wiped away invisible tears.

'Yes. I'm fine, Mum. And you?'

'I'm OK too, love. Really I am.'

The two woman separated, a fleeting moment of awkwardness between them, and Kath said, 'Did you find out who bought the house?'

'Willie doesn't know. It was bought by a telephone bidder and he can't find out who it was.'

'Did anyone else bid?'

'A few chancers who dropped out when the bidding went above three fifty. And Richard McGarel.'

'The pharmacist?'

'That's right.'

'I bet that Rosemary McGarel couldn't wait to get her hands on our house.'

'Well, she didn't get it. Thank God.'

'The house should've gone for half a million at least,' said Kath.

'Well, it's immaterial to us, isn't it? It's not as though we're going to benefit from the proceeds.'

'No, we're not. That's it then.' She turned to face her mother and continued brightly, 'What about you, Mum? Have you had any luck finding somewhere to live?'

'I have as a matter of fact. Do you remember that flat I went to see in the new development in Mill Street?'

'Is that the one I went to see with you? The one where the family bought it for the old mother and she was never well enough to move in?'

'That's right. It's in immaculate condition.'

'It is. It's lovely.'

'Well, I'm going to put in an offer. The estate agent says there's nobody else interested at the moment so I'm in with a good chance.'

'Oh, Mum, that's great news,' said Kath, feeling more optimistic than she had in weeks. She went over to her mother and gave her a hug. 'Things are starting to get better, aren't they?'

'They couldn't have got any worse, Kath,' said Fiona, smiling wryly and displaying a rare flash of her dry humour.

Kath laughed. 'So long as we have somewhere to live and we're safe, that's all we need, isn't it, Mum?'

'Yes, it is, love,' said Fiona and she caught hold of Kath's hand and gave it the briefest of squeezes. 'Now, come and get the rest of your house-warming present. Don't get too excited — it's only a box of groceries.'

She led Kath outside to where her car was parked with the boot open. Inside was a cardboard box full of basic supplies from the supermarket.

'Oh, thanks, Mum,' said Kath, reaching in and lifting out the box. 'You know I was just thinking that I'd have to go out and get things for the morning. And to tell you the truth I'm too tired to face it.'

'That's what I thought. I'm afraid I had to

267

guess what you'd need. I'd have called to ask but you've no phone and you must've had your mobile switched off.'

'The battery's flat again. I must put it on charge,' said Kath absentmindedly, carrying the box through to the kitchen where she began taking things out and putting them away. 'The phone's a bit of a nuisance,' she said, referring to the lack of one in the house. 'I'm relying on my cell phone for the time being. I'll have to see Mike about installing a landline. I can't see that he'll object if I pay for it, can you?'

'No.'

'I need it pretty urgently for the business. I have to contact staff and speak to the contractors lined up to do the painting and whatnot. They're supposed to start next week.'

'Are you thinking of rehiring all the staff?'

'Most of them — that's if they haven't got new jobs already. And John Routledge, of course, is coming to work for me.'

'And you want him to?'

'Of course. I think he's crucial to the success of the hotel. Quite frankly, I don't think Dad could've managed without him. Oh, toilet roll! Thanks, Mum. You know, I'd completely forgotten about that.'

'Hmm,' said Fiona, and she scowled, ignoring Kath's last comment. 'I wouldn't take John Routledge back,' she said in a low voice.

'Why ever not?' said Kath incredulously, freezing momentarily with a tin of baked beans in each hand.

'Just. I don't . . . I don't trust him.'

'Why? What did he do to you?'

'Nothing. I just think he's a bit — a bit shady.'

'Well, Dad thought very highly of him,' said Kath, completely confounded by her mother's irrational prejudice. She placed the tins in a cupboard and had turned, ready to interrogate Fiona further, when Mike Mulholland appeared in the doorway.

He said hello, cast a glance around the room and, when his gaze fell on the daffodils, said, 'Nice. I like flowers in a kitchen.'

'Mum bought me them as a house-warming gift,' offered Kath and there was pause during which Mike looked from Kath to Fiona.

'Have I come at a bad time? I can pop back later.'

'No, no, not at all,' said Fiona, before Kath had time to speak. 'I was just leaving. Now that I know she's safely settled in I can rest easy. Oh, Bridget said she'd pop over sometime tomorrow, Kath.'

'Great. I need to talk to her about something.' She opened the fridge and placed a carton of milk in the door.

'And good luck for tomorrow, love.'

'Thanks, Mum. Bye.'

Kath wiped her hands, wet from the condensation on the milk carton, on a cloth and wondered why she felt slightly uncomfortable in Mike's presence. He hadn't moved from the doorway, standing aside only to let her mother pass, and she was sure that if she looked at him directly, he would be staring at her. Suddenly she remembered that

269

she was wearing an old-fashioned flowery apron of her mother's — quickly she undid the ties and pulled it over her head.

'Is everything OK then?' he asked.

'Yes, it's . . . it's great,' she said, pulling stray strands of hair off her face. 'Thanks for putting on the storage heaters and the fridge.'

'The heaters are on all winter — to stop the place getting damp.'

'Oh, I see.'

'But I turned them up for you yesterday.'

'Thanks.'

Mike smiled and walked into the room with his hands still in his trouser pockets. He pulled out one of the kitchen chairs with his foot and sat down, little dried chunks of mud flaking off his boots onto Kath's newly cleaned floor. She found, to her surprise, that this didn't bother her in the least.

'I like you being here,' he said and she held her breath. 'I mean, it's nice to see someone living in the old place again.'

Kath exhaled slowly.

He was silent then and looked about the room, nodding his head in approval. For some reason that really pleased Kath.

'Mike?'

He returned his gaze to her and raised his eyebrows slightly in response.

'I was just going to pop over and see you about something.'

'Sure. What is it?'

'Would you mind if I put in a phone line?' Then she added hastily, 'I'd pay for it, of course.'

'That's absolutely fine.'

'And,' she said, reaching for a folder that lay on the kitchen counter, 'would you supply the hotel with meat?'

'Of course. I'll do you a discount too.'

'That's really good of you. Thanks. Can you do poultry and game?'

He nodded.

'And organic eggs?'

'Everything.'

'Great, that's one less thing to worry about,' she said with satisfaction, fumbling through her papers for a computer-generated checklist. She ticked a box and said, 'I'm looking forward to getting access to my own computer once I get into the hotel. You don't realise how much you rely on the things until you don't have one. Ned — he's my brother-in-law — '

'I know.'

'Well, I've been using his for spreadsheets and the like and storing them on CD but it's not the same as having your own — ' She stopped abruptly, aware that she was rambling.

'Have you given any thought to fruit and veg?' he said suddenly.

'Oh, I was going to use Anderson's, like before.'

'Hmm,' he said thoughtfully.

'What?'

'I wouldn't use them, Kath. Dick Anderson is a lazy so-and-so. He doesn't go to the market every day — I've heard that some of his customers aren't very happy with the quality.'

'Who would you recommend then?'

271

'Niall Lennon. His produce is far better and his prices are fair. What are we talking about?'

Kath passed him a note, compiled by John Routledge, of the hotel's weekly requirements. 'It's just an estimate at this stage. Based on previous usage. I'm hoping that we'll attract more trade than in the past.'

'Listen, I know Niall pretty well. Would you like me to have a chat with him? See if I can get him to do you a deal. He owes me a few favours.'

'Oh, would you, Mike? Would you really? Money is tight and every little bit saved will make a difference.'

'Leave it with me,' he said as he folded the piece of paper and put it in the pocket of his battered brown Barbour jacket. 'Did you ever get builders and decorators sorted out?'

'Yes, I took your advice and went for the Flynns. Their quote was the most competitive and they said they could start tomorrow. They were the only ones who'd do everything, from the floor to the painting and decorating.'

'Good,' he said, sounding satisfied. 'They'll do a sterling job.'

'Listen, Mike, I want you to know that I'm really grateful for all the help you've given me with the hotel. I don't think I could have got this far without you. You've been a true friend.'

'But I haven't done anything.'

'Yes, you have. The advice you've given me has been invaluable — joiners, plumbers, glaziers. The list is endless — and what do I know about these things? And I don't think the suppliers would've got involved with the hotel again after

... after what happened, if it hadn't been for you.'

'Oh, I don't know about that.'

'No, it's true. Why would they trust Brendan O'Connor's daughter to make a go of it? I know that people think I haven't got the experience to succeed.'

'Who said that?'

'Nobody's said it outright. But I can see it in people's faces. For example, the bank would only lend me the money I needed when I came up with a watertight guarantor. And the bank has security over the hotel.'

'Well, I think a lot of it had to do with your mother, Kath. By paying off all the creditors she made sure there was no ill will towards the family.'

'I know. Mum's been so selfless and I'm really proud of her. I thought at first that she was mad when she proposed to do that. But I see now why she did. However, I still think you've had a big part to play in things.'

He shrugged off her praise.

'Look, why don't you come for dinner tomorrow night, Mike? It won't be much — just a light supper and a glass of wine. My way of saying 'thank you'.'

'OK. I'd like that.'

'I'll see you tomorrow night at eight then,' she said, smiling.

22

The next morning at seven thirty Kath crossed the threshold of the Sallagh Braes Hotel yet again, but this time she was the legitimate holder of the key in her hand. The first thing she noticed on stepping inside was that the air wasn't as cold as outside — Frank Morrison must've attended to the heating as she'd advised. She flicked a wall switch on her right and the chandelier in the reception hall lit up. He'd connected the electricity too — good. She stood in the hallway and breathed in the stale air and couldn't quite believe that the place was hers.

'I'm doing the right thing, aren't I, Dad?' she said into the silence, as her stomach churned with anxiety. 'I haven't taken on too much, have I?'

In the silence that followed she pondered the fact that her father, with decades of experience, hadn't been able to make the business work and she was consumed with panic. She was mad to think that she could succeed where he'd failed.

She looked at the keys in her trembling hand and firmly reminded herself that she had plenty of experience in turning businesses around. That had been her job as a management consultant — going into a failing business, identifying its weaknesses and making it a success. She'd seen plenty of family concerns, like the Sallagh Braes Hotel, which had somehow lost their way. The

274

introduction of new blood, new ideas and new money could transform any enterprise.

The difference with this one was that she'd invested her entire life savings in it, and a lot more was riding on it than financial success. Her entire future for one thing. And the hopes and dreams of her family.

But, she reminded herself bravely, it was too late to run away now, even though she could have done so right at this minute. She told herself that she could do it. There would be problems, yes — nothing ever ran smoothly in life, did it? But she would come through it and so would the hotel.

Kath took a deep breath and opened the door to the office.

In spite of constant interruptions from the workmen who turned up at nine o'clock, including cutting the power supply off twice, she became totally absorbed in deciphering the files, both paper and on computer. She had to think about administering wage, National Insurance contributions, insurance and registering for VAT. All different, of course, from the States. And there were still furniture and fittings to be sourced. In short, there was a lot to be done — too much for one person. She would need some help.

Thankfully one of the office girls who'd worked for Brendan, and who knew the systems inside out, had agreed to come back and John Routledge was starting on Monday. She could delegate a lot to him. And Willie Ross was coaching her through the intricacies of the

British company tax system as, under his advice, she'd set up a limited company — The Sallagh Braes Hotel Limited.

That night, she was much later getting back to the farmhouse than she'd planned. At a quarter past six she marched quickly up the track home, her leg muscles protesting at the steep incline and her brain buzzing with all the things she had to do. She tried to switch off by cooking. She'd just finished preparing a simple pasta sauce, put it on to simmer and set the fire in the sitting room when there was a loud rap on the door. She froze for a moment, fearing that it might be Mike — here far too early — and then went to answer it.

She was relieved to find Bridget standing on the doorstep, her shoulders hunched against the chill, damp wind coming in off the sea.

'Sorry I'm calling in so late, Kath — I meant to get over earlier,' she said breathlessly, entering the house without waiting for an invite and peeling her black reefer jacket off in the hall. 'It's just been all go today.'

'It's OK, Bridget. Really.'

'God, this place hasn't changed much, has it?' she observed, hanging her coat over the post at the bottom of the banisters.

'Apart from a lick of paint, no, I don't think so,' said Kath, following her sister's gaze up the shadowy stairwell.

'Are you sure you're going to be alright living up here on your own?'

'I'll be perfectly fine. The Mulhollands are only down the lane.'

'Oh yes,' said Bridget, eyeing Kath keenly and then glancing away. 'Well, it's a bit too rustic for me.' Then she added, after the briefest of pauses, 'But each to their own.'

Kath suppressed a smile. Bridget never could resist telling Kath exactly what she thought. Kath wondered if she was as blunt with other people or if she reserved such candidness only for her family.

'I was helping Mum choose some furniture for her new flat,' said Bridget as Kath led her into the sitting room where she put a match to a piece of twisted paper. Flames licked hungrily around the kindling arranged in the grate. 'And I've been ferrying the children from one thing to another all afternoon. Sometimes I feel like an unpaid taxi driver.'

She sighed heavily and flopped into one of the brown velour armchairs, sending up a faint, but discernible, cloud of dust. Kath frowned, thinking that she'd have to get the Hoover out tomorrow and give the chair and sofa a good going over.

'God, you're going to have to get a new suite, Kath. This is absolutely vile!' Bridget pulled a face as Kath sat down in the armchair by the window.

'There's nothing wrong with it,' laughed Kath, thinking that she had a lot more important things to worry about than buying new furniture. 'It'll do just fine. Now what were you saying about Mum buying furniture? She's a bit premature, isn't she? She hasn't even put in an offer for the flat yet.'

'Ah, but she has,' said Bridget, with an air of mystery, delighted to be the bearer of breaking news. 'She did it today.'

'Really? She didn't hang about.'

'I know but it'll be a while before she hears anything back. The children of the old lady all have to be consulted and agree to accept the offer. But the estate agent said that the family were keen to sell quickly and she thinks Mum'll get it.'

'That's brilliant news, Bridget,' said Kath.

'I just hope she's not rushing into anything.' Bridget's brow furrowed with concern. 'She seems awfully keen to buy something and move in as soon as possible. Why, I don't know. She's perfectly welcome to stay with us as long as she wants.'

Kath bit her lip and looked at the clean, but rather worn, rug on the floor, thinking of something diplomatic to say. Something that wouldn't hurt Bridget's feelings. For Kath knew fine well what was motivating her mother — she found it suffocating staying at Bridget's.

'I imagine Mum just needs to have a place of her own. It must be unsettling for her living at yours in a sort of limbo,' she ventured. 'It's probably better that she's settled in her own flat.'

'I suppose so.' Bridget glanced at her watch. 'I need to keep an eye on the time. I have to pick Alex up from karate in an hour, so I can't stay too long.'

An hour? thought Kath with dismay. She'd wanted time to get herself ready for Mike's visit. At the hotel, the builders had started by pulling up all the old carpets and sanding the oak floorboards. They were coming up a treat but it was a messy job — she felt grimy with dust. She wanted to have a shower and put on some make-up.

'Listen, how did you get on at the hotel today?' asked Bridget.

'Oh, fine, fine,' said Kath, reluctant, for some reason she couldn't quite put her finger on, to share her plans for the evening with Bridget. She just knew that she didn't want her sister to know that she cared what Mike thought of her. She felt like she was a teenager again, trying to hide a crush. But she didn't fancy Mike — she really didn't. She still thought of Carl every day. And the very last thing she needed in her life was a man.

'Tell me more,' said Bridget's voice, interrupting her thoughts.

'Well, the workmen started on schedule. They've sanded about a quarter of the floorboards. Once they've finished that off they'll need to be varnished and then they can start on the rest rooms — they need updating.'

'You mean the toilets,' said Bridget, correcting Kath's American euphemism. 'What're you going to do?'

'Put in new sanitary wear, new mirrors, retile and re-carpet,' said Kath, resigning herself, as the conversation dragged on, to the fact that she'd have to make do with a squirt of perfume and a dab of lipstick before Mike's visit.

'That'll cost.'

'That's the most expensive job. The rest's just

279

cosmetic. The idea is to bring all the public areas up to scratch first. I'll have to tackle the bedrooms later.'

'Well, good luck to you,' said Bridget, not quite managing to sound as though she really meant it. 'Now Mum said that there's something you wanted to talk to me about.'

'Well, yes, there is. It's about the hotel actually.'

'Really?'

'I was wondering if you'd like to get involved, Bridget? Maybe work a few mornings in the office and on reception. I could do with some help. And it'd be nice to have some family involved.'

'Oh,' said Bridget, seemingly lost for words.

'You were saying the other night how you'd love a part-time job. And I'd pay you, of course,' added Kath hastily, not wanting her sister to think that she was trying to take advantage of her. 'Not a lot. But the going rate for office work.'

'What would you want me to do?' said Bridget warily.

'Anything and everything. Take customer bookings, I guess. Place orders. Pay invoices. That sort of thing. It would free me up to be a bit more front of house. I think that's partly where the success of the business depends.' When she saw Bridget hesitating she added, 'Do you remember Moira Dobbin? She used to work in the hotel.'

'Yeah. Sam Dobbin's daughter.'

'That's right. Well, she's agreed to come back

full-time so she'll be essentially running the office. You'd be helping her out where needed.'

'But I'm not sure I'm qualified, Kath.'

'You're as qualified as I am.'

After a pause, Bridget said with a smile, 'You know, I'd love to, Kath. But,' her face fell again, 'I'd need to speak to Ned about it.'

'Of course.'

'I don't know if he'll want me to do it. I'd need to arrange childcare for Charmaine, you see.'

'Isn't she in pre-school nursery in the mornings?'

'Yes, but only from nine till a quarter to twelve.'

'I'm sure Mum would love to help out, Bridget. She could collect her and give her lunch. It'd give her something to do. Something to look forward to.'

'Do you know what? I think that's a brilliant idea! And I think Mum'd love it. Only thing is I couldn't do Fridays. Charmaine's not in nursery then and school finishes at lunchtime.'

'How about working Monday, Wednesday and Thursday then?'

'Sounds good. Oh, but what about the summer holidays?' Bridget's hands flew up to her face. 'They're only round the corner.'

'Listen, Bridget, why don't we jump one hurdle at a time? You know, if you keep putting obstacles in your way, you'll never get back out to work.'

'You're right. Let's do it!' said Bridget, her face breaking into a big smile.

281

'Great!' said Kath, pleased. Then, all of a sudden, she leapt to her feet. 'Oh my God, I left something on the cooker!' She ran from the room. In the kitchen, she pulled the big stainless-steel pot off the gas burner and lifted the lid. Steam billowed out, causing her to arch her head backwards until it had dispersed. Cautiously, she gave the contents of the pot a stir with a well-worn wooden spoon. Then she replaced the lid, put the pot back over the flame and turned the control down as low as it would go.

Bridget came into the kitchen.

'It's alright. It's not burned!' said Kath with a sigh of relief.

'You know, I'm really excited about working in the hotel,' said Bridget. 'It'll be a bit like old times — you know, when we used to help out in the holidays. But without Dad of course . . . ' Her voice trailed off.

'You know,' said Kath thoughtfully, 'I like to think that he'll be watching over us. And that he'll be pleased.'

'And telling us what to do like he used to!' said Bridget, forcing a note of cheerfulness into her voice.

'Yes, something like that,' said Kath and smiled.

'Well, now, something smells good,' said Bridget, changing the subject quite abruptly. 'What's in the pot?' She lifted the lid and peeked inside. 'Pasta sauce. You've enough in here to feed an army! Are you expecting company?'

'Well, I am, as a matter of fact.'

Bridget looked at Kath over the lid suspended mid-air in her hand. 'Who?'

Kath paused. She'd spent all day telling herself that it was only a casual supper with a good friend. She had nothing to hide from Bridget. From anyone.

'It's only Mike Mulholland,' she said as she placed two tablemats on the table.

Bridget replaced the lid with a loud clang and said, her voice full of incredulity, 'You've invited him over for dinner?'

Kath, who was taking cutlery out of a drawer, paused momentarily. 'It's supper, not dinner. And why not?'

Bridget raised her eyebrows, lifted a spoonful of blood-red tomato sauce out of the pan, blew on it and put it to her lips. 'Hmm . . . good. But it needs a little salt.'

Kath folded two napkins, laid them beside the forks and rummaged in a cupboard for a tea-light holder. 'He's been really good, you know — he offered me a discount on meat supplies for the hotel.' Then she added, a touch defensively, 'This is just my way of thanking him for all the help he's given me over the last weeks.'

'And that's all it is?' said Bridget, going over to the table and examining one of the knives.

'What do you mean?'

'Well,' said Bridget, watching as Kath lit candles and placed them strategically on the table, 'it looks a bit like a date to me.'

Kath took a few paces back and stared at the table as though seeing it for the first time. Bridget was right — Kath blushed, hurriedly blew out the candles and put them back in the cupboard.

'There, does that look better?' she said anxiously.

'You know, Kath, Mike's not everything he appears to be,' said Bridget ominously. Her eyes, that curious mixture of grey-speckled brown, narrowed. 'You should be careful.'

'What do you mean?' Kath followed Bridget into the hall and watched her pull on her jacket.

'Let's just say he's not very good at keeping promises,' replied Bridget, swiftly fastening the row of silver buttons that glinted against the black wool fabric of her coat.

'Bridget, I never did get the full story of you and Mike Mulholland. I know you dated him for a bit years ago. Did he do something to you? Did he break a promise?'

'Well, if you really want to know, he did as a matter of fact. But I don't want to talk about it. That's all in the past now,' she said, the emotion in her voice betraying the fact that this was far from the truth.

'But, Bridget — ' protested Kath as her sister stepped outside into the March chill.

'Oh, here he is now,' said Bridget, raising her right arm in salute to the figure at the end of the track.

'Shit!' said Kath under her breath. 'I'll speak to you tomorrow, Bridget. Bye!' And, slamming the door, she ran inside.

23

Kath flew up the stairs and into the bedroom where she hastily brushed her hair, slapped on some lipstick and doused herself in perfume. She would have to wait until another day to find out the nature of this puzzling misunderstanding between Mike and Bridget. Whatever it was, Bridget seemed to harbour no rancour towards him now — she was always friendly enough towards him. Maybe Mum could shed some light on the mystery . . .

Kath gave herself a quick once-over in the mirror and groaned. Her turquoise top was splattered with the dark red stains of dried tomato. She hauled it off, heard Bridget's car driving off and a confident rap on the red wood-panelled door.

'Shit!' she said again.

She grabbed the first thing that came to hand from a drawer — a plain unbecoming white T-shirt — and pulled it over her head. There was no time to change the worn denim jeans she'd been wearing all day. She ran to the bottom of the stairs, paused to compose herself and opened the door.

Mike was standing there, freshly shaved, and holding a bunch of pink tulips in his hand. He leaned forward and pecked her on the cheek. He smelt faintly of pleasant aftershave.

'Hello,' she said with her biggest smile,

accepting the flowers and realising, with dismay, that underneath his battered Barbour jacket he was dressed nicely in smart cords and an open-necked shirt. She, on the other hand, looked like she'd just been mucking out a pig-sty. 'Come in,' she said when she realised he was staring at her expectantly. She stood sideways to let him pass through the narrow door and said, 'Sorry about this.'

'About what?'

'The state of me,' she said pulling at the hem of the T-shirt with one hand, the flowers in the other. 'I wasn't expecting Bridget to call and, well, I kind of ran out of time to get ready.'

'Well, I think you look great,' he replied. He took off his coat and was about to throw it over the newel post when he paused. 'Sorry, old habit. Is it OK to put it here?'

'Absolutely fine.'

At the door to the sitting room he hesitated and she said, 'Yes, go on in. Why don't we have a drink before we eat? What'll you have, Mike?'

'Have you any beer?'

'Just bottles of Stella.'

'That'll be grand, thanks.'

She went into the kitchen where she hastily rammed the bunch of flowers in a vase and filled it with water. She left them on the kitchen counter and collected a beer and a glass of wine for herself.

She returned to find Mike peering at the photos displayed on the old pine dresser that had once housed his mother's collection of colourful china.

'Is it strange being a visitor here?' she asked and he nodded.

'I never did like that bungalow, you know,' he said, sitting on the sofa.

Kath took a seat in what was now her favourite armchair by the window.

'It was my mother's idea,' he went on. 'I think she wanted something a bit grander than this old farmhouse. But I'd rather be living here any day. It reminds me of my father.'

Kath looked into the straw-coloured liquid in her glass and thought of Brendan.

'I'm sorry,' he said hastily. 'I didn't mean to be insensitive.'

'You weren't. It's OK.'

'How did it go up at the hotel today?' he said, changing the subject.

'Good,' said Kath, brightening. 'So far so good, anyway. The workmen started on time and that's something.'

Mike yawned and Kath squirmed uncomfortably in the seat. Was she that boring?

'I'm sorry for being so rude, Kath. It's just that I've been up half the night with one of the calving cows.'

'Oh, there's no need to apologise,' she said, relieved by his reply. 'Tell me all about it.'

She listened, fascinated, while he told her all about the calving and some of the other things that were happening on the farm — the vaccination of breeding ewes and the trimming of ewes' feet against foot-rot, whatever that meant. His life was so far removed from the life she'd lived in metropolitan Boston that they

287

might as well have lived on different planets.

But all that was set to change. She was no farmer but her income, and survival, now depended on the land too. It was the renowned beauty of this area that drew visitors both locally and from all over the world — visitors that she hoped to lure to the revamped Sallagh Braes Hotel.

When their glasses were empty they went through to the kitchen where they sat opposite each other at the rectangular pine table. They drank wine and ate a simple supper of pasta, salad, cheese and luxury shop-bought ice cream.

When the food was finished, Kath opened another bottle of wine and topped up their glasses.

'So, tell me,' said Mike. 'What made you decide to stay and take on the hotel?'

'Well, for one thing, I couldn't bear to see it fall out of the family. My father loved that place. So does Mum. And I guess I do too.'

Mike cocked his head to one side before asking, 'But it's a huge decision just to pack in everything and start a new life. What about your home in Boston?'

'I sold it.'

'And all your possessions?'

'Likewise.'

He sucked in air through his teeth and jerked his head slightly to the left. 'That's brave, Kath.'

'Well, it's not strictly true,' she said, not feeling brave at all, just reckless. Stupid, even. 'I'm waiting on a shipment of personal belongings. But all the big things, like my furniture, I sold with the apartment.'

Kath was silent for a few moments while she dithered over whether to tell him about Carl — the true motivation behind her decision to emigrate back to Ireland. She stared at his open, earnest expression and his clear, dark brown eyes set under heavy brows. You didn't keep things like Carl a secret from true friends. He had been too much a part of her life, for too long, to pretend he never existed. She took a deep breath.

'There was another reason I decided to leave Boston, Mike. I broke up with my long-term boyfriend.' Then, deciding that this didn't convey the enormity of what had actually happened, she started over, tracing the grain of the pine table with her finger. 'No, it was more than that. It was much more than that. Something terrible happened to me . . . ' She took a deep breath and went on to tell him the whole sorry tale of Carl and what she saw now as her utter gullibility.

She had to stop once or twice to keep her emotions under check, but the telling wasn't as painful as the last time when she'd broken the news to her family. She realised suddenly that the old adage was true — time was a great healer, albeit a painfully slow one. When she finished speaking, Mike was quiet for so long, his lips pressed together into a thin line, that he seemed lost for words.

'Kath,' he said at last. 'I am truly sorry. I really am.'

'You know, I'd always thought of myself as

pretty worldly-wise,' she said, glad of the opportunity to talk about Carl — something that she'd tried not to do too much around her family. They had enough to worry about without burdening them with her problems. 'At first I was just so hurt, so terribly wounded. It was only later that I realised what a complete fool he'd made of me. Because he did, didn't he? Making me believe that he loved me. And telling me all those lies.'

'He never made a fool of you, Kath. The only person he made a fool of was himself.'

'Well, I feel like a complete and utter idiot. All that nonsense about flying to Wisconsin every weekend to see his mother . . . ' she took a slug of wine and shook her head, 'and there was me thinking he was God's gift because of it. Any half-sensible person would've smelt a rat months ago.'

'I think you're being a bit hard on yourself, Kath. If someone's determined to deceive you they can make anything sound plausible.'

'You know it's made me very — very wary of people. And I wasn't like that before. That's one of the reasons I like being here. I'm among people I grew up with — my family and you and Gladys for example — and I know who they are and where they come from. And there's something very reassuring about that.'

'I know what you mean. But you shouldn't let Carl — what's-his-name?'

'Scholtz.'

'You shouldn't let him change the type of person you are. For every Carl Scholtz there's a

290

thousand decent blokes out there who would never do what he did to anyone.'

Kath sighed. 'I know. It's just going to take me a little while to trust people again.'

'Promise me you won't let him turn you into a cynic?' Mike said with a grin, breaking the sombre tone of the conversation.

'I promise,' she said, returning his smile and a little of the misery that had engulfed her since the Carl Chapter, as she now referred to it, lifted.

The few seconds of silence that passed between them was broken by Kath.

'Coffee?' she said and he nodded. She got up, put cups and saucers on the table along with milk, sugar and a small plate of foil-covered chocolate mints. Then she poured them each a cup of black coffee and sat down.

'Oh, did you hear?' she said, remembering suddenly. 'Highfield House was sold at auction yesterday.'

'Was it?' he said and lifted a fine, gold-rimmed coffee cup to his lips. It came from a set Fiona had salvaged from the house and insisted on giving to Kath. It wasn't really to her taste but she would never throw it out.

Quickly she filled him in on the few details she'd learned about the auction from her mother.

'I wish I knew who'd bought it,' she said.

'Would it make any difference if you knew who it was?' he said, helping himself to a mint.

'Not if it was someone I didn't know.'

'And if it was someone you knew?' he asked,

peeling the foil off the chocolate and popping it in his mouth.

'I think I'd probably hate them.'

From his expression Kath realised she'd made him feel uncomfortable. She imagined it was because what she'd just said sounded so petty and downright horrible.

'I'm sorry,' she said quickly. 'That wasn't a nice thing to say, was it? But I'm only telling the truth, Mike, I can't pretend I don't care.'

'Of course you care about the house,' he said reassuringly, as he scrunched the foil wrapper in his hand. 'It's only natural. It's where you grew up. It's — it was your home.'

'I'm just annoyed with myself that I wasn't able to buy it. But I didn't have enough resources for the house and the hotel.'

'You can only do so much,' he said kindly.

'Well, you never know,' she said brightly. 'Who knows, maybe one day I'll get Highfield House back.'

'You never know,' he agreed, looking at the tight, hard little ball in his hand that had once been the foil wrapper.

'I guess we'll know the identity of the purchaser soon enough. I imagine they'll be moving in once the legalities are sorted out. That shouldn't take more than a few weeks.'

'Well, I'll need to be getting back,' he said, changing tack suddenly.

Kath glanced at the new-looking chrome kitchen clock on the wall above the sink, incongruous in the authentic farmhouse kitchen. It was nearly midnight.

'Of course,' she said, pushing the chair back and getting to her feet with a little difficulty. Had she really had that much to drink?

'Have you an early start in the morning?' she enquired politely.

'I think there might be another calf on the way,' he said, rising from the table. 'I'll have to keep an eye on it overnight.'

'You must be exhausted!'

'I am, but this is one of the best bits about my job. I moan a lot but really I wouldn't miss it for the world. I could always get one of the farmhands to do it, if I wanted to.' He paused and added, 'That was a really lovely meal, Kath. Thank you. I really appreciate it.'

'Thanks for coming. It was nice. I really enjoyed talking to you, Mike. I hope I didn't bore you with all my problems.'

'No, not at all. I had a really lovely evening. I'd like to return the favour sometime. I'm no cook though. Maybe we could go out somewhere instead.'

'That'd be nice,' she replied and waited, but no offer of a future rendezvous was forthcoming.

Leaving the zip of his jacket unfastened, he reached into the inside left pocket. 'I wanted to give you this,' he said, pulling forth a small volume. He held it out and Kath put out both her hands to receive it.

'*Penguin Classics: The Metaphysical Poets,*' she read and looked at him quizzically.

'It's not exactly a housewarming present,' he explained. 'Someone gave me a copy when Dad died and I found some of the poems — helpful.

But maybe it's not your sort of thing,' he added, suddenly bashful.

'Oh no,' said Kath quickly, thinking that he'd misread the vacant look on her face for disinterest. 'It's just that I've never heard of them, that's all. I don't know a thing about metaphysical poetry but I'd love to learn.'

'Some of the later John Donne ones, and Andrew Marvell, deal with the subject of death. I found them kind of . . . well, soothing, even though the language is a bit overdone. You have to try and imagine them within the context of seventeenth-century England when they were written.'

'I am deeply touched,' said Kath, holding the book to her chest. 'And it's a very, very thoughtful gesture.'

He leaned forward suddenly, gave her a quick peck on the cheek and opened the door. 'Goodnight,' he said and stepped into the darkness.

'Goodnight,' she called after him and closed the door.

She stood in the hall and looked at the cover of the book. The image on the front was of a gloomy medieval painting of a deathbed scene. A person — man or woman, she could not tell which — lay in a bed with a lacy nightcap on his or her head. To the left was the dark figure of a man, holding a briefcase and a skull — the physician perhaps? And to the right, a woman, dressed also in black and with tight ringlets in her hair, knelt on the floor.

What an enigma Mike Mulholland was

turning out to be! Birthing cows one minute and reading seventeenth-century poetry the next. In truth she was astounded. She wouldn't have described him as cerebral but there was obviously a lot more to him than she'd given him credit for. Turning out the lights, she climbed the stairs, suddenly overcome with fatigue, and in spite of her best intentions, fell asleep with the light on and the volume of poetry, unopened, on her chest.

24

'Other people manage, Ned, why can't we?' said Bridget, as she rummaged in the walk-in dressing room off the bedroom she shared with her husband.

She flicked quickly through the rails of neatly arranged clothes, mentally discarding most of them as possible workwear. The few suits that might've been suitable were too small for her now. She used to be a size ten, now she was more like a fourteen. She sighed. It was a crying shame what having children did to your figure.

'Term-time's absolutely fine. I don't have a problem with that. But the holidays are only a couple of months away. Why start working now?'

'Because I'm needed now,' said Bridget, coming out of the room with a jacket in each hand. 'If I don't take this job Kath'll have to recruit someone else.'

'Let her then.'

'But I don't want her to. Don't you see — this job is perfect.' Then she added rather darkly, 'Apart from anything else, it'll enable us to keep an eye on our investment. We've a big financial stake in this business.'

'That's true,' said Ned, and he rubbed his chin thoughtfully.

Bridget walked back into the wardrobe quickly so that Ned could not see the smile on her face. Appealing to his sense of financial prudence was always an effective strategy.

'But you still haven't answered my question. What are you going to do with the children come the summer holidays?'

'Apart from the two weeks we're booked to go to Sardinia,' shouted Bridget pointedly, from inside the wardrobe, 'we, not *I*, will arrange for the children to go to summer club at school.'

'They'll hate it.'

'It's only for a few mornings a week. And maybe, if Mum feels she can cope, she'll mind them the odd time too.'

'Well, Bridget, it's up to you,' he said, sounding as though he didn't mean it.

Bridget's stomach tightened into a knot but she resisted the bait. She bit her bottom lip and pulled two shoeboxes off the top shelf. They were covered in dust.

She heard the click of the bedroom door as Ned shut it behind him and sighed. How had she ended up married to a chauvinist? Ned wasn't like that when they'd married, was he? Maybe he was and she'd not noticed. Maybe love made you blind to people's faults. It was, she acknowledged, his only flaw but it was an extremely irritating one.

She opened the first shoebox and smiled. Inside was a pair of pillarbox red, kitten-heeled slingbacks from LK Bennett. She lifted one shoe out and admired it. One of the reasons for her love affair with shoes was that they never got too small for you, no matter what happened the rest of your body. She slipped her feet into the shoes and skipped around the room.

She didn't care what Ned said — she was going to do this. She wanted to have a bit of fun. She wanted to meet people and go to work in the morning dressed in a smart suit, like all the other professional women out there. Dynamic women with successfully balanced work and home lives. She wanted to be one of them. OK, this was a pretty lowly job but it was a start. It would give her what she wanted — some sort of life outside the home.

★ ★ ★

The next morning, once she'd dropped Alex and Laura at school and Charmaine at nursery, Bridget drove the few miles out of Ballyfergus to the hotel. She pulled up in the large tarmacked forecourt, her spirits high in spite of the dull, overcast day. She noticed that the broken skylight above the door had been repaired. There were workmen in white overalls visible at the windows and, in the walled garden, a curl of grey smoke rose into the still, damp day. The smell of burning wood reminded Bridget of the bonfires they used to have here on Halloween night.

She got out of the car and her gaze was drawn involuntarily to the white bungalow further up the hill. She wondered if Mike was there now. Or out in the fields. Or at the butcher's shop in town . . . She sighed, reminding herself that she was a happily married mother of three. Mike hadn't wanted her love — he'd made that very clear all those years ago.

How she wished she could forget about him

but she knew that was impossible. He was her first true love and he would always occupy a special place in her heart. It was something she would just have to learn to live with. No, she corrected herself — it was something she *had* learnt to live with. She'd learned to cope without him.

He wasn't the marrying type anyway — rumour had it that he always had some girl or other on the go, but the relationships never lasted. And Bridget drew some comfort from that. She liked to believe that he regretted losing her. That, in spite of his rejection and the cruel things he'd said to her all those years ago, he still held a candle for her. Just as she did for him.

Tearing her gaze away from the hillside, she walked into the garden, through the gap in the six-foot-high stone wall. David, wearing blue overalls and a green fleece, was tending the bonfire which was smoking rather than burning. She crossed the lawn and stopped some distance short of him, not wanting to end up stinking of the fire. When he saw her, he came over and said hello.

'What're you doing?' she asked.

'Just clearing out the worst of the overgrown bushes and trees.'

'Aren't you supposed to be at work today?'

'Day off,' he replied and wiped the sweat from his brow with a forearm. His hand was sheathed in a well-worn leather gardening glove. 'I promised Kath I'd give her a hand with the garden. The old man let it go a bit . . . ' His voice trailed off.

'Yes, it's quite a job,' agreed Bridget, after an awkward pause. 'There's a lot of bare patches visible now,' she added, noticing the new-looking gaps in the borders where David had ripped out overgrown specimens. 'They'll need replanting. And,' she poked a clump of moss underfoot with the toe of her black patent boot, 'the lawns could do with a bit of TLC.'

'Kath's got someone coming in to do all that. I'm just giving a hand with the rough stuff. Anyway, enough about me. What's this I hear about you working in the office?'

'And on reception,' said Bridget proudly.

'Good for you, Bridge,' he said using her nickname from childhood and she flushed with pride.

'You know, David, I'm really looking forward to it. I've been wanting to get a part-time job for ages. And this suits me perfectly.'

'How d'you think it'll work out having Kath as your boss, though? You two rub each other up the wrong way sometimes.'

'No, we don't,' said Bridget, slightly irritated. She did not like David pointing out the flaws in her relationship with Kath nor putting a dampener on her high spirits. 'Well, OK then, maybe we don't always see eye to eye but that's because Kath's so strong-headed. She never wants to take advice.'

David sucked air in through his teeth. 'Sparks might fly.'

'Oh, it'll be absolutely fine,' said Bridget dismissively. 'Now, what about you and Simone? Have you set a date yet?'

'No,' he said and grinned. 'I suppose because we're living together we both feel there's no real rush.'

'I wish you'd hurry up! I'd love an excuse for a new outfit.'

'Oh, well, in that case,' he said, in a mock serious tone, 'we'd better get a move on. I'll tell Simone tonight that we have to get married so you can get a new frock!'

Bridget threw her head back and laughed. 'Listen, I'd better get up to the hotel. The boss'll be wondering where I am.' She gave him an exaggerated wink, then turned on her heel and started walking back over the grass towards the front of the hotel, the heels of her boots sinking into the soft earth.

'Bridget?'

'Yes?' she said and stopped, looking over her shoulder.

'Do you think Murray looks like me?'

'Of course he does. He's your son.'

'I suppose,' mumbled David and Bridget frowned, remembering that awful incident in her house when Mum had said Murray wasn't her grandson. Clearly, it had deeply bothered David.

'David,' she said, walking towards him again on the balls of her feet, 'you mustn't pay too much attention to Mum. We all say stupid, cruel things we don't mean sometimes.'

'Do you? I don't.'

Bridget sighed, acknowledging the truth of this, in his case at least. 'All I'm saying is that you shouldn't read too much into what she said. She was under a lot of stress and I'm quite sure she didn't mean it. She's still tetchy even now. Once she's settled in that flat of hers, I'm sure we'll all see a big difference in her.'

'Maybe,' said David and he walked back to the bonfire and threw on a bundle of sticks, indicating that the conversation was over.

Bridget left the garden and made her way into the hotel foyer, thinking that she was a good liar. Although Mum refused to admit anything to her, she suspected that she had good reason for saying what she did. You don't say something like that without having reasonable grounds. What did she know about Murray that the rest of them didn't?

'Hi, there,' said Kath's voice, interrupting her thoughts. 'You look smart.'

'Oh, well, I thought I'd start off as I mean to go on.'

'You didn't need to get all dressed up. We're not opened yet,' said Kath and Bridget bristled.

But she let the comment go unchallenged because her attention was taken up by the transformation around her. Gone were the flock wallpaper, the patterned carpets and the ornate red and gold curtains; everything was new and unfamiliar. Newly varnished oak floorboards gleamed in the warm pools of light emanating from wall-mounted fixtures.

The partition between the old sitting room and the reception area had been knocked through into one cavernous space. Light flooded in through a skylight inserted over the reception desk and all the walls were in the process of being painted pale cream. Two men up a ladder were adding finishing touches to a gorgeous distressed chandelier hanging in reception.

'Kath,' she gasped, 'it's going to be beautiful. What are the curtains like?'

'Like this,' said Kath, reaching behind the reception desk and handing her a swatch of fabric. It felt like moleskin, in the softest shade of taupe. Kath brandished a pair of mahogany holdbacks which resembled enormous mushrooms. 'And these are instead of tiebacks. Much more modern, don't you think?'

'I think it's going to look fantastic! It's all so exciting! So where will I be working?'

'In here.' Kath led her sister into what used to be their father's office. It was unrecognisable — there were three modern desks squeezed in where the antique mahogany one used to be, each one sporting a brand new computer atop. The oak panelling had been painted white and Brendan's old chair was gone.

At one desk sat a woman with red hair shorn into an elfin bob, no make-up and thick black-rimmed glasses.

'You remember Moira Dobbin?' asked Kath and Bridget shook Moira's hand.

Moira was in her early forties, divorced with two teenage daughters. She was still as quiet and self-effacing as she'd been as a girl.

Bridget and Moira made polite small talk for a while, then Moira then excused herself and left the office.

Bridget turned to her sister and hissed, 'But what did you do with Dad's desk, Kath? And his chair?'

'Keep your hair on,' said Kath, lowering her voice in case Moira should hear. 'They're up at the farmhouse for the time being, in the spare room. We're tight for space down here. The old desk was far too big. I couldn't keep it.'

'It's just a bit of a shock,' said Bridget, noticing too the brand new beige carpet on the floor and the discreet buttermilk blind on the window. 'Everything's different.'

'Everything has to be different, Bridget,' said Kath gently, 'if this place is to succeed.'

'It's just really weird seeing it like this. I never imagined it could look so . . . so . . . '

'Cool?' said Kath, finishing the sentence for her with a word Bridget never used, but did indeed sum up the new look.

'Yes, that's about right,' she agreed.

'Even better than that,' said Kath excitedly. 'Let me show you our new website.'

Bridget sat down in front of one of the computer screens while Kath typed expertly on the black keyboard. In a few seconds a soft-focus picture of the hotel appeared, accompanied by background music — the sound of traditional Irish instruments.

Quickly, Kath pressed a series of buttons, bringing up page after page of well-presented, accessible information about the hotel and the surrounding area.

'Who did this for you, Kath? It's brilliant!'

'Do you remember me talking about Steve, Emmy's boyfriend?'

'I do. He's American, isn't he?'

'That's right. Well, setting up websites isn't

304

only Steve's job — it's his passion. He did this for me in his spare time. All I did was send him some photos, our tariff, blurb about the facilities and the local area, etc., and he set up the whole site. Look,' she said, hitting a couple of keys and bringing up a page headed *Make Your Booking Now.* 'You can even book online. We've had over a hundred hits already and the site's only been up and running a few days. Oh, and I've been talking to some travel companies in the States — ones that do upmarket package tours of Ireland. I'm trying to persuade them to come over and check out the hotel with a view to using us next season.'

'That sounds fantastic,' said Bridget, impressed with her big sister's dynamism — a trait that she, unfortunately, did not share. Not for the first time, she felt inadequate in Kath's company. All she'd done with her life was get married and have kids.

'Hi, Kath — Bridget — Moira,' said a familiar man's voice from the doorway and Bridget looked up to see John Routledge standing there. He had a file in his hand and was dressed in a pale blue open-necked shirt and navy chinos.

'Kath,' he said, 'the chef's here for his interview.'

'Oh, great,' said Kath and then, turning to Bridget, she explained, 'This is an old college friend of John's we're hoping to recruit for the head chef's job.'

'Really?' said Bridget without taking her eyes off John.

Although not to Bridget's taste, he was a

handsome man. She wondered if he and Kath, working so closely together, might hit it off. Relaxed and informal in each other's company, they certainly seemed to like each other — in spite of John being seven years Kath's junior.

And it would help take Kath's mind off Mike Mulholland for, in spite of her sister's protestations to the contrary, Bridget was quite convinced that Kath had a soft spot for him. She could tell Kath that she was wasting her time, but she didn't want to hear it. And worst of all, Bridget had seen Mike Mulholland look at Kath in a way he'd never looked at her . . .

'Righto then,' said John. 'We're in the meeting room along the hall when you're ready.'

'I'll be along in just a minute,' said Kath.

As soon as John had left the room, Bridget said, 'He's much better looking than Mike Mulholland, isn't he?'

Kath shrugged and scooped some papers off the desk. 'I hadn't noticed.'

'How did your romantic dinner go the other night?'

'Really well,' said Kath, apparently oblivious to the sarcasm in Bridget's question. A secret smile spread fleetingly across Kath's face and Bridget could have sworn she blushed.

She felt her cheeks flush with rage at the thought of Mike and Kath together. She resolved there and then to have John and Kath over for dinner one night, even though John Routledge had never before set foot in her house. She had to do something — she couldn't just sit there and let Mike Mulholland fall in love with her sister.

'Are you feeling OK?' said Kath and Bridget flushed even more, this time with embarrassment.

'Sure! I'm absolutely fine,' she said cheerfully.

'OK,' said Kath doubtfully and then went on, 'Well, about this Ben. He's at Shu just now and he's worked in some other great restaurants in Belfast like Cayenne — that was called Roscoff's before.'

'I know,' said Bridget, remembering the days when she used to go to the hip and happening restaurant with her fashionable colleagues from work.

'He's worked at Apartment and The Old Inn at Crawfordsburn,' went on Kath. 'All really top-notch places. Anyway, the point is that he has loads of experience. He's perfect for the job. I just hope we can persuade him to come and work for us.'

'And how are you planning to lure him away from the big smoke?'

'Ah, well, love's already partly done that for us. Apparently he's engaged to a girl from Ballyfergus and she doesn't want to move to Belfast. So at the moment he's commuting and it's an absolute nightmare, as you can imagine, with the long hours.'

'Sounds promising,' murmured Bridget but her mind was still on Mike and Kath. She felt sick to the stomach when she thought of the two of them together.

'I'm hoping John can do the rest of the

307

persuading,' said Kath, raising her eyebrows to indicate the enormity of the task ahead. 'Well, I suppose I'd better not keep them waiting. Moira'll show you the ropes. Wish me luck!'

Bridget smiled thinly and Kath left the room.

For a moment Bridget hated herself. She knew that what went on between Mike and Kath was really none of her business. She should keep her nose out of it and get on with her own life — hadn't she everything a sane woman could wish for? She listed her assets: a lovely family, good husband (albeit a little flawed), no money worries, gorgeous home, brand new Volvo XC 90 and now the little bit of independence she so desperately craved.

'Now,' said Moira, 'you're sitting here and that's John's desk. But Kath'll use whatever computer's free when one of us isn't here. How long is it since you used a computer?'

'It's been a while,' said Bridget, as panic took hold. It had been a damn sight more than a 'while' — it had been years. She hoped things hadn't changed too much.

'Right then. Let's start with the booking system,' began Moira.

Bridget balled her fists while she listened to Moira and dug her painted nails into her palms until they hurt. The problem was, no matter what she did, she just couldn't let go of Mike Mulholland . . .

25

Over a week had passed before Kath had a minute to turn her attention to the book of poetry Mike had given her. On Saturday, after locking up the hotel, she climbed up the hill and let herself into the empty farmhouse. In spite of the fact that work at the hotel was progressing to plan, she was wracked with anxiety lest something go wrong. And it was all such a steep learning curve.

Her head ached with facts and figures and the hundreds of things on her extensive 'to-do' list. She'd interviewed sixteen staff during the week with John's help and recruited eleven of them. At least Moira was now setting up wage accounts and putting things straight in the office. And Bridget was on board now too. It was all coming together nicely. She told herself to stop worrying.

She threw the tome Willie Ross had loaned her — a book on setting up and running a limited company — on the hall table and sighed. Too exhausted to think about cooking, she decided to treat herself to a deep bubble bath. Upstairs, she arranged lit candles on the side of the bath and watched the bubbles froth and multiply like yeast in warm water, as the room filled with hot steam.

Later on, she would drive into Ballyfergus to the supermarket for food — the cupboards were almost bare — and maybe she'd hire a DVD and pick up a takeaway. Changed days indeed, she thought wryly. Only a couple of months ago she'd have thought anyone who spent her Saturday nights alone, curled up in front of the TV, a sad case. If she thought about her situation too much, she would begin to feel sorry for herself.

Clearing her head of the self-pitying thoughts that threatened to consume her, she eased herself gently into the bath, taking care to keep Mike's book clear of the water. She leafed through the pages, found the poems of John Donne and started to read. The poem 'Song', appeared to be about love, but the language was archaic and the verses obtuse and complex.

She read the poem over several times, referring frequently to the notes at the back of the book. In truth, she found it hard to understand it, never mind take comfort from it. Poetry had never been her thing at school — but still, it was a nice gesture of Mike to give her something that obviously meant a lot to him. She yawned and resolved to try again another day when she wasn't so tired.

She threw the book gently on the floor, away from the bath in case it got splashed. It landed with a flop beside the pedestal of the hand basin and fell open at the title page. Kath noticed some sort of inscription scrawled across the paper in a large, loopy hand and her interest was aroused. She leaned out of the bath, stretching as far as she could, and just managed to pick up the volume with her damp fingertips. She lay back into bath and peered at the careless blue handwriting in the dim candlelight. It took her a

310

few moments to decode it: '*On the death of your father* — *In the hope you find some comfort from the pages within. Love you always, Anne.*'

Kath frowned. Why had he given her what clearly had been a special gift? She wondered who Anne was and decided that she couldn't possibly keep the book. It was sweet of him to give her something so personal but she'd have to return it.

Thinking of Mike gave her an idea. She could stop by his house, using the book as a pretext, and then casually ask him if he'd like to share a takeaway. She hadn't seen him since the beginning of the week and it'd be nice to end the week with someone to talk to.

Kath lay on in the hot water a few minutes longer, unable to entirely relax now that she had a plan for the evening. So she got out of the bath and dried herself with a rough towel. Her skin tingled and she felt revived. In the bedroom, she slipped on a pair of jeans and a long-sleeved T-shirt, tied her hair back and put on some lipstick. She stopped short of full make-up. She didn't want to look like she'd made an effort. She didn't want Mike thinking she was asking him on a date. They were just friends after all.

Downstairs in the kitchen she made a mental note of the few essentials she mustn't forget, like milk and bread, put on her jacket and went outside. Even though Easter was fast approaching, and the worst of the cold weather was over, it was still dark at seven thirty.

She pulled the car keys from her pocket, stumbled over to the dark hulk of the car and found the keyhole by feel. She hopped in and drove the short distance to the Mulhollands' house. There were lights on inside. She parked the car, turned off the engine and noticed that her heart was pounding. What was she so nervous about? She told herself not to be silly; she must make her invitation sound casual, as though it was something she'd only thought of on the spur of the moment.

She rang the doorbell and fixed a smile on her face. Gladys opened the door and ushered her in. After exchanging a few pleasantries in the hallway, Kath asked if Mike was in.

'He's in the study down there,' said Gladys, pointing to a door at the end of a hallway. 'Just you go on in. Here, let me take your coat, love.'

'Oh, I can't stay, Gladys. I just wanted to speak to him about this,' she said, raising her right hand in which she held the book he'd given her.

'OK. I'll see you later then. If you'll excuse me, I'm just watching *Coronation Street* and I don't like to miss it.'

Gladys disappeared into the lounge, shutting the door on the sound of the TV.

Kath walked down the hall and knocked on the door.

'Hi,' she said cheerily, opening the door in response to a grunt from within. The first thing that struck her about the room was the books. Hundreds of them lined the walls on groaning bookshelves.

Mike was seated at a desk. 'Oh sorry! I thought it was Mum. Come on in,' he said.

312

She stepped inside, leaving the door open behind her.

Mike leaned back in the office chair and ran his fingers through his hair. 'Sit down, Kath. How are you?'

'I'm good,' she said, scanning the titles on the shelves. She saw volumes by Dickens, Chaucer and Hardy as well as modern classics by Rushdie, Self and Welsh. 'What a lot of books! Have you read them all?' She took a seat on the opposite side of the desk from him.

'Pretty much. Though I keep meaning to read some of them again but I never have the time.'

'I hope I haven't disturbed you? Were you reading just now?'

'No, chance would be a fine thing,' he said, glancing at the official-looking forms strewn over the untidy desk and yawning. In the corner a computer screen flickered. 'I was doing farm stuff. You wouldn't believe the amount of paperwork we have to file nowadays, Kath. Every calf that's born has to be issued with a government passport within twenty-eight days of birth. It's a real job keeping on top of it.'

'A passport. What on earth for?'

'It's part of the Cattle Tracing System administered by the BCMS — sorry, that's the British Cattle Movement Service. It's all to do with tracing cattle quickly in the event of an outbreak of disease.'

'Like foot and mouth?'

'Exactly. Every time cattle are moved you have to inform the BCMS.'

313

'And what happens if you don't get a passport?'

'Then you can't move the animal off the farm unless it's to a knacker's yard and it can't enter the human food chain.'

'So it's pretty much worthless to you.'

'That's right.'

'And you have to fill out all these forms?' She indicated the mound of untidy papers, suppressing a sudden urge to straighten them. Kath was a great believer in 'tidy desk, tidy mind'. Mike obviously worked differently.

'Not necessarily — you can do it online. Saves on postage but you still have to sit and key it all in. Thank God I have someone who comes in to help. An older lady, Cynthia — you might have seen her around?'

Kath shook her head.

'Well, I couldn't manage without her, that's for sure.' He rubbed his chin with his hand.

'Don't let me hold you back,' said Kath.

'It's OK. You're not. I've done enough for today. I was just finishing off.'

Kath nodded, took a deep breath and said, 'I was passing and, well, I wondered if — '

The doorbell went and Kath froze, the words 'join me for a curry' stuck in her throat like a piece of popcorn gone down the wrong way.

'Ah, that'll be Anne,' said Mike, looking past her up the hall as he got to his feet.

Kath remembered that Anne was the name of the person who'd given Mike the book of poetry. Whoever she was, she must mean a lot to him.

Maybe it was a thoughtful aunt or a friend of the family.

She turned and watched with growing interest while Gladys opened the door and a tall, slim young woman stepped across the threshold into the hall. She wore hipster jeans with legs so long they trailed the ground, ballerina pumps and a short khaki-coloured military-styled jacket. Her sandy-coloured hair was secured in a pony-tail and round her neck was a skinny multi-coloured woven scarf. She looked like a student.

'Hello, Gladys,' she said, and the two women embraced each other with great familiarity.

'Anne!' said Mike and walked up the hall to greet her. She threw her arms around his neck and kissed him on the cheek. He responded by lifting her off her feet for a few seconds and then releasing her from his embrace.

Kath's heart sank. The girl must be half Mike's age. What was he doing with a kid like her? Then she glanced down at her own dowdy clothes and realised how frumpy she looked. Mike might be a farmer but he obviously liked his women trendy. And young. What on earth made her think that he might've been interested in her?

'Kath, this is Anne,' said Mike proudly and the girl advanced on Kath with a wide, genuine smile on her pretty face.

Up close she wasn't quite as young as Kath had first thought — in her early to mid-twenties perhaps. She took the girl's hand in hers and shook it limply.

'Mike's told me all about you,' said Anne,

315

pumping Kath's hand energetically. 'Can't wait to see the hotel once it's opened again. Mike says you're doing it all up.'

'That's right. It'll be quite a change. Wooden floors, subdued lighting, modern furnishings.'

'Wow!' she exclaimed as though Kath had just said something astounding. Her blue eyes flashed with energy. 'We could do with somewhere different to go for a nice meal, you know. You get a bit fed up with the same old places. Well, I do anyway.'

'I was thinking of running a free mini-bus service for big groups,' said Kath, not sure why she offered that nugget of information. To hide her disappointment, perhaps.

'That's a wicked idea,' enthused Anne. 'Isn't it, Mike?'

He laughed indulgently and Kath's stomach churned with jealousy. 'Yeah. Kath's got some great ideas for the hotel. And I'm sure it's going to be a big success.'

Kath smiled weakly. 'What is it you do then, Anne?' she asked, unable to curtail her curiosity.

'Anne's just qualified as a solicitor,' said Mike proudly, while Anne blushed and looked at the floor. 'And she's started her first job with Crawford and McCann up in Belfast.'

'How interesting,' said Kath with a forced smile. Not only was Anne young and beautiful, she was clever too. How could she possible compete with her?

'Right,' said Anne, glancing at her watch and adding in a teasing tone, 'are you ready to come

316

now or what, Mike? I can't hang around here all night, you know.'

'Sure,' he said, pulling on a coat. 'If you'll excuse me, Kath. We're running a bit late . . . '

'Oh, sure. Of course,' she mumbled, took a step backwards and bumped into a plant stand that she hadn't noticed before.

'Careful, love,' said Gladys, reaching out with one arm to steady the wooden pillar.

'Oh, I'm sorry,' said Kath, annoyed at her clumsiness.

'There, I've got it,' said Gladys, smiling. 'No harm done.'

'Kath, weren't you just about to ask me something when the bell went there?' said Mike.

'Oh, it — it was nothing. It doesn't matter.'

'Yes, it does,' he said, pulling up the zip on his coat. 'Look, why don't you go on out to the car, Anne, love, and I'll be there in a minute.'

The girl said goodbye to Kath and Gladys and went outside. Gladys stood in the hall with her arms folded against the chill that came through the open front door.

'What was it you wanted to ask me?' said Mike.

'Oh, I was going to ask . . . ' she said, very slowly, giving herself time to think.

'That's a chilly night out there,' observed Gladys to no one in particular.

'I was going to ask . . . ' Suddenly she remembered the book in her hand. 'If you really meant to give me this for keeps? I just noticed the inscription and realised it was a gift so I

317

came to say that I'll give it back to you once I've finished with it.'

'I meant for you to keep it.'

'No,' said Kath too loudly and Mike looked at her oddly. 'What I mean is, I couldn't possibly keep it. Not when it's something so — so personal. I'm grateful to you for lending it to me, though.'

He shrugged as though he didn't care one way or the other and said, 'Have you had a chance to read much yet?'

'I've just started dipping into it.'

He nodded and said, 'The rain's just coming on. Are you going back up to the farmhouse? We can give you a lift. Save you getting soaked.'

'No, thanks. I'm fine,' she said brightly. 'I've got the car. I was just on my way into Ballyfergus. Thanks anyway.'

'Listen, I owe you dinner from the other night. Are you free next Friday or Saturday?'

'Sorry, Mike,' she said, determined to salvage any dignity she could. 'I'm up to my eyes right now with the hotel.'

'Another time then?'

'I just can't see me finding the time,' said Kath, realising as she said it how inexcusably rude she sounded. But it didn't matter now. 'Have a good night. Bye, Gladys. Bye, Mike.'

She ducked her head and shot out of the doorway before Mike could say another word. The security light was on outside, illuminating everything in a harsh white light. She made for her car and opened the door, glancing up once to see Anne sitting in the driving seat of a small

318

red, car. She waved furiously at Kath, her features blurred by the rain streaming down the window. Kath smiled cheerily and waved back in response. Then she hopped in her car and drove off down the track as fast as she could.

She followed the coast road that snaked into Ballyfergus, not sure if her vision was impaired more by the rain outside or the tears streaming down her face. In spite of her attempts to play down her expectations of Mike, she realised now that she did care for him. She thought she loved him. But you can't love someone you've only just known for a few months, she told herself crossly. And then she remembered that wasn't true. She'd known Mike all her life.

But she couldn't blame Mike for misleading her. He'd done nothing, after all, to encourage her — he'd been gentlemanly and polite, nothing more. It was her desperation that had caused her to misread his friendly concern as something more. He was only helping her because of who she was — Brendan O'Connor's daughter — not because he had any interest in her.

Anyway, if Anne was typical of the type of girl he liked, Kath would never even get off the starting blocks with him. She was too old and too conservative in her tastes. And Anne and Mike were obviously very well suited — they shared a passion for literature which Kath couldn't even understand, never mind enthuse about.

The wipers whipped the rain off the windscreen and Kath stared into the darkness ahead. She saw clearly what had led her to such

319

foolishness — loneliness. The desire for a loving, intimate relationship had not evaporated with Carl's absence. All she'd done was project those desires onto Mike. You are pathetic, she told herself angrily. Can't you live without a man in your life?

Annoyed with herself, she wiped the tears from her face with the back of her hand and told herself that she'd better watch the road or she'd end up getting killed. She took her foot off the accelerator until the car was cruising safely within the speed limit.

It was better that she'd found out now before she'd fallen in too deep. Before she'd made a complete fool of herself. She shivered when she imagined how embarrassed Mike would have been if she'd made it clear she was interested in him. How he would have tried to explain, in the gentlest terms, that he did not care for her.

She pulled into the supermarket car park and sat stony-faced in the car for a few moments, composing herself. She would be forty years old on the eighth of November. Her chances of finding the kind of happiness she'd thought she'd found with Carl were slipping away. It was something she was going to have to accept. Her life would not follow the traditional path she'd hoped for.

Kath took a small mirror from her handbag and checked her appearance. She rubbed at the mascara smudges under her eyes until they disappeared and retouched her lipstick. She couldn't expect love to fall into her lap on a half-deserted hillside in East Antrim, could she?

And her chances of meeting someone in a small community like Ballyfergus were slim. She would have to face facts. She was on the shelf.

But, she told herself firmly, it could be a happy and fulfilling life all the same. She had her family: her mother, sister and brother, nieces and nephews. She had the hotel and an exciting future ahead of her. She must start focusing on the blessings she had, rather than those she did not.

And, perhaps, somewhere down the line she might meet a lovely man in the course of her work at the hotel — someone in the hotel trade or even a guest.

Fifteen minutes later she was in a supermarket aisle, extracting a bag of frozen peas from the bottom of a freezer cabinet. This was only her third trip to the supermarket and she was still getting used to the layout and stock. Fresh herbs weren't always available and she had to adapt her favourite recipes according to what she could find. She realised that living in a big city, with easy access to all manner of exotic ingredients, had spoiled her.

Suddenly she felt a sharp tap on the shoulder. She stood upright with the bag of peas in her hand and turned to find a small, rather dumpy woman about her own age standing before her. She was flanked on either side by two children: a boy and a girl.

'I heard you were back,' she said and Kath returned the stranger's smile.

The woman was well dressed in a smart navy suit and heels and her hair was severely scraped back off her pretty face. She looked like she worked in a bank or a building society. On her arm was a wire shopping basket containing two frozen pizzas and a bottle of Coke. Kath had absolutely no idea who she was.

'It's me,' said the woman and her face creased into a familiar grin. Kath recognised those dimples but could not place the face. 'Sharon O'Neill.' The woman laughed. 'Course that's not my name now. You didn't recognise me, did you? But look at you — you've hardly changed at all.'

'Sharon!' said Kath, suddenly recognising her old school friend. Overcome with the emotion of the last few hours, she reached out and gave her a firm hug. 'It's great to see you? How are you? And who are these two?'

'Ryan! Celeste!' barked Sharon. 'Mind your manners. Say 'hello'.'

'Hello,' mumbled the two children and Sharon scowled, clearly not impressed by their response. 'I blame their father,' she said cheerfully and grinned. 'Now what's all this I hear about you taking on the Sallagh Braes?'

'Oh, Sharon. It's a long story. I don't know where to begin.'

'I was sorry to hear about your dad, Kath.'

'Thanks,' said Kath and looked at the ground. The pain of Carl's betrayal might have lessened a little, but the hurt of Brendan's death was as raw as ever.

'Can I have an ice-cream?' said Ryan, who looked about six or seven.

'No, you cannot,' growled Sharon at the boy and then, to Kath, 'I need to get these two home

322

soon. They haven't had their tea yet.'

'Well, it's great to see you, Sharon,' said Kath with genuine enthusiasm, as a flood of happy memories of her schooldays came flooding back. 'Do you still keep in touch with the other girls? Donna and Eileen?'

'Donna's living in Scotland but Eileen came back after university. Do you remember Alan Fairweather, the doctor's son?'

'Oh, yes. He was the year above us at school, wasn't he?'

'Well, she married him.'

'I'm terrible,' confessed Kath. 'I haven't been very good at keeping up with everyone.'

'Mum!' whined Celeste, pulling at the hem of her mother's jacket. 'Can we go home now?'

'In a minute,' said Sharon, shooting a warning glance at her daughter.

'I'm fed up,' chimed in Ryan.

'Don't let me keep you,' said Kath.

'Tell you what — are you doing anything tomorrow night?'

'No.'

'Why don't you come over to mine for a glass of wine then, and we can catch up properly. Let's say around eight. Here, I'll write down my address. Andy'll be out — that's my husband — so we'll have the place to ourselves.'

'Oh, Sharon. I'd really like that. It's great bumping into you, it really is.'

Sharon fumbled in her handbag and pulled out a biro and a scrap of paper. She scribbled an address and phone number on it and handed it to Kath.

'It's great to see you too, Kath. I dare say we've a lot of catching up to do.'

You don't know the half of it, thought Kath, as she watched Sharon shoo her reluctant brood down the aisle towards the checkout. Kath smiled and continued with her shopping.

The encounter with her old school friend had lifted Kath's spirits. She'd been too wrapped up with her plans for the hotel to realise that she missed having friends close by. She spoke to Emmy on the phone once a week, but it wasn't the same. She needed friends here too, as well as family, and Sharon was one of the nicest people she'd ever known.

Right now she was working the longest hours she'd ever worked in her life but she knew that wouldn't, and couldn't, go on long term. Once the hotel was established, she resolved to join some clubs or maybe the local gym. She needed to carve out a social life for herself, just like she had done when she first moved to Boston. It was foolish to place all your expectations for happiness on one person — that was the mistake she'd made with Mike Mulholland.

On the way home, she stopped for a takeaway, picked up a DVD and drove home, determined not to let depression get the better of her. She passed the hotel, took the track to the farmhouse and, through sheer force of will, drove past the Mulhollands' bungalow without giving it so much as a second glance.

26

Many weeks had passed since that incident at Bridget's house, but David couldn't put it out of his mind. Absentmindedly, he put the car into third gear and the diesel engine whined in protest. He braked until the noise stopped and the big Land Rover was barely nudging thirty miles per hour. He wanted the journey to Viv's sister's house, where he was due to pick up Murray, to last a little longer. He wanted time to think.

He rolled the window down, leaned his brown arm on the sill and inhaled the fresh crisp air. May was the most beautiful month, he thought. Spring was well under way with the promise of summer and the long light-filled nights just round the corner. The trees were in almost in full leaf, the air temperature was rising daily and, in his forest, the noisy hordes of summer visitors had yet to arrive. He passed one of the Mulhollands' fields full of ewes and their six-week-old lambs frolicking in the warm sunshine. And yet the beauty of nature around him wasn't enough to quell his troubled thoughts.

What exactly was it his mother had said? 'He is no grandson of mine' or words to that effect. Several times since, he'd questioned her about why she said it. She'd said that it was simply a reaction to the stress she was under at the time.

She'd said that she was sorry. She'd said that they were only words, that they didn't mean anything. But he didn't believe her. He knew that his mother and Murray didn't exactly hit it off together. Murray was — well — sometimes he was a difficult child. Perhaps Fiona simply meant that she disowned him because of his bad behaviour, which was a horrible thing to say to your own flesh and blood. Or maybe she meant it in the most literal way possible — that the child was not his son but another man's. His stomach tightened into a ball at the idea and he told himself to calm down.

And then he allowed himself to consider, for just one minute, how he would feel if this were true. If he knew for certain that Murray was not his child, would he still feel the same about him?

David swallowed and blinked away the tears that threatened to blur his vision. He wished he was a better man, but he wasn't. He was only human with the same frailties and flaws as any other man. For when he asked himself this question the truthful answer was he didn't know.

Carol, Viv's elder sister, lived in Seacliff Estate, a sprawling council housing scheme that had been built in the 1980s to house the ever-burgeoning population of Ballyfergus. It had originally been populated by many out-of-towners and the estate soon became run-down with drug, drink and crime problems linked to Loyalist paramilitary organisations.

The ongoing Peace Process aimed to find a way for Catholics (many of whom were Republicans) and Protestants (many of whom were Loyalists) to live together in harmony. But parts of Ballyfergus remained resolutely Loyalist strongholds where paramilitaries ruled the streets.

However, in spite of its problems, the little community at Seacliff had resurged in recent years, setting up a community council, badgering official bodies for funding for a play park and multi-sports facility for teenagers. The residents had planted flowerbeds and trees and this year the estate had won the Northern Ireland Amenity Award for Best Kept Large Estate, an accolade that would've been unthinkable only a decade before. The pride of the community in their achievement was well deserved.

David pulled up outside Carol's house, got out of the car and surveyed the street. Even though the Twelfth of July, the anniversary of the 1690 Battle of the Boyne and the start of the 'marching season' which celebrated it, was nearly two months away, Carol's house, like many others along the tidy street, sported flags. The 'Red Hand of Ulster' flag flew proudly from the flagpole on Carol's well-kept mid-terraced house, declaring to the outside world that the residents within were loyal to the crown.

All the way along the little street, the kerb was carefully painted red, white and blue and similarly coloured bunting was strung between the street lamps. Though David wasn't a Republican, or a Catholic, he found the display faintly threatening. He attributed this to the fact that he held liberal, middle-of-the road political views and to the fact that his father had been a Catholic.

David locked the car, walked up the short drive, rang the doorbell and waited. Carol opened the door to him and immediately a look of surprise registered on her face. She was wearing tight jeans and a baby-pink jumper and fluffy socks, the same colour as the jumper, on her feet. Similar in build to Viv, they shared the same dyed-blonde hair. But Carol's face was altogether softer and the contrast didn't stop with appearances — Carol was a warmer, nicer person than her sister. David used to think that he'd chosen the wrong sister and, even though he now loved Simone, he still had a soft spot for Carol.

'Ach, David,' she said, sounding exasperated, 'did she not phone you?'

'Viv? No.'

'Ach,' she said again and tutted. 'She was supposed to phone you to tell you that there'd been a change of plan.'

He looked at her blankly and felt the familiar anger, that only Viv could induce in him, start to simmer.

'Look, you'd better come on in. We can't stand in the doorway discussing this for all the world to hear,' she said and peered out, as though checking for eavesdroppers in the deserted street. She stepped back to allow him entry to her neat little hallway, shut the door behind him and said, 'I'll make you a cup of tea.'

David opened his mouth to protest and then shut it again. There was no sound from inside,

328

indicating, as he already suspected, that Murray was not here.

Maybe Carol might be able to shed some light on the truth about Murray. She was a woman who called things as she saw them and, unlike Viv, found it difficult to tell lies convincingly.

He went into the tidy lounge, placed his car keys on the glass-topped coffee table and listened to the sounds of Carol making tea. The room was dominated by an oversized state-of-the-art TV. The silver monster looked incongruous amongst Carol's silk flower arrangements, bold-patterned sofas and fussy ornaments. By the time Carol came into the room with two mugs of hot steaming liquid in her hands, David's anger had abated somewhat.

'Where's Peter and the kids?' he asked, referring to Carol's husband and their two young children, Rachel and Craig.

'He took them to the swimming pool,' said Carol, handing him a beige earthenware mug. 'He always does on a Sunday afternoon.'

David nodded. 'So tell me, what's going on with Viv?'

'Well,' said Carol, sitting down opposite him on the sofa, 'Viv said she had to go up to Belfast and she wouldn't be back in time to collect Murray from you so she'd have to take him with her.'

'But we arranged last week that I'd take him to see that new film at the IMC in Ballymena! And I'm not late,' he said, glancing at his watch.

'I know. I know,' said Carol with a big sigh.

329

'What can I say, David? She changed her mind and she shouldn't have done. She said she'd call you.'

'When was this?'

'About an hour ago.'

'I never got a call.'

'Maybe she called your mobile.'

David unhooked his mobile phone from his belt, pressed a few buttons and shook his head. 'Nope. Nobody's called, sent a text or left a message. I'll try her now.'

He speed-dialled Viv's mobile number and waited, while Carol looked on in silence. The phone tripped immediately to Viv's answering service.

Ending the call, he said, 'She's switched it off.'

'Maybe she couldn't get through on your mobile.'

'That's utter bollocks and you and I both know it,' he said with feeling.

Carol bowed her head and her face coloured. Not because of David's profanity — she was quite capable of dishing them out herself — but because, he guessed, she was embarrassed by her sister's behaviour.

'I'm sorry, Carol,' he sighed, 'for taking it out on you. I know it's got nothing to do with you.' He would save his anger for the next time he saw Viv.

'I really don't know why she didn't call you,' said Carol, shaking her head. 'Making you drive all the way out here for nothing.'

'I think I know,' he said darkly and she raised her eyebrows in surprise.

330

'You do?'

'Yes. Did she tell you that Simone and I are getting married?'

'She did. Congratulations. Simone's a nice girl,' said Carol openly. 'I was in the same year as her at school.'

'Did Viv tell you how she felt about it?'

'Mmm,' said Carol and she put the rim of the mug to her lips, so hiding her face. Between sips of tea, she mumbled, 'She mentioned something about it,' which David suspected was more than a slight understatement.

'Well, she had plenty to say about it when I told her. She wasn't one bit pleased and I think this is her way of getting back at me.'

Far from defending her sister, Carol said, 'Perhaps you're right, David. To tell you the truth she wasn't happy when she told me.'

'I don't know why it should bother her. Apart from the fact that she seemed to think I might not keep up the maintenance payments.'

Carol pursed her lips, as though trying to stop herself from speaking, nodded slowly and looked at the floor. Then she shuffled her feet and fiddled with the armrest cover with her free hand even though it wasn't out of place.

'Why she should think that, I've no idea,' David added and waited. When she said nothing he decided to tell her something that he and Simone had not yet shared with anyone. 'Did she tell you that Simone's expecting?' he said, well aware that Viv knew nothing of it.

'No, no, she didn't,' said Carol and she put the mug down carefully on the coffee table and clasped her hands together between her knees. 'Viv didn't mention that at all. Why, that's — that's wonderful news.'

'Thanks, Carol. It's the first time for Simone. For me, too, of course.'

'Hmm,' said Carol, examining the skin on the back of her right hand.

He waited again but she said nothing more.

'Well . . . thanks for the tea, Carol.' He set the mug down on the coffee table, collected his keys and stood up.

'I'm sorry you've come all this way for nothing,' she said, getting out of her seat.

'And I'm sorry to involve you, Carol. I know Viv often leaves Murray with you. Thanks for looking after him. He loves you, you know.'

'And I love him,' said Carol simply.

David smiled at her and walked into the hall. He pressed his back against the wall to allow her access to the front door. She'd just placed her hand on the latch, when he said, 'A few weeks ago my mother said something really strange about Murray.'

'Oh, what was that?' said Carol, looking up at him with her hand frozen on the door handle. In her stocking feet she was only five foot three inches in height to his six feet.

'She said that Murray wasn't her grandson.'

Carol let out a little strangulated sound like a puppy's yelp and stared at David. For a moment she seemed lost for words — her face contorted and she chewed her bottom lip. At last she spoke.

'I've always liked you, David, and I'm sorry

that things didn't work out for you and Viv.' She took her hand off the latch and played nervously with one of her gold hoop earrings. 'David, maybe you and Simone . . . what I mean is, I think you both deserve a fresh start.'

'A fresh start?' he said and held his breath.

'David, there's something you should know about Murray.'

'What, Carol?'

'You should walk away now,' she blurted out suddenly and then put her hand over her mouth.

'What is it that I should know, Carol?' he said calmly, while the blood pounded in his head. He felt his brain was about to explode.

'It's just . . . I can't tell you that,' she said and blushed. 'No. Forget I said that. I shouldn't have said anything!' He opened his mouth to speak but she said very firmly, 'You'd better go now, David. Please go.'

David stepped outside and heard the door close quietly behind him. Now that he was out of Carol's sight, his composure evaporated. He put his hands over his eyes and dragged them down slowly his face. His face was covered with sweat. He tried to think of all the possible reasons for what Carol had just said.

Was there something wrong with Murray? Some sort of inherited trait on Viv's side that the family were embarrassed about? Something that they didn't want him to find out about? Like mental illness or a low IQ — that might explain why he found it difficult to connect with him. But as far as he knew Murray was doing OK at school. And though he tried to fight it, David's

333

mind kept coming back to the most obvious and the most feared explanation — that the child was not his.

He knew only one other person who might be able to shed some light on the mystery — Simone. With her level-headedness and common sense he trusted her judgement more than he trusted his own.

He got back in the car and glanced at the house. He was sure he caught a glimpse of Carol's face at the window, behind the net curtains. He turned on the engine and pulled away from the house.

This time he drove the ten miles home as quickly as he could, frustrated by the Saturday afternoon drivers snaking slowly along the coast road. There were few opportunities for overtaking but, when they did present themselves, he took them recklessly and incurred a chorus of angry toots and beeps from the oncoming cars he only just managed to miss.

Normally he loved this journey and, like the other drivers, relaxed into a slower driving pace that permitted the enjoyment of the dramatic scenery. But today all he could think about was getting home to Simone and finding some way to quell the torment inside his head.

He found her upstairs resting on the bed, still wearing her pyjamas and a fluffy, white dressing-gown. She lay with her head propped up on two pillows and in her hands was a magazine titled *25 Beautiful Kitchens*. For a few fleeting seconds he wondered why she was reading about kitchens when they had a perfectly good one downstairs. But he had no time to discuss such frivolities now.

'Hi there,' she said pleasantly, without lowering the magazine. 'Where's Murray?'

'Viv cocked up the arrangements. She's gone and taken him to Belfast.'

Simone put the magazine to one side and sat up, resting on her elbows. A frown appeared across her brow and she said, 'But why did she do that? Didn't she know that you were supposed to be taking him to the cinema?'

'She did. But never mind that now.' He threw the car keys on top of the dresser by the door and sat down on the edge of the bed. 'I've something much more important to tell you.'

As he related the conversation he'd just had with Carol, Simone's expressive face reflected her changing emotions — first surprise and annoyance at Viv's behaviour, and then confusion and shock at Carol's revelation.

'And that's all she said?'

'Yes. 'There's something you should know about Murray' and 'You should walk away now'. She clammed up after that. Wouldn't say any more. In fact she asked me to leave straight after that.'

'Hmm,' said Simone.

'Well, what do you think? After what Mum said at Bridget's house . . . don't you think it's odd?'

'Yes. I do, David,' she said and stared at him for a few seconds, concern clouding her face. 'Listen, I'm gasping for a cuppa,' she said

335

suddenly. 'You wouldn't make us one, would you, love?'

'Sure,' he said, standing up and remembering that he'd left her only an hour ago suffering from morning sickness. 'I'm sorry. How thoughtless of me! How are you feeling?'

'Oh, I'm fine now. The sickness has all gone. I'm just being lazy really, lying here. You go on down and put the kettle on and I'll be ready in a minute.'

'And then we can have a proper talk about it,' he said.

'Yes.'

He left her and descended the stairs, put the kettle on and laid out some biscuits on a plate. By the time he'd made the tea, laid a tray with mugs, spoons, sugar and the plate of biscuits, Simone was in the lounge fully dressed in brown cords and a cosy-looking cream jumper.

'I would've brought it upstairs,' he said. 'You didn't need to get out of bed.'

'It's OK. It was about time I got up anyway.' She took a custard cream and a mug of tea and sat down on the olive green sofa that had seen better days. 'Come and sit beside me,' she added and patted the seat.

David obeyed, ignoring the tea and biscuits. His stomach was in too much turmoil to contemplate eating or drinking a thing.

'Well?' he said impatiently, anxious to hear her assessment. 'What do you think?'

She munched on the biscuit thoughtfully.

'David,' she said at last, in a measured tone he'd not heard her use before, 'I don't know

336

what these things mean. What do *you* think they mean?'

'They could mean a lot of things. Or they could mean nothing. It could just be careless talk. Nothing more than that,' he said, trying to convince himself more than her. 'But . . . '

'But what?'

He sighed heavily and said in a quiet voice, 'I think the most likely explanation is that Murray isn't my son.' Voicing the thought for the first time made him ashamed. He felt like he had disowned the child before he even had any proof of his true identity. Simone continued to stare at him until he said, 'You're not saying much, Simone.'

She coughed. 'David, there is something I've thought about Murray for a long time.'

David sat bolt upright. 'What?'

'Look, the reason I didn't say anything before was that it's not always true. And it just didn't seem important. I thought Murray was the exception to the general rule.'

'What rule?' he said as his impatience grew.

'Well, you know the way that Murray has a double crown?' she said, touching the top of her head.

'Yes?' said David, instinctively touching the top of his own head. 'You mean his swirlies?' he added, using Murray's term for them.

She nodded. 'Well, the thing is, generally speaking, that's a trait normally inherited from one parent.' She paused. 'And neither you nor Viv have it. I looked.'

'So you're saying that one of his parents must

337

have had a double crown?'

'No, not necessarily, but it's usually — no, almost always — the case. Ask any midwife.' She stared at him in silence for a few seconds and then went on. 'Look, it's not an exact science. But there have been some experiments carried out on mice and a gene called Frizzled 6 was identified as being responsible for mutations of hair growth — '

'Why didn't you tell me this before, Simone?' David interrupted, full of hurt. 'We promised that we'd always be truthful with each other. That we'd never tell lies.'

'I haven't lied to you, David. It just never occurred to me until recently that Murray's double crown could be significant. It was only after your mum said what she did at Bridget's that I started to think about it seriously. And,' she added hastily, 'I didn't want to say anything until — ' She stopped.

'Until you knew all the facts?' he asked and she nodded.

David stared at her — she met his gaze steadily and bit her lip.

'So,' he said slowly, 'what you're saying is that you have doubts that Murray is mine?'

Simone shut her eyes and nodded slowly. 'I do. And it's as much a gut feeling as based on anything concrete. I just don't see any resemblance between you and him. Not in looks, temperament, manner. Nothing. But all of that is just speculation. The thing about the double crown, well, I think it's significant. I've done quite a bit of research into it.'

'You have been busy,' observed David dryly.

'I didn't mean to keep all this from you, David. I started to read up on it and, well, one thing led to another.'

David got up and took a lightweight fleece from the back of the front door which opened directly onto the outside.

'Where are you going?' asked Simone.

'Out for a walk. I need to think.'

'There's just one more thing, David. And then I'll not say another word on the subject. Unless you want me to.'

'What?'

'You and Viv weren't together when she announced she was pregnant.'

'No, but we got back together as soon as she told me.'

'I see,' said Simone and David opened the door and went outside, fully aware of the point Simone was trying to make.

In the two months during which he and Viv were apart he had no idea what she did or who she saw. It was entirely conceivable that she'd gone out with someone else — and it was also possible that she'd slept with him.

David ambled slowly through the trees, avoiding the well-trodden paths through the forest where he was bound to meet people he knew out for a Sunday walk. The fun-filled day he'd planned for Murray and himself had turned to misery and the beauty of the day had evaporated.

He tried to imagine how he would feel if someone told him for sure that Murray was not his. Would he still love him? Would he feel the same about him? He couldn't answer those questions. He didn't want to. Even the possibility that it might be true made him feel physically ill. He shoved his hands deeper into his pockets, even though it was not at all cold, and walked on through the quiet forest. The silence was broken only by the crack of twigs underfoot, the call of birds and the occasional far-off shriek of a child playing somewhere in the dense woodland.

Then he told himself to calm down and think rationally. What was the evidence on which his doubts were based? Two throwaway comments, from his mother and Carol, both of which could mean any number of things or nothing at all. And Simone's speculations based on nothing more than the fact that Murray had a double crown. That, basically, was it.

David sighed and felt the tension leave his shoulders. He had allowed his imagination to run away with him. Maybe the prospect of marriage and another child on the way had unsettled him. He wanted Simone and the baby more than anything in the world, but he'd made a complete mess of his relationship with Viv. He couldn't bear for that to happen again. He was, he conceded, a little anxious about the future. And this had made him irrational.

Now, he could see quite clearly. The truth was that, much as he admired and trusted Simone, she too, like him, had simply got a bit carried away. Once the tiniest doubt about Murray had seeded itself, they'd simply sought out the evidence to support that theory. It would be just

340

as easy to find hundreds of pieces of evidence to disprove this premise. Like Murray's brown eyes, a trait he shared with David.

A wave of love washed over David when he pictured Murray's nervous little face and he felt utterly ashamed of himself. He resolved there and then to put all speculation about his son's parentage out of his mind.

Soon he would have a new wife and a new family and Murray was very definitely going to be a part of it. This nonsense about his firstborn son would have to stop now. He turned on his heel and, with a renewed sense of purpose and a lighter heart, he headed back to the cottage to tell Simone his decision.

27

The official opening of the hotel on Sunday 7 May at seven in the evening was a low-key affair. Kath had arranged a cocktail party for friends, family, staff and the local businesses which had either helped with the renovation or would be supplying the hotel with goods and services.

By seven thirty the chic foyer was filled with the eighty or so invited guests and buzzing with the hum of conversation and murmurs of admiration. Kath's stomach churned with nerves. She noticed the absence of only one guest — Mike Mulholland — and wondered where he was. Gladys was already here, chatting to Fiona and Bridget over by the trays of drinks arranged on the reception desk.

'I didn't expect such a big turnout,' Kath whispered to John Routledge. 'I think practically everyone we invited has turned up!'

'Sure people in Ballyfergus would come to the opening of an envelope if there's free booze and food involved,' he said with a mischievous smile and Kath giggled. 'Anyway,' he went on, talking to her in a side whisper while they continued to scan the room. 'Half the town's talking about you and this hotel. Do you think they were going to give up the opportunity for a good old gawk?'

'Oh, John. You're terrible,' she laughed, finding that his humour helped to disperse her nerves. She sighed, smoothed imaginary creases from her clothes and said, 'Well, I suppose I'd better go and circulate.'

'Mmm,' said John, taking a gulp of champagne, 'me too. See you later.'

Kath moved amongst the guests, exchanging small talk and eavesdropping on conversations as she passed through the small crowd. Overhearing the genuinely enthusiastic comments about the hotel lifted her spirits. Hopefully these people would go home tonight and tell all their friends and family how great it was. If each person told ten other people, that was seven hundred people. And word of mouth recommendation was, by far, the most effective form of advertising.

'Thanks for joining us,' she said to Ben, the new chef, and stopped to chat with his pretty, pregnant fiancée. Then she spied Bridget coming towards her and excused herself.

'I love your dress,' said Bridget, eyeing the wrap dress Kath had bought last Christmas for her office party.

Kath looked down at the dress and her knee-high black boots and remembered that she'd bought the outfit to impress Carl. She needn't have bothered — he backed out of the party at the last minute. When she came to think of it, he very rarely accompanied her to public events. And he never, ever invited her to his works 'dos'. He said she'd be utterly bored — but now, of course, she knew the real reason he didn't want her there . . .

'Is it a real Diane von Furstenberg?' said Bridget, fingering the sleeve of Kath's dress — it

343

was vintage-patterned silk jersey in grey, black and white.

'Sure is,' said Kath, remembering that she'd paid over three hundred dollars for it in Bloomingdales. 'But it'll be a while before I'll be able to afford clothes like this again.' Then, changing the subject, she said, 'You look nice too, Bridget. Where did you get that suit?'

Bridget was wearing a tight, short pinstripe skirt with a matching fitted jacket.

'Karen Millen,' said Bridget, opening the jacket to reveal a leopard print camisole, trimmed in hot pink. The inside of the jacket was lined with the same fabric.

'Wow!' said Kath, surprised that the rather conservative mother-of-three would wear something so bold.

'You don't think it's too 'footballers' wives', do you?' said Bridget anxiously. 'I'm trying to update my image.'

'No, not at all,' said Kath, not as convinced as she sounded. British footballers' wives had a reputation for extravagant, glamorous clothes that could sometimes be a bit on the tarty side. And this suit came dangerously close to that category. 'I think it looks great!' She believed that, in this instance, her sister's confidence was more important than the truth.

'Wow, this is great!' said Sharon, who was dressed up to the nines for the occasion and holding a full glass of champagne in her hand.

Although Kath's bank balance screamed that she could ill afford to be splashing out on real champagne, she felt it was important to create the right first impression.

'Aye, it is,' agreed Sharon's tall, gentle husband, with a nod of his head.

Kath had come to know, and like him, as a man of sound heart but few words.

'Good luck, Kath,' said Ned, when Kath came within earshot.

'Thanks, Ned. And thank you. Without your support, I couldn't have done this.' She resolved to persuade the bank to discharge Ned's letter of guarantee just as soon as she could.

'I really appreciate your help in the garden, David,' she said to her brother, who was sitting with his arm wrapped protectively around Simone on one of the new sofas.

'Oh, it was nothing,' he replied, brushing off her thanks. 'You take full credit for all this, Kath. You deserve it.'

'Darling!' cried Fiona, coming over and surprising Kath by giving her a hug — an uncharacteristic gesture from a mother who was not normally demonstrative in public. 'This is . . . what you've done is just amazing, Kath. I can't get over it. I'm so proud of you.'

'Do you think Dad would've liked it?' said an embarrassed Kath, deflecting the focus from herself.

'I'm sure of it,' Fiona said decisively and then added, blinking back tears, 'I heard some good news today.'

'What's that?'

'The estate agent phoned just after five. I got the flat!' And she beamed, happier than Kath had seen her in months. 'The daughter that thought my offer wasn't enough finally caved in and agreed to sell.'

'Oh, Mum, that's wonderful news,' said Kath with relief, knowing how her mother yearned for a place of her own. 'When do you move in?'

'Beginning of June, as soon as the legalities are all sorted out.'

'That's still a month away, though,' said Kath thoughtfully. 'You know, my offer of a room in the farmhouse still stands, Mum.'

'No, I couldn't move out now — much as I'd love to. It would be too much of a snub to Bridget and Ned. Anyway, it's only for a few more weeks. Don't worry about me, love. I'll be fine.' She squeezed Kath's hand and wandered away to talk to Willie Ross.

'Your father would've been very proud,' said Frank Morrison, during a quiet moment when Kath managed to catch him standing alone.

'I just hope we can make it pay, Frank,' said Kath in earnestness, the smile falling from her face for the first time that evening. 'You know I've put every last penny into the hotel. It has to start making a profit soon or I'm in deep trouble.'

'I know,' said Frank, popping one of Ben's exquisite canapés — crayfish and chive salad in a pastry cup — into his mouth. He chewed and swallowed. 'Lovely,' he said, smacking his lips. 'Well, you're putting a brave face on it, Kath. If you're anxious, it doesn't show. Not to them anyway.' He indicated, with a wide sweep of his hand, all the people in the room.

'That's something I learned from Dad. Always

put on a cheerful front, no matter what's happening in the background.'

Frank laughed, and Kath realised that she regarded him more as a friend than a bank manager now.

'That was your dad, all right,' he said. 'He was always a good front man. Right up until the end.'

By eight thirty some guests were starting to leave. Kath had just said goodbye to Mr and Mrs Lennon, the fruiterers, when she heard a familiar voice from behind that stopped her in her tracks.

'Hello, Kath,' said Mike, and she turned to greet him with a big smile pasted on her face, ready to face Anne too.

But he was alone and she noted immediately that he'd made a big effort. He looked out of place in his suit and tie, as he had done at Brendan's funeral. In his hand was a full glass of champagne — he twirled the thin stem of the glass between his strong forefinger and thumb.

'Oh, thanks for coming, Mike,' she said brightly. 'I thought maybe you weren't going to make it.'

'Sorry I'm late. I got held up. But I wouldn't have missed this for the world.' He cast an approving glance round the room.

'Where's Anne?' said Kath.

'Anne?' he said, his brow furrowing into a frown. 'I didn't know she was invited?'

'Oh, I just assumed . . . never mind. It's good to see you.'

'And you too,' he replied and stared at her.

Kath looked away.

'What — ' she began.

'Kath — ' he said at the same time and they both stopped.

'Sorry,' she said, 'you go first.'

'No, you,' he said and the awkwardness between them made Kath wish for their former intimacy.

But the unease that now existed between them was entirely of her doing. She had started to love him and then found out that he wasn't free, just like Carl. She'd given herself a good talking to and resolved to keep her distance — it would be better for all concerned. That was why she had declined his invitation to dinner. After that, while he'd remained as cordial as ever and continued to take a keen interest in the hotel, he'd never broached the subject again.

'I was just going to ask you what you thought of the finished product?' she said. 'You haven't seen it since the curtains went up and the soft furnishings were delivered.'

'I think it's great,' he replied without taking his eyes off her. 'I'm sure it'll be a great success.'

There was a short pause and she said, 'Oh, I meant to say — thanks for the Farmers' Union booking.'

He shrugged. 'We always go out for a meal when we have our annual meeting. We might as well make it here,' he said, downplaying his role in what Kath imagined must have been a difficult task: persuading the rather conservative farmers to change from their traditional venue, and now her rival, the Marine.

'Well, I really appreciate the business.'

'I'm sure the food here'll be better than the

Marine anyway. John was telling me you've got a great chef.'

'Yes, he's marvellous. He did the canapés. Here, have you tried them?' She lifted a tray off a nearby coffee table and proffered it to Mike.

'No, thanks,' he said without looking at the contents.

She set the tray back down, feeling snubbed. She found her glass, put it to her lips and took a sip of the fizzy champagne.

'Kath?'

'Yes?'

'Have I done something to upset or offend you?' he said carefully.

'Yes,' she said quickly, playing for time. 'You wouldn't try one of my canapés!'

'No,' he said, quite serious. 'That's not what I mean.'

He paused then and she felt obliged to fill the silence.

'Of course you haven't done anything to upset me, Mike!' she said brightly and forced a little laugh. 'What makes you think that?' She tried to avoid eye contact.

'It's hard to say. Over the past few weeks, I just got the impression that maybe you didn't want me around.'

'Don't be daft, Mike,' she said, dropping the forced jocularity and looking directly at him. 'Nothing could be further from the truth.' Briefly she placed her hand over his — the one holding the glass — and said, struggling to control the emotion in her voice, 'You are a very dear friend, Mike. And I hope you always will be.'

349

Suddenly the tension in his face disappeared and he revealed his teeth in a wide grin. The weathered skin round his eyes crinkled like a fan and his dark eyes twinkled. All of a sudden, the air around Kath became thick like syrup. She felt she might faint and steadied herself by holding onto the back of a sofa.

'That's alright then,' he said.

Kath smiled and blinked. Why oh why could she only fall for men that were already taken? Was there something wrong with her that made decent bachelors run a mile? Well, she just bloody well hoped that that Anne 'whatever-her-name-was' realised what a very special guy she had in Mike Mulholland!

★ ★ ★

Fiona took a sip of champagne and listened as Gladys and Bridget shared anecdotes about children — Gladys's grand-daughter Joanna and Bridget's Laura were the same age and good friends at school. Fiona relished the sensation of the bubbles bursting on her tongue and the light-headedness that accompanied each glass. She had never been drunk in her life — this was the closest she'd ever come and she wondered why she'd never tried it before.

She straightened the sleeve of her Jacque Vert black dress and idly watched the well-dressed, familiar figures in the beautiful room. It reminded her of similar soirées in the days when the hotel was making money and she and Brendan were the toast of Ballyfergus.

Fiona's spirits were higher than they'd been in months. Of course she would never again feel as safe and as secure as she had before the tragedy. Brendan's death, the loss of the hotel and, most of all, her home had stripped away the security that she'd once taken so much for granted. She had not yet forgiven him for all the things that he'd done. She wondered if she would ever find inside herself the grace that was necessary to do that.

But tonight, for once, the gloom and despondency with which she battled daily had lifted a little and she was happy. She looked around the room with satisfaction. The transformation in the décor was utterly amazing and, while it had at first come as a shock, she could see that it was necessary to bring the business into the twenty-first century. She loved the serene, restful tones of brown and beige and the beautiful chandeliers and the simplicity of the design. She was so very, very proud of Kath.

She wondered what Brendan would make of it all and tears sprang to her eyes. Quickly, she wiped them away discreetly and told herself firmly that this was not the time or the place. So she put a big smile on her face and tuned back into the conversation.

'Give them a few years and they'll change their minds about that one,' laughed Gladys.

'What's this?' said Fiona brightly.

'I was just telling Gladys that Joanna and Laura have decided that they will never like boys,' explained Bridget.

Just then Gladys said, 'Oh, excuse me a

351

moment I must go and talk to Ester Crawford. Haven't seen her for ages. Great party!'

'Gladys always loved a good party,' observed Fiona, giving her friend a little wave.

'It seems to be going very well, doesn't it?'

'Mmm,' murmured Fiona, catching sight of Kath and Mike Mulholland engaged in deep conversation on the other side of the spacious room.

She thought they made a lovely couple but, although Fiona thought Mike had a soft spot for Kath, she had shown no interest in him. She was probably still pining after that Carl Scholtz. Fiona pursed her lips and took another mouthful of champagne. If she could get her hands on him, she thought angrily, she'd give him a piece of her mind. He'd broken her daughter's heart and she would never forgive him for that.

She'd never taken to him in the first place. She thought back to the last time she and Brendan had visited Kath. Carl had taken them all out for lunch at some swanky restaurant in a big hotel overlooking the public gardens in the centre of Boston. What was the hotel called? The Four Seasons.

The restaurant was awash with florals, frills and flounces and old portraits on the walls. Carl had insisted on ordering a tasting menu for them all, which meant that they got five very small courses of fussy, complicated food that was outrageously priced. It was all too pretentious for Fiona — she'd have much preferred a decent steak and some vegetables she recognised.

Carl was at pains to demonstrate he was on

first name terms with the staff and blethered on about all the awards the restaurant had won. Fiona came away with the distinct impression that Carl thought they were country bumpkins. Of course, she'd tried to voice her reservations about Carl to Kath, but she was having none of it. She was in love with the man and, in her eyes, he was faultless.

'Mum, you're away with the fairies,' said Bridget good-humouredly, interrupting Fiona's thoughts.

'Sorry, what did you say?'

'Would you like another drink, Mum?'

'Oh,' said Fiona looking at the near-empty champagne flute in her hand. 'No. I think I'd better leave it at that. I don't want to end up embarrassing myself.'

Bridget lifted a fresh glass off the tray behind them on the reception desk and said, 'What were you thinking about just then?'

'Oh, nothing much. Well, actually, I was thinking about Kath and Mike Mulholland,' said Fiona, watching as Kath laughed at something Mike had said.

'What about them?'

'I think they'd make a lovely couple, don't you?'

'No, not at all,' said Bridget quickly. 'Mike's not Kath's type. She likes her men much more sophisticated. Men like Carl Scholtz. Why would she be interested in a farmer from Ballyfergus?'

'He's an intelligent man. He's been to university and he's a very successful business-man. She could do a lot worse.'

'Don't forget I know Mike better than you do, Mum. And I really don't think he and Kath are in the least bit suited.'

'Well, you may be right, Bridget. If it's meant to be, it'll be. If not, it won't. Simple as that. There's nothing you or I or anyone can do to alter the course of true love.'

There was a short silence which Bridget broke suddenly. 'Did I tell you I was having a dinner party soon? I've asked John Routledge and I'm going to ask Kath.'

Bridget put her glass down on the desk as a sickening feeling engulfed her. She wished it was just the effect of too much champagne but it was more than that.

'I might as well go and do it now while I remember,' she said and took a short step forward.

'Wait a minute,' said Fiona sharply, and she touched her daughter lightly on the sleeve of her jacket.

'What?' said Bridget a little irritably, not taking her eyes off Kath and Mike.

'I didn't know John Routledge was a friend of yours and Ned's.'

'He's not.'

'So why are you inviting him to dinner?' Fiona held her breath as she waited for Bridget to answer.

'I fancy doing a little bit of matchmaking,' said Bridget with a mischievous glint in her eye. 'Don't you think they'd make a great couple? They get on really well together.'

'Bridget, I really don't think that's a good

idea . . . ' began Fiona, unsure what to say next.

'Why ever not? They're both single and John's a lovely guy. You know how highly Dad rated him. I think that Kath doesn't even see him — you know, in a romantic way. At the hotel it's all business. In a different environment, over a few glasses of wine, maybe she'll notice him.'

'But . . . but . . . ' stammered Fiona, struggling to think of a valid objection to Bridget's plan.

'You just wait and see,' said Bridget, patting her mother's hand, which was clasping her arm.

Fiona responded by clasping her arm more firmly.

'Let go, Mum! You're hurting me!' Bridget stared at her mother in alarm.

'Sorry,' said Fiona, forcing a thin smile and reluctantly withdrawing her hand.

Fiona stood quite still and watched as Bridget moved away into the throng. Suddenly, in the crowded room, she felt utterly alone and helpless. She thought about the letter she'd found in the envelope along with Brendan's will. Thank God none of the children had opened it that day in Brendan's office, when she'd broken the news to them that the family was ruined. Apart from their solicitor and Willie Ross, no one else had read the note and she knew that she could rely entirely on the discretion of both men.

After much soul-searching, she had finally decided to keep the contents of the letter a secret. It was addressed to her after all and Brendan had given no indication as to what he expected, or wanted, her to do with the information contained within it. So it was up to

355

her to decide. There was nothing to be gained from making the contents public — indeed much harm would result to her reputation and Brendan's memory if she did.

She wished he'd never written the damn thing. Why had he done it? Had off-loading his sordid little secret made him feel better? She counted to ten and let the anger disperse. Right now she didn't have time to think about Brendan. Right now, it was the living, not the dead, who needed her attention.

Until tonight she had not imagined any circumstances where she might be forced to reveal the contents of the letter. But now, with Bridget's meddling, she sensed real danger. She told herself not to panic. It was, after all, only a dinner party. There would be other guests and most likely nothing would come of it. But she would have to be alert and watch things closely — and keep her mouth shut.

She remembered the upset she'd caused by letting slip what she knew, or thought she knew, about Murray. She wasn't going to make that same mistake twice.

★   ★   ★

Kath was telling Mike all about the hotel's website and how successful it was proving, when Bridget came up to them.

'Hi, Mike,' she said and then, turning to her sister, she went on, 'Kath, we're having a dinner party on Saturday and I just wondered if you're free.'

356

'Free? Next Saturday?' said Kath and she paused for a moment as though consulting a mental diary — which of course she wasn't because her social diary had just about zilch in it. 'Hmm,' she said, wondering why Bridget had chosen to discuss her dinner party in front of Mike. She wasn't about to ask Mike and Anne, was she? The thought filled Kath with dread — she felt her face turn pink.

'I don't think I've anything on,' she said feebly, unable, on the spur of the moment, to invent a valid-sounding prior engagement. 'I think that should be OK. Thanks.'

'Good,' said Bridget, looking directly at Mike in a weird sort of triumphant way, 'because John Routledge is coming too.'

'Oh, that's nice,' said Kath, wondering what on earth Bridget was up to.

'Well,' said Mike, setting his glass down carefully on a glass-topped side table, 'I suppose I'd better be going.'

'Oh, you don't have to go!' said Kath before she could stop herself and she laughed. 'I mean, the party's not over yet.'

'I think,' he said, glancing over her shoulder, 'that you'll find it is, Kath. Most of the guests have gone.'

'Have they?' said Kath, spinning round on her Gina heels. He was right — only Gladys, John, some staff members and her family were left. She realised with horror that she'd been too busy talking to him to notice. She hoped nobody had noticed what a poor hostess she'd been.

After Mike had said goodnight and left with

357

Gladys, Kath turned to Bridget and said, 'What on earth were you doing talking about a dinner party in front of Mike and then not inviting him and Anne?'

'Anne?'

'You know. His girlfriend.'

Bridget hesitated just for a moment and then said, 'Did you want me to?'

'No,' she answered truthfully. 'But it was a bit rude, Bridget.'

'Was it?' she replied airily.

'Well, I thought so,' said Kath, bewildered by her sister's behaviour. 'Anyway, who else is coming to dinner?'

'The McAlisters and Sheila and Tom Todd,' said Bridget in a tight, pleased-with-herself voice.

'You're not by any chance trying to match-make, are you?' said Kath.

'No, of course not,' said Bridget calmly. 'Now keep your voice down. Here he comes.'

'I'll give Eric and Sandra a lift home now, Kath,' said John, jingling a set of keys in his right hand. 'Unless there's anything else?'

'No, no, you go on home.' She smiled at the two serving staff. 'You've done a great job tonight — thank you. And thanks ever so much, John. I'll see you in the morning.'

'Bright and early,' he replied chirpily. 'We've a big day tomorrow. Our first guests arrive!'

After everyone but immediate family had gone, and the door had been shut and locked behind them, Kath collapsed onto one of the coffee-coloured sofas. She peeled off her boots, wriggled her toes and rested her tired feet on the big wooden coffee table. She folded her arms across her chest, still annoyed with Bridget.

She was perfectly capable of choosing her own men, thank you very much. But then again, she hadn't a very good track record at it, had she? It wasn't that she'd any objection to spending an evening in John's company — far from it. It was just that she would be mortified when he realised it was a set-up. Sometimes Bridget could be a real pain.

While Kath pondered all this Fiona made tea for everyone and then they all sat down around the big coffee table in the lounge area.

'Well, Kath,' said Ned when they all had hot cups of tea and coffee in front of them, 'I think that was a great success.'

There were murmurs of assent around the table and Kath said, 'Thanks, Ned. And thanks to all of you for coming along and supporting me.' She yawned and added, 'Well, I don't know about the rest of you, but I'm absolutely exhausted.'

'It'll be all the worry catching up with you,' said Fiona. 'Your father — well, he used to be the same. Responsibility can be very wearing.'

Everyone looked at the table and Kath said, after a pause, 'You're right, Mum. I never relaxed all night, trying to make sure I spoke to everyone and making sure it all went to plan. I'm glad it's over now. That's us officially opened and now we can get on with the business of running the hotel.'

They sat in silence for a few moments and

then David coughed.

'I have some news for you,' he said.

Kath's interest quickened. Her brother was a man who used words both sparingly and accurately.

'We wanted to wait until tonight was over before telling you.'

He smiled and looked at Simone who sat beside him — she returned his smile with one of her own goofy ones. Kath saw Simone's fingers tighten around David's in the gentlest squeeze. Something about that loving, tender act made her realise how much she missed being loved.

'We're going to have a baby,' said David and Kath leapt from her chair and shrieked with delight. She knelt down and put her arms around her brother and Simone and found that she was weeping with joy.

'I'm sorry,' she said and wiped away her tears. She got to her feet and let the others bestow their hugs and kisses on the parents-to-be. 'I'm sorry,' she said again, more to herself than anyone else. 'It's just everything. It's just everything happening all at once.'

When everyone had recovered from the shock, Bridget said, 'So when's the baby due?'

'December — the week before Christmas,' replied Simone. 'I'm two months pregnant.'

'A Christmas baby,' said Fiona and sighed. 'How lovely!'

'Well, you'll be more prepared than most mothers, Simone. You'll know exactly what to expect in the delivery suite,' observed Bridget, referring to Simone's career as a midwife.

'That's true,' agreed Simone and she laughed. 'I'm sure I'll be a really annoying patient. I'll be telling the midwives how to do their job!'

'You'd better get the credit card out, Ned,' said David in a deadpan voice.

'Why's that?' said Ned, looking perplexed and more than a little guarded.

'Because Bridget's going to need a new frock. We're getting married!' said David and laughed.

Fiona clapped her hands and cried, 'Oh, what wonderful news! When?'

'Well,' said David, glancing at Simone and then addressing Kath, 'we were kind of hoping that we could have the wedding here. So it would depend when you can fit us in. We were thinking sometime in July maybe?'

'Of course it'll be here,' said Kath firmly. 'Where else would an O'Connor get married? Hold on. Wait a minute.'

She ran into the office, switched on the computer and consulted the screen for a few minutes. Then she came back out into the lounge area and announced, 'We've got weddings on the last three weekends in July but Saturday the eighth is free.'

'Does that sounds OK to you, Simone?' said David.

'Absolutely.'

'The eighth of July it is then!'

'The eighth of July,' mused Fiona. 'We haven't long, girls. That's only two months to get things organised.'

Bridget, Fiona and Simone immediately started discussing the details of who should do the dress, flowers and cake while Kath found a box of cigars and handed one each to her brother and brother-in-law. Then she went through to the bar and came back with bottles of spirits — she poured whisky for the men and Drambuie for the women and they all toasted the happy couple.

Kath curled up on the sofa, looked round at her family and beamed with happiness. The hotel had opened on time and Fiona finally had a place of her own to call home again. And now there was a wedding and a new baby to look forward to. Things were definitely looking up for the O'Connor family.

28

The hotel had only been open a fortnight and, like a duck on a pond, everything on the surface appeared to be sailing along smoothly, while under the surface Kath and the staff were peddling furiously to keep the whole thing going.

'I don't know what happened to the wages, Kath,' said Moira on Monday morning, peering at the computer screen in front of her. 'They should've been in everybody's bank accounts on Friday but for some reason the money hasn't gone through.'

'OK. Get on the phone to the bank right away and find out what's going on, please, Moira,' said Kath, wishing John didn't have a funeral to go to today. She could've done with his help.

Moira picked up the phone, dialled and was soon engaged in a lengthy conversation with one of the bank staff.

'That's the third call I've had about the website this morning,' said Bridget from the other side of the room.

'What about?' said Kath, lifting her head yet again from the marketing strategy she was trying to devise for the hotel. How could she plan long term when all her time was being taken up with day-to-day crises?

'There seems to be something wrong with the site. You can get so far with the booking system

363

but when it comes to accepting payment details the thing goes all haywire.'

'Have you emailed Steve?'

'Yes, I'm just waiting on him to get back to me.'

'Good.'

Ben, the chef, came into the office wearing his kitchen whites and holding an A4 sheet of paper in his hand.

'The special's off tonight, Kath,' he said. 'The fish hasn't arrived and won't be available until Thursday.'

'Don't you have something else in mind instead?' Kate said brusquely.

'Yeah, I could do something with game and a redcurrant sauce.'

'That sounds great, Ben,' said Kath quickly, realising too late that she'd been rude. 'I'm sorry for being short, Ben. It's just been one of those mornings.'

'No worries,' he said calmly and set the piece of paper down on Kath's desk. 'I've written down the name of the dish. *Pan-seared Venison with Rosemary and Redcurrant sauce.* But someone'll need to run off the new menus.'

'That sounds delicious, Ben. Bridget, can you do that just now?'

'Sure,' said Bridget.

'Thanks, Bridget,' said Ben.

'Kath,' said Moira as soon as Ben had left the room. 'It looks like the bank's computer system crashed on Friday and the payments haven't gone through. They said they can put them through today but the money won't be in the staff's bank accounts until tomorrow.'

Kath pulled a face and considered whether that was acceptable.

'Some of the staff won't be happy,' offered Moira.

'You're right, Moira,' said Kath, remembering that the hotel was only as good as the staff working in it. Treating them as she would like to be treated herself was Kath's main priority. 'We'll have to make up wage packets in cash today. You work out what change we need, phone the bank and I'll go down and collect the money.' Then she added crossly, 'And tell the cashier that I'll be speaking to Frank Morrison about this.'

An hour later Kath got into her buttercup-yellow car and sped into town. By the time she'd parked, made her way into the bank and listened to the profuse apologies of the cashier, her anger had subsided. It was, after all, nobody's fault. Machines made mistakes and there was nothing to be gained from giving Frank an ear-bashing over a central computer fault.

The cashier stuffed the money into a cream-coloured canvas sack and Kath heaved it into a capacious shoulder bag, which she'd brought with her specifically for this purpose. Weighed down by the coinage, she made her way back to the car park at a deliberate pace, feeling deflated. She got into the car and drove slowly back along the coast road to the hotel, thinking.

The whole business of running a hotel, it seemed to Kath, meant lurching from one crisis to the next. So far every day had been the same. She thought of her father and, for the very first time, gleaned a tiny insight into his state of mind before his death. She could see how working under this sort of pressure could get to you, especially if imminent bankruptcy loomed over the horizon. Poor Dad.

Of course Kath understood stress. She had worked under pressure before, from demanding bosses and ridiculous deadlines, but, at the end of the day, it had only been a job. She could have walked away at any time. But for her father the hotel had been more than just a job.

The future of the O'Connor family had depended entirely on its success for many years and, even after his children were all grown, he probably still felt that weight of responsibility. And that must have weighed so heavily on his mind. If only he'd been able to share the burden with his wife and family. They would have saved him somehow.

Suddenly Kath realised that she was driving so slowly she was holding up a queue of six cars. She told herself to snap out of her melancholy and accelerated until the car was cruising just under the speed limit.

It was still early days, she reminded herself. The hotel had only just opened and there were bound to be teething problems. Sure she was entirely responsible for the hotel and she was in debt to the bank. But she told herself, with a shaky confidence, it was only money. There were worse things than being bankrupt. Like taking your own life . . . The trick, she told herself firmly, was to keep things in perspective.

Back at the office, Kath and Moira made up the wage packets and Kath personally distributed them to the staff with her apologies. Then she took a short break for lunch, grabbing a sandwich from the kitchen, and returned to her marketing plans.

It was mid afternoon by the time Tommy McMurtry, the old part-time gardener, appeared in the doorway of the office. He shuffled his weight from one foot to the other, looking uncomfortable. He'd retired from his job as a groundskeeper with Ballyfergus Council ten years ago and had worked for her father until finances forced him to lay him off last winter. He came in two days a week to cut grass, keep the borders tidy and, in dry spells, water plants. Kath noticed that he'd trailed mud in on his boots. She bit her lip to stop herself from saying something.

'Yes, Tommy?' she said, as patiently as she could. 'What is it?'

'Sorry to bother you, Miss O'Connor.'

Kath had given up trying to get him to call her by her first name, realising, in the end, that he was more comfortable addressing her in this formal manner.

He squeezed the cap he held in both his hands. 'But there's something I think you should come and see.'

Kath stood up straightaway, a sense of foreboding taking hold. Happy to potter away undisturbed in the garden, Tommy avoided

367

communication if he could. Something must be very wrong.

He led her out the front door of the hotel into the bright sunshine, through the gap in the wall and over to the farthest corner of the garden, which abutted one of Mike Mulholland's fields and looked out over the North Sea.

'Look,' he said and pointed at a patch of grass beside the wooden pergola.

The surface of the grass was covered in a shallow, still layer of water. She took a few steps forward and her black court shoe sank into the soggy ground. She extracted it and took a few paces back onto firmer ground.

'I would've told you earlier but I've been weeding those borders all day,' he explained, indicating the far corner of the garden. 'I only noticed it just now.'

'But there hasn't been any rain for days, Tommy, unless you count that shower last night. Where's the water coming from?'

Tommy paused a while and stared at the ground as if searching for an answer there. 'Leak in your mains pipe, I would say,' he said at last. 'I'm sure it runs under here.'

A leak in a mains water pipe! Kath felt her underarms suddenly damp with perspiration. That sounded serious. And serious meant expensive. She hoped Tommy was wrong. It could be something else, couldn't it? Maybe water running down from the Mulhollands' farm or somewhere else? She'd been in the hotel all day and no one had mentioned any problems with the water supply.

'If there's a mains leak, why hasn't the water supply to the hotel been affected?'

'If it's a small one you'd not necessarily notice.'

'Oh, dear,' said Kath, with only the vaguest idea what one did in a situation such as this. She folded her arms and stared at the smooth surface of the water and added, 'We can't leave it like this, that's for sure. I'd suppose I'd — I'd better call the water board, then.'

When Tommy did not reply she smiled grimly at him, turned and took one pace across the grass.

'They won't repair it, Miss.'

Kath froze. She turned to face him once more.

'Not if it's on your land,' he said. 'Not for free anyway.'

Kath put her hands up to her face and rubbed her brow, frowning. She didn't have the money to call in someone to deal with this. She was certain it would cost hundreds of pounds! And there was a wedding on Saturday. The bride and groom wanted to take wedding photos in the grounds of the hotel. She couldn't have the wedding party squelching their way through a quagmire!

'The copper pipes running up here are pretty old,' continued Tommy. 'We've had several leaks over the past few years.'

'And what did you do?' said Kath, disappointed to hear that this was a common occurrence, but relieved that Tommy must know what to do about it.

'Oh, your father and I used to put on a

temporary repair. I know a wee bit about plumbing. Of course, the pipes really need replacing but . . . '

'Well, that's what we'll have to do,' said Kath decisively.

There was no money to pay for a professional repair, let alone new pipes. That would cost thousands. It was something she'd have to factor into next year's business plan, she thought miserably. Or the year after . . . But right now, she told herself, she didn't have time to worry about that.

'Where do we start, Tommy?' she said, turning her thoughts to addressing the immediate problem to hand.

'Well,' he said, rubbing his clean-shaven chin, 'we'll need to find it, first of all. That'll mean digging up this section from here to here,' he indicated a four-yard stretch of grass, 'to a depth of about two feet.'

'And that turf's just been laid,' said Kath with exasperation.

'If we're careful we can just roll it up and put it back when we're finished,' he said and looked at his watch. 'And if I leave now I could get to JP Corry's before closing.'

'What's that?'

'Builder's merchants in Ballymena. They'll have what I need.'

'Oh but Tommy, you're supposed to be finishing at five,' said Kath, consulting her watch and beginning to panic. Without Tommy's help she knew she'd be completely lost. 'And it's half four already.'

'It's alright, Miss. I can't leave you to sort this out on your own, now can I?'

'Oh, thanks, Tommy,' said Kath, flushed with relief. 'You've saved my life.'

'Well, I don't know about that,' he said and smiled shyly at her exaggeration, his face reddening a little.

'Well, you know what I mean. It's really good of you to stay and help me. I'll make sure you get overtime.' And she'd get him a really good bottle of whiskey and his wife, Muriel, a bunch of flowers. While Tommy was dashing halfway across the county Muriel would be sitting at home wondering what was keeping him and trying to keep his tea warm without ruining it.

'Now you'll need some money for the plumber's, Tommy. Come on up to the hotel and I'll get you some cash. And then I'll start on the digging.'

'Ach, you're only a wee lassie,' he said, using one of the colloquialisms that people from Ballyfergus shared with their Scottish neighbours across the Irish Sea in Stranraer and Cairnryan. He placed his flat cap on his head and pulled it down firmly. 'You can't go digging a big hole in the ground like that.'

'Well, someone has to do it,' she said, thinking that old Tommy looked as slightly built as she. It was one thing employing him to do light gardening, quite another asking a man of his age to dig a four-foot trench. 'There's only you and me here. And I don't know a thing about plumbing.'

Tommy pursed his lips in protest and shook his head.

'It'll be alright,' urged Kath, then added reassuringly, 'I'll see if I can get someone to help.'

After Kath had given Tommy some money, he went back outside to peel the turf away from the affected area of the garden while she returned to the office.

She phoned David both at home and on his mobile but there was no answer. She thought of asking Mike for help but decided against it. She was trying to keep her distance from him and, anyway, she'd seen no sign of him around the farm all day. The only male members of staff working in the hotel right now were in the kitchen, and they couldn't be spared — they were preparing for thirty covers booked in for tonight. There was nothing for it, she'd have to tackle it herself.

She made her way quickly up to the farmhouse where she changed her black trouser suit for a pair of old jeans, pale blue T-shirt and wellington boots. By the time she got back to the hotel, Tommy had gone and the turf was rolled up neatly at the end of the strip of bare earth. He'd laid a big sheet of blue polythene on the grass beside the bare patch where, she presumed, she was to place the dug-out earth.

In one of the sheds at the back of the hotel she found a rusty spade and carried it round to the part of the garden that was flooded. She needed both hands to carry the heavy shovel. She hadn't been to the gym in months — her muscle tone wasn't what it used to be. How on earth was she going to dig a two-foot deep ditch? She quelled the panic that started to rise inside her and told herself it was a case of mind over matter.

Kath positioned the spade over the ground and, using her right foot to push down on the metal shoulder of the shovel, she dug into the soil. It sliced easily through the soft ground, but lifting out the saturated mass of earth was a different matter altogether. Clumsily she heaved several spadefuls of wet mud onto the polythene, covering her T-shirt with smears of mud. Soon she was sweating.

The mud stuck to the spade and she used her right boot to scrap it off — the sticky mud clung to her boot in great sodden lumps. The wind picked up and her hair fell loose of the twist she'd put in it that morning — she removed the clips that had held it in place and put them in her back pocket, pushing her hair back behind her ears. She hoped she could get most of the digging done before Tommy returned. She feared he'd insist on doing it himself and the last thing she needed was him having a heart attack on her.

Once she reached a depth of eighteen inches she proceeded cautiously, probing with the spade until it touched something hard that sounded like metal. Excitedly, she scraped away the last few inches of soil with her hands to reveal a greeny-black pipe. As far as she could see, there was no sign of a leak in this section, but at least she'd located the pipe.

She stood up to ease the ache in her back with her legs astride the exposed pipe. The mud stuck to her hands like wet bread dough — she looked at them indifferently for a second and then wiped the soil on the thighs of her jeans. A loose strand of hair had escaped from behind her ear — she hooked it back into place, aware that she'd probably covered it, and the side of her face, with mud. She didn't care. No one was going to see her doing this. Only old Tommy. She made another incision in the earth, wondering if she'd locate the leak before he got back.

Twenty minutes later she was still digging, with her head bent over the spade and her face hidden by her loose hair, when she heard a voice very close by that made her cringe with embarrassment.

'What on earth are you doing, Kath?'

It was Mike Mulholland.

Kath froze. She didn't want anyone to see her like this, least of all Mike. Then she realised that the voice had come from behind her and, right now, his view would be of her rear end.

She stood up abruptly, turned to face him and squinted at his silhouette in the late afternoon sun. Her hair whipped wildly around her face in the strengthening breeze. Mike was standing at the side of the ditch which, despite her best efforts was still less than two feet deep and four yards long. She shielded her eyes from the glare of the sun with her arm and saw that he was wearing work trousers and a threadbare checked shirt and on his feet, like her, he wore wellington boots.

'We've got a mains leak, we think,' she said between gasps, and leaned on the handle of the spade, exhausted. 'Tommy's gone to get stuff from the plumber's merchants to fix it.' She paused to catch her breath, hooked a hank of hair behind her left ear and went on, 'I'm trying to locate the source of the leak. Tommy thinks it must be in this section here somewhere.'

'Yep. Looks like it,' said Mike, surveying the ground. 'How long have you been digging?'

'Half an hour, I guess.'

He smiled briefly. 'You'll be here all night at that rate,' he said, adopting a serious expression once more. 'Here, let me give you a hand.' He offered her his outstretched arm.

She hesitated for a moment, thinking that she really ought to insist that she was fine, that she didn't need any help. But that was blatantly not true. And, if she didn't accept his help, poor old Tommy would end up finishing the job and that, really, was out of the question.

So she swallowed her pride and extended her muddy hand. Mike grabbed it and pulled her effortlessly out of the shallow ditch. His hand was rough and his grip firm — her entire body thrilled at his touch. She blushed with embarrassment but Mike was too busy springing into action to notice.

'Here, let me have that spade,' he said, taking the implement out of her hand. 'And you have a rest. You look like you need it.'

Kath blushed again and said, 'I don't look that bad, do I?'

'What are you talking about?' he said, sounding utterly genuine. 'You look absolutely fine to me. Just tired.'

'Look at the state of me!' she said, looking down at her stained top.

'Well, you're hardly going to dig a ditch wearing your best Prada, are you?' he said and Kath laughed and thought how sweet he was.

Suddenly she relaxed. What did it matter what Mike saw her wearing or doing? He wasn't interested in her except as a friend, so why should he give a toss what she looked like? And, from what she knew of him, he wasn't the type of man to be impressed by appearances anyway. His interest in people went much deeper than that.

She watched him attack the soil purposefully with the spade, slicing through it as easily as a warm metal scoop through soft ice cream. He threw the sods of earth onto the blue plastic sheet and she watched the muscles in his back ripple with the effort. She moistened her dry lips with her tongue and bit her lip. She realised that she longed to touch his body.

'What're you thinking?' he said as he carried on working.

'Oh, I was just thinking that it's lucky you came along when you did. I was worried about Tommy having to dig the rest of it.'

'Old Tommy's stronger than he looks.'

'Still, I would've felt guilty all the same.'

'Hey, hold on a minute,' said Mike excitedly. 'It's wetter round this bit . . . yep, I think this is it here.'

Kath stepped into the shallow ditch beside Mike and crouched down beside him.

'Let me see,' she said and, in her eagerness, tipped forward onto her knees. The cold water seeped through the fabric of her jeans.

'See just there,' he said, scraping the mud off the part of the pipe he'd just exposed. 'You can see the water bubbling out. It's not coming that fast but overnight it's been enough to flood the garden.'

'Oh, Mike, that's brilliant!' cried Kath and spontaneously she threw her arms around him and gave him a hug. His torso was dense with solid muscle.

She looked into his face and he stared at her with a peculiar expression. Suddenly she realised that she was making him feel uncomfortable. She withdrew her embrace as quickly as she'd bestowed it.

'Sorry. I got a bit carried away,' she said, making light of their awkwardness, and stood up quickly. The wet bits of her jeans clung cold and uncomfortably to her knees. 'Now all we need is Tommy,' she added and turned to see a man striding purposefully across the lawn towards her.

'You're right,' said Mike. 'There's not much more we can do here until he gets back.'

But it wasn't Tommy McMurtry who was coming towards her.

It wasn't anyone from the hotel.

It was the last person on earth Kath expected to see in the garden of the Sallagh Braes Hotel on a sunny afternoon in May.

'Oh my God,' said Kath.

'What is it?' said Mike, and she heard the

377

sound of him stepping out of the ditch and the squelch of his feet on the wet grass as he came and stood beside her.

'It's Carl,' said Kath, her voice little more than a whisper.

29

The middle-aged cab driver had done nothing but chatter all the way from the airport and Carl found it difficult to understand half of what he said. He had a head of steel-metal hair, a face weathered like a cliff face and he wore a battered brown leather bomber jacket. His accent was so thick and he spoke so quickly that the words merged unintelligibly into one another, and Carl wondered when he found time to draw breath. He might as well have been speaking Irish. Maybe he was.

Carl squirmed in the back seat of the cab and tried to get comfortable. But his knees were jammed into the back of the passenger seat and his head nearly touched the headcloth. The cab seemed small and alien compared to the spacious instantly recognisable yellow sedans that served as cabs in Boston. Pale blue in colour, only a discreet plate on the bumper distinguished this vehicle from the family cars on the narrow roads.

And when Carl did decipher what the cab driver was saying, he discovered that he was extraordinarily inquisitive. He wanted to know what Carl did, where he was from, whether he was married or not and why he was visiting Ballyfergus. Carl found this unnerving. He was used to the anonymity of Boston where you were lucky to get so much as a grunt out of a cab driver.

He gave the driver monosyllabic answers, not wishing to appear rude but also not willing to divulge the nature of his business. And, when Carl was not forthcoming with information, the driver simply launched happily into a monologue about the tourist attractions of the north-east and what Carl must see: the Glens of Antrim, the Giant's Causeway, Bushmills Distillery and strange-sounding places whose names Carl couldn't catch.

He looked out the window and watched the rapidly changing weather. They drove through black clouds and heavy rain and then, a few moments later, the rain cleared and the sky was full of luminescent fluffy white clouds. The sun peeked out from behind the clouds and bathed the Lilliputian landscape in bright sunshine. Carl slipped on his shades and took it all in. The small scale of it astounded him as did the lush greenness — he could see now why it was called The Emerald Isle.

Here were fields half the size of a soccer pitch, there a quarter the size of his front yard, all neatly delineated with low stone walls and small scrub-like bushes. And the land undulated gently like a natural rollercoaster, up and down, quilted by these little fields.

He saw a sign for Ballyfergus and tried to imagine Kath in this landscape, the place of her birth and childhood. The land where she'd grown up and which had formed her, in the same way so much of his character was moulded by his background. He realised suddenly that the simple act of being here would help him understand her more.

It was a pity that this visit had to be so short — he could only stay a few days. But that would be all this trip required. There would be other visits here, vacations when he would have the time to get to know Kath's family — and Ireland too. It looked like an interesting place.

When they reached Ballyfergus the driver ignored the signs for the town centre and took a gently curving bypass that seemed to skirt the town. To his left Carl glimpsed the roofs of buildings of varying heights, old and new, and three tall apartment blocks that seemed incongruous in this small-town environment.

To his right glittered a stretch of water and he wondered what it was.

'That's Ballyfergus Lough,' said the driver, as if reading his thoughts. 'And just behind that cluster of buildings there,' he pointed, 'are the docks where the boats leave for Scotland.'

Carl remembered then Kath telling him that Ballyfergus was on the coast. He peered out the window. In the distance, on the other side of the wide stretch of water, he could see the ugly chimneys of some sort of factory.

Carl was surprised when they passed a sign for a Kentucky Fried Chicken outlet and, a few moments later, when they came off the bypass and waited at a small rotary, a closed-down McDonald's fast food restaurant.

They drove a short distance up a street that the driver informed him was the High Street. It was busy with shoppers but, to Carl's sophisticated eyes, they and the town itself seemed dull and unattractive. He saw a boarded-up shop with 'Graham's' above the door and a cluster of small shops selling fresh produce, electrical goods, meat and what looked like a bookshop.

Then they took a long straight road bordered on either side by an assortment of old-looking houses, terraced and detached. They drove past clusters of plum-clothed schoolchildren dawdling on the sidewalk, then a park on their right and soon they left the town behind them.

'Not long now,' said the driver and glanced at Carl in the rearview mirror. 'The hotel's just a few miles out this road.'

The muscles in Carl's stomach tightened and he remembered that he hadn't had anything to eat since a late breakfast at Heathrow airport. It was late afternoon now but he'd no idea of the exact time — the watch on his wrist was still set to Boston time. He couldn't remember if it was five or six hours ahead.

He wondered if Kath would be at home when he arrived, presuming she was staying with her family — he couldn't remember the name of the house but recalled that it was just a stone's throw away from the hotel. Kath could be anywhere of course, doing anything, but the hotel was a good starting point.

The car sped through a short tunnel that was too narrow for two cars to pass safely. Driving through it, the driver tooted his horn, the noise resounding off the black stone walls, and grinned at Carl in the mirror. Ignoring him, Carl strained

382

to take in the scenery. Steep black cliffs rose up on the left and to the right was an expanse of cold-looking sea.

'See yon o'er there,' said the driver, pointing across the water and drawing Carl's attention to a hazy landmass in the distance. 'That land ye can see there is Bonnie Scotland.'

Carl nodded and went over in his mind for the trillionth time what he would say to Kath. For he knew that it would be the most important speech of his entire life. At first, he'd expected her to come back to him after a suitable period had passed and she felt he had learned his lesson. But, as the weeks passed with no word from her, he began to realise how deeply he had wounded her. It was obviously important to her that she demonstrated how much he'd hurt her — and he understood that, he really did.

Selling her apartment, packing in her job and moving here were dramatic gestures — but he hoped and prayed that that was all they were. Deep down he believed that she still loved him. But he knew that he had to convince her of more, much more, than his love. He had to make her believe that he was capable of being the kind of man she wanted and, deep down, he wanted to be too — good, loyal, honest, trustworthy, moral. He had to make her understand that, without her, his life was meaningless.

And he'd give her what she wanted — the news that he and Lynda were to get divorced. And this was true, though it would be unwise, at this juncture, to disclose the likely bitter and protracted nature of that divorce. And then, thank God, this whole nightmare would be over and they could get back to living a normal life again. They wouldn't be able to get married for a while, but he'd ask her to move in with him. That would give her the sense of security he imagined she needed.

They passed through a pretty village called Ballygally. Carl played with the sound of the word inside his head, aware from listening to the cab driver that he could not mimic the local pronunciation of place names, with all their 'achs' and hard vowels.

Then the car slowed and the driver flicked on the left-hand turn signal. Carl peered out the window and saw a freshly painted sign swinging in the strong breeze. 'The Sallagh Braes Hotel' it said along with a phone number and, surprisingly, a website address. Carl realised that his notion of Ireland was probably very outdated, stuck in some sort of idealised time warp.

'That's us here now,' said the driver, stating the obvious and pulling into the driveway. 'So, how long are ye staying here?'

Carl replied, surprised by how quickly his ear had attuned to the unfamiliar accent, 'I'm not staying here. I'm just here to see someone.'

'Business?' said the driver, ascending the drive at a snail's pace and peering at Carl in the rearview mirror.

'You could say that.'

'D'ye want me to wait, then?'

'No, thank you.'

The driver screwed up his face and said, 'Will that be Brendan O'Connor's wee girl you're after? The one that's bought the hotel and taken over the running of it? Now let me think . . . ' He brought the car almost to a complete halt on the narrow drive and paused. 'What's her name? Kathleen. That's it! Kathleen O'Connor.'

'That's right,' said Carl, taken by surprise. 'How did you know?'

'Didn't ye hear me telling ye that I come from round here? We don't get that many American visitors out this way. I suppose you're one of her friends from the States.'

'That's right,' said Carl, anxious now to end the conversation.

Kath was running the hotel! He imagined her in one of the business suits she wore to work, with a white silk blouse peeking out and her hair pulled off her carefully made-up face. She always looked so well-groomed — that was one of the things that had attracted him to her in the first place. But the driver had said she'd bought the hotel, hadn't he? That sounded worryingly permanent and a little of Carl's confidence crumbled.

'I hear she's made a real go of it,' said the driver. 'You can't get a table in the restaurant at the weekend.'

'You don't say,' said Carl, peering through the windshield as the car pulled up in front of a large Victorian building that looked more like a well-to-do farmer's house than a hotel. Four tall, spindly palm trees swayed in the breeze at the front, looking exotically out of place in this agricultural landscape. A handful of cars was parked in a neat row to the left of the entrance.

Carl took a deep breath. Extracting Kath from here might prove more of a challenge than he'd expected. He'd imagined her holed up and jobless in her mother's home pining for him — not running a hotel.

He fumbled in his wallet with the unfamiliar currency and managed to extract the correct combination of notes for the fare, along with a generous tip. Then he stepped out onto the hotel forecourt, slammed the door shut and stretched his cramped legs. He set his grey leather Louis Vuitton holdall down on the ground and looked about. He realised that the cab was still idling on the blacktop. When he turned to look, the driver gave him a friendly wave and drove away slowly.

Carl turned his attention back to his surroundings. On his left was a shingle track leading further up the hill, where he could spy a cluster of farm buildings and the top half of a largish Victorian house proudly facing out to sea. From Kath's descriptions, he guessed that was her family home. To his right the land fell away sharply to the road and the coastline below.

He looked around. The scenery was stunning — beautiful and wild. And quite different from anything he'd ever seen. Kath was a city girl through and through — she loved Boston. But she had always pined for the place where she'd grown up and now that he was here, he could see why. And it worried him. Maybe she wouldn't want to leave it a second time?

Suddenly he heard a woman's voice coming over a tall stone-built wall to his left. He could've sworn it was Kath. His heartbeat quickened and he walked towards a gap in the middle of the wall. He found himself standing at the edge of an attractive walled garden with a lawn in the middle, dissected by a gravel path and bordered by shrubs and plants just coming into flower. He set his bag down on the ground by the edge of the wall. At one end of the rectangular-shaped space, a man and a woman crouched down in what appeared to be a ditch of some sort.

He watched as the woman placed her arms around the dark-haired man and then he realised who she was. Kath. His heart sank and, for a moment, his confidence teetered on the brink of collapse. Then he found himself striding towards the pair of them, his putty-coloured Burberry trench coat flapping in the wind. Who the hell did that guy think he was?

As he drew close Kath stood up and, putting her hand up to her face, stared directly at him. She was wearing muddy galoshes on her feet, the knees of her jeans were stained brown and she seemed to be smeared from head to foot with something black — was it mud? Her hair, the colour of polished mahogany, blew wildly around her head in the wind, like a character in a cartoon who's just received an electric shock. She'd put on a little bit of weight since the last time they'd met. In short, she looked like he'd never seen her before.

Carl felt the toe of his Tod's tan suede loafer sink into something wet and cold. He looked down and realised he'd just waded into a pool of brown water on the top of the grass.

'Damn!' he said, lifted his foot out of the water

and shook off the excess. His four-hundred-dollar shoes were ruined.

Kath put her hand over her mouth and, for a moment, Carl thought she was laughing at him. But when she removed it, her expression was serious and her face was pale and drawn.

'This whole bit here's flooded,' she said, indicating the grass around her which was covered in water. 'There's been a leak and we're trying to fix it. You'd better go back.'

He took a few paces backwards onto drier ground and immediately regretted storming in here so impulsively. This ignominious arrival wasn't exactly what he'd had in mind for their reunion.

Kath turned and said something to the man beside her and Carl stared at him. He was short and stocky and badly dressed in worn-out clothes and green galoshes. The sleeves of his frayed shirt were rolled up to reveal strong hairy arms. He had a wild, unkempt look about him and his expression, as he stared at Carl, was challenging. Carl suppressed the urge to strike him.

Kath and the man came forward a few paces until they were standing right in front of him. She had mud in her hair and smears of mud on her face. But she didn't seem to care.

'Carl,' she said, 'I'd like you to meet my neighbour, Mike Mulholland.'

Carl nodded at the Irishman but did not extend his hand.

'Mike, this is Carl Scholtz.'

The Irishman said something unintelligible,

388

which Carl assumed was a greeting but there was no warmth in his voice nor in his still, black eyes. Carl gave him a hard stare and then turned his attention to Kath.

'Your neighbour?' he said, looking round at the empty slopes around them. 'Up here?'

'Yes, that's right. I live in that farmhouse up there. See?' She pointed to the cluster of buildings Carl had noticed earlier. 'And Mike lives in that white bungalow beside it.'

'What about the house? That's your family home, isn't it?' said Carl, ignoring the reference to the Irishman and pointing at the large Victorian house that loomed above them.

'It was,' said Kath sadly, shielding her eyes with her hand as she stared up at it. Her nails were short and unpainted and her hands were encrusted with mud. 'It's a long story, but the long and the short of it is that dad was bankrupt. The house had to be sold.'

'I'm sorry, Kath,' he said quickly. 'I'd no idea.'

She inclined her head slightly to the left in acceptance of his commiseration. 'It's a crying shame — the house has lain empty for months and nobody seems to know who bought it. I don't understand why people would buy a house like that and then not live in it.' She was talking more to herself than to Carl. 'Anyway, as it turned out, Mike had an empty farmhouse for rent.'

'Did he now?' said Carl, thinking that this was another worrying development.

Not only had Kath got herself embroiled in a business, she'd set up home on her own as well.

389

But worst of all, she was living right next door to this man he'd just seen her embrace. Jealousy gripped him.

'Yes,' he said, before he could stop himself, 'how handy to have a farmhand on your doorstep when you need a manual labourer.'

'Mike's not a farmhand,' said Kath too quickly, too defensively for Carl's liking and he immediately regretted his outburst.

Mike, his square jaw jutting forward like the prow of a boat, took a step forward with the spade balanced lightly in his left hand, as though it weighed no more than a toothpick. The muscles round his left eye twitched and he stood poised for action on the balls of his feet.

Kath placed a hand on his shoulder and said with a sigh, 'Carl, what are you doing here?'

'I came to see you, of course.'

He was about to suggest they go somewhere to talk when they were joined by a wizened old man — he had a cap on his head and he carried a battered toolbox in his right hand.

'Hi, Tommy,' said Kath. 'How did you get on?'

'Grand,' said the old man and he nodded a friendly greeting to Mike. 'Did ye find the leak?'

'Yes, Mike just found it,' said Kath and then, turning to Carl, she added, 'Oh, Carl, I'm afraid I'm busy right now. We have to get this fixed.'

'Shall I go into the hotel and wait then?' said Carl, feeling out of place. He realised that something fundamental in his relationship with Kath had changed. Before he'd held the balance of power; now it was she who was very much in control. It unnerved him.

'Is this one of your friends from across the pond?' said the old man, suddenly taking an interest in Carl on hearing his accent.

'Yes, he's just arrived.'

'I was in New York for a few years in the fifties,' said the old man. 'Worked on the docks. Didn't like it much, I have to say, so I came back here.'

Carl nodded and gave him a thin smile but remained silent — he was too worried to engage in idle conversation right now.

The old man went over, looked in the ditch and called out to Kath, 'It's alright, Miss O'Connor, I should be able to fix that easy enough. And Mike'll help me fill it in after, won't you, Mike?'

'Sure I will, Tommy,' said Mike in a soft voice and his stance relaxed. He ambled over to the edge of the ditch and looked in.

'There ye are now, Miss O'Connor,' said the old man, sounding pleased with himself. 'Now you go and get that man a drink.' Then he added with a chuckle, 'He looks like he could do with it!'

'Are you sure?' said Kath, not sounding at all keen to leave the two men.

Carl felt the irritation creeping up again. Didn't she realise that he'd come halfway round the world to see her? And all she wanted to do was stand around a hole in the ground talking!

'Yeah, we're fine,' said Mike, staring directly at Kath, and then he added softly, as though giving her license to leave him, 'You go on.'

Kath looked at Carl and he swallowed the lump in his throat and said, 'Can we go

391

somewhere where we can talk?'

She glanced at the hotel, then at the farm buildings and finally she looked down at her clothes and grimaced. 'I suppose you'd better come up to the farmhouse. I need to change out of these wet things.'

'OK.'

She led the way through the gap in the wall. Carl collected his bag and followed her up the track that led to the farmhouse. It was rutted and full of potholes and Carl had to watch his step in his soft-soled shoes.

'It's good to see you, Kath,' he said, falling in beside her.

She glanced quickly at him, opened her mouth to speak but all that came out was, 'Hmm . . . ' She pulled nervously at the hem of her T-shirt. 'How long are you planning on staying?' she asked then, glancing at his small holdall.

'Just a few days. Maybe longer. I don't know.'

There was a pause and then she said, 'How was your journey?'

'OK.'

'And when did you arrive in Ireland?'

Carl responded to her question with details of his travel itinerary, thinking that this was the sort of conversation strangers had with each other. Thankfully Kath soon abandoned the small talk and they fell into an awkward, but preferable, silence.

It wasn't long before they reached the farmhouse, a small stone-built affair on two floors that sat right on the edge of the track. Kath pushed open the front door, which was unlocked, and said, 'Go through there to the lounge. I'll be down in a minute.'

She disappeared up the narrow flight of stairs and, leaving his bag by the door, Carl took the opportunity to explore downstairs. There were only two rooms — a rustic kitchen and a small living room. They were furnished in the most basic style with little regard for modern tastes — so unlike Kath's stylish apartment in Boston. The house was cold, even in May, and smelt faintly musty. On the floor were worn rugs, and drapes which must have dated from the seventies graced the windows. What had happened to Kath? The woman he'd fallen in love with in Boston could not have lived like this.

He moved through the rooms, picking up items here and there, opening cupboards and scrutinising the contents of the decrepit fridge. He realised he was looking for evidence of a man living here and told himself to stop it.

In the living room he idly picked up a photograph of two elderly people standing on the steps of the hotel. He recognised them as Kath's parents — he'd once taken them all out to eat at Aujourd'hui, one of Boston's top-class restaurants, in the Four Seasons Hotel. They were pleasant, if quiet, people and he knew he'd impressed them with the window seat overlooking the public gardens and the fact that he was known to all the staff by name. He felt that Kath's mother liked him.

So this, he thought, looking at the faded wallpaper on the walls, was what Kath chose to call home — this little cottage on a windswept hill in the back of beyond. When he thought of the lifestyle he could offer her, even after the expense of a divorce, he allowed himself a chuckle. Surely she wouldn't say no to that?

'Is something funny?' said Kath's voice.

He turned around sharply and said, 'No. I . . . I was just thinking about something.'

She came into the living room and took the picture out of his hand. She placed it carefully back on the side table and said, 'That was taken the summer before last when they came to Boston. Do you remember?'

'Of course I remember.'

She was barefoot and wearing simple grey sweat pants and a matching zipped top. Her hair was pulled back into a pony-tail and the mud had been removed from her face. She looked tense, which Carl took to be a good sign. She must still care for him.

'You look like your father,' he said.

'Is that what you were laughing at?' she said defensively.

'No, not at all. It was just something I thought about. It amused me. It was nothing.' He put his hands in his pockets and walked to the window. He saw an elderly woman come out of the white bungalow, get in a car and drive off. 'How are you doing, Kath? I hear you've bought the hotel.'

'News travels fast. Did Emmy tell you?'

'No, your Emmy's as tight-lipped as an oyster,' he said and a smile flitted briefly across Kath's face. 'It was the cab driver from the airport. I couldn't get the guy to stop talking. And he seemed to know a lot about you and the hotel.'

Kath, standing with her arms folded across her chest and her hip jutted out to the right, smiled again, but not entirely pleasantly. 'That's Northern Ireland for you. It's a small place.'

'You're telling me.'

'That's one of its charms, Carl,' she said, the smile falling from her face. 'It's not big and impersonal. Here you know everybody, or you can very easily find out who they are. It means that people can't pull the wool over your eyes or make a fool of you so easily.'

'Kath, let's not go over old ground. I never meant to deceive you or make a fool of you. I never meant for any of that to happen.'

'Of course you did!' she said, her voice full of venom. 'Don't lie to me, Carl. You intended to carry on as long as I was fool enough to let you.'

He walked over to her and stood, looking down. She did not lift her eyes to meet his gaze and so he found himself addressing the top of her head.

'I know what I did was terribly, terribly wrong. And I am so sorry that I hurt you. I promise you that I will never lie to you again. I love you, Kath.'

'You have a funny way of showing it,' she said and her eyelashes flickered rapidly.

'Look,' he said, taking her gently by both hands, 'come and sit down here.'

He led her over to the hideous brown sofa and sat down, pulling her down beside him. She did not resist. Now their heads were more or less level and he could see her face properly.

'I've had a lot of time to think, Kath, and — '

'So have I,' she interrupted and slid her hands out of his grip and folded them on her lap.

'Let me finish. Please,' he said, paused and then went on, looking at the wet toes of his fancy suede shoes. 'I've had a lot of time to think about things and I know now what it is that I want. Before I was confused, messed up, living in a sort of fantasy world where I thought I didn't have to face up to the realities of my life.' He looked at the grey ashes in the empty fireplace and said, 'I got married simply because it seemed like the right thing to do at the time. I was at that age when everyone around you seems to be married or engaged and Lynda and I had been dating for quite a while. I was successful, I had everything that I wanted materially and I simply wanted the next thing on the check list — a wife and family. And Lynda was there and she was willing and we did get on, then anyway. I thought I loved her.'

'So what changed?'

Detecting a softening in her, he went on eagerly. 'I don't really know. Truth is, I don't know if it was me that changed or Lynda. But since the children were born we've drifted apart. I hardly know her now. She's like a stranger to me.'

He stopped speaking then and Kath was silent.

'And then I met you,' he went on. 'And my world came alive. And I realised what real love was.' He paused then and waited for her to speak.

'That's sad, Carl. But I don't know what you

want from me,' she said at last and shrugged. 'I don't know what you want me to say.'

He folded his smooth hands over her work-roughened ones. He looked her deep in the eyes and said, 'I want you to say that you'll come back to me, Kath.'

Kath shook her head slowly and there were tears in her eyes when she spoke. 'No, Carl. No. I can't.'

'Yes, you can, Kath,' he said, his voice breaking. 'There's nothing stopping us now.'

But she continued to shake her head sadly while he tried to explain, not listening to what he said.

'Kath,' he said loudly then and she was motionless and stared right at him. 'I've asked Lynda for a divorce.'

'Oh,' she said abruptly, the exclamation sharp and high-pitched. 'Lynda's agreed to a divorce?'

'So you see, we can get married,' he said smoothly, avoiding her question, and Kath's eyes grew wide like saucers. 'Just as soon as the divorce comes through. That's why I'm here, Kath. To take you back with me.'

Kath looked away, clearly agitated. She put her right thumb in her mouth and chewed on it the way he'd seen her do before when stressed or anxious. From the pocket of her jacket she pulled out a scrunched-up tissue and squeezed it in her left fist.

Outside Carl heard a tractor trundle past, darkening the room for a few seconds as it growled up the track. Kath glanced quickly out the window and then as quickly back at Carl, as though she'd been caught doing something she oughtn't. He realised she'd been looking at the driver of the tractor and he immediately thought of the Irishman in the garden.

'So tell me,' he asked, trying to sound casual. 'Who's this Mike Moholland?'

'*Mul*-holland,' she corrected him. 'Just a neighbour, like I said.' She looked at her fists now curled up together in her lap.

'And that's all he is? Just a neighbour?' said Carl, thinking that he didn't go round hugging his neighbours.

'Well, he's a friend too, of course. He's helped me a lot with the hotel.'

'I bet,' said Carl flatly, failing to hide his jealousy.

'Oh, Carl,' she said sounding exasperated, 'Mike is just a friend, nothing more. He has a girlfriend called Anne.'

'I'm sorry,' said Carl, full of relief. 'I didn't come here to talk about him. It's just that I love you so. I can't bear to think of you with anyone else.'

'There isn't anyone else,' she said and her eyelids flickered like butterflies' wings.

He coughed and cleared his throat. 'Will you come back to me, then?' he said and paused for dramatic effect. 'Will you marry me, Kath?'

'Marry you . . . ' she said, as though mesmerised by the words and then she broke eye contact with him and looked about the room. All of a sudden she became animated and said, 'But I can't just up sticks and leave here, Carl, even if I wanted to. It's not as simple as that. I've only just opened the hotel. I'm up to my eyes in debt. Too much is at stake, not just for me but for the rest of the family, to walk away now.'

Carl looked about the scruffy little room and said with a laugh of incredulity, 'Are you asking me to come and live here?'

'No, Carl, I'm not,' said Kath coldly and she stood up. 'I'm not asking you to do anything. You're the one doing the asking right now — not me.' She sighed then and said in a softer voice, 'To tell you the truth, I can't think about this any more. I need to be on my own.'

She walked to the front door, leaving him with no option but to follow her.

'Would you mind leaving me now, please?' she said. Gingerly, she touched her right temple with the tips of her fingers and her brow creased into a frown.

'Are you alright?' he said.

'I have a headache.'

'I'm sorry. Maybe we can talk about this later?'

'Yes. Tomorrow.'

'Well, goodbye — for now,' he said, picked up his bag and stepped outside.

The sun had gone to be replaced by a canvas of grey, against which black clouds skittered in the wind.

'Carl — where are you staying?'

'Hadn't thought about it,' he said, hoping that she was about to invite him to stay in her house.

'You can stay in the hotel, if you like. I don't mind. I'm sure there are a couple of rooms available.'

'Thanks. I'd appreciate that,' he said, trying to hide the fact that her offer was a let-down.

'Right. I'll give reception a ring to say you're on your way.' And she closed the door without another word.

Carl set off down the track. In spite of Kath's cool reception, which was only to be expected, he descended the road with a lighter tread than when he'd climbed it. He had engaged her in dialogue and, though she tried hard to hide it, he could tell that she was deeply affected by his presence. Especially when he mentioned marriage.

Her love for him was bound to be dented, but he was still confident that it could be fully restored. He would have to work quickly though. He hadn't much time and she was right about one thing — there were a lot of practical issues to be solved. She'd have to sell that stupid hotel for a start.

Carl scrutinised the white bungalow where the Irishman lived on his way past. Dwarfed by the landscape around it, up close the house was much larger than he'd first thought. This was no hillside farmer's cottage. It was a substantial modern building with two wings jutting out at the back. At a glance he guessed it offered three-and-a-half, maybe four, thousand square foot of living space. Nothing like his own property at Williamstown, but big compared to the properties he'd seen on his way here from the airport.

Carl wondered who the elderly woman was he'd spied leaving the house earlier and frowned as he pondered the nature of Mike Mulholland's relationship to Kath.

He recalled the scene that had greeted him in the garden — Kath leaning close to the man, her arms around him, relaxed and familiar. Carl swallowed the lump that formed in his throat and took several deep breaths. He told himself to calm down — this delicate situation required rational, logical thought. In spite of Kath's protestations to the contrary, clearly the Irishman was closer to her than she was prepared to admit.

Kath had put up a much greater degree of resistance than he had expected — and he was quite sure that Mike Mulholland had something to do with it. He remembered the way the Irishman had squared up to him, insolent and taciturn. Women rarely noticed the subtleties of these things, but men did — Mike Mulholland was making a claim on Kath.

Carl told himself that Kath couldn't possibly prefer that country hick over him. But there was still a nagging doubt in his mind. If Kath wasn't prepared to tell him the truth, then maybe Mike Mulholland would. And, if the Irishman did have designs on Kath, then it was high time that Carl put him very firmly in the picture. Because one way or another, he was going to get Kath back.

30

Kath sat on the edge of the bath, a towel wrapped round her, and watched the water cascade noisily into the tub. Opening the hotel, in spite of all the challenges and vicissitudes, had provided her with a sense of purpose and a sense of certainty about the future. She was enjoying her life here — something that she had thought would never be possible again after Carl's duplicity.

But Carl's sudden appearance in Ballyfergus had stripped away these certainties, rocking her confidence and making her feel once more like the wreck she'd been only a few months before, when that fateful telephone call from Lynda had pulled her world apart. She frowned, thinking about that awful time, and tried to put it out of her mind.

Of course, she hadn't let Carl see the effect his presence had on her today, but that was how she felt. Vulnerable and afraid and doubting her own mind.

Suddenly she couldn't remember if she'd locked the front door. She ran downstairs to see, braving the relative chill of the air outside the steamy bathroom. The door was locked and bolted. She sighed, climbed the stairs wearily, turned off the taps, discarded the towel on the bathroom floor and eased herself into the bath.

She didn't want to see or speak to anyone

— she wanted to be entirely alone. For she knew that the dilemma she faced was one that only she could solve.

She lay back and watched the candles flicker in the draught and tried to relax, but her shoulders were so tense they felt as though they were tied to the ceiling with elastic bands.

Once more the future was in doubt and her options stretched out before her like paths in a dense forest. She could not see where they led, but she would have to choose. And she would have to make that choice soon.

'Will you marry me, Kath?' she said out loud, echoing Carl's question, and momentarily she allowed herself to fantasise. She imagined herself, elegant and ladylike in the most chic wedding gown, sailing down the aisle to the tear-filled smiles of her friends and family. Then she blushed at her foolishness.

The reality was that, much as she'd yearned for so long to hear those words from Carl, they had brought no elation or joy. They no longer held any magic for her — they were tarnished with the memory of his betrayal.

She closed her eyes and immersed her head slowly under the water, angry with herself for allowing Carl to get under her skin. She felt her hair around her shoulders like silky seaweed and, when she could hold her breath no longer, she broke the surface of the water and gasped for breath.

She wiped the water from her eyes with wet fingers and rested her head on the edge of the bath. She tried to calm herself but, much as she willed it, her heartbeat wouldn't slow down and she couldn't quell the queasiness in her stomach. And although her heart was a pathetic jumble of conflicting emotions, she knew the issue hinged on three very straightforward questions.

Firstly, did she still love Carl?

Secondly, could she forgive him?

And thirdly, could she ever trust him again?

Everything else — including the future of the hotel, where they might live, careers — was irrelevant. Difficult issues to be solved certainly, but not insurmountable problems.

If she could answer yes to these three critical questions then her future was decided — she would go back to Carl. She would be a fool to say no. If she loved him, forgave him and trusted him, then that was more than enough for a secure and happy future together.

But, if she couldn't say yes without reservation then her future wasn't so clear-cut.

The distance in time and place had allowed her hurt to heal, but the wounds were still raw. She still loved Carl — she probably always would — but her love was tainted by the negative emotions she felt towards him. Sometimes it felt more like hate.

Like today, when he'd been so downright rude to Mike for no reason whatsoever. She wondered if, blinded by love, she'd simply never noticed his faults before. But then everyone had faults — she had plenty of her own. She thought of how impatient she'd been with the staff in the office today and cringed with regret. It only went to show that no one was perfect.

But she certainly hadn't forgiven Carl. To be fair, she acknowledged that she hadn't actually tried to see the situation from his point of view. And there was a certain visceral pleasure in holding onto the hurt and the indignation. Was she capable of letting that go?

But the question that vexed her most was the one about trust. Even if she loved him and forgave him, would she ever be able to fully trust him again? What he'd done was so audacious, on so dramatic a scale and carried out over such a prolonged period that she feared he was corrupted to the core.

But maybe her expectations of him were too high. He said he'd made a mistake and he said that he was sorry. He'd promised that he would never lie to her again. Shouldn't that be enough for her? Maybe her ideas of what a man should be — upright, honourable, honest and utterly incorruptible — were old-fashioned and unrealistic in today's world. Everyone made economies with the truth; we all told white lies — that was part of human nature.

But she'd put Carl on a pedestal and now she would never be able to idolise him the way she once had. Looking back, she realised now that he had been almost too perfect and hero-worship was not the basis of a lasting relationship. And yet the prospect of a life without him, now that he had offered himself unconditionally to her, seemed bleak and lonely. Should she simply suppress the doubts she harboured and learn to live with his flaws?

He could give her the companionship and the

family life she so craved. Was it better to compromise than live a life alone and unloved? Because the way things were going, if she didn't accept Carl Scholtz, Kath reckoned she would end up a spinster for the rest of her life.

★ ★ ★

The next morning Kath went to work with a head that felt like cotton-wool. She dreaded meeting Carl again, for the night had brought with it no resolution to her dilemma.

Bridget and Moira were already in the office when she arrived through the back door. Bridget was peeking round the door into reception and gestured for Kath to join her as soon as she entered the room.

'Is that him?' shrieked Bridget in a voice not unlike a foghorn. 'Oh, he's better looking than his photo and he's very tall! What's he doing here? Did you know he was coming?'

'*Sshh!*' said Kath, joining her sister at the door to the office where she was just in time to see Carl's tall, well-proportioned figure heading in the direction of the restaurant where breakfast was served. 'He'll hear you,' she added, thinking that he'd need to be deaf not to have heard her sister's comments.

'Have you spoken to him yet?' said Bridget and Kath was aware that Moira, in spite of her eyes being glued to the computer screen, was hanging on every word. She could tell this by the light-fingered way she brushed the keys rather than her usual pounding action.

'Yes, I saw him as soon as he arrived yesterday,' she said, rubbing her brow. 'He came up to the farmhouse to talk.'

'And?'

'And what? We talked. That's all.'

'What did he say?'

Kath glanced at Moira and gestured at Bridget to follow her out of the office through the back door. They stood in the narrow corridor that led to the kitchen.

'He apologised for what he'd done and asked me to go back to him,' she said, picking imaginary dust off the sleeve of her jacket. 'He said that he'd asked his wife for a divorce.'

'So he's going to divorce her,' said Bridget thoughtfully and her eyes narrowed.

'That's what he said,' said Kath suddenly realising that, with Carl, there was every possibility of a big difference between what he said and the truth.

'Why are you pulling that face? Aren't you pleased he came all this way to tell you that. He must think a great deal of you.'

'I suppose so.'

'It means he'll be free to marry again,' said Bridget and waited for her sister's reaction.

'I know. He already asked me to marry him,' said Kath flatly.

'Oh my God!' said Bridget excitedly and she put the shell-pink-painted fingers of her right hand to her lips. 'What did you say?'

'I told him I needed time to think.'

'What's there to think about? It's either 'yes' or 'no'. Look, do you love him?'

407

Kath sighed. 'Yes, yes, I think so.'

'So the answer's got to be 'yes', hasn't it?'

'Not necessarily. It's just not as straightforward as you make it sound, Bridget. I'm not sure that love on its own is enough. You see, I don't know if I can forgive him for what he did. And there's the question of trust. How do I know he's not going to deceive me again?'

'OK,' said Bridget forcefully. 'He did something astoundingly foolish but he realises that now. He's leaving his wife and kids for you!'

Kath closed her eyes for a second, wishing that Bridget hadn't reminded her about Carl's two little daughters.

'He's said he's sorry,' continued Bridget, ticking off Carl's actions like achievements on her fingers, 'and he's trying to make things right between you. What more do you want him to do? It's not like he's going to have another wife up his sleeve.'

Kath shrugged. 'When you put it that way Carl's offence doesn't seem so — so horrific. Am I really just being obstinate? Would other women simply forgive and forget and welcome him back with open arms?'

'Yes, they would,' said Bridget decisively.

Kath felt slightly irritated by her sister's apparent self-assurance on this subject. She wished she could see the situation in the clear-cut black-and-white way that Bridget obviously did.

'I don't know that he can do any more to convince me,' she said, more to herself than to Bridget. 'I think it's down to me now. And I

408

can't do something unless it feels instinctively right. And right now, if Carl pressed me for an answer it would have to be 'no'.'

'Well, I think you're absolutely mad,' snapped Bridget. 'If I was in your shoes I'd take him back without question.'

'Bridget,' said Kath, her hackles now up, 'how can you possibly know how you'd feel if you were in my position? And why are you defending Carl's corner so passionately? You don't even know him.'

A scowl passed briefly across Bridget's countenance and then her expression softened. 'I just want you to be happy, Kath. And I don't want to see you throw away your only chance of happiness, that's all. Promise me you'll think about it a bit longer.'

'OK. I'll not do anything hasty,' said Kath with a deep sigh, feeling utterly drained by the conversation. With nothing left to be said she followed Bridget back to the office.

But instead of returning to her seat Bridget went out into the reception area through the other door and Kath heard her engage someone in conversation.

'Ah, I thought it was you,' she said.

'Sorry?' said Carl's puzzled-sounding voice.

'From the photos. I recognised you from the photos Kath sent. I'm her sister. Bridget.'

'Hi! Great to meet you,' said Carl, his voice now flooded with warmth and Kath cringed with embarrassment.

She stood behind the white panelled door and listened while Bridget engaged Carl in small talk as though he was your average American tourist here for a holiday. After a few minutes of this, Bridget moved the conversation on and Kath was astounded to find herself the topic of their dialogue.

'I'm sorry we never met before,' said Bridget, 'and I really hope you and Kath can sort things out between you.'

What the hell did Bridget think she was doing?

'Yeah. Well. So do I,' said Carl, not sounding too hopeful. 'You've heard what happened between us?'

'Oh, yes. I know all about it.'

'I'm afraid I made a bit of a mess of things,' said Carl, and Kath bit her hand.

'Well, yes, you did, didn't you? But we all make mistakes,' said Bridget and Kath felt her palms go clammy with sweat. 'I've been trying to get Kath to see that. I mean, I know that what you did was terrible but I think she should forgive you. And you wouldn't have come all this way to see her if you weren't serious about her, would you?'

'I've never been more serious in my life,' said Carl solemnly.

'Well, let's hope that Kath sees sense.'

'Yes, let's hope so,' said Carl, sounding as puzzled by Bridget's forthright intervention as Kath was incensed. 'But I wonder if you could help me?'

Kath put her hands up to her face in a prayer-like pose, fully expecting him to ask to speak to her. She wasn't ready. She had nothing to say to him that hadn't been said last night.

'Is there anywhere around her I could rent a car for a few days?' said Carl and Kath breathed a sigh of relief.

'Of course,' said Bridget smoothly the model of efficiency. 'If you ask at reception here Jeannette will get you all sorted out.'

Seconds later Bridget appeared back in the office, looking bright-eyed and pleased with herself.

Kath felt like smacking her.

'I do not believe you!' she hissed. 'What the hell do you think you were doing out there?'

'Talking to Carl,' said Bridget innocently. 'You can't expect me to completely ignore the poor guy, can you?'

'I never asked you to ignore him. But who gave you license to discuss me with him? And in front of staff as well.'

'I'm your sister, Kath,' said Bridget in a hurt tone of voice. 'If I can't talk to him about you, who can?'

And with that she returned to her seat and calmly started to type the figures from handwritten bar and restaurant receipts into the computer.

Kath caught Moira's eye and gave her a brief, strained smile. Sometimes Bridget was a complete pain in the behind. Regardless of what Kath said to her, Bridget acted like it was her job to sort out her sister's love life. But this time she'd really gone too far.

It was several minutes later, when Kath was back at her desk and her annoyance with Bridget had lessened a little, that she wondered why Carl wanted a car. He'd hardly be going sightseeing, would he? Then again she couldn't expect him to sit around all day waiting for her to show up. She put the knuckles of her right hand in her mouth and wished with all her heart that she knew what to do about Carl.

★   ★   ★

Carl had woken very early, his internal time clock not yet adjusted to UK time. His large, but slightly shabby, room was in the old part of the hotel, with a bay window overlooking the sea. In the early morning gloom, he had pulled a club chair, upholstered in floral fabric, over to the window, opened the thin curtains and sat and watched the sunrise.

The sun, a quivering orange sphere ringed in ruby, rose over the distant Scottish shoreline casting an ethereal red-tinged glow over the calm waters and the sleeping landscape.

Carl opened the creaking casement window and the crisp clean air and the sound of birds welcoming in the new day came in. Down by the sea, the black-topped road that hugged the coastline was deserted of traffic. He listened to the creaking of the old pipes as the hotel slowly came to life and watched as the day took shape.

Slowly the sun became too bright to watch and soon disappeared into a mass of ghostly cloud that appeared to rise like a fog out of the sea. He could see silver dew glistening on the leaves on the tree outside his window and on the spiders' webs spun between its fragile twigs. He

412

heard the lowing of far-off cattle and the fields glowed a bright paintbox green almost too intense to be real.

He tried very hard to imagine himself living in this place. For Carl recognised that he might have some difficulty persuading Kath to leave her family, and the hotel, after she had invested so much. And he could see why. It was indeed beautiful here but, even though he had only set foot in the country less than twenty-four hours ago, instinctively he knew that it could never be home to him. It just didn't feel right. But if it was what it took to get Kath back, then he might have to resign himself to a life in this foreign place. The important thing was to get Kath to agree to take him back. Maybe he could persuade her to go back to Boston later.

When the bedside clock said eight o'clock, Carl showered, shaved, dressed and put on his coat. He went downstairs and walked straight out of the front door of the hotel into the cool, calm morning. Thick cloud filled the sky but there was no rain yet. Carl took the track to the white bungalow on the hill and in a few very short minutes he was knocking on the door.

'I'm looking for Mike Mulholland, ma'am,' said Carl to the well preserved, snowy-haired woman who opened the door to him.

She looked doubtfully at Carl for a few seconds and then a smile rose to her lips.

'You must be one of Kath's friends.'

'That's right, ma'am.'

'You're up early,' she observed, then extended her hand and said cheerfully, 'Pleased to meet

413

you. I'm Gladys. Mike's mother.'

Carl shook her hand briefly and said the usual civilities, while thinking that it was weird for a man of Mike Mulholland's age to be living with his mother. He, on the other hand, couldn't wait to get away from his alcohol-dependent mother just as soon as he'd been able.

'You said you were looking for Mike,' prompted Gladys, interrupting his thoughts. 'I'm afraid he's not here right now. You've just missed him.'

Carl glanced briefly down the track that led to the main road and then back at Gladys. He was annoyed that he'd just missed Mike — this wasn't something that could wait until he chose to show up at the farm again. Carl's flight back to the States left the following morning. He was running out of time.

'Do you know where I can find him?' he asked.

'Oh, Mike's never hard to find,' she replied pleasantly. 'If he's not here he's either at the processing plant or the shop.'

'Shop?' repeated Carl and, seeing his puzzled expression, she elaborated.

'The butcher's shop in town. Mulhollands' on the Main Street. It's not hard to find. Ask anyone.'

'Thanks. I'll do that,' said Carl with a smile.

He wanted to drive straight into town and find Mike but of course he didn't have a car. Without wheels at his disposal, he felt reliant and frustrated. He would put that to rights straight away.

Back at the hotel, he downed a quick breakfast of toast — made from a heavy but not unpleasant sort of wholemeal wheaten bread — some too-strong coffee and orange juice. The waitress pressed him to try a Full Cooked Irish Breakfast, whatever that was, but he didn't have time. She seemed a little deflated at his decision and he almost wished he'd ordered it just to please her.

In reception, he encountered Bridget, a plumper, slightly less pretty version of her sister. She seemed a pleasant sort of person and engaged him in conversation. He was surprised to learn that she was keen to see him and Kath reunited — he'd expected all Kath's family to have a vendetta against him. He hoped she exerted some influence on her sister.

After arranging rental of the car, the problem of how to get into Ballyfergus to pick it up was quickly resolved by the resourceful receptionist. The night porter, who was heading home, gave him a ride into Ballyfergus and chatted almost non-stop for the entire ten-minute journey. Carl was struck, once more, by the friendliness and openness of the people.

The porter dropped him on the outskirts of town where, after a few formalities, he picked up a BMW saloon. It took him several minutes to reacquaint himself with a stick-shift — he hadn't driven one since his student days — and then he drove carefully into the town centre.

It took him several attempts to wedge the rental car into a ludicrously tight parking lot in the centre of town. He opened the door of the car as far as he could, without bashing into the adjacent vehicle, and just managed to squeeze out of the driver's seat in the narrow gap. He was amazed at the meanness of the parking spaces and marvelled that all the cars weren't permanently marked by scrapes and bumps as a result of parking in such tight quarters.

On the High Street he stood and stared in one direction, then the other, deciding which way to explore first.

'Are ye lost?' said an elderly man, pulling some sort of trolley behind him. On his head was a cloth cap and he wore a tweed jacket.

'Yeah, I guess so. I'm looking for a butcher's shop called Mulhollands'.'

'Oh, it'll be Mulhollands' you're after,' said the old man with a laugh, correcting Carls' pronunciation.

Carl gave him a pained smile.

'It's up that way,' said the old man, raising a gnarled finger as he leaned for support on the wheeled trolley in which Carl could see a loaf of bread and cans of food. He pointed to the right. 'Fifty yards or so on your right. You can't miss it.'

Mulhollands' was an unassuming store which faced a road junction and fronted a stretch of sidewalk much wider than that which lined the rest of the street. Carl stood outside for a few moments composing himself. He reminded himself of his twin objectives — to find out the nature of the relationship between Mike and Kath and to warn the Irishman off her.

A blue van pulled up and he watched a white-coated man get out. The man went to the

416

back of the van, opened the doors and hoisted the carcass of a hog on his shoulders. He carried it through the open front door of the butcher's shop.

Carl took a deep breath and followed him inside.

Inside there were half-sides of cattle carcasses hanging from meat hooks against a white tiled wall at the back of the long, narrow space. In the glass display cabinet that separated staff from customers was a tidy display of fresh cuts of meat, sausages, hams and bacon, each separated from its neighbour by bright green plastic strips of grass. There were three men behind the counter busy cutting and weighing slabs of meat. They wore white shirts, blue striped aprons and small hats on their heads. All of them had their sleeves rolled up, revealing beefy, muscled forearms.

'Mike! That's Billy here now!' shouted one of them, referring to the man with the hog.

'About time,' came the good-natured reply and Mike Mulholland appeared in a doorway at the back of the store, with a notepad in his hand and a pencil lodged behind his left ear. He was wearing a green checked shirt and brown corduroys. The smile fell from his face as soon as he saw Carl.

'What can I get you, sir?' said one of the butchers but Carl did not take his eyes off Mike.

'It's all right, Ian,' said Mike, carefully removing the pencil and laying it, and the notepad, on a table at the back of the store. 'I think the man's here to see me.' He came round to the customer side of the display cabinet and said quietly to Carl, 'You'd better come through to the back.'

Then he led Carl through the door at the back of the store, along a narrow corridor and into a small paved courtyard with nothing in it but some old wooden pallets stacked against one wall. It was bordered at the back by a tall fence and on the other three sides by the age-stained grey walls of adjacent buildings. The slabs underfoot were wet and smelt strongly of disinfectant.

Mike folded his arms across his deep chest and, very deliberately, positioned his feet about eighteen inches apart.

'What can I do for you, Carl?' he said.

Carl pulled himself up to his full height and looked down at his adversary.

'I need to know about you and Kath,' he said, his voice full of disgust. 'I need to know if you're seeing each other.'

Mike cocked his head a little to one side and laughed. 'You need to know? Or you want to know?'

'Don't play games with me,' said Carl menacingly. 'You know why I'm here in Ireland.'

'I'm not sure I do, as a matter of fact,' said Mike and waited.

'I'm here because I want Kath back. And believe you me, I will have her.'

'Oh, will you now?' said Mike with a cocky sneer.

'Are you and she seeing each other, or are you not?' demanded Carl, resisting the urge to punch the little squirt in the face.

Mike blinked, breaking the eye contact into which they'd both been locked since entering the courtyard. He looked at the ground and said quietly, 'No, I'm not seeing Kath.'

Carl took a step backwards as relief washed over him. Momentarily he felt dizzy — he bent forward and rested his hands on his thighs. He hadn't realised how wound up he'd been.

'But tell me something, Carl, what makes you think that Kath's going to take you back after what you did to her?'

'What did Kath tell you about me?' said Carl, eyeing Mike intently from his half-crouched position.

'She told me enough to know that you're the biggest lying, cheating, two-faced shite I've ever had the misfortune to meet.'

The sentence hadn't finished leaving Mike's lips before Carl lunged forward and had him by the throat.

Carl's vision was suddenly blurred by a bright white light that obliterated his peripheral sight. All he could see was Mike's face and his ears filled with a sound like gushing water. He gripped the collar of Mike's shirt and, exerting every muscle in his body, lifted him bodily off the ground. There was a ripping sound as the right side of the collar gave way and partially detached itself from the body of the shirt. Carl lost his balance and released his grip on Mike.

Immediately, a powerful arm shot out and something hard connected with Carl's mouth. He felt a sharp stab of pain and fell backwards to

419

the ground, breaking his fall just in time by reaching out backwards with his hands, palms downwards.

He put his hand to his lip and when he looked at his fingers, they were splattered with blood. Mike was standing menacingly over him with a look of pure rage on his face. His left fist was balled so tight that the knuckles were white.

'You split my lip!' cried Carl in astonishment.

'Hey, what's going on out here, Mike?' said a deep voice and Carl looked up to see a squat, heavily built butcher filling the doorway into the store. The rage leached quickly from him to be replaced with a simmering anger.

The fat man stepped into the courtyard as daintily as a ballet dancer in his polished black brogues. 'Is he causing you bother?' he said to Mike, as his fists curled into meaty balls and he loomed over Carl.

'It's all right, Ian. Nothing I can't deal with,' said Mike, his voice full of contempt. He stepped away from Carl and unfurled his fist. 'Go on back inside.'

Ian hovered for a few seconds more and then, with a reluctant glance over his shoulder, obeyed. As he watched the man's broad back disappear, Carl ran his tongue over his rapidly swelling upper lip. The blood was warm and tasted like metal.

'I don't want to see you here again,' said Mike, panting. 'Or setting foot on my farm. Do ye hear me?' His shoulders were tensed and his arms remained crooked in a boxer-like pose, ready for further service.

'I'm warning you! You stay away from her.'

'You can't tell me what to do, Carl Scholtz. And the only person who can tell me to leave Kath O'Connor alone is Kath herself.'

Quickly, Carl picked himself off the ground, conscious that his recumbent pose placed him in a position of weakness relative to Mike. Back on his feet, he stood nearly four inches taller than the Irishman.

'She'll never have you, you know,' said Carl, looking down at Mike with a sense of superiority. 'You're wasting your time.'

'Maybe. Maybe not. But I'm in with a damn sight better chance than you are.'

'That's where you're wrong. I think I know what Kath wants. Don't forget that I've known her for three years and we were together for nearly two of them.'

'Don't forget that I've known her all my life.'

'She'd never choose you over me.' Carl searched for just the right term of abuse. 'I mean, what would she want with an ignorant Irish pig-farmer like you?'

For a few seconds the air between them was static with tension. Mike stood immobile, his face frozen, his eyes sparking like firecrackers.

Then he uttered a loud, disdainful noise, a sound somewhere between a snort and a guffaw.

'You might as well get your facts right,' he said scornfully. 'I don't keep pigs.'

'Whatever,' said Carl, disappointed that Mike had not risen to the bait.

'I think we should both let Kath decide what she wants, don't you?' said Mike coldly, took

421

another step away from Carl and folded his arms again. His shoulders dropped noticeably and the heaving in his chest abated. 'Now get out,' he said, his voice a hoarse whisper.

Carl straightened his coat, which had slipped off one shoulder in the tussle, and examined the palms of his hands. They were streaked with dirt. He glanced about futilely for somewhere to clean them and then wiped them on his dark blue jeans.

Then he turned and walked back through the store, with as much dignity as he could muster, staring straight ahead and ignoring the mur-mured whisperings of the staff inside.

Out on the sidewalk he checked himself for damage and was enraged to find the raincoat ruined. The back of the garment was stained with dirty water and the front was splattered with spots of bright red blood. He cursed Mike Mulholland out loud and his upper lip began to throb painfully.

By the time he got back to the car, his pulse had stopped racing and his head was clear again. He sat in the driver's seat and reflected on what had just transpired between him and Mike. He regretted letting things get out of hand. It wasn't the first time his quick temper had landed him in trouble but, he told himself, Mike had asked for it. Unfortunately though, Carl had come off the worst.

He examined his injury in the rear-view mirror — it wasn't serious enough to warrant medical attention but there was no way he could hide it from Kath. Though perhaps that wasn't a bad thing. Kath had always been squeamish about violence in movies and on TV. What would she think of Mike Mulholland when she found out that he'd assaulted him? Yes, decided Carl, firing up the car engine, if he chose his words carefully, he could definitely make this work to his advantage.

And, in spite of the set-to with Mike, he'd found out what he wanted to hear. Mike had confirmed that he and Kath were not a couple. The man most certainly had designs on Kath but, so far, it seemed she had not returned his affections. With this comforting revelation fresh in his mind, Carl drove slowly back to the hotel, planning what he would say to Kath when he saw her next.

31

A piece of paper, folded precisely in two, was waiting on Kath's desk when she came back from lunch. She picked the paper up. It was a handwritten note from Carl — she recognised his distinctive hand at once. She stared at it for a few seconds and then glanced furtively round the office. Only Moira was there and she was engaged in a prolonged and animated discussion with the laundry, which kept muddling the hotel's linen up with other customers', including the Marine Hotel.

Will you do me the honour of joining me for dinner tonight? said the note in Carl's elegant, cursive hand, full of the dramatic loops and curls that she'd once thought so romantic. She folded the note and held it briefly against her chest, remembering similar messages written in happier times. Then she smiled sadly, opened the piece of paper again and read on.

Please join me at 8 p.m. in the hotel restaurant, Yours always, Carl.

Kath frowned. She had no objection to meeting Carl for dinner — at the very least he was due the courtesy of a decent interview given that he'd travelled halfway round the world to find her. But not in the hotel restaurant. It would have to be somewhere else, away from the prying eyes, and ears, of the hotel staff.

She thought for a few moments, then picked

up the phone and dialled by memory.

A few minutes later she made a second call.

'Hi, it's me. Kath. I hope I didn't wake you.'

'No, not at all,' came a sleepy reply, sounding just the way Carl always did first thing in the morning. 'Just resting.'

'Listen, it's about tonight . . . ' She cleared her throat. His voice evoked the sensuous memory of dreamy early morning lovemaking sessions. She forced the images quickly from her mind and went on, 'I think we should meet somewhere else. Somewhere other than the hotel, I mean.'

'That's cool. Anywhere in mind?'

'There's a little place I know out the Drumnagreagh Road where I think we would have a bit more — more privacy to talk.'

'Oh, yes, of course. I would've suggested somewhere else but — '

'Well, you don't know the area. How could you?' she said, thinking that it was just as well that he'd left the choosing to her. There were few really good places to eat in Ballyfergus and most of the gems were well known only to locals. Linn Heights, tucked away in the countryside on a little-used country road, was one such place. 'I've booked a table for eight o'clock.'

'Good. So what time shall I pick you up at your house?'

'Quarter to the hour should give us plenty of time.'

'Right. I'll see you then,' he said and she was about to hang up when he added, 'Kath, I'm really looking forward to talking to you.'

'OK. I'll see you later.' She put the receiver

down. She noticed that her right hand was shaking. Quickly, she hid it under the desk.

Carl's voice still had the power to evoke such intense emotions in her. And in spite of her calm-sounding performance on the phone, her insides were all tangled up like a plate of buttered spaghetti.

She hadn't a clue what she was going to say to him when she met him. If he pressed her for an answer, as he surely would do, then she really didn't know what her reply would be. Common sense told her to say yes. After all, Carl was offering her everything she wanted: a clean slate, marriage and, hopefully, children, and all the warmth, love and companionship that came with family life.

But when she thought about these things she couldn't get the image of his wife and children out of her mind. She imagined a dark-haired Lynda, slim and pretty, with the children carbon copies of their mother. And when she thought about them she felt ill. Gut instinct warned her to be cautious. Carl could just as easily dump her the same way he'd dumped poor Lynda and the kids.

That night Kath dressed for dinner in a slapdash fashion, not because she didn't care but because she couldn't concentrate on the task. In the end she opted for a safe black trouser suit worn over a simple red camisole and high heels. It wasn't particularly flattering, she thought as she looked in the mirror, but it would do.

She heard a car pull up outside the farmhouse and looked out her bedroom window. With six weeks to go until the summer solstice, the days were getting longer and outside it was still light. Down on the track below a big flashy BMW purred quietly. The car door opened and Kath saw Carl step onto the flinty path. He was wearing dark-coloured trousers, an open-necked shirt and a jacket. He pulled the edges of the jacket together and approached the front door.

Kath collected her bag and went downstairs. She arranged a pleasant expression on her face, even though she felt seriously stressed, and prepared to exchange small talk. But, when she opened the door, the very first thing she noticed was Carl's lip — it was cut, and the area around the wound was red and swollen.

'Oh my God! What on earth happened to you?' she said and instinctively she touched her own lip in empathy with him.

'How are you, Kath?' he said, ignoring her question. 'You look lovely tonight.'

'Did you have an accident?'

'Sort of. Look, let's not stand here talking about it,' he said, glancing somewhat nervously over his shoulder. 'I'll tell you all about it at the restaurant.'

'OK,' said Kath, feeling slightly annoyed by his put-down. She pulled the door shut behind her and said, 'Let's go then.'

Carl walked round to the passenger side of the car, opened the door, waited for Kath to get in and then closed it gently. She placed the beaded evening bag awkwardly on her knee and realised how long it was since a man had taken her out to dinner. The last time in fact had been the night she'd misguidedly asked Carl to marry her. She shivered at the awful memory of that night and the following morning and tried to put it out of her mind.

Under normal circumstances she loved the whole ritual of going out — the dressing up, the pre-dinner drinks and the poring over the menu followed by a delicious meal with wine. But tonight she was a bundle of nerves. Carl got in beside her and directed the car quickly down the track towards the main road. In close proximity to him, Kath's composure all but evaporated and she began to perspire.

'I ate in the hotel restaurant last night,' said Carl and Kath was grateful to him for offering up a relatively banal subject for discussion. 'After I left you at the farmhouse.'

'What did you have to eat?' she asked and some of her nervousness evaporated as she awaited his response. She might mistrust some aspects of Carl's character but his educated palate was always reliable.

Just then they came to the bottom of the track and Carl said, 'Which way?'

'Right,' said Kath, just as Mike's muddy Land Rover pulled into the entrance where there was only just enough room for the vehicles to pass one another safely. Mike glanced into the car but did not acknowledge either occupant. Kath was surprised and then disappointed. She glanced at Carl but he was busy looking for traffic on the road and appeared not to have noticed Mike.

'Remember, drive on the left!' she cried as Carl pulled out on the wrong side of the road.

Quickly he corrected his mistake.

'So?' said Kath eagerly, after a few moments of silence had passed. 'What did you think of the food?'

He paused for a long time and then said slowly, 'It was OK,' which Kath took as a guarded compliment. Carl was a harsh critic.

'Truthfully?'

'Truthfully. Good local ingredients simply cooked and presented. It was more like farmhouse cooking than haute cuisine but I suppose that's not what you're aiming for.'

'I'm just trying to serve quality food that represents good value,' said Kath, slightly peeved by his snobbish comment. 'People around here are very canny.'

'Canny?' said Carl, not understanding.

'Careful with their money. Price is important. People like to think they're getting value for money or they won't come back. And outside of the summer season, the success of the restaurant depends on local business.'

'I see.'

After that they drove the short distance to the restaurant in an awkward silence broken only by Kath's intermittent directions.

Linn Heights was nothing to look at from the roadside. It was simply another spacious white villa, like many of the new properties springing up all over the countryside in Ireland. And that's what it had been until a few years ago when the owners, Bill and Jackie Cosgrove, built a big conservatory on the back of the house and decided to open a restaurant.

It was now very popular with locals who were always ensured a warm welcome and good, hearty food. If Carl thought the hotel food was rustic he would find the cooking in this place positively prehistoric. The signature dishes were steak and chips, an authentic Irish stew and apple and blackberry crumble. The restaurant's charm lay in the honest simplicity of the fresh, wholesome food and the feeling that you were a valued guest in someone's home rather than an impersonal restaurant.

Carl pulled into the small shingled car park and said with surprise, 'Is this it?'

Kath couldn't help but laugh. 'Yes, this is it. It's a very small family-run affair. A taste of real Ireland for you.'

Inside, the bald-headed, rotund figure of Bill Cosgrove greeted Kath warmly by name and spent a few moments conversing in general terms with Carl. After that he led them to their table by the window with lovely views of the green rolling countryside, placed a bottle of red wine on the table, along with handwritten menus, and left them in peace.

Family pictures were dotted along the deep windowsills along with china ornaments and small dried-flower arrangements, contributing to the feeling that you were in someone's personal space. Kath watched Carl with interest as he looked about the room with its shabby-chic mismatched china and cutlery, realising how things had changed. Before, if she'd taken Carl to a new restaurant, she'd have been on edge, fretting about whether he liked it or not. Now, she didn't really care what he thought. If he didn't like it, that was tough. She did.

'This all looks . . . very interesting,' he said.

'It is,' said Kath, picking up the menu. 'Why don't we order?'

Choosing from the menu didn't take long. There were three starters, four mains and three desserts to choose from. Kath choose the soup and lamb chops, Carl the mussels followed by medium-rare steak and chips. Bob sourced all his meat from Mulhollands' — she wondered how Carl would feel if he knew that. For some reason he'd taken an instant dislike to Mike.

'So,' said Kath. 'Are you going to tell me what happened your face?'

'It can wait,' he said, fixing her with a piercing stare. 'We've more important things to talk about.' He paused, ran his tongue over his sore-looking lips and began, 'Kath, I love you more than anything in the world — '

But Kath put her index finger to her lips, silencing him. 'Sshh,' she said quietly and shook her head. She closed her eyes briefly to fend off the tears that were gathering like storm-clouds in her eyes. 'Please, I don't want to hear that right now . . . '

'OK,' he said softly and then added with passion, 'but you must know how I feel about you, Kath.'

She silently nodded her assent. He took a sip of wine and allowed her a few moments to compose herself.

'Are you OK, Kath?'

'Yes, yes, I'm — I'm fine. I guess I'm still in

shock. I never expected you to turn up out of the blue like this.'

'Did you think I'd let you go so easily?' he said and placed his hot hand over hers where it was resting beside the breadbasket. She looked at the fine fair hairs on the back of his hand, swallowed and looked into his eyes.

'Why didn't you come sooner?' she asked, voicing the thought that had haunted her over the last few months.

'I didn't think you'd be ready to listen. And I needed time to sort things out — you know, between Lynda and me,' he said and had the decency to look down, shamefaced, at the lilac tablecloth.

Kath slipped her hand out from under his and said, hesitantly, 'And things are all . . . sorted out? You're definitely getting divorced?'

'Oh, yes,' he said brightly. 'It won't be easy but I think Lynda and I can come to some sort of arrangement.'

'But what about your daughters, Carl?' said Kath, her eyes filling with tears. 'You can't just walk out on them.'

'Kath,' said Carl patiently, but with an undertone of annoyance in his voice, 'believe me, I'm not walking away from my marriage lightly. That's why it's taken me so long to come and get you.'

Kath was slightly taken aback by the certainty, bordering on arrogance, reflected in this last statement. But Carl appeared not to notice her reaction and went on.

'I knew there was no point in coming here

until I was able to offer you a legitimate relationship. I had a lot of things to get straight in my own mind, and discuss with Lynda, before I was ready. This is just so difficult for me,' he went on, his voice softening. 'If only the children weren't involved . . . ' His voice trailed off.

It was a difficult decision, Kath didn't doubt that, but if he loved her the way he professed to, surely it was crystal clear what he had to do? It wasn't an easy choice by any means, but it was a clear-cut one. It was either his wife and family or her. Or had he been hoping to find a solution that would allow him to have his cake and eat it?

'Kath?'

'Sorry. What did you say?'

'Would you like some more wine?'

'Mmm — please,' she said and watched as he filled her glass with the ruby red liquid. The wine had certainly helped her to relax and her nerves had nearly gone. And far from the alcohol dulling her senses, she found her mind was suddenly very alert.

The starters came and they both ate in silence. Kath had two-thirds of the bright green pea and ham soup, then put her spoon down on the table.

'How is your soup?' asked Carl.

'It's lovely,' she said and nibbled on an oatcake that had come with the soup. 'How are your mussels?'

'Delicious.'

Carl stopped eating, dipped his fingers in the bowl of warm water Bob had delivered to the table along with the food, dried them on a napkin and said, 'You know how I feel about you, Kath, don't you?'

'I think so.'

'Well . . . ' he said and paused to glance up briefly as four diners were shown to the table next to them. He lowered his voice and went on, 'Do you remember what I asked you yesterday?'

Kath nodded and felt her face colour.

'My offer still stands,' he said and paused.

All of a sudden the oatcake felt like sand in her mouth.

'So what do you say, Kath?'

Kath swallowed with difficulty, took a sip of wine and said truthfully, 'I don't know what to say, Carl. I can't say 'yes' but I don't want to say 'no' either.'

'What the hell does that mean?'

'It means I can't give you an answer. Not yet anyway.'

'But I fly back to the States tomorrow. I need an answer by then.'

'I'm not sure I can give you one,' she said, nervously matching his even stare.

'Are you worried about what would happen with the hotel?'

'The hotel?' she repeated stupidly. 'Well, I suppose it would be very difficult to leave it right now — '

'I really admire what you've done with it, Kath,' he interrupted. 'The girl on reception was telling me how you've transformed it and that the restaurant's the talk of the town.'

'Thank you,' she said, wondering if he really meant it or was merely trying to butter her up.

'I can see how much effort you've invested in it and how much it means to you. But you shouldn't let it come between us. It could easily be sold — it's a very attractive property — and you know I would take care of any financial loss, if there was any. You don't need to worry about that.'

The idea of selling the hotel filled Kath with panic. It wasn't just her hotel: it was her life now. 'But it's not just about money, Carl. It's about what I want to do and where I want to do it. Right now, I can't imagine ever going back to Boston or doing anything else with my life.'

'So you want to stay here then?'

'Yes. I can't expect you to understand, Carl, and I know it sounds silly, but when I set foot on the Sallagh Braes, it felt like I'd come home.'

'You were home,' said Carl flatly.

'I mean in a spiritual sense, not literal,' she said quickly. 'After I found out about Lynda and the girls, and then my father died as well, I was . . . ' She paused and stared at the floor, as she searched for just the right word. 'Broken,' she said at last, meeting his gaze again. 'I was broken. And coming back here helped that pain to heal. I remember taking a walk on the Braes and feeling that everything was going to be alright. And though I was still hurting at the time, I felt strangely at peace. It's like the land is part of me and I'm part of it. This is where I'm meant to be.'

'OK,' he said, raising both his hands in the air in an impatient gesture. 'If that's what you want. Fine.'

435

'Fine?'

'It'll make things very difficult,' he said, sounding a little like a parent addressing a wayward child, 'but not impossible. I could sell the business and start up over here. Maybe in London or Dublin.'

'But they're miles away.'

'I could commute,' he said, but he didn't sound very convincing.

'Maybe that's not such a good idea,' observed Kath with a hint of bitterness. 'Look where weekly commuting got you the last time.'

'I'm trying to find solutions here, Kath,' he said shortly. 'What do you suggest?'

'I don't know,' said Kath flatly, genuinely perplexed.

Just then Bob came to clear the starters away and returned shortly thereafter with the main courses. Kath requested water and he went to get it, along with a selection of sauces — Dijon and hot mustard, horseradish and mint.

Kath put a piece of potato in her mouth and watched Carl cut open his steak and examine it closely. Satisfied, he put a large dollop of horseradish on the side of his plate and began to eat. Marriage, she reflected, was supposed to be a magical union of souls. Why were they talking about it in such clinical, practical terms?

'Carl, it's not meant to be like this,' she said suddenly, setting her cutlery down on the table.

'Pardon?' he said, with a full mouth.

'Marriage is supposed to be about love. It's supposed to be spontaneous and romantic. And all I'm worried about is how we'd shoehorn two

436

careers into our relationship. It just doesn't feel right.'

'Well, you're the one that's being so stubborn about everything. I don't see why we can't just go back to Boston and carry on — '

'Where we left off?' said Kath.

'Well, yes. Apart from the fact that we'd be married.'

Kath sighed.

'It's not just about the hotel, is it?' he said.

She shook her head and said, 'No.'

Carl put his cutlery down and said, 'You asked me what happened to my face today?'

'Yes,' said Kath warily. Though curious, she wondered what this diversion had to do with the serious topic under discussion.

'I went into Ballyfergus today.'

'Fur-gus,' she said. 'Not Fear-gus.'

'Whatever,' he said, sounding piqued. 'I went to see Mike Mulholland.'

Kath's heartbeat quickened. 'But why?'

'I saw you with your arms around him in the garden yesterday. I wanted to find out what was going on between you two. He did this to me.'

'But Mike's not a violent man,' said Kath disbelievingly. 'And I told you that nothing was going on,' she added, crossly. 'Why didn't you believe me?'

'I wasn't wrong,' he said and Kath's heart skipped a beat. What was he talking about?

'He did this when I told him to leave you alone.'

Kath sat back in her chair, shocked. Why would Mike do such a thing? Unless, of course, he cared about her . . .

'He's not the gentleman you seem to think he is. So if you have any feelings for him, I suggest you forget them. And, as you say, he has a girlfriend already.'

Kath was filled with rage at Carl's patronising manner. 'It's not because of Mike Mulholland that I can't say yes to your proposal, Carl,' she said coldly. 'I loved you so much and part of me probably always will. But that doesn't mean I'll marry you. After what you did to me,' she shook her head sadly, 'I don't really see how I can ever trust you again. And without trust what do we have? I'd spend the rest of my life looking over my shoulder, clock-watching when you're late, wondering who you're with and what you're doing. I don't think I can live like that.'

Carl sat back in his seat and stared at her. Then he leaned across the table and pleaded, all arrogance in his manner gone, 'Please, Kath. Can't you find it in your heart to forgive me?'

'I'm sorry, Carl. I really don't think I can,' said Kath and she dabbed away a tear that threatened to run down her left cheek. 'I want to. I want to so much. But I just can't.'

'I love you more than life itself, Kath. I'd do anything to get you back. Anything.'

'That's what worries me,' said Kath, with sudden clarity. 'I believe you would. Including lying and cheating and hurting other people just to get what you want.'

'That's not fair, Kath.'

'It's the truth, Carl. Isn't that what you've done up to now? The lies you told your wife and me to keep us both where you wanted us — her at home with the kiddies and me in your bed.'

'Oh, Kath! Don't throw away what we had because of bitterness. I am not the person you think I am. I can make you happy and we can have a wonderful life together. We can have children together too. A proper family.'

Kath blinked and said, 'I think I can give you your answer now, Carl.'

He stared at her and said, 'Think about it, Kath. Don't make the biggest mistake of your life.'

'Was everything alright?' said Bob, interrupting them and looking with concern at the half-eaten meals.

'It was absolutely lovely, Bob,' said Kath quickly. 'Really. It's us, not the food. It's just that we're not very hungry.'

Carl nodded in agreement.

'Can I get you any puddings then?' said Bob.

'Dessert, Carl?' said Kath.

'No, not for me,' he said, with a little wave of his left hand. 'Just a black coffee.'

'Same for me, please,' said Kath brightly and gave Bob a reassuring smile.

They were silent then for a few minutes and Bob came quickly with two coffees.

As soon as he moved on to serve the adjacent table, Kath said, 'I have thought about it. I've thought about little else for the last few months.' She cleared her throat and said, 'I can't marry you, Carl.'

'I see,' he said grim-faced and he tapped the teaspoon repeatedly on the cloth-covered table.

'And that's your final word?'

'It is,' said Kath, as she struggled to keep her voice steady.

'Tell me something. What made you make up your mind?'

'I don't know,' said Kath, not altogether truthfully. 'It just seemed clear to me all of a sudden.'

Carl drained his cup of coffee, threw a wad of notes on the table and said, 'Let's go. I'll take you home.'

'I can't let you pay,' said Kath, reaching for her handbag.

He stood up abruptly. 'What does it matter, Kath? It's only money. Come on, let's get out of here.'

He opened the restaurant and car doors for Kath, treating her with the same careful courtesy he'd always done. In the car on the way home neither of them spoke. Carl rested his right arm on the narrow windowsill and stared straight ahead, repeatedly rubbing his mouth with his right hand.

Kath looked out into the pitch-black darkness that surrounded them and thought about all the things she'd missed about Carl over the last few months. And all the things she would continue to miss when he was no longer part of her life — his generosity, his laughter, the warmth of his embrace, being loved — physically and emotionally. Having someone to share everything with — from her most intimate thoughts and secrets, to dull everyday events.

But she couldn't stop thinking about Mike

440

Mulholland. He would never have got into a fist-fight with Carl over her if he didn't care about her. And if he cared about her, maybe there was hope that his feelings might one day develop into something more. Kath had tried so hard to suppress her feelings for him, but it was no use. She realised that she was in love with him.

Carl turned the car in the yard behind the farmhouse and doubled back down the track where he pulled up outside the Kath's front door. He got out of the car without turning the engine off, opened Kath's door and helped her out of the car.

They walked back round to the driver's side of the car together and Carl put his hand on the open door. Inside, the instruments on the console glowed like the cockpit of an aircraft.

'So this is goodbye, then,' he said.

'Yes,' said Kath, wanting to say so many things but knowing that the time for talking was over. 'I'm sorry, Carl,' she said simply.

Then she stood on her tiptoes and placed a soft kiss on his stone-cold cheek. 'I hope you find happiness with someone who can love you back.'

He got in the car without another word and she watched until the car's tail-lights disappeared out of sight behind the wall that separated the hotel garden from the car park. From here the hotel, illuminated by ground level floodlights, looked serene and handsome in the darkness.

Kath stood there in the cool, calm night and watched Carl's tiny figure get out of the car, enter the hotel and disappear from sight. In the

441

morning he would be gone and she would never see him again. She bit her lip and mourned the passing of their love.

Then she stood in the darkness and listened to the heavy silence and realised that she had made the right decision. For she felt as though a great weight had been lifted from her shoulders. She felt free.

32

'So you sent him packing?' said Bridget, unfolding a pair of curtains that used to hang in one of the attic bedrooms at Highfield House.

It was the first Sunday in June and she and Kath were helping their mother move into her new flat. David and Ned had arranged all the heavy things, like the bed, sofa and other furniture, and now the women were adding the decorative touches.

'It didn't feel like that at the time. But yes, I suppose I did,' replied Kath, taking a well-wrapped bundle out of a brown cardboard box. She peeled off the layers of bubble-wrap to reveal a Lladro figurine of a small girl with a puppy at her feet. She placed it carefully on the dresser, aware of the great sentimental value each piece held for her mother.

'He asked her to marry him, you know, Mum,' shouted Bridget into the small kitchen that was directly off the lounge.

'I'm not surprised,' said Fiona, coming into the room with three mugs of hot coffee. She handed them round and said, 'He didn't come all the way across the Atlantic just for a chat and a cup of tea. He must've been very disappointed.'

'I don't know,' said Kath. 'With Carl, it's hard to tell. I don't think it'll take him long to get over me. He might even go back to his wife.'

443

'If she'll have him,' said Fiona.

'I still think you were mad to turn him down,' grumbled Bridget, examining the curtains.

'I don't,' said Fiona. 'Sure the man was a liar and a cheat. What sort of husband material is that?'

'Mum, what did you bring these curtains for?' said Bridget. 'They won't fit anywhere.'

'Yes, they will,' said Fiona. 'I measured them and they'll be perfect for my bedroom. Don't you remember? The attic ceilings weren't as tall as in the other rooms at Highfield House.'

Kath fished in the box for another ornament and thought how brave her mother was about moving in here. It was a perfectly serviceable, clean little flat but what a come-down from the house on the hill. Still, if her mother could put a brave face on things, so could she.

'These look nice here, don't they?' she said brightly.

'Yes. It's all starting to look more like home,' said Fiona, and she changed the position of the ornaments Kath had so carefully positioned, so that they were facing each other in pairs.

Inwardly, Kath smiled. She took a sip of coffee, set the mug down on a coaster on the dresser and continued on with her task, which she found mildly therapeutic. There was something very rewarding about making things right.

Bridget bustled across the floor with the curtains bundled in her arms. 'Well, I'll go and see if I can put these up,' she said cheerfully on her way out of the room. 'You don't want the neighbours gawking in at you in your undies!'

'Chance would be a fine thing,' said Kath and giggled.

Fiona gave her daughter a playful smack on the bottom. 'Don't you be so cheeky! I'll have you know that I have a pair of legs that any forty-year-old would be proud of!'

The women grinned at each other and Kath carried on with her task, while Fiona opened a box of books and began stacking them in piles on the coffee table.

After a few moments, Fiona glanced over her shoulder at the door. Then she went over to it, peeked into the hall and closed it gently.

Kath stopped what she was doing and looked at her mother.

'Kath, I haven't had a chance to talk to you since that dinner party at Bridget's,' said Fiona, picking up a book. 'How did it go? Bridget seemed to think it was a great success.'

Kath laughed and picked the Sellotape off another well-wrapped parcel with her fingernail. 'She's something else, Mum. Do you know that she told me there were going to be two other couples there? But when I arrived she said that they'd called off at the last minute. So it was just her, Ned, me and John Routledge. I don't believe that she'd invited anyone else.'

'So how did you and John get on?' said Fiona, her fingers inching their way blindly round the edges of the small hardback volume she held in her hands.

'It was actually a very enjoyable night. John's a nice guy and good company. He'll make someone a great husband one day.'

'But not you?' said Fiona and pressed the book to her chest.

'Oh, no, Mum,' said Kath with a laugh. 'I like John a lot but not that way.'

'Good,' said Fiona with what sounded like a sigh of relief. She set the volume down on the coffee table.

'What do you mean 'good'?' said Kath with a frown.

'Oh, just that I think you could do better than John Routledge, that's all.'

'John's a very nice person, Mum,' said Kath, thinking that there was a little bit of the snob about her mother. She wasn't prepared to let her get away with a comment like that. 'You'd be lucky to have him as a son-in-law.'

Fiona blinked and raised her eyebrows but said nothing.

'Anyway, with my non-existent love life, I'll be lucky if I ever get married,' said Kath, trying, and failing, to inject humour into the words.

'Don't say that, love,' said Fiona gently and momentarily she placed a reassuring hand on Kath's arm. 'There's someone out there for you. You just haven't found him yet, that's all.'

Kath gave her mum a small smile to show that she was grateful for her encouraging words. But, though kindly meant, they gave Kath no comfort. She knew time was running out.

She thought about Mike every day, but she couldn't summon up the courage to approach him. What would she say? 'Do you fancy me?' Or, 'I know you've a girlfriend, Mike, but would you like to go out with me?' Or how about going for the kill? 'Would you like to marry me and have children together?' The poor guy would run a mile.

'You're miles away. What are you thinking about, love?' said Fiona.

Kath stared at her mother for a few seconds and then said, 'I was thinking about Bridget and Mike. There was something I wanted to ask you about them. They went out together for a few months, didn't they?'

'That's right. You'd just gone to the States,' said Fiona, taking another book out of the box.

'Tell me about it,' said Kath, gently setting a partially unveiled ornament back in its wrapping so that she could concentrate on listening.

'Well, there's not an awful lot to tell. Mike used to call at the house a lot. It was a bit like having another son around, actually. You know how I've always liked him. They went out to discos and the pictures — all the usual things. It lasted about two and a half months.'

'And then what happened?'

'Mike broke it off.'

'Why?'

'I got the impression that Bridget was getting too serious and all he wanted was a laugh and a bit of fun.'

'And was she serious about him?'

'Oh, yes. She was in love with him.'

'I wonder why she never told me?' said Kath.

'But you did know they went out together.'

'I meant that she never told me she loved him,' said Kath, suddenly realising that she didn't

447

know her sister as well as she thought she did.

Fiona shrugged, removed the last volume from the box, placed it on one of the stacks of books and threw the empty container in the corner of the room along with the others.

'Maybe it was too painful for her, Kath. She hardly talked to me about it. It took her a long time to get over him. But she did, eventually, and then she met Ned. And now it's all history,' said Fiona and she paused, eyeing Kath keenly. 'Why do you ask?'

'You don't think she still holds a candle for him, do you?' said Kath, avoiding her mother's question.

'Oh, Kath, don't be ridiculous. Sure she's a happily married woman with three lovely children. What would she be hankering after him for?'

'Yes, yes, I suppose you're right,' said Kath, feeling a little foolish.

There was a long pause and then Fiona said, 'You know, Mike's an awful nice guy, Kath. And I think he likes you.'

'Oh, I don't think so. Anyway, what about A — .' began Kath but just then the door burst open.

'Right, that's the curtains up. You were right, Mum. They do fit and they look great. Hey,' Bridget paused, looking from her mother to Kath, 'what are you two talking about?'

Fiona's mouth moved like a goldfish's but no sound came out.

Kath said quickly, 'Emmy and Steve. You must remember — my friends from the States?'

'Oh, yes,' said Bridget. 'I've heard you mention them once or twice.'

'Well, I was just telling Mum that they're coming over to Ireland in a couple of weeks. I was thinking of having a party for them.'

'I think it's a great idea,' said Fiona, recovering her composure. 'Emmy's a lovely girl.'

'Great,' said Bridget. 'When were you thinking of having it?'

Bridget listened with interest while Kath invented plans for the hastily improvised party on the spot. By the time their brief conversation was over, the arrangements were planned in their entirety.

'But will you have time to do all that, as well as prepare for David and Simone's wedding?' said Fiona.

'The wedding doesn't take that much planning as far as the hotel is concerned. John'll do most of the work — I'll just be keeping an eye on things. And they want it to be pretty low-key anyway.'

'I don't see why, just because Simone's pregnant, they can't do it properly,' said Bridget.

'I don't think that's got anything to do with it, Bridget,' said Fiona. 'I think it's just the way both of them are — you know Simone doesn't like a fuss. And neither does David. It's just not their style'

'It'll be lovely,' said Kath confidently. 'Just you wait and see. Now have either of you given any thought to a wedding present?'

★ ★ ★

449

Carl spent the next few weeks back in Boston. He went about his business in a state of suspended disbelief, refusing to accept Kath's rejection. He wrote her a long letter, once more apologising for what he'd done and begging her forgiveness. He received no reply.

He tried to think of other ways to reach her heart and drew up plans for another trip to Ireland, only to abandon them a few days later. What could he say to her that he hadn't already said? He'd offered to marry her, pack in the business, move country, have children with her. And still that had not been enough. He had nothing more to offer.

After he'd left Ireland, he'd gone over and over their last conversation in his mind, recalling every detail of the exchange. And as he did so, the memory crystallised, and eventually he was left with one overriding recollection — the subtle change that took place in Kath at the mention of Mike Mulholland's name. The downward glance, the faint flush that came to her cheeks. He had been looking for it, that was true, but the signs were there all the same. Even if she didn't realise it herself, she was in love with Mulholland. It was only then that Carl realised that he would never win her back.

He went to work as usual, numbed with shock, and had the kids for the weekend. He brought them down to the apartment in St Botolph Street where they sat indoors, because there was no garden to play in, and Daisy complained that she was bored. They missed their friends and their toys and, at night, Jasmine cried for her mother. Carl crawled into the single bed with her and held her in his arms and wept silent tears for Kath into her soft, fine hair.

The next day he took them to the movies and for lunch at one of his regular haunts — Angelo's Ristorante on Boylston Street — where they wouldn't eat anything but plain buttered spaghetti. They sat like little women with beaded handbags on their laps in the pretty dresses their mother had packed for them, looking wary and confused. Carl's heart ached. Then, with no warning, Jasmine wet herself, a sign of her insecurity. Carl realised he hadn't brought a change of clothes and they had to go straight home in a cab.

In the cab Jasmine insisted on sitting on his knee and he stared out the window as the cold, bitter-smelling urine soaked through his cream linen trousers. He knew more than most how much children needed a secure and stable home. And there were worse things than staying in a loveless marriage, weren't there? Like being alone.

He thought of other cultures where arranged marriages were based on common shared values, class and wealth. Most of these marriages were successful — love was not a prerequisite but something that grew over time. This proved that love, if properly nurtured and fostered, could grow in the most sterile of environments. There was no reason why, if he and Lynda tried, they could not resurrect the love they'd once shared. He held Jasmine tight and kissed the top of her golden head and resolved to try and make his

451

marriage work. For their sake as much as his own.

Back at the apartment, he let the girls watch the cartoon channel on TV and fed them Ben and Jerry's ice-cream until Jasmine vomited all over the cream carpets and cried, yet again, for her mother. He would have taken them back to Williamstown straightaway because he knew that they were not enjoying themselves. Nothing he did pleased them because they simply did not want to be here. But taking them home now would be a sign of failure — and a victory to Lynda. So he gritted his teeth and tried to do his best.

'You shouldn't give her so much ice-cream to eat, Dad,' said Daisy, once Jasmine was happily settled again in front of the TV screen. 'It always makes her sick.'

Carl rubbed at the carpet with a wet cloth where Jasmine had vomited, ashamed that he did not know this simple fact about his own daughter. He realised he was little more than a stranger to Daisy and Jasmine — more like a fond uncle than a real dad.

'Mom has a secret and she says I'm not to tell you,' said Daisy suddenly. She pulled her legs up under her on the sofa and giggled.

Fear gripped Carl. What was Lynda up to that she didn't want him finding out about it?

'But I'm your dad. It's OK to tell me,' said Carl, feeling like a complete heel coaxing the secret out of her. 'Mom and I don't keep secrets from each other.'

Daisy put her hands over her mouth and

mumbled something.

'What did you say, darling?'

'Come over here. I'll whisper.'

Carl crawled on his knees over to the sofa and leaned close to Daisy.

She cupped her small hands around his ear and said quietly, 'Mom's got a boyfriend.'

Carl pulled away and smiled at Daisy, not wanting to alarm her or make her think that she had done wrong in telling him.

'Really?' he said and swallowed the lump in his throat. 'Have you met him?'

'Yes.'

'How many times?'

Daisy picked at the big toenail on her right foot and said, 'I don't know. Just once, I think.'

'Is he nice?'

'I don't know,' she said again and shrugged.

'What's his name?'

'Bob.'

'I see.'

Carl took the cleaning things back into the kitchen, rested his hands on the counter and hung his head. Lynda hadn't wasted any time, had she? They'd only started talking about divorce and already she had another man on the go. He wondered if he'd been to the house in Williamstown and how often. He wasn't happy about the idea of a strange man being round his daughters.

Then the thought suddenly struck him that this might not be a new relationship. He couldn't imagine Lynda introducing a man she'd only just met to her children. That was rich — after the hard time she'd given him about Kath! But all was not lost, he told himself, as he started to panic.

Even though Lynda had known about Kath for some time, she had not demanded a divorce. And now that Kath was out of the picture perhaps she would be willing to return to the status quo. This Bob, whoever he was, was probably an attempt at getting back at him. Why else would she have allowed Daisy to meet him, knowing full well that the child would probably spill the beans to her father?

That night, after he'd read the children what felt like a hundred stories and tucked them up in bed, he sat with a glass of bourbon on the sofa and resolved to return to Williamstown as soon as possible the next day. He'd learnt from his mistake with Kath not to hang around.

As soon as the children were dressed and breakfasted, Carl packed the car. It was a gorgeous bright, early June morning with the heat of the day still to come when they set off. In the back seat Daisy played with the Gameboy Carl had bought her and Jasmine soon fell asleep. They reached Williamstown just before noon.

The first thing Carl noticed was the unfamiliar car in the driveway — a sand-coloured luxury pick-up truck, the kind used for posing in rather than a workhorse. It didn't belong to Lynda's parents or anyone he knew. He wondered if it was one of her 'weekday' girlfriends from school or nursery — women he rarely met. Daisy got out of the car with him — Jasmine was still

454

asleep — and together they approached the door to the kitchen.

'Carl!' cried Lynda when she opened the door to them, wearing grey jogging pants and a red T-shirt. Her hair was hanging loose like she'd just got out of bed. She put her hand up to her neck.

Standing behind her was a man of about Carl's age, rather heavily built with a pug nose and dark curly hair. He was wearing a short-sleeved pink polo shirt and cream chinos. His hands were in his pockets but, as soon as he heard Lynda's exclamation, he pulled them out and looked at his toes.

'Oh, look, it's Bob,' said Daisy and she ambled past her mother into the room.

Instantly Carl filled with rage. He opened his mouth to speak, closed it again and then, with the greatest act of self-control that he had ever brought to bear, he simply turned on his heel and walked away. He stormed round the back of the house, ran for several minutes through the trees and stopped to catch his breath in a sunny clearing.

Sweat beaded his brow. He wiped it away with his bare forearm and took several deep breaths. The initial surge of anger subsided and rational thought took over instead. How he handled this situation would determine the success of his discussions with Lynda — and therefore his entire future. He reminded himself that he was the one who had asked for a divorce. She was perfectly entitled to do what she wanted and see whom she wished. It was none of his business. It wasn't important either — what mattered was getting the result he wanted.

With these shaky resolutions fresh in his mind, he walked straight back to the house and, when he got there, the girls were inside with their mother and Bob was gone.

'You should have called, Carl,' said a red-faced Lynda, busying herself with clearing away the breakfast remains. 'I wasn't expecting you until this afternoon. I thought you said you were going to take the girls to the museum today.'

'Change of plan. Look, forget about it, Lynda. It was my fault. You're right, I should've phoned. I wasn't thinking.'

She looked at him as though he'd gone crazy and said, 'He stayed here last night, you know.'

'I guessed as much,' he said, struggling to appear calm. 'Where are the girls?'

'In the play room.'

Carl sat down heavily on the barstool that Bob must have recently vacated. There was a half-empty cup of coffee on the breakfast bar along with the Sunday edition of the *Boston Globe*, opened at the sports page.

'Who is this Bob anyway?' he said, thinking that he looked like a used-car salesman.

'He owns Beaverbrook.'

Beaverbrook was one of The Berkshires top-class skiing resorts, catering mainly for upper-class weekend skiers from Boston. So he was loaded — why did that not surprise him? It must be something in her genes — she was attracted to rich men like a moth to a flame.

'And a couple of lakeside resorts in New Hampshire.'

'Lynda, let's not talk about Bob. Let's talk about us.'

'There isn't an 'us',' snapped Lynda. 'Unless you mean the divorce. You should've heard from my lawyers by now.'

'Yes, I got a letter. But I haven't instructed my lawyers yet.'

'Why not?'

'Because we need to talk,' he said and paused. 'Come and sit beside me. Please.'

Lynda perched warily on the barstool beside him and he went on.

'Look, I understand about Bob, Lynda. I know that you're only seeing him to make me feel jealous. Why else would you have introduced him to the girls? You must've known that Daisy would tell me about him. And I am jealous. There, are you happy?'

Lynda looked at him in disbelief. She probably hadn't realised that her actions were so transparent.

'And I guess I deserve it, after what I did to you. I can't explain why I did it and I certainly can't ask you to understand it. I don't understand it myself. All I can say is that I'm truly sorry if I hurt you.'

'What is it that you want, Carl?' said Lynda slowly, her brow furrowed in concentration.

'Lynda,' he said and paused before going on, 'I want to put the past behind us and make a go of our marriage. I want to us to rediscover the love we once had.'

'She's dumped you, hasn't she?' said Lynda triumphantly and Carl felt his face colour.

'This isn't about Kath,' he said evenly.

'Like hell it isn't,' said Lynda, her eyes boring into him like drills. 'Answer me. Has she blown you out or not?'

'Kath and I don't have a future together,' answered Carl evasively. 'My future is here with you and the kids.'

'Oh no, it's not,' said Lynda and then she laughed so loudly Carl looked over his shoulder to make sure she hadn't attracted the attention of the children. She threw her head back as she laughed, then brought her gaze back to rest on Carl. Abruptly she stopped laughing.

'You are so absolutely full of it, Carl,' she said. 'And you are completely wrong about Bob. I've known him all my life — we were in high school together, our parents socialised together and we used to date long before I had the misfortune to meet you. And before you think about citing him in any proceedings, nothing happened between us until Bob heard you'd walked out on me. He came to see me that very same night. Bob loves me, Carl, really loves me. Not your kind of love that transfers so easily from one person to another like lipstick. I should have married him, not you.'

'But, Lynda, think about the girls!' cried Carl, the only line of defence he could think of in the face of her unexpected outburst.

'The girls like Bob. They'll be absolutely fine

about it. The reason I introduced him to them is so that they get used to him being around.'

'But, Lynda, they need their father.'

'Don't worry,' she said in a soothing voice, but her eyes were as cold as a Berkshire winter. 'You'll get perfectly reasonable visiting rights. And let's face it, Carl, they hardly saw you when we were together. To be honest, I doubt that they'll notice that much difference as far as you're concerned. And Bob will make a wonderful stepdad.'

'But I love you, Lynda. And you're — you're my wife.'

'Love!' she said and she slammed the flat of her hand down on the breakfast bar. 'You don't know the meaning of the word, Carl. Bob does. He's loved me all his life and he's waited for me all these years. And do you know what?' She leaned forward until her face was inches from his.

He shook his head, unable to think of anything to say to douse the fire of her uncharacteristically fierce emotions.

'I love him!'

Lynda stood up then and pulled the hem of her T-shirt over her slim hips. 'So if you don't mind I'd like to set the divorce proceedings in train and I'd advise you to start talking to your attorney.'

'You would?' he said stupidly.

'Yes. Because I'm going to take you to the cleaners.'

★ ★ ★

Carl pulled the dustsheet off the aggressive-looking Harley Davidson Fatboy in the lock-up garage he rented for a small fortune just a few minutes from St Botolph Street. The garage was specially insulated and in the winter he paid for it to be heated. He stood perfectly still for a few moments, savouring the curves and lines of the beautiful machine.

The bike had been fully customised over the course of a year and a half so that it was now a unique reflection of his personal taste and preferences. The engine had been fully rebuilt for added performance, the bodywork airbrushed with a specialist flamed-effect finish and every component possible had been replaced with chrome accessories from the world's best-known Harley customiser. The bike glittered like a piece of expensive jewellery, the tyres were black as wet coal and every inch of her shone like the sun.

He liked to imagine that his father had had a hand in assembling the original bike, now unrecognisable under twenty-four-thousand-dollars' worth of chrome and mechanical refinements, but he knew that the likelihood of that was slim. Nowadays the Milwaukee factory manufactured bike parts — engine and transmission components. Assembly took place at other locations across the US.

Still, if he was ever telling anyone his 'poor boy made good' story he liked throw that in as a one-liner — 'My old man built this bike in the factory in Milwaukee. Worked there, doing damn near the same job, for nearly forty years.' His father did not even know that his son owned a

Harley. Keeping this information secret was a satisfying little bit of personal revenge.

In the game of poker that was Carl's life, he'd taken many chances and, more often than not, the gambles had paid off. But this time he'd lost. And it couldn't have been a more spectacular failure — he'd lost his wife, family and Kath. And all the money in the world couldn't put his world to rights again.

He grieved for Kath. He had truly loved her. He loved her still. He would never stop loving her and the pain would be with him always. He found it hard to concentrate much on anything — his life seemed pointless. When he thought of the sheer effort, brainpower and energy he'd exerted in maintaining his parallel lives for so long, he marvelled that he'd ever found the resources within himself to do it. Now he just felt worn out and empty. Everyday tasks — like shaving and getting dressed — seemed to take so much out of him.

But he was an adult and his pain was self-inflicted — he would learn to live with it. He had no choice. Lynda and Kath were certainly better off without him — he hoped they could see that. And he was sure that they would, in time, rebuild their lives with men more worthy of them. He wished them well. He wished them the happiness that seemed beyond his grasp.

Of all his regrets, the one that pained Carl the most was the knowledge that he'd failed his daughters. When he'd held them in his arms as tiny babies he'd resolved to provide them with a loving and stable home, because he had been denied this himself as a child. He remembered the desperate longing for normality — a mom and dad who came to parents' evenings and sat round the dinner table at night over a home-cooked meal and doted on their only son. He bit his lip to stop himself from breaking down.

The girls were probably better off without him too. What kind of a father and role model was he for them anyway? A liar and a cheat. He'd rarely been there for them and, when he was there physically, he was often mentally preoccupied with work and Kath. He would maintain contact with them, of course, but he knew he would never have a close relationship with them. He didn't know how to be a good father. Bob would probably do a better job than he.

For the first time in nearly thirteen years Carl was alone again. Entirely alone — no one to care what time he came in at night or how his day at work had been. And the thing that had once driven him so hard — the acquisition of material things — now seemed an empty, shallow pursuit.

At Carl's feet was a black nylon holdall. Already he was perspiring in the heat of the hot July day. He would have to work quickly if he wasn't to end up drenched in sweat. Biking leathers, though essential, were heavy and cumbersome and murder to wear on a day like this. But, once he was out on the open road with the wind blowing through his half-unzipped jacket, he knew that he would be comfortable.

He stuffed the contents of the bag into the tassel-trimmed leather panniers flanking the back wheel. He travelled light — a couple of T-shirts, shorts, a light sweater, one pair of long pants, light footwear, underwear and a small soap bag. He could buy anything else he needed along the way.

A psychiatrist had once told him that he would never be truly happy until he came to terms with his childhood. She was right — at his core was a miserable boy, rejected by his father and, in her less obvious way, by his mother. All his life Carl had avoided moments of quiet reflection because he did not like what he saw — a man with everything and satisfied with nothing.

He knew he wasn't capable of loving in the selfless way he had observed in other people. It was true that you could only truly love when you loved yourself. But if as a child you were not the recipient of unconditional love, then how could you learn how to return love? All he had learnt was to manipulate people to get what he wanted. But this, as he'd so disastrously proved, was no road to happiness.

Carl eased an open-faced helmet over his damp hair and snapped the catch under his chin. He donned a pair of black goggles and positioned them carefully over his eye-sockets. He felt in his back pocket for a black leather wallet and checked that it was chained securely to a belt loop on his chaps. He pulled a bandana up over his mouth and eased his hands into a pair of lightweight summer biking gloves.

His mother was dead but his father was still very much alive and living in Wisconsin. He'd remarried and outlived his second wife, Bella, whom Carl had never met. They'd had two sons together but Carl did not know where they were now. The only reason he knew his father was still alive was because they exchanged Christmas cards every year.

Or rather, against his wishes, Lynda exchanged a gilt-edged, personalised card from the family on Carl's behalf. From a close and loving family herself, she could never understand Carl's estrangement from his only remaining parent. Now he was grateful to her for the fact that he and his father had never lost touch.

In the inside zipper pocket of his jacket was a scrap of paper with his father's address written on it. It burned against his chest. He hoped that it held the key to the questions that had haunted him all his life.

Carl threw his leg over the bike, pressed the ignition switch and the machine barked into life. He twisted the throttle — she growled like a beast, then the engine settled into the distinctive Harley 'potato-potato-potato' rumble he loved so much. He wrestled the bike into an upright position, flicked the side stand up with his left heel, clunked the bike into first gear and she cruised, smooth as an ocean-going liner, out into the brilliant sunshine.

Carl did not know how long this journey would be, where it would take him or if he would ever come back. He only knew that his hope for the future lay in facing up to the ghosts of his past.

33

'Thanks for the drinks party, Kath,' said Emmy with a big wide grin, looking around the small function room. It had yet to be refurbished in line with Kath's ambitions but it was serviceable enough and on just the right scale for the small party. 'It's been really nice to meet all your family and friends like this.'

Everyone had assembled to give Emmy and Steve a big send-off. All Kath's family were there as well as friends, both old and new. In the morning they were taking the train to Belfast and then on to Dublin where they would be met by Emmy's brother, who'd drive them on down to Waterford.

'It wasn't much,' said Kath, referring to the simple supper she'd laid on. 'But I wish you could've stayed longer. I've really enjoyed having you here. But it just hasn't been long enough.'

'I know,' said Emmy, pulling a face. 'But the family are dying to meet Steve. And we've only got two weeks to see everybody. There's so much to squeeze in.'

'I miss you,' said Kath, her eyes beginning to fill up with tears, lubricated by several glasses of white wine.

'Me too.'

'But you have Steve,' said Kath and sniffed into her wineglass, feeling sorry for herself.

'And you've got all your family around you

465

and these great friends,' said Emmy, determined to pull Kath out of her melancholy.

'It's not the same as having you,' said Kath, sounding like a petulant child. Then she smiled at her foolishness, put her arms round Emmy and gave her a big hug.

When Emmy had extracted herself from Kath's embrace she said quietly, 'Are you sure you've made the right decision coming back here?'

Kath nodded and said, 'Absolutely. I've made a lot of mistakes but coming here isn't one of them.'

Emmy stared at her friend for a few seconds and then said, 'Have you dated anyone since Carl?'

'No,' said Kath, shaking her head and wrinkling her nose.

Out of the corner of her eye she noticed Anne, Mike's girlfriend, talking with Bonnar, one of the hotel staff. As Kath watched them she opened her eyes in amazement. Anne's body language was subtle but she was clearly flirting — at one point she put her hand on his shirt and stroked Bonnar's chest. He reciprocated by leaning forward and whispering something in her ear that made Anne laugh. Immediately Kath sought out Mike's face in the crowd.

'Why not?' said Emmy.

'There's no one in the least bit interested in me,' she said, without taking her eyes off the little drama unfolding in the corner of the room.

'Isn't there?' said Emmy and her eyes twinkled mischievously as she scanned the faces in the room. 'What about him over there?'

'Who?' said Kath, amazed that Mike didn't seem in the least bit concerned at Anne's behaviour. In fact, if anything, he was watching her with something akin to amusement on his face. They must have a weird sort of relationship if he was happy to let her go chatting up other men. Maybe it turned him on. Kath shivered.

'That man in the suit with the glasses,' said Emmy, drawing Kath's attention away from Mike.

'Frank Morrison?' said Kath. 'Oh, no. You've got to be joking. He's my bank manager, for heaven's sake.'

'Well, he's been watching you all night.'

'No, he hasn't. You're imagining things, Emmy.'

'I'm not, you know,' she replied knowingly. 'Anyway, what's wrong with him? Is he married or something?'

'No — for a change,' said Kath, referring sarcastically to Carl and this raised a rueful smile from Emmy. 'It's just there's absolutely no chemistry between us.'

'Well, what about that Mike Mulholland then? Remember when you came back to Boston you told me you fancied him. He seems really nice.'

'Well, I've gone off him a bit,' said Kath truthfully, though only because of Anne. She glanced back at Mike who was now engaged in conversation with David. 'He's got a girlfriend. That's her over there — she's just walking towards the door. The tall good-looking one with the long hair.'

'Looks a bit young for him.'

'Mmm. That's what I thought. Anyway, he's already taken.'

'Well, I've news for you, Kath. He hasn't been able to keep his eyes off you either!'

'Now you really are letting your imagination run away with you,' said Kath, and she burst out laughing, more out of nerves than humour. She so desperately wanted Emmy's observation to be true but she knew it was impossible. She caught Mike's eyes, blushed and looked away.

'Listen, Kath,' began Emmy, after a few moments had passed. Then she clamped her lips shut as though trying to stop herself from blurting something out.

'Yes?' said Kath and waited.

Emmy hesitated, lowered her voice and then went on, 'There's something I want to tell you. Though it's not official yet and we haven't even told my parents.'

'What?' said Kath, fully expecting an engagement announcement.

Emmy set her untouched glass of wine on the table beside them. Her hand was shaking and suddenly Kath was alarmed.

'I'm expecting,' said Emmy.

'A baby?' cried Kath, in utter surprise.

'What else, you twit?' said Emmy goodnaturedly and she smiled. Kath glanced down at her friend's stomach, though of course there was no visible evidence to be seen.

'But you said you didn't want children,' said Kath, as she battled with the twin emotions of joy and jealousy. She was the one who wanted

468

kids, not Emmy. It wasn't fair.

'I know,' said Emmy and she shrugged her shoulders. 'But it happened.'

'And you're pleased?'

'Delighted.'

'Then so am I,' cried Kath unreservedly, and she gave Emmy a brief hug and a kiss on the cheek, ashamed of her initial reaction. She took both Emmy's hands in hers and said, 'That is the most wonderful, wonderful news. Now tell me all about it. When's it due for a start?'

She listened carefully while Emmy told her all about the new baby and how she and Steve were hoping to buy a bigger home. Kath remembered the dreams she once had about a similar future and put them firmly out of her mind. She determined to take pleasure in Emmy's happiness. She would not dwell on her own disappointments. She would not allow herself to become bitter and resentful.

While Emmy chatted away happily, Kath looked for Mike at the spot where she'd last seen him but he was gone. A few seconds later she spotted him by the supper table engaged in a tête-à-tête with Bridget. Ned was nowhere to be seen and Anne was still practising her seductive charms on the waiter.

Mike was leaning in close to Bridget, talking quickly and using his hands now and then to elaborate on a point. Kath wondered what on earth they could be talking about in such an animated manner.

' . . . so you'll have to come over and visit when the baby comes. It'll be February though,' said Emmy, and her expression darkened. 'You might not want to come when the weather's so miserable.'

'Don't you worry, I'll be there,' said Kath firmly, with a reassuring smile. 'Whenever that baby chooses to appear!'

It was late when the last of the guests finally left, Frank Morrison lingering until the bitter end. Emmy and Steve had already gone up to their room and Kath had just said goodbye to Lorna, her beautician friend, and her partner, which left her alone in the room with Frank.

'Kath,' he said and she froze on the spot.

She turned to face him with a cheery grin on her face. 'Did you have a good time?' she asked, determined to make light conversation in spite of Emmy's observation ringing in her ears.

'The party? Yes. It was great,' he said, as though he was thinking about something different altogether.

'Good,' said Kath, and she moved towards the door, although she sensed that he had not finished speaking.

'There was something I wanted to ask you,' he said and she was forced to stop and turn around once more.

'I . . . ' he said and stopped as a waitress came into the room.

They watched while she stacked dirty plates on a tray and carried them away.

'I wanted to ask you — ' said Frank and paused.

Kath stood with a stupid grin on her face and prayed that he would not ask her on a date. She liked Frank a lot and considered him a friend. She did not want the easy nature of their relationship to change. She did not want things to be spoilt.

'I wanted to ask you,' he repeated and Kath's heartbeat quickened, 'if you'd like to have dinner with me sometime.'

He coughed and momentarily Kath considered pretending that she thought he meant a casual dinner as mutual friends. But it would be cruel to do so — there was no mistaking his intent. He shuffled nervously from one foot to the other, put his right hand to his mouth, the fingers curled into a tube, and coughed again.

'I'm sorry, Frank,' she said, feeling his mortification as she delivered her rejection. 'Thank you but no. I'm very fond of you as a friend but nothing more. I'm sorry.'

'No, no, it's quite alright,' he said with a big, false smile, as his face flushed red. 'It was just a thought. Never mind. Look at the time. I'd better go now.'

'Yes, it is late,' said Kath, trying hard to act normally and pretend she did not notice his excruciating awkwardness.

'Goodnight, Kath,' he said quickly, planted a chaste peck on her cheek and disappeared quickly through the door.

Kath touched her cheek where he had kissed her and sighed. She sensed that it had taken a lot of courage for him to approach her. How she wished she could've saved him from the hurt and embarrassment.

And it was funny, she thought, as she switched

out the lights and left the room, how Emmy had seen what Kath could not. She never in a million years would have thought Frank Morrison fancied her. But Emmy had been right.

And then Kath wondered if her friend's intuition was as accurate when it came to Mike Mulholland . . .

34

'Of course, we shouldn't really be staying in the same place tonight,' called Simone from the steamy bathroom, where she lay in the bathtub, neck-deep in bubbles. 'I mean, it's not traditional for the bride and groom to see each other on the morning of the wedding, let alone wake up in the same bed together! My outfit is supposed to be a secret too. Still, I suppose it's a bit late for false modesty and all that.'

David sat on the bed and pulled off his sock. He put it to his nose, sniffed and said under his breath, 'Jesus!' He threw the sock at the laundry basket, where it landed a foot short on the rust-coloured carpet, and repeated the procedure with the other one.

'Can I get in that water after you?' he called.

'Are you listening to a word I'm saying?' said Simone, sounding indignant, and David smiled.

He wandered through to the bathroom, naked, and knelt down at the side of the bath. He scooped up a handful of bubbles.

'Hey, what do you think you're doing?' she said.

He smiled at her and dotted her upturned nose with suds, ignoring her remark. Then he put his hand in the bath and felt the slippery curve of her large left breast, suspended like a pendulum in the water. He tweaked the nipple

473

until he felt it go hard like a leaf bud. His penis stiffened.

'Do you want to get in?' she said, her voice dropping an octave.

He had lifted his leg to step into the bath when the shrill sound of the phone rang out like an alarm. Simone locked eyes with him.

'Don't,' she said.

'What if it's something to do with the wedding?' he said, his foot suspended inches above the sea of foam.

'Oh, it's probably your mum or my mum or somebody getting into a state about nothing. Whatever it is, it's too late to do anything about it now anyway.'

David smiled at Simone's composure and he loved her for it. Nothing was going to spoil her special day. He remembered all the palaver Viv had wanted at her wedding — a church ceremony, a big white dress, four bridesmaids and a horse-drawn carriage. She had it all planned out. Not that the marriage itself had ever materialised — thankfully he'd realised his mistake before things had gone that far. But, in spite of its humble beginnings — a low-key civil ceremony and reception attended only by family and close friends — he knew that his marriage to Simone would last forever.

'I'd better get it just in case,' he said, grabbing a pea-green towel from the rail and walking back into the bedroom. He wrapped the towel round his waist, sat on the bed and picked up the phone.

'Yes?' he said.

'It's me,' said a slurred-sounding voice. 'Viv.'

'Viv!' he exclaimed and his heart pounded. 'Is Murray OK?'

'Yesh, yesh, he's absolutely fine. Been fasht asssleep for hours. He'ss really looking forward to your *Big Day tomorrow*,' she said, enunciating the last three words with exaggerated diction. Her voice was full of bitterness.

'Viv,' said David crossly, 'what are you doing phoning at this time of night? Do you realise it's eleven thirty? You had me worried sick something had happened to Murray.'

'I am ringing you about Murray, acshully,' she said, slurring her words. 'I'm ringing to tell you that if this wedding goes ahead, you'll not see him again.'

'Now, I've had just about enough of your nonsense, Viv. You can't use Murray as a weapon against me. Stop playing games. You're drunk. Now put the phone down and go to bed.'

'I am not drunk,' said Viv more intelligibly, 'and I'm not talking nonsense. I mean it.'

'Viv,' said David calmly, 'you're talking out of your arse.'

'No, I'm not!' she shouted and he held the phone away from his ear and shook his head. After a few moments her voice quietened and he put the handset back to his ear just in time to hear her say, 'And I'm warning you, David O'Connor — don't think I won't do it!'

'And I'm warning you, Viv,' retorted David, the anger bubbling up like froth on a pint of lager, 'this wedding is going ahead whether you like it or not. Don't you dare come on the phone

475

and try to threaten me! Two can play at that game. If you try and stop me seeing Murray,' he said and paused — then inspiration struck and he added quickly, 'I'll have a DNA test carried out and seek a court order granting access.'

There was silence on the phone for what seemed like several minutes. That's shut her up, thought David. He could hear her breathing and a soft moaning sound came down the line.

'Viv? Viv? Are you still there?'

'You think you're so clever, don't you?' she said and paused again. Her breathing was heavy in the silence that followed. 'Alright,' she said suddenly. 'Have it your way. I'll not stand in your way. You can see him whenever you want.'

And with that she slammed the phone down. David replaced the handset in the base unit slowly and, when he looked up, Simone was standing in the bathroom doorway with a large towel wrapped around her. Her shoulders glistening with water and a slick of suds dripped onto the floor from her elbow.

'What the hell was all that about?' she said and David shook his head.

'I have absolutely no idea,' he said and scratched his head. 'It was Viv. She was drunk. I don't know what the hell she wanted. One minute she was talking about not letting me see Murray if we get married — the next minute she'd changed her mind.'

'The woman's a flaming lunatic,' said Simone and then she added thoughtfully, 'Do you think Murray'll be alright with her? I mean, how drunk did she sound?'

'Ach, he'll be alright. He's in his bed and you know he's a sound sleeper. She'll probably go to bed herself now and sleep it off.'

'She's really pissed about you and me getting married, isn't she?' said Simone, and she came and sat on the bed beside him. 'I suppose it's hard for her. Maybe she's jealous.'

'Maybe, but I'm convinced it's mostly about money. She's worried that I might stop paying maintenance.'

'But you wouldn't, would you?'

'Of course not. What do you think I am?'

Simone looked down at the bedspread and traced the swirly pattern with her fingertips.

'I'm sorry,' he said at once. 'I didn't mean to be short with you.'

Simone looked up at him and gave him a weak smile. 'David, it's our wedding day tomorrow . . .'

'I know. I know,' he said and dragged his hands down his face. 'I won't let her spoil it for us. I promise.'

Then he tugged gently at the towel draped loosely around her until it came free and revealed her plump, damp body.

'You are beautiful,' he said and, as he kissed her, he forced all thoughts of Viv from his mind.

★　★　★

David sat at the computer on the landing outside the bedroom, almost exactly two weeks later, unable to get the last conversation with Viv out of his head. On honeymoon in Mallorca her

477

words had played on his mind and he'd forced them out of his thoughts. He had told Simone nothing of this, determined that Viv would not come between them. But the more he thought about it, the more he came to realise that something was not quite right.

Why did she back down so quickly as soon as he mentioned a DNA test? He could think of only one reason. She believed the test would come back negative. No matter how hard he thought about it, he could think of no other plausible explanation.

He thought of all the other things that had happened over recent months — his mother's comment about Murray, Carol's warning to 'walk away now' and Simone's intelligent observations about Murray.

He rubbed his eyes with the tips of his fingers. The scales had finally been tipped. He had enough circumstantial evidence to cause grave concern. There was no going back now. Guiltily, David glanced over his shoulder and his fingers hovered over the computer keyboard.

'What are you doing, darling?' said Simone, and he jumped.

'You gave me a fright,' he said, as she placed a mug of hot tea on the coaster beside his elbow.

'Sorry.'

'Thanks for the tea. I'm just downloading the snaps from Mallorca,' he said brightly and shifted in the chair.

'Oh, let me see them when you're done. It was a wonderful holiday, wasn't it?' she sighed.

Her arm was brown as a nut. He caught her

hand and placed a gentle kiss on her forearm.

'Honeymoon,' he corrected and she beamed at him. He placed a hand on her slightly swollen belly. He loved being part of this pregnancy, involved in every stage, something he had missed out on with Murray. 'I love being married to you.'

'Me too.'

'I'll give you a shout when they're ready to view.'

'Thanks, love,' she said and went back downstairs. The theme tune of *Eastenders* floated up the stairwell and he knew that she would be occupied for the next thirty minutes.

He plugged a grey cable into the digital camera and watched as the computer down-loaded the holiday pictures. Then, when it was done, after only a few seconds, he unplugged the camera and went online.

Quickly he typed in a search for 'paternity kits' and instantly the search engine called up over ten thousand results. He drew in his breath. He clicked on the first site on the list and, instantly, there before him was a special offer for a 'Peace of Mind' kit — reduced from over two hundred to just one hundred and ninety-nine pounds. It involved nothing more than a simple swab test taken in the mouth. All he had to do was click the order button.

He paused, his fingers suspended in the air. Was he doing the right thing? He decided to read some of the information on the site before proceeding. Four per cent of fathers were raising children that were not their own, it said.

Twenty-five per cent of fathers who suspected infidelity were proven correct. Was he one of that twenty-five per cent? In the face of such statistics he knew that he had no choice — he had to find out the truth.

David took his hands off the keyboard and rested them in his lap. He tried to imagine how he'd feel if Murray were not his son, but his brain refused to compute this possibility. Deep down, he didn't believe that it could possibly be true. He just needed to put those fears to bed once and for all, he told himself, so he could get on with the business of being a father to his son.

He clicked on the order button, pulled his credit card out of his wallet and followed the simple instructions.

'David,' said Simone's wary voice behind him, and he realised that she had been standing there for some minutes, 'what are you up to?'

'I'm ordering a paternity testing kit,' he replied evenly.

'David! Wait a minute. Do you have any idea what you're doing?'

David hit a few more keys on the keyboard, completing the transaction, then swivelled round in the chair to face her. 'I'm going to prove once and for all that Murray is my son.'

'But what if he's not, David?'

'He will be. I'm ninety-nine per cent sure of it.'

'If you're so sure of it why do you need a test to prove it?'

'Because . . . because of other people,' he said, angrily. 'Mum and Carol and even you, Simone.

I'm sick of people insinuating that he might not be mine.'

'And you have no doubts yourself then?' said Simone softly.

David hung his head and his whole body tingled with fear. 'If I had no doubts about Murray, I wouldn't be ordering a DNA test, would I?' he said quietly. 'But the doubts are only there because of other people.'

Simone knelt down beside him and leaned on the arm of the chair, her earnest face looking up into his. 'You have to think through the implications of this, David. Not just for you but for Murray. It takes more than a genetic link to be a father. You've cared for him and nurtured him and he believes that you are his dad. What effect do you think a negative result would have on your relationship with Murray? And can you imagine how devastated he'd be?'

David blinked and shrugged his shoulders. His eyes were hot with staring at the computer screen and his shoulders taut with tension. Simone was right. He hadn't really thought it through. If it was positive, then everything would be rosy. If it wasn't, he really didn't know how he'd handle it.

'I'll have to jump that hurdle when I get to it, Simone. All I know is that I have to find out the truth. I can't go on like this, wondering if he is mine or if he isn't. It's eating away at me. I've thought of little else for the last two weeks, since that bloody phone call from Viv.'

'I guessed as much.'

'You did?' said David in surprise. 'How?'

481

'You were preoccupied a lot of the time in Mallorca. And I guessed it was about Murray.'

'I'm sorry, Simone. I didn't spoil our honeymoon, did I?'

'No, no you didn't,' she said and patted him on the back of the hand. 'Maybe you are right about this test, David. If it's bothering you so much then you have to do it.' She pulled herself to her feet again and folded her arms. 'So what happens next?'

'I'll have the test kit in a couple of days. Thursday at the latest, according to the website. Then all I have to do is take a swab from my mouth and Murray's.'

'And Murray's coming to spend the weekend,' she said, consulting the calendar on the wall.

'That's right.'

Simone put her knuckles in her mouth and thought for some moments. 'Are you going to tell Viv what you're doing?'

'What do you think?' said David incredulously. 'I'll tell her if and when there's something to tell.'

'It doesn't seem right somehow, doing it without her knowledge.'

'She'd never consent to it, Simone. Not if she's something to hide.'

Simone nodded slowly. 'I suppose not. And what about Murray? What are you going to tell him?'

David shook his head. 'Nothing.'

'But if the result is negative — '

'It won't be,' said David, cutting her off mid-sentence. 'It simply won't be.'

He was confident that all would be well. And he would soon be able to put this period of worry and uncertainty behind him.

★ ★ ★

For the next four days all David could think about was the DNA test. When the kit arrived on Wednesday by special delivery he hid it guiltily in a kitchen cupboard and waited until Simone had gone to work before pulling it out again. Then he locked the front and back doors, went upstairs and opened the package. He laid the contents out carefully on the bed.

There were two long swabs, like big cotton buds, sealed in plastic wrappers and two long, hard plastic cylinders for the return of the swabs once the samples had been taken. There was a leaflet with detailed instructions inside. David read this carefully, twice.

It was as simple as the website had promised. All he had to do was wipe the swab on Murray's inside cheek and place it in the cylinder. Then he would do the same for himself and post the samples off. In less than ten days he would know the truth.

On Saturday morning David picked Murray up as arranged and took him to the swimming pool. On the way there and on the way home, David stole glances at Murray, who was absorbed in a Tamagotchi, his latest palm-sized electronic toy. At the cottage Simone was packing things for a barbecue.

'Why don't we go to Carrickdun?' she said.

'It's such a lovely day.'

Carrickdun was an old estate a few miles outside Ballygalley. It had been gifted to the local council some years ago and the extensive grounds turned into a public amenity. There was a beautiful walled garden, an outdoor amphitheatre, which hosted bands and concerts in the summer, a café and shops, a children's playground, putting green, golf course and miniature railway. It was very popular with people from Ballyfergus.

They drove along the coast with the car windows down and Murray's favourite band, Busted, playing in the cassette player. The fresh sea air tousled their hair and Simone sang along with Murray. When they got there it was busy — David had difficulty finding a parking spot and all the picnic tables were taken. They parked in the farthest corner of the car park and got out.

'Let's sit here!' said Murray excitedly, pointing to a patch of grass between other picnicking families on the grassy bank that framed the car park.

'Sure,' said Simone and she carried a blanket and the picnic basket up the slope. David followed with the rest of the supplies and set about preparing the disposable barbecue.

'Can I help cook the sausages, Dad?' said Murray, jumping up and down on the spot. He put his hands together in a prayer-like gesture and smiled angelically. 'Please, Dad? Please?'

'Of course you can, son,' said David and the last word caught in his throat. He swallowed and looked at the little boy. He wore a dinosaur

T-shirt and shorts, with thin legs sticking out below like matchsticks. On his head was a camouflage sunhat David had bought him in Gap. His fragile face looked so happy.

'Are you all right, David?' said Simone.

'Fine,' he replied with a brave smile. 'Here, Murray — you carry this up to the edge of the grass there,' he handed Murray the barbecue, 'and look for some stones to prop it up on so it doesn't burn the grass.'

Murray followed his father's instructions, scouring the area until he found six small rocks. David balanced the small foil rectangle on the stones and allowed Murray to strike the match and light the piece of fuel-soaked paper just under the metal grill. In seconds the paper shrivelled up and turned to black dust. The flames were almost invisible in the bright sunlight but the heat was fierce.

'Careful, now,' said David. 'It's very hot. The instructions say we've to leave it for twenty minutes before we cook the sausages.'

'Is that long, Dad?'

'Quite long.'

'But why do we have to wait?'

'To allow the flames to die down. You're supposed to wait until the charcoal's gone grey before cooking.'

'Why?'

'If you don't you'll burn the food on the outside and it won't be cooked on the inside.'

Murray knelt and watched the flames intently, every now and then poking a blade of dry grass into them.

485

'Keep an eye on him,' said Simone. 'He'll set the place alight if you're not careful.'

'Simone's right, Murray. Don't be sticking anything into the barbecue. You might hurt yourself.'

When fifteen minutes had passed and Murray could contain his excitement no longer David opened the pack of sausages.

'Let me put them on! Let me put them on!' squealed Murray.

David laughed and handed Murray the tongs. He dropped the first sausage on the grass, picked it up with his fingers and placed it gingerly on the barbecue.

'That's hot!' he cried.

'Told you,' said David, resisting the urge to intervene. He watched while, with painful slowness, Murray extracted each sausage and placed them haphazardly on the barbecue.

The sausages split and the hot fat hissed and spat.

'You need to keep turning them,' instructed David. 'To stop them burning.'

'OK, Dad.'

Soon the skins turned black.

'I think that'll do them now,' said David.

Murray picked the charred sausages one by one off the hot grill and transferred them to a plate, dropping two once again on the grass. David picked the bits of grass off them and returned them to the plate. Then Murray carried it like a trophy down to the spot where Simone had laid out the rest of the food. Then they all tucked in like they hadn't seen food in days.

'Well, boys,' said Simone with satisfaction, putting her empty plate down on the grass. She patted her stomach and said, 'That was just the best barbecue I've ever had. Those sausages were cooked to perfection, Murray.'

Murray, munching like a mouse on a hot dog, beamed with happiness.

'And this is just the most perfect day, isn't it, David?' she smiled at him.

David forced a smile in return and wished that he could agree with her. He could not see the beauty around him for all he could think about was the two swabs laid out on the top of the dressing table in the bedroom at home.

Was he doing the right thing? Why couldn't he just put the doubts out of his mind and forget about the whole thing? What would he do if the test was negative?

'Dad?' said Murray, interrupting his thoughts. 'Can we go and play golf now?'

'Of course we can. And after that you can have a go in the playground.'

'I love the big slide!' shouted Murray.

'And then we can go on the miniature train.'

'Brilliant!'

'And after that you can have an ice-cream.'

'Can I choose?'

'You can have anything you want, Murray,' said David. 'Now come on and give us a hand packing all these things away.'

That night Murray was exhausted and, by teatime, his eyes were rolling in his head.

'Early night,' mouthed Simone silently across the table to David and he nodded.

As soon as the meal was over David said to Murray, 'Come on. Time for bed.' And for once the boy didn't argue with him — an indication of just how tired he was.

Upstairs David told him to change into his pyjamas and he went and sat on the closed toilet seat. On top of the cistern lay the opened packet with the swab inside it. David's heart pounded in his chest. For a moment he toyed with the idea of putting it in the bin. But he knew that wasn't a realistic option. Not now that he had come so far. He would only suffer the same anguish over again and be forced to resort to a test at some point in the future. He might as well get it over and done with now.

'Murray! I haven't got all night. I'm waiting to do your teeth.'

'You don't have to do my teeth, Dad,' said Murray, coming into the bathroom. 'I can do them myself.' He saw the swab in David's hand and said, 'What's that for?'

'Oh, it's a special thing for cleaning your teeth. I saw it in the chemists and thought we could try it out. Here, open your mouth.'

Murray stepped forward cautiously and opened his mouth wide. David brushed the wrong end of the swab lightly over Murray's teeth. Then he flipped it round the correct way and rubbed it quickly across the inside of the boy's cheek.

He pulled it out of Murray's mouth and said, 'That's not a lot of use, is it?'

'It tickled,' said Murray. 'And it didn't feel like it was cleaning anything,' he added, running his

488

tongue over his bottom teeth.

'Yep, you're right. I think I wasted my money on that, didn't I? An ordinary toothbrush does the job much better.'

He handed Murray his Toy Story toothbrush, already loaded with a blob of red, white and blue striped toothpaste and said, 'Here, you brush your teeth and I'll go and pop this in the bin.'

In the bedroom he slipped the swab inside the cylinder and closed the tight lid. His hands were shaking. He steadied them on the dresser and looked into the mirror. A terrified face stared back at him. It was half done now. He only had his own to do and there was no time like the present.

Quickly he removed the second swab from its sealed packet, inserted it in his mouth and rubbed it firmly against his cheek. He withdrew it, slipped it into the cylinder and closed the lid. He threw the packaging in the bin, put both cylinders in the padded envelope provided and sealed it. It was done.

Then he took a deep breath and went back into the bathroom.

'That'll do, Murray. It's late.'

'No, it's not,' said Murray, his mouth full of froth. 'It's still light outside.'

'Time for bed,' said David sternly. 'If you hurry up I'll read you a story.'

Murray finished brushing his teeth and came through to his bedroom. He sat on the bed beside David and said, 'Where will I sleep when the new baby comes?'

'Why, here, of course,' said David and he put

his arm around the boy's shoulders.

'Where will the baby sleep?'

'In a cot in the same room as me and Simone.'

'Why?'

'Because that's where babies sleep when they're tiny.'

'Will it always sleep there?'

'No. When it's bigger it'll need a bedroom of its own like you have.'

'But there aren't any more bedrooms in this house, Dad.'

'I know. Don't you go worrying about that — I'll sort something out,' said David with a certainty about the future that he didn't feel. If Murray wasn't his, would he still come and stay? Sharply he told himself to stop it.

He read two chapters of *Charlie and the Chocolate Factory*, which had become Murray's favourite book after seeing the film with Johnny Depp in it on DVD. Then he tucked the boy up in bed, kissed him on the forehead and said, 'I love you.'

'I love you too, Dad,' said Murray and David slipped quietly out of the room and closed the door behind him. He stood on the landing with his sweaty fingers on the doorhandle and his head throbbed with anxiety. He told himself he had done the right thing. The only thing he could do, under the circumstances.

'He was a wee angel today, wasn't he?' said Simone as soon as David came downstairs. Then she saw the look on his face and said, 'What's wrong?'

'I did it. I took the swabs.'

'Where are they?'

'Upstairs in the envelope ready to be posted on Monday.'

'Did Murray suspect anything?'

'I don't think so. I told him it was a new thing for brushing his teeth. He believed me.'

'Oh, David,' said Simone and she got up off the couch and put her arms around him. 'I'm so sorry that you're having to go through all this. It's awful for me — I can't imagine how you must be feeling. My stomach has been tied up in knots all week.'

'Don't get upset about it, Simone. It's not good for you or the baby. It's done now. All we have to do now is wait.'

'How long?'

'A week to ten days,' he said and raised his eyes to the bedroom above where Murray was sleeping. 'And it's going to be the longest week of my life.'

35

It had been a very long day and Kath was the last person in the office when John Routledge appeared at the door.

'I thought you'd gone home, John,' said Kath, glancing up from the computer screen where she was penning a marketing letter she planned to send out to local businesses, encouraging them to use the hotel for conferences, Christmas parties and the like. 'It's after eight.'

'No,' he said and coughed, as though clearing his throat. 'I had a couple of things to do.' He stood in the doorway for some moments without speaking, as though he was deep in thought. Then he closed the door firmly behind him.

The door to the office was never shut and immediately alarm bells went off in Kath's head. She tried not to look surprised and carried on with her work. John came into the middle of the room, pulled a chair out from under Bridget's desk and sat on it, facing Kath.

She stopped what she was doing and looked up at him, unable to ignore this uncharacteristic behaviour any longer. His arms were folded defensively across his chest.

'What is it, John?'

He rubbed his mouth with the back of his hand, looked at the floor and then back at her.

492

Clearly something was bothering him. John was the easiest-going, most goodnatured person she knew.

'I don't know how to tell you this,' he said and Kath's heart sank.

'You're not leaving me, John, are you? I couldn't run this place without you. I know you could get a job anywhere — '

'No,' he said, interrupting her with a vigorous shake of his head. He ran a big freckled hand through his neat thatch of thick hair, leaving it sticking up on end.

Kath noticed a ring on his right hand which she was sure she hadn't seen him wearing before. For a brief moment she thought it looked familiar. She shook her head. She must be imagining things.

She stared at him and a thought, just as bad as the first one, crossed Kath's mind. What if he was about to ask her out? Maybe Bridget's meddling had worked and she'd persuaded John that Kath was interested in him. If that was the case, she'd kill her.

'John,' she said and looked at the clock on the wall, 'I'll have to be heading home now.'

'I don't even know if I should tell you,' he said and Kath froze.

This wasn't the preamble to a romantic proposal.

'Tell me what?' she said and the room was a silent as a cave.

'I've battled with this for months. It feels . . . it feels dishonest somehow working with you and having this secret between us.'

493

'What secret, John? I don't have any secrets from you.'

'But I have from you,' he said and his face was as white as a sheet. His blue-green eyes were moist with emotion.

Kath could not imagine what the secret could be but, from John's stressed appearance, she feared it was not going to be a pleasant one. Her heartbeat quickened and she bit her lip. 'John,' she said, as calmly as she could manage, 'Will you please tell me what you're talking about? I have no idea what you mean.'

'He said that it would reflect badly on my mother and that people would talk about her,' said John, as though he had not heard Kath's question. 'He said that it was best kept secret. Why he told me I don't know. But he did. And I've had to live with it for all these years.'

Kath sat bolt upright in her seat. The muscles in her face were so tight she felt her face would crack. Who was he talking about? For some reason she thought of her father. 'Live with what?' she whispered.

'My mother's very frail now and I don't think she'll last much longer.'

'Yes, I know she's been ill. I'm sorry,' said Kath, remembering that Mrs Routledge was in a nursing home.

'And when she goes I'll have no one. I'm her only child,' he said and wiped the tears from his eyes with his hand.

'John,' she said gently, 'where did you get that ring? I haven't seen you wearing it before.'

'Brendan gave it to me.'

494

'When?' she said accusingly.

'He left it for me in an envelope. I found it after he died.'

'Was there a note?'

'Yes.'

'And you never said anything!' cried Kath as jealousy seized her. 'My father left you a note and he didn't leave one for his own family? What did it say?'

'Not a lot. Only that it was up to me to tell the truth when I thought the time was right.'

'Jesus Christ!' exclaimed Kath, unable any longer to contain her frustration. 'What truth? Will you stop talking in riddles, John? Whatever it is you're trying to tell me, will you please spell it out?'

'I'm trying to tell you,' he said and paused. He sat upright in the chair and composed himself, then began again. 'I'm trying to tell you, Kath, that I am your half-brother. Brendan was my father.'

Kath face cracked into a grimace of disbelief. 'No,' she said. 'You can't be.'

'I am and I can prove it. Here,' he said, his expression stiff as stone. He took a small piece of crumpled paper from his pocket and handed it to Kath. His hand was trembling.

Kath looked at the paper and then into John's anxious face. It simply couldn't be true that this big man was Brendan's son and her half-brother. The idea of her father having a relationship with Ellen Routledge was laughable! But then, she thought, you didn't need to have a relationship with someone to father a child — you only needed to sleep with them . . . Still, it was simply unbelievable. She remembered seeing Ellen in the hotel where she'd worked for a few years as a chambermaid. A nice, homely woman — plain and unassuming. She looked nothing like a seductress.

'Read it,' prompted John.

Kath swallowed her disbelief and focused on the paper in her hand. For some reason her vision was blurred and she had to blink several times before she could read the familiar, elegant script.

'*I'm sorry, son, for taking the coward's way out,*' it said. '*Wear this and remember me always. I was never ashamed of you, only concerned for your mother's reputation. It was all my fault — not hers. You are free to tell the truth now that I am gone — it's your truth after all. Your loving father, Brendan.*'

Kath started to cry and John came round and put his arm around her shoulder. Her disbelief crumbled. She didn't want it to be true — but here was indisputable evidence in her father's own hand. Had her father been a seducer? A lecherous creep who preyed on simple women like Ellen Routledge? The idea filled her with shame. She dropped the note like it was a red-hot ember — it fluttered to the floor and landed face down on the carpet.

'I'm sorry,' said John. 'This must be a terrible shock.'

She looked at him through her tears. Though she hated herself for it, she was filled with envy that he had been accorded the honour of a

496

written suicide note from Brendan. Had her dad loved him more than the rest of his children?

'It's seeing Dad's writing. It's the only note he left, John,' she said, in between sobs. 'It would've meant so much if he'd done the same for the rest of us.'

'I'm sorry that he didn't,' said John. He bent down and picked Brendan's crumpled note off the floor, then sat back down in the chair. 'Perhaps it was because he knew that I wouldn't be able to grieve him publicly, like the rest of you. I don't know.'

Kath took a hankie from her handbag, which was sitting on the floor at her feet, and wiped her eyes. She blew her nose and dabbed under her eyes where she knew the mascara would have run.

'How long have you known, John?' She was trying to take in the fact that this big man sitting in front of her was her own flesh and blood.

'Since I was twenty.'

'As long as that! That explains why you stayed at the hotel all those years, then. But why did he tell you? And why then?'

'I'm not sure he meant for me to find out. We got into an argument about my driving. Brendan told me not to drive so fast and I said, 'Who do you think you are, my father?' And then there was this deathly silence and he just stared at me and instantly I knew. He'd always taken a big interest in me — much more than the other staff at the hotel. And when I asked him he said it was true. He said that I was his son.'

'And your mother and he . . . ' said Kath and

497

her voice trailed off. She had always believed that her parents' marriage was perfect — now that picture of familial bliss was shattered. Maybe that was why Dad worked such long hours at the hotel when they were children — not out of necessity but because he was having an affair. Maybe he had more than one . . .

'They met at the hotel,' said John. 'My mother worked here for five or six years. I don't know how long the affair went on — he never told me and I didn't really want to know. He said that he'd loved her but it took me a long time to forgive him for what he'd done.'

'But you did eventually?' said Kath, thinking that the relationship sounded more like a love affair than a sordid one-night stand. Her father rose a little in her estimation.

'He was good to me, and my mother, when my dad died. And after that, well, we became quite close. I loved him in the end.'

'It must've been hard for you not being able to tell anyone,' said Kath, trying not to focus on her own misery and reminding herself that, of all those involved in the sleazy business, John was the innocent victim.

'It was. To this day my mother doesn't know that I know.'

'Are you going to tell her?'

'I don't know that it would serve any purpose. She's become quite confused lately and I think it might just cause her anxiety. If she'd wanted me to know she'd have told me before now, wouldn't she?'

'I suppose so,' said Kath, feeling desperately

let down by her father. Like Carl, she had put her father on a pedestal and believed him to be perfect. But, if she'd learnt one thing over the past few months it was that no one was flawless. Everyone was prone to weakness and that, in the end, was what made us all human. Maybe Brendan had truly loved Ellen Routledge. Maybe she had been the love of his life. Suddenly she felt sorry for her father — and Ellen.

And she felt sorry for John, carrying the burden of such a secret for so long. Suddenly she recalled with horror that it was John who'd found her father's body and cut it down from the tree.

'Oh, John,' she said and she put her hand over her mouth, 'I've just remembered — it must've been awful for you finding Dad's body.'

'It was,' he said with a little shiver and a brief flutter of his eyelids. 'The worst bit was not being able to tell anyone what he was to me. Not being able to share the grief.'

'But you can do that now,' said Kath gently, and she placed a hand on his knee. 'I'm glad that you're my brother. I like you a lot, John. And you were a loyal friend to my — our — father. I'll always be grateful to you for that.'

He smiled weakly and there was a short, but not uncomfortable, silence between them.

Then Kath said with a hollow little laugh, 'Do you know that Bridget was trying to set us up together?'

'I guessed as much,' he grinned. 'It's one of the reasons I decided to tell you. In case she tried it again!'

'So what do we do now? Do you want to tell the rest of the family?'

'I'd like to but I'm not sure. What do you think?'

Kath frowned and said, 'My guess is that my mother doesn't know a thing about this, John. And she's going to be devastated when she finds out.'

John nodded gravely.

'But, that said, it's not right to keep this a secret from your half-brother and half-sister. David and Bridget have a right to know about you and you have a responsibility to tell them.'

'But what about your mother? I don't want to cause her any pain. If she can't deal with this, then maybe it's best that we don't tell her.'

Kath sighed, took a deep breath and said carefully, 'I loved my father dearly, John. But he was wrong to keep your existence a secret from my mother. And if anyone is responsible for causing her pain, it's him, not you. Look, why don't you let me tell her? I think it would be — be easier if she heard it from me.'

'Would you?' he said, his eyes lighting up with expectation.

'I will. I promise,' said Kath confidently, but inside her stomach was churning with dread. 'I'll go and see her tomorrow, once I've had a chance to let all this sink in. And wait until I've spoken to her before telling David and Bridget.'

'OK. Thanks, Kath,' he said and stood up. His manner was entirely different from earlier. He looked tired and washed out but also relieved. He looked like what he was — a man who had

500

just freed himself of a very great burden. 'You know no one outside your immediate family need know about this, if it makes it easier for your mother. She'll probably be . . . embarrassed about it.'

Kath nodded and stood up. Hesitantly they embraced.

'Thanks for telling me, John. I know it can't have been easy for you.'

'Thanks for making it so easy, Kath,' he said and folded the note and put it back in the inside pocket of his jacket. 'And thanks for — for accepting me.'

After he'd gone, Kath sat in the office listening to the sounds from the hotel and thinking about John and her father. She heard the scuffle of feet over the limestone floor as staff scurried back and forth from the kitchen to the restaurant and the clatter of cutlery on china. She heard the clink of glass as diners gathered in the bar for drinks and then, later, the sound of soft chatter from the lounge as they congregated for after-dinner coffee. The restaurant, her greatest success, was busy every night. Dusk fell and still she sat on in the gathering darkness.

Part of her envied John and the close relationship he'd obviously shared with Brendan. She wondered if her father had loved John more than his other children. He was obviously very fond of him. She was full of pity for John, having this truth thrust upon him at such a young age.

And now she felt a little as John must have felt. The burden he'd so gratefully unloaded was now sitting on her shoulders and she felt its cold weight like a stone. She would have to face her mother with this devastating news and she was quite sure that Fiona would not take it as calmly as she had.

She was sure her mother knew nothing about her husband's infidelity, let alone the existence of a love child. But she had promised John and she could not see how this truth could possibly be kept from her mother.

This year was proving to be the most extraordinary one of her entire life. Everyone, it seemed, had secrets — was she the only person in the world with no skeleton in her cupboard?

⋆　⋆　⋆

It was with a heavy heart that Kath drove into Ballyfergus early the next evening. It had been a long, hot sunny day and the coast road was busy with day-trippers returning home from visits to the beaches at Cushendun and Cushendall. There were several foreign-registered cars on the road also — a welcome sight to Kath. The hotel was far from full to capacity but that was to be expected — this was only her first season. Next year would be different.

Kath got stuck behind a battered old blue Volvo estate, the rear window partly obscured by a blown-up beach ball and lilo. She slowed her speed and made no attempt to overtake — Kath was in no hurry for this interview with her mother. She wished she didn't have to do it at all but she could see no way out of it.

She watched while arms flailed in the back of

the car in front and the driver, a woman with dark curly hair, nearly crashed trying to mediate between the squabbling children in the back seat. She kept turning her head to look at them and reaching back with one hand, probably to smack the bits of them that she could reach. She was, most likely, shouting.

Kath remembered similarly fraught summer outings in the car with her mother in the driving seat and smiled. Then she thought of John — his childhood must've been a lonely one with no siblings. In spite of her recent misfortunes, Kath knew she had been lucky. She had been raised in a happy home. Or what she had thought, until yesterday, was a happy home.

Then she found herself challenging her own assumption. Did marital infidelity necessarily make a marriage an unhappy one? Her father *appeared* happy but he must have been dissatisfied at some level. And what about her mother? Did she view her marriage as a success? The only person who could answer these questions, now that Brendan was gone, was Fiona.

Kath practised what she would say to her mother, trying to cloak the message in softening euphemisms — 'relationship' instead of 'affair', 'love child' instead of 'bastard son'. But it was no good. No matter how she put it, the facts of Brendan's duplicity could not be disguised. Kath imagined the effect her words would have on her mother and her heart ached.

For the hurt of Carl's betrayal was never far from her mind and she winced when she recalled how she'd felt on discovering Carl's infidelity. The anguish and the rage when she'd first found out — and the feelings of hollowness and worthlessness that followed.

She wiped the tears from her face with the back of her hand and sniffed. Now she was about to deliver the same terrible blow to her own mother. She prayed that Fiona would not hate her for being the bearer of such loathsome news. She wished for a way out — but she knew there was none.

At last she reached Ballyfergus. The Volvo turned up Victoria Road and Kath drove on to the centre of town. She pulled up outside the complex where her mother now lived and sat grimly in the car, steeling herself for the inevitable.

She dreaded this meeting — how on earth could she break the news to her mother? If Fiona didn't know about the affair, then it would come as such a shock. And if she had known about it at the time, it would be just as painful having all the old wounds opened up again. And then she would have to come to terms with the fact that she now had a stepson, the child of another woman, whom her husband had loved.

Kath closed her eyes and prayed for strength but when she got out of the car her legs felt shaky. She steadied herself by holding onto the side of the car, took a deep breath and climbed the short flight of stairs to her mother's flat.

'Hello, love, what a surprise,' said Fiona with a relaxed smile when she opened the door. She had settled well into her new home and now seemed more like her old self.

'Did you bring the wedding album? Simone said she'd left it with you.'

'Sorry, I forgot.'

'Oh,' said Fiona, sounding very disappointed, 'I was really looking forward to seeing the pictures. Never mind. I'll get it next time. Come in and see what I've done with the place since you were last here.'

Kath followed her mother into the small lounge which now looked like a scaled-down version of the grand drawing room in Highfield House.

'I've rearranged things a bit and some of the pieces work well in here, don't you think?' said her mother with pride.

Kath's mouth went dry. She opened her mouth to speak but nothing came out.

'Kath, are you feeling alright? You look like you've just seen a ghost.'

'I'm fine,' said Kath and she sat down abruptly on the sofa, one of a pair which used to grace either side of the fireplace in her mother's former home. The room was too small to house the other one, which had gone to auction along with so many of her mother's beloved things.

'Shall I get you a cup of tea?' said Fiona.

Kath nodded and Fiona rushed off to the kitchen immediately.

How Kath wished she didn't have to add to her mother's troubles! She'd had so much to deal with already and she was coping so well. She worried that this revelation would prove too much for her to bear. She knew her mother was a strong, capable woman but everyone had their breaking point.

'There you are,' said Fiona, handing her daughter a fine china cup of black tea on a matching saucer. She placed a small jug of milk on the table beside Kath. 'Now,' she said, when Kath had poured her milk and taken a sip of the hot liquid, 'are you going to tell me what's wrong?'

'Mum,' said Kath and the blood pounded in her ears. She set her cup and saucer on the table, not certain that she could hold them steadily. 'I have some news for you. Not bad news exactly. But something that I don't think you're going to like very much.'

'Oh,' said Fiona and the smile fell from her face. 'What's that then?'

'I had a long chat with John Routledge today,' said Kath and, at the mention of his name, her mother's lips fixed themselves into a thin line. 'He told me some things about himself and Dad.'

'What did he tell you, Kath?' said Fiona and her voice was as calm as a BBC broadcaster's. She put her cup and saucer down on the table beside Kath's and her hands, spread out like starfish, gripped the arms of the chair.

'He told me that Dad was his father too.'

'I see,' said Fiona, sounding not in the least bit surprised.

'You probably know his mother. She worked at the hotel for — '

'I know who his mother is,' Fiona snapped and then said, less irritably, 'Anything else?'

'He showed me a ring Dad had given him — I thought I'd seen it before and then I remembered Dad used to wear it — and a note that he wrote to him just before he died.'

'He left John Routledge a note?' said Fiona and her eyebrows arched in annoyance.

'Yes. I was surprised too.'

'Did you see it?'

'Yes,' said Kath and she relayed the contents of the note as accurately as she could remember them.

Fiona looked into space and said nothing. Kath was astounded by her reaction or rather the lack of it. Then she suddenly remembered how her mother had snubbed John at her father's wake. At the time Kath had put her mother's behaviour down to stress.

'You knew this already, didn't you, Mum?'

'Yes,' said Fiona, focusing at last on Kath. Her forbidding expression relaxed a little. 'I've known for several months. Since just after your father died, in fact.'

'But how did you find out? John said that only he and his mother knew the truth and she never told a soul, not even him.'

'Your father left me a letter, Kath. It was with his will. It was short and to the point and it was written, I believe, long before he ever contemplated suicide. He wanted me to know about John but he didn't want me to know until after he was dead. What exactly he expected me to do with the information I have no idea.'

'But why would he do that?'

'I can only guess that he wanted to pass over

507

to the other side with a clear conscience.'

'Did you know about the affair before then?'

'No.'

'So the letter was the very first you knew about either the affair or John?'

'That's right,' said Fiona matter-of-factly. She picked up her cup and saucer and took a sip of tea. 'I didn't see a lot of your dad then. It was the early seventies and, with the onset of the Troubles, the hotel nearly went under. Things were really bad. You had just started school and I was at home with Bridget and David. Brendan was working all hours at the hotel trying to keep it afloat. At least I thought he was working . . . ' Her voice trailed off. She sighed and went on, 'He was stressed a lot of the time but he seemed happy with his home life and he loved you children.' She pursed her lips and an angry frown creased her brow. 'You know, he never even said he was sorry,' she said, and her steeliness wavered. She touched the corners of her eyes with a hankie and said, more forthrightly, 'You said that John told you all this yesterday.'

'That's right.'

'And did he say why he told you? What does he want from us?'

'I'm not sure that he wants anything. Maybe just to be accepted by the family. He's an only child and his mother's in Gillaroo Lodge now. He doesn't expect her to last long.'

'He can't be part of our family,' said Fiona with a dismissive snort. 'He may be Brendan's son but he's not an O'Connor. And he never will be.'

'Oh, Mum, how can you be so cruel? It's not John's fault. If you want to blame anyone, blame Dad.'

'Oh, I *do* blame him! Believe me, I *do*,' said Fiona and Kath was shocked by the vehemence in her mild-mannered mother's voice.

'Mum, why didn't you tell us about the letter?'

'Why do you think? I didn't want you to know what your father had done. I have my pride, you know.'

'Didn't you suspect anything at the time?' said Kath gently.

'No,' she said, paused and added abruptly, 'No, that's not entirely true.' She sighed deeply. 'I didn't know about the specifics of this affair and I didn't know about Ellen Routledge. But you don't live with someone for over forty years without knowing every nuance of their behaviour. There were times during our marriage when I suspected something wasn't quite right . . . call it a sixth sense or whatever. But I chose not to look any further. I put his odd behaviour down to the pressures of running the hotel and being responsible for his family. I never entertained the idea that he might be having an affair. I knew your father would never leave me — he loved his family too much — and I believed he loved me too.'

'I'm sorry, Mum,' said Kath, not quite understanding how a woman could sense something amiss in her marriage and choose to turn a blind eye to it.

After a pause, Fiona added, 'I suppose I feel a bit of a fool, really. Believing in him all those years. I wish he'd never told me.'

'You would've found out eventually. You can't keep something like that a secret forever.'

'Some people do, Kath. Your father obviously couldn't. He should never have told John. The boy grew up believing Dennis Routledge was his father. What right did your dad have to shatter his illusion? He never paid a penny in maintenance or had anything to do with the boy when he was growing up.'

'You have a point but John doesn't seem in any way bitter towards Dad. He says he loved him.'

'Well,' said Fiona and she looked around the room as though wishing the conversation over, 'it's all out of the bag now. I suppose John's going to tell half of Ballyfergus.'

'No, not at all,' said Kath, jumping to John's defence. 'He said that he only wanted Bridget and David to know and that it need go no further. And he has no desire to upset his mother at this late stage.'

'Well, that's something at least.'

'You know we can't keep John a secret forever, Mum,' said Kath gently. 'It wouldn't be fair. He has a right to be acknowledged by his brother and sisters.'

Fiona scowled and then sighed, sounding defeated. 'Yes. I suppose you're right.'

'John's a good person, Mum.'

'I know he is. When the hotel went under I tried to give him that black marble antique clock that used to sit on the mantelpiece in the drawing room at Highfield. Do you remember?'

Kath nodded.

'I wanted him to take it in lieu of the unpaid staff wages. But he wouldn't take it. He was very . . . compassionate.'

'Then you'll make more of an effort with him?' probed Kath.

Fiona nodded. 'I will.'

'Thanks, Mum,' said Kath. She patted her mother's knee, knowing that it would take a great deal of courage for Fiona to publicly acknowledge John. It meant that people would know her husband had been unfaithful.

There was a short silence between them which Kath broke by asking gently, 'In spite of the affair, were you . . . was your marriage a happy one, Mum?'

Fiona frowned before answering, as though giving the question a great deal of thought. 'I thought it was,' she said at last. 'I thought your father was happy too. But . . . '

'But what?' said Kath softly.

'I think I was very hard on him. I wasn't as supportive as I could've been. I was always criticising the way he ran the hotel. I think, deep down, that I wanted to be running it myself but in my day that wasn't the done thing.'

'You mustn't be too hard on yourself, Mum.'

'You don't understand, Kath,' said Fiona and her eyes filled with tears. 'I think it was because of the way I was that your father took his own life.'

'Mum, don't be ridiculous!'

'You don't understand, Kath. Don't you see? If he had been able to confide in me that things were as bad as they were, he would never have been forced to take his own life. If I had been a supportive partner instead of always nagging, he could have discussed his problems with me. If he had been able to share the burden, I'm convinced he wouldn't have killed himself.'

'Mum,' said Kath gently, 'we can all find reasons to blame ourselves if we look hard enough. If I'd been a better daughter, visited more often, taken more of an interest, perhaps I could've seen this coming. Perhaps I could've done something to prevent it happening.'

'Don't be silly, Kath. You had your own life to lead.'

'I'm being no more silly than you are,' said Kath evenly. 'I did think that for a while and I felt very guilty about it.'

'Oh, Kath, love,' said Fiona and she sighed, 'your father's death had nothing to do with you.'

'And it had nothing to do with you either, Mum,' said Kath, kneeling in front of her mother and taking both her hands in hers. The skin on the back of her hands was soft, the result of religious daily applications of Crabtree & Evelyn handcream, her mother's favourite brand. Kath had given her some at Easter, mindful that she could no longer afford to buy such luxuries for herself. 'No one is responsible for Dad's death except Dad himself,' she went on. 'Whatever pressure he was under, he chose the route he did all by himself. No one forced him down that road, least of all you.'

'You really think so?' A tear ran down a crease in Fiona's face.

'Yes,' said Kath, wiping it away with her finger. 'You were a good wife and a good mother, Mum. And I love you.'

'I love you too,' said Fiona and she gave Kath's hands a firm squeeze. 'Now,' she said, brightening, 'you haven't told me how you feel about John. It's not every day you discover that you have a half-brother.'

Kath forced a thin smile at her mother's quip, rolled back on her heels and sat in the chair. 'I like John, Mum. I don't have a problem with him at all and I'm happy to welcome him into our family. But I feel a little bit, well . . . disappointed in Dad and I feel guilty for thinking it. You see, I thought you had a perfect marriage. And I can't help but think about what Dad was up to and wondering how many other affairs there were . . . '

Fiona bowed her head.

'I'm sorry, Mum,' said Kath quickly. 'I shouldn't have said that.'

'No,' said Fiona bravely. 'It's OK. You go on.'

Kath let out a long, sad sigh. 'Part of me wishes that I'd never found out.'

'It must've been quite a shock for you, love.'

'It was. And yet in a way, apart from the existence of John, it's got nothing to do with me. What I mean is that what went on in your marriage is between you and Dad. He was a good father. Nothing changes that. And he could have done worse things, couldn't he? He could have walked out on us.'

513

'Would that have been worse?' said Fiona, sounding bitter.

'Maybe not for you, Mum. But for us children it would've been worse. For all his faults, he did keep the family together.'

'That's true,' agreed Fiona reluctantly.

'And yet . . . ' Kath looked at her tightly clasped hands, feeling disloyal towards her father.

'What, love?'

'I can't help being angry with him — for hurting you and for the spineless way he told you.'

'Try not to be too hard on him, Kath,' said Fiona, leaning forward earnestly in her seat, her turn now to be the defender of Brendan. 'Leave that to me. I'm the one he deceived — not you. And for all his faults, he was a good father and he loved you all dearly. Don't take that away from him. Don't spoil the memories.'

Fiona's generosity of spirit, in the face of her husband's wretched and cowardly infidelity, filled Kath with awe. She felt a lump in her throat and started to cry. Fiona came over and patted her shoulder.

'There, there,' she said.

'You're so good, Mum. I don't know if I could be as forgiving in your shoes.'

'I didn't say I'd forgiven him, love. Don't forget I've had nearly six months in which to come to terms with this. You will too, in time.'

'I'll try,' said Kath, sniffing back her tears. But, though her love for her father would never change, she knew that she would never remember him in quite the same rosy glow as she had done before. She wondered if her brother and sister would feel the same when they found out. 'What about Bridget and David? How do you think they should be told about this? Do you think John should do it?'

'I think it might be time to call a family conference, Kath. And perhaps it would soften the blow if you told them rather than John. In case one of them says something . . . insensitive in the heat of the moment.'

'What makes you think either of them would do that?'

'You know David and your father didn't always see eye-to-eye. Brendan was angry when David wouldn't join him at the hotel. And I think David was hurt that his father wouldn't support him in his chosen career path. He simply had no interest in the hotel business but Brendan took it as a personal insult.'

'I know that. But what's it got to do with John?'

'John became Brendan's protégé — a substitute son for David, in your father's eyes at least. I think that was why he told John that he was his father.'

'I'm not sure about that, Mum. The way John told it, it sounded like it just slipped out.'

'Your father was an intelligent man, Kath. Believe me, he wouldn't have let slip a secret that he'd kept for two decades unless he meant to.'

36

'I know it seems like ages away,' said Kath to Bridget, 'but we need to start thinking about the winter now. We're planning a party night for every Friday and Saturday in December and we need to start selling those tickets soon. Here, have a look at these draft leaflets.'

There was no one else in the office — Moira was on her lunch break and John was showing a new member of staff the ropes on reception.

'I see,' said Bridget, feigning an interest in the pamphlets that Kath placed on her desk. They featured a close-up photograph of the hotel's front door, slightly ajar, offering a glimpse of a warm, glowing interior. The door was flanked on either side by two small lit-up Christmas trees, sprinkled with digitally enhanced snow — the scene was nostalgic and welcoming.

Bridget opened the first one and pretended to read but the words were just a series of smudged lines. Her vision was blurred from lack of sleep and anxiety.

She couldn't understand how it had happened. She'd been taking the pill for years and it had always been reliable. She was sure she hadn't forgotten to take it. She never did — the fear of getting pregnant concentrated her mind like nothing else.

'The way I see it,' Kath went on, 'the most crucial time for us is the month of December, including Christmas itself and the New Year. I'm not expecting that we'll have many guests staying but there's a great opportunity for local trade. Think of all the local clubs as well as staff in all the local businesses that'll be booking a big night out.'

'Mmm,' said Bridget and she thought back over the last month. Suddenly she remembered the terrible bout of vomiting and diarrhoea she'd suffered after a dodgy carry-out from a new Chinese that had opened up, and closed down again just as quickly, on Market Place in Ballyfergus. It must've been that. Bridget put her hands over her face and groaned inwardly.

'I want to put you in charge of sales for the party nights as well as the Christmas lunch bookings,' went on Kath, oblivious to her sister's distress. 'If we make a go of this, we can generate enough income to get us through the first three months of next year, when things are going to be pretty dead.'

How could she have been so stupid? thought Bridget angrily. She was just getting her life together, just learning to keep all the balls in the air and now she'd gone and dropped them. The prospect of another baby and being trapped in the treadmill of domestic misery for the foreseeable future filled her with dread. How could she do it? It would drive her mad.

Ned, of course, would be delighted. He'd have her back in the house morning, noon and night, chained to the kitchen sink — where he wanted her. He thought babies were wonderful but he wasn't the one that raised them. Bridget loved

517

her children with a passion, but she was a woman who could never understand the ecstasy that overcame other new mothers facing a tiny, vulnerable baby.

Bridget adored newborn babies but only when they belonged to someone else. When they were yours, you were too stressed out, worried and exhausted all the time to really enjoy them. She'd been looking forward to the prospect, perhaps ten or fifteen years from now, of being a grandmother. Not a mother all over again! She was nearly thirty-eight years old — she knew there were lots of women just starting their families at that age, but she'd considered her family complete. She just felt too old and worn out to do it all again.

She thought of all the lovely clothes she'd just bought and looked down at her figure. She'd worked so hard to get down to a size fourteen. Another baby at her age would blow all that good work to smithereens. Her body would never recover from it. She looked at Kath, slim as a pencil in her smart business suit, and was filled with envy.

Kath would never be stupid enough to get herself pregnant when she didn't want to be. Kath was the smart one in control of her life. The one who went to university and got the high-flying job. Even the hotel, when she touched it, turned to gold. She'd even got the best name — Kathleen — that could be abbreviated to the chic and modern Kath while Bridget was stuck with an old woman's name that people insisted on shortening to Bridie or

Bridge or, even worse, Biddy.

As a child, Kath had been her father's favourite. He never sat Bridget on his knee in the office and fed her sherbet lemons, like he did with Kath. She remembered the time he came home with a bright yellow dress for Kath and bar of chocolate for Bridget and David.

Bridget had seethed with anger until her clenched teeth hurt and had thrown the chocolate in the stream. Maybe it wouldn't have pained her so much if she'd been a less observant child. But she'd always been quick to notice when slights and preferential treatment were being handed out. And she knew when she was being palmed off with second best.

'Bridget, are you listening to a word I'm saying?'

'I'm sorry,' said Bridget. 'I've just got a lot on my plate at the moment.'

'Like what?'

Bridget blinked like she'd been caught in headlights and said, 'I'm finding it hard to juggle work and home life. I'm still running the house single-handedly and no one does anything to help. I was up till one o'clock on Sunday night doing the ironing. And that's only summer clothes. Wait until they're all back at school and it's umpteen sets of school uniforms every week on top of casual clothes — not to mention sports, ballet and rugby kits.'

Kath set the leaflets in her hand down on the desk beside her computer. 'Doesn't Ned help?'

'Only if I tell him exactly what to do. He maintains he doesn't see what needs doing and

519

he can't iron or cook. Sometimes it takes more energy nagging him to do things, so I just end up doing them myself.' Bridget felt her eyes filling up with tears. 'And I really loved working here. That's the hardest bit. Having to give it up.'

'You're not seriously thinking of giving up work?' cried Kath. 'It's only a few mornings a week and it's good for you to get out and meet people, Bridget. Look, I know it's hard going, working and running a home, especially now during the holidays when you've had to make all sorts of complicated childcare arrangements. But come September, Charmaine starts school and you'll have loads more time on your hands. Things will get better, you'll see.'

'No,' said Bridget, fighting back the tears.

'Well, why don't you get someone in to help with the cleaning, then? It would take a bit of pressure off and — '

'Kath,' Bridget interrupted in a deadpan voice. 'I'm pregnant.'

'But Bridge, that's wonderful news,' said Kath spontaneously, using Bridget's pet name from childhood which she hated. Then she paused and said, 'But you don't seem very happy.'

'I'm not. I can't have this baby. I think I want an abortion.'

She heard Kath's sharp intake of breath and she hung her head. She wasn't sure she could actually go ahead with terminating the pregnancy but right now she wished the foetus didn't exist.

'Bridget!' cried Kath in horror. 'You can't do that. Have you told Ned how you feel?'

'He doesn't even know I'm pregnant.'

'But why haven't you told him?'

The answer was that Bridget had been hoping it wasn't true, despite a late period, tender breasts, morning queasiness and the feeling that her limbs were made of lead. She had only just become convinced of it after she'd remembered the bout of illness the previous month.

So why she said what she said next, Bridget would never be able to adequately explain to herself or anyone else. It was something that she was powerless to stop — it was, she thought later, the result of many years of pent-up frustration, jealousy and anger. She wanted to hurt Kath and she knew how to do it.

She had seen the way Mike looked at Kath and the way Kath searched for him in a room. She wasn't prepared to stand by and let Kath have Mike. As long as he remained single she could cope but, if he married her sister, she wasn't sure that she could bear that. Why did Kath always have to win?

'Because the baby's not his. It's Mike Mulholland's,' she blurted out.

As soon as she'd said it, she wished that she could take it back. She knew that she had gone too far. But how could she? How could she explain her bitter, twisted mind to Kath? What would Kath think of her?

Bridget's relationship with her sister was complex — she was insanely jealous of her but she admired her too. She wanted Kath to think highly of her. She wanted her to think that a man like Mike Mulholland would desire her, love her even. She couldn't admit to such a terrible lie.

Kath stared at Bridget and blinked and there was some satisfaction in seeing her composure crumble. She stretched out her arms behind her, felt for her chair and lowered herself gently into it.

'Mike Mulholland,' whispered Kath, more to herself than Bridget. 'I can't believe it.'

Bridget bowed her head. Kath would never have anything to do with Mike after this. And if she got her to agree not to tell anyone, no one need ever know.

'I wondered what you were talking about at Emmy's party,' said Kath. 'Now I know.'

Bridget thought back to the party and remembered having a discussion with Mike about a rumour she'd heard that someone was going to build another wind-farm on the blustery Sallagh Braes. Mike argued that it was an SSSI — a Special Site of Scientific Interest — and that unsightly developments like this should be banned. He said that they were a scar on the landscape — he'd become quite heated during their conversation.

'You mustn't tell anyone,' said Bridget. 'I haven't decided what I'm going to do.'

'Of course,' said Kath. She stared blankly at the wall behind Bridget and then focused on her sister's face. 'Do you love him?' Her voice was devoid of emotion.

Bridget hesitated, not sure how to answer this. If she said yes, then that would lead her down a whole avenue of complications, such as whether she would leave Ned, which of course she had no intention of doing.

'No,' she lied. 'It was just a one-night stand. It was a — a mistake.'

'Does Mike know?'

Bridget thought about this and decided that if she said no, Kath would insist that she tell him. 'Yes.'

'And what does he have to say about it?'

Bridget shrugged and wished Kath would stop asking all these questions. From one small, but deadly, lie she was becoming entangled in a whole web of them.

'He said he'd support me in whatever I want to do,' she said, her voice little more than a whisper.

'You weren't serious about an abortion just then, were you?'

'No,' said Bridget with a sigh. 'I don't think I could do that.'

'Oh my God,' said Kath and she put her face in her hands. 'What a complete and utter mess.'

⋆　⋆　⋆

When Simone walked through from the lounge with a bundle of envelopes in her hand, David knew straightaway from her expression that the letter had arrived. She laid the narrow white envelope on the table in front of him, not noticing that the sleeve of her dressing-gown trailed in the leftover milk at the bottom of his cereal bowl.

'I think this is it,' she said.

'I wasn't expecting it so soon.' He stared at the

address label, then back at Simone's face. He realised he was waiting for her to tell him to open it. He could not touch it.

'Me neither,' said Simone with a gloomy expression on her face.

She sat down opposite him and they both stared at the envelope.

'Will you open it?' he said. 'I'm not sure I can bear to read it.'

Simone shook her head. 'It's not too late, David. We can open the door of the range right now and throw it in the flames and be done with it.'

David followed her gaze to the old stove, grumbling away in the corner. Because it was the only method of cooking food in the cottage it was kept lit, even in summer.

'Is that the answer?' He did not expect her to reply. 'To hide the truth? To go back to wondering and doubting and never being sure?'

'All I'm saying is that before you open that envelope, you should consider your options.'

'What options, Simone? I don't have a choice. I can't go on like this. And you have doubts about him too. Don't put this all on me. It was you who noticed the double crown thing.'

She licked her lips and said very slowly, 'I just think you've rushed into this, David. I read the website, you know, after you'd ordered the kit. And it put a lot of emphasis on getting proper counselling and considering things very carefully before embarking on a test. You've just ploughed ahead without taking the time to think about the implications. You don't even know what you're going to do with the information if it's negative. Will you tell Viv? Or your family? And what about Murray? You won't be able to keep this from him forever.'

'I don't know the answer to any of those questions, Simone,' he said truthfully. 'But I know one thing. Inside that envelope is the truth and it's too late to go back now. I simply have to know.'

She stared at him, her eyes moist with tears, and said softly, 'I know you do, love.'

'I can't bear this any longer. Will you read it, please?'

Simone nodded and slid the envelope over to her side of the table. She sniffed, coughed and picked it up in her left hand. She flipped it over and pushed her thumb under the unstuck bit of the flap at the back.

She paused and glanced at him and he rocked back and forth in the chair, his fist shoved into his mouth. He tried to prepare himself but it was impossible to calm down.

He felt the way he once did on the rollercoaster at Blackpool Pleasure Beach when he was twelve. That awesome combination of terror and fear, and the adrenaline coursing through his veins, as the car climbed the steep bank and paused for a millisecond on the apex of the highest curve. He experienced the same dizziness, the feeling of being trapped and the same terrifying anticipation of what was to come next.

Simone ripped the envelope open, using her thumb as a letter-opener. She pulled out the contents — some leaflets fell onto the table — and opened an A4-sized sheet of white paper. She glanced at David, then looked back at the paper and frowned in concentration as her eyes quickly scanned the page and came to rest at the bottom of it.

Then she folded the paper, set it down on the table and he stopped breathing. He realised suddenly that, just as he knew exactly what to expect on the rollercoaster as the car began its descent downhill, he knew what the result would be.

'It's negative,' she said, her voice shaking with emotion. 'Murray is not your son. And that's proven to a hundred per cent accuracy.'

David covered his face with his hands and started to cry. He felt Simone's arm around him and he buried his face in the folds of her sleeve. And then he realised just how much he wanted Murray to be his child.

He remembered how he'd felt the day Murray was born and he'd held him in his arms for the very first time. The wave of tenderness and joy and the wonder at the little howling scrap of life that was his flesh and blood. He recalled the overwhelming feeling of pride and the sense that this child was the greatest achievement of his life. And now, to find out that it had all been built on a falsehood! It was unbearable.

'I'm sorry, David. I'm so sorry,' said Simone and she pulled his head to her breast and cradled it. He could feel her body trembling and her warm, wet tears on his forehead.

They remained like that for some time until, at

last, David pulled away. The tears were gone only to be replaced by an ache in the middle of his chest, like heartburn. He touched himself lightly on the breastbone, knowing instinctively that this pain would never go away.

'I'll make us some tea,' said Simone despondently, after a long silence had passed.

David picked up the sheet of paper and read the result for himself, too shocked to speak. His senses were suddenly, painfully heightened. Every scrape sounded like a screech, the drip, drip, drip of the tap was like a bass drum and the soft sounds of Simone at work were like someone hammering a sledgehammer into his head. Even the dull early morning light of a wet, grey summer morning hurt his eyes. He closed them and cupped his hands over his ears. But the noises continued inside his head.

When he opened his eyes there was a chipped mug of tea in front of him and he heard Simone say, 'Are you OK?'

He removed his hands from his ears and sighed heavily in response. He felt as though he would never be OK again.

'How could she do this to me?' he said.

'Perhaps Viv didn't know, David. It's quite possible she didn't.'

'No,' said David and his grief hardened into anger, 'she knew all right. And she had absolutely no intention of ever telling me, or Murray.'

'Oh, David, that's a terrible thing to say about Viv. Most probably she believes Murray is your child. I imagine this'll be as much of a shock to her as it is to you.'

David shook his head. 'You don't know Viv the way I do, Simone. She's quite capable of lying like this.'

'Well, if she has, she won't be the first women in that position. I imagine she did what she thought was best for Murray.'

'And for herself,' said David darkly.

'I'm sure she had his best interests at heart. Maybe she knew his real father wouldn't want to have anything to do with him.'

'Why are you defending her?' said David, his voice choked with emotion.

'I'm only trying to — to help. To see things from her point of view.'

'OK. Let's say that all the things you've said are true. Maybe she was motivated by concern for Murray. But it doesn't make any difference. If she had any doubts — and she must have had — she should've made it her business to find out. What she did was wrong. Just plain wrong. It wasn't as if we were even together at the time. I still think that she used Murray to get me back so that I would support her and her child.'

'David,' said Simone with a sigh, 'has it ever occurred to you why Viv acts the way she does towards you?'

'Because she hates me?'

'No. Because she's still in love with you, silly. If she did know Murray wasn't yours — and I'm not suggesting that she did — that's a very sound reason for letting you believe he was.'

'I don't follow.'

'You can be dense sometimes, David. Don't you see? Murray might have been her way of getting you back.'

'That's unforgivable.'

'She's to be pitied more than anything, David.'

'I can't forgive her for this. And what about Murray? Doesn't he have a right to know who his real father is?'

'Yes, he does,' said Simone sadly.

'I have to tell her what I've done,' he said decisively.

'She might stop you seeing him if you do that,' observed Simone wisely.

'If I know Viv, not as long as I pay maintenance.'

He'd given Viv thousands over the years in support of Murray, often leaving himself short of money to treat Simone the way he would have liked. And how much of Viv's maintenance money had been spent directly on the boy? She was unemployed and yet she managed to run a car and was never stuck for money for new clothes and her regular nights out. He would never stop paying maintenance of course — even now in his anger he resolved to do right by Murray — but it irked him nonetheless.

'David, you don't have to tell her.'

'I can't do that.'

'Yes, you can,' she said earnestly. 'If you tell her, it'll change things forever. You know it will. You love Murray, don't you?'

'Of course I love him, Simone, but he's not mine. Don't you see what that means?'

'I see a crushed man who loves a little boy. It's

529

up to you how you go from here. You can either carry on as though nothing's changed or — '

'I can't do that,' he said, interrupting her. 'You know I can't.'

'Or,' continued Simone as though he hadn't spoken, 'you must accept the consequences of telling her. If you go ahead, if you make this public, Viv might well make sure you never see him again.'

'I'm telling you, she won't do that as long as I keep paying maintenance. Besides, I don't think she's vindictive enough to do it.'

'Isn't she?'

'But don't you see, if I don't tell the truth then I'm as bad as she is. And I have to be honest, Simone, I can't keep this a secret. It's just too important. I can't carry on as though nothing's changed when everything has.'

'And what about Murray? Surely it's better not to tell him now? He's so young!'

'I don't know. I know he's only five but it's wrong to let him grow up thinking I'm his dad. I'm going to have to tell him — if not now then at some point in the future. And I think it's better to tell him the truth while he's young and better able to cope with it, than wait until he's older and then tell him. I think it would be even more traumatic for him then than now.'

'You don't ever have to tell him.'

'I can't do that.'

'Oh, David, just think, will you? I know you're angry with Viv and you may have good reason to be. But don't make Murray suffer for that.'

'I'm not making him suffer for it!'

'You will be if you tell him.'

David stared at the untouched mug of tea and examined his conscience. True, he was very angry with Viv, but he simply could not live with the lie. In the long run, it wasn't fair on Murray.

'No, Simone,' he said at last. 'I don't think that's fair. I am furious with Viv but, putting that aside, I still think it's better that I tell him now than let him grow up believing a lie. My love for him won't change — I'll still continue to see him and he'll come to stay here. It won't change our relationship.'

'I think you're kidding yourself, David. I think it'll break his heart.' A tear leaked out of the corner of her eye. She put her hand up to her face and brushed it away.

'It's breaking my heart, Simone,' said David softly.

★   ★   ★

David spent the next three days off work sick, holed up in the cottage, hardly speaking to Simone and refusing to leave the bedroom. He lay on the bed and stared at the wall and tried to sort out the confusion in his head. He never imagined that he would be so traumatically affected by the knowledge about Murray. Simone had been right. He hadn't appreciated the devastation that would accompany a negative result. He tried very hard to take Simone's advice on board about not telling Viv and Murray. But it was no use. He simply couldn't do it.

531

But now he had to face the consequences of his actions. He would tell Viv when he'd calmed down enough to talk to her. He decided to tell her over the phone. He could not tell her face-to-face because he knew he wouldn't be able to control his temper. When he thought about her, he truly wanted to kill her. He hated her like he'd never hated anyone in his life.

And when he thought of poor, innocent little Murray the tears would come again. How would he feel when the man he knew as his dad told him he wasn't his biological father? Was a child of that age even capable of understanding the concept? Was he asking too much of a five-year-old?

But, he told himself, children were very resilient. The only thing that would change for Murray was the knowledge that he was not related by blood to David. And what did that really mean to a child of his age?

What mattered was that Murray knew he was loved — not what label he knew David by. David resolved that he would continue to treat Murray exactly the way he had always done. Nothing would change — their trips to the cinema, Murray's stay-overs at the cottage, the hugs and kisses, the love between them. He just wished with all his heart that he did not have to tell him but he knew he must.

When his mother phoned on the third day asking him to come and see her he put her off.

'I can't come, Mum. I'm not well.'

This was not a lie for David was physically incapacitated by his grief. His legs felt like lead and his brain keep playing the same cycle of thoughts over and over again — as though it was one of Murray's battery-powered toy trains going round and round the same old loop of track — until it was worn out. His head was full of 'what ifs' and 'buts' and his heart ached with regret.

'I'm sorry to hear that, son. What's wrong with you?'

'I'm not sure. Just a flu bug or something.'

'What are your symptoms?'

'Sore head. Temperature. You know, the usual.'

'Well, you wrap up warm now and stay in bed. The weather's turned cold all of a sudden.'

David hadn't noticed.

'But I really must see you soon, David. I have something very important to tell you. Do you think you'll be well enough at the weekend?'

'I don't know, Mum.'

'Please, David. It's really important.'

'Can't you just tell me over the phone?' said David irritably and he was quite certain that if she didn't get off the phone soon, he was going to scream at her.

'No, I can't,' she said firmly. 'Just make sure you're at the hotel on Saturday at two o'clock.' With that, she put the phone down.

On Friday evening Simone made him a comfort meal of macaroni cheese and bacon and brought it up to the room on a tray.

'Here,' she said, standing by the bed. 'Sit up and eat this.'

'I'm not hungry.'

'I insist. I'm worried about you.'

533

David rolled onto his back and looked at her. Her face was drawn with worry and he was full of guilt that he'd caused her so much anguish.

'I'd be a lot happier if you ate this,' she said. 'I made it specially for you.'

He hauled himself into a sitting position and she placed the tray on his lap. Then she left the room and he surprised himself by eating the entire meal. When he was finished he swung his legs over the side of the bed and carried the tray downstairs. He found her in the kitchen on her knees stuffing clothes into the washing machine.

'Here, let me do that,' he said gently, setting the tray on the table. He helped her to her feet and took over the task. He threw washing tablets into the machine, closed the door and set the dial. The machine gurgled into life.

'I'm sorry that I've been so — so useless,' he said, standing up.

Suddenly she grasped his hand and placed it on her belly. 'This,' she said fiercely, 'is your child, David O'Connor. And it's time you woke up and realised it. You did what you thought you had to do as far as Murray is concerned but now you've got to learn to live with it.'

'I know that,' he said and put his hand up to her tired-looking face. 'You look exhausted, Simone. I've been neglecting you, haven't I?'

'I'm exhausted with worrying about you. I can't go on under this pressure, David. It's making me ill.'

'Look, I'm sorry,' said David, suddenly coming to his senses. 'I've been wallowing in self-pity. But that's over now, I promise.'

'Thank God for that,' she said without irony and her shoulders visibly relaxed.

She sat down in one of the kitchen chairs and David started to clean up the mess in the kitchen.

'Your mother was on the phone again,' she said after a few moments had passed. 'She's very anxious to see you, David. She says she must see you tomorrow and she was getting quite upset when I said I didn't know if you'd make it or not.'

David sighed and said, 'OK. I'll go and see her. Whatever it is that's bothering her, she obviously needs to get it off her chest.'

After lunch the next day, David shaved and showered and drove the Land Rover along the coast road in the direction of Ballyfergus. He had put on a brave face for Simone, because he was worried about her, but inside he felt just as devastated as he'd been the day he found out about Murray. He could think of nothing else. At five minutes to two, he pulled into the hotel car park. He sat in the car staring at the familiar façade and wondered why his mother had asked to meet him here.

He sighed heavily, got out of the car and went inside. He was always taken aback by the new sleek interior, part of him still expecting the old chintzy hotel he'd known as a child. What Kath had done with it was marvellous. She had a real gift for business — he wished his father had recognised that talent in her, instead of automatically assuming that his only son would want to follow in his footsteps.

'Mr O'Connor,' said the girl on reception, 'your mother and sisters are waiting for you in the small function room just down the corridor.'

He walked down the hall, surprised to hear that Kath and Bridget were involved as well. His curiosity aroused, he opened the door to the room and went inside. The three women were facing each other on chairs arranged in a small circle. Kath was in a business suit, looking like she was about to chair a meeting, while Bridget and Fiona were casually dressed. The fourth chair in the small circle was empty. It looked like a group therapy session was about to take place and he was the last participant to arrive.

David greeted his mother and sisters and said, 'What's all this about then, Mum?'

'Thanks for coming, love. Are you sure you're OK? You don't look very well.'

'I'm fine,' he mumbled. 'Just haven't got over this bug yet.'

He sat down in the empty chair and Fiona said, 'Kath, would you like to start?'

Kath cleared her throat and said, 'Mum's asked you both here because she, well, both of us really, have something to tell you about Dad.'

Kath glanced at Fiona and she nodded and briefly closed her eyes, a signal for Kath to go on. Bridget looked at David and raised her eyebrows questioningly, a nervous little smile on her lips. David shook his head to indicate that he knew nothing of what this was all about.

'I was in the office one evening last week and someone came to see me. It was John Routledge,' said Kath, her voice not as confident as usual, and she paused.

What did Kath's staff meetings have to do with Dad? David wished she would get on with it so that he could get out of here and back to the cottage. He wondered how they would all feel when he eventually told them about Murray.

'He told me something that came as a quite a shock as I'm sure it will to you two as well,' said Kath.

'What?' said Bridget, barely managing to disguise her impatience.

'Sshh, Bridget,' said Fiona, raising a hand to silence her daughter. 'Let her tell you.'

Would Fiona be pleased, David thought darkly, that her suspicions about Murray had been confirmed? She'd never liked him, a fact that hurt David deeply.

'He told me . . . ' said Kath and now she appeared quite agitated. Her face was flushed and she wrung her hands together nervously.

David's interest quickened.

'He told me,' she repeated, 'that Dad was his father.' She paused a moment to let the information sink in and then added, 'He said that he was my half-brother, and therefore yours too.'

David put his hand to his brow and closed his eyes. His thinking was fuzzy from grief and lack of sleep. Dad had fathered Ellen Routledge's son, John? The dirty old bugger! That explained why Brendan had been so fond of John. David had often envied the close relationship between the two men, imagining that his father preferred a stranger to him. This proved his suspicions had been correct. Had he loved John more than he'd loved him?

'I don't believe it,' said Bridget with a short, hollow laugh and David opened his eyes. Bridget turned to her mother and said, 'Tell Kath it's not true.'

'I'm afraid it is true, Bridget. You know your father left a will?'

Bridget nodded dumbly.

'Well, inside that will was a letter from your father addressed to me.'

'You never said anything about a letter, Mum,' said Bridget accusingly.

'I didn't want you, or anyone else, to know about it. I was ashamed of what your father had done and how it would reflect on me. But when John told Kath . . . ' said Fiona and stalled. 'Anyway, in the letter your dad told me about John.'

Bridget sat back in her chair looking stunned while David tried to absorb the facts. How must poor Mum feel, he thought, glancing up at her proud face, rigid as stone, knowing that her husband had been unfaithful? And how must John feel about it all? David had never liked him but only, he had to admit, because he was jealous of his closeness to Brendan. But now that he knew he was his own flesh and blood, could they ever be friends?

'But how did John find out?' said Bridget.

'Dad told him.'

'When? Just before he died?'

'No. He told him years ago, when John was just twenty.'

'John's known for that long?' said Bridget in astonishment.

As Bridget interrogated Kath about the unfolding of events, David's thoughts drifted back to Murray. He realised that, in twenty or thirty years from now, a similar scenario to this one might be played out in another room somewhere in Ballyfergus or beyond. Except it would be poor Murray who would be the bastard son trying to find his place in the world and acceptance amongst his own flesh and blood. David put his hands over his face and started to cry.

'David!' cried Fiona.

Kath and Bridget stopped talking at once.

Fiona got out of her chair, came over to him and put a hand on his shoulder.

Quickly David wiped his eyes, embarrassed at losing control in front of his family. He was a grown man, for Christ's sake, he told himself crossly. He felt like he was falling apart.

'I'm sorry that this has been such a shock to you, David,' said Fiona. 'I know that you and your dad had issues. But he did love you.'

'Mum . . . ' said David and his voice was a whisper. He took a deep breath and tried again. 'Mum, it is a shock. But I'm not upset about Dad or John Routledge. It's — it's Murray.'

'What's wrong with him?' cried Bridget.

'Is he hurt? Ill?' said Kath.

'No,' said David and he felt a cold tear trickle down his cheek like melting snow. 'Nothing's wrong with him. But I just found out that he's not my son.'

'Did Viv tell you this?' said Fiona, almost as though she had been expecting it.

He shook his head and swallowed the lump in his throat but it did not go away. 'I did a DNA test on him,' he said with difficulty. 'You know, one of these paternity tests where you take samples of cells from inside your cheek. I did it and sent it off and it came back negative.'

There was a long stunned silence.

Then Bridget said, 'Have you told Viv?'

'Not yet.'

'Jesus Christ,' said Kath and she sat down abruptly and put her face in her hands.

'Oh, David, darling,' said Bridget with compassion, 'I'm so sorry.'

David nodded and then looked up at his mother, who was still standing with her hand on his shoulder as though using it to support herself.

'So you were right, Mum,' he said bitterly, 'Murray is not your grandson after all.'

Fiona's eyes flickered with hurt and she removed her hand. 'I never wished this to be, David,' she said in a breaking voice. 'I wish with all my heart that he was your child. And I'm sorry that he's not because I know that you love him dearly.'

David's eyes burned hot with unshed tears and he looked away.

'Kath,' said Fiona, recovering her composure, 'I think you'd better go and tell John that we're sorry, but we'll have to talk to him another day. I'm sure he'll understand.'

'Yes, of course,' said Kath and she slipped

quietly from the room.

'Oh, David,' said Bridget and she knelt in front of the chair and embraced him, 'what are you going to do?'

David pressed his hot face into the shoulder of his sister's black cord jacket. It smelt of dry-cleaning fluid and expensive perfume. 'I'm going to do what I have to.'

'You mean tell Viv?' she said, pulling away to look into his face.

'Yes. And Murray too.'

'Murray?' she repeated, sounding shocked.

'I have no choice, Bridge. Don't you see? I can't go on pretending I'm his father when I'm not. He'll find out one day and it's better that he's told now, when he's young and able to adapt to the truth. If I wait until he's older it could inflict untold psychological damage, especially if he knew that the truth had deliberately been kept from him. And maybe one day, just like John,' he added, not entirely believing it himself, 'he'll find out who he really is.'

37

Kath sat alone in the kitchen on Monday morning drinking coffee and watching the phone on the dresser. She glanced at the big chrome clock — it was eight thirty. She was still unwashed and undressed — she wore a white towelling dressing-gown over her pyjamas. She was utterly worn out by the events of the previous week.

The revelation about John had taken a lot of adjusting to, mainly because it required Kath to recalibrate her entire catalogue of memories about her father. She found herself pulling out specific ones and examining them under a spotlight, much as forensic scientist would, looking for evidence of his crime.

She tried to recall if she'd ever seen him with a woman at the hotel but she could recall nothing suspicious. Of course, as a child, she would've been blind to the subtleties of adult behaviour and Brendan probably took great care to be discreet around his children. It was the idea that he had been furtive and untruthful to Fiona that hurt the most.

She remembered asking him, on many occasions, why he couldn't be home for tea or home in time to read her a bedtime story. 'I'm sorry, I have to work, darling,' he would say and pinch her chin with his forefinger and thumb. Now she knew that, on a few of those occasions at least, he was lying. Just like Carl. Had she, unwittingly, gravitated towards a man just like her father as, according to popular wisdom, all women did? A man capable of living a double life, apparently without suffering from a guilty conscience, and sustaining lies for years.

But, she reminded herself, he probably acted as he did to protect her and her siblings — and Fiona — from hurt.

For all she knew he could have been in love with Ellen. With both of them married to other people, and him the father of three young children, it would have been impossible for them to be together. Ellen might have refused to leave her husband for him — divorce wasn't as common thirty years ago as it was today.

Kath realised that, speculate as she might, she would never know the entire truth. And without knowing the whole story, it wasn't fair of her to judge her father's actions.

But she felt terribly sorry for her mother, finding out the truth after all these years. If Brendan had never written that letter and never told John, only Ellen Routledge would have known about the truth. And it would most likely have gone to the grave with her. She'd kept her silence for all this time — she wasn't going to break it now.

The most difficult part was trying to come to terms with the fact that her father had not been perfect — he was just a man as flawed as the next one, prone to human weaknesses and failings. She wondered if guilt about what he had done had anything to do with his suicide and then as quickly dismissed the idea. He'd successfully kept Ellen and John a secret for over thirty years. Why would that suddenly drive him to take his own life?

She thought back to the recent conversation she'd had with Fiona about the reasons for his suicide. Poor Mum, imagining that she was responsible. She wasn't, of course, but it must be hard, as Brendan's widow, not to feel in some way guilty. Not to feel that you could, and should, have done something to stop him.

But it wasn't all bad news, Kath told herself, in an effort to drag herself out of the despondency that consumed her. On the up side, she had a new and lovely half-brother, whom she was genuinely fond of. And it would've been very sad for John not to find out that he was part of the O'Connor family. For when his mother passed away he would have nobody to call his own.

Now he had a new family to get to know properly. It would take all of them a while to adjust to the new order, but Kath was sure that she and her siblings would rise to the challenge. She was sure they would all learn to love him. Even David, the one Fiona had worried about the most, appeared to have accepted the idea readily enough. But then again he had other things on his mind.

Kath ran her hands through her dirty hair and sighed heavily.

'Poor little Murray and poor David,' she said out loud.

The news about Murray had shocked Kath to

the core and her heart ached for her brother's misery. She found it inconceivable that Viv could have done such a wicked thing. Even if she thought David was the father of her baby, she must have had very strong doubts. You don't go around getting amnesia about who you've slept with and when. She should have been honest with David about her doubts — she should have given him the opportunity, at the outset, to carry out a paternity test. Or done it herself. Before he came to love the boy and call him his own.

But just as she would never know the truth about her father's relationship with Ellen Routledge, she would never know what motivated Viv. Perhaps she had been desperately in love with David and saw Murray as the only way to make him love her. Perhaps she was terrified by the prospect of being a single mother and raising a child alone — Kath knew she herself would be. Viv may well have done what she did out of fierce maternal love for Murray. Her desire to provide him with a loving father might have overridden any qualms she had about her actions.

But what was done could not be undone, and now the future for David and Murray looked uncertain. He was quite determined that the child should be told and, after the recent experience with John, Kath agreed with him. It would be wrong to keep the truth from Murray — and better that he should absorb the idea when he was still very young. But where would it leave him? Confused, hurt and fatherless. And what about his real father? Did Viv even know who he was? It was far too much for a little child to cope with, especially with only a stupid, selfish woman like Viv as a mother. It was all a terrible mess.

The hands on the clock inched towards nine o'clock and Kath went over to the dresser and picked up the phone. She dialled the hotel office and waited.

Moira answered it after four rings and said, 'Are you OK? We wondered where you were.' Kath was always in the office by eight.

'Actually, I'm not feeling too good. Is John there?'

'Sure.'

John came on the line. 'How are you?'

'John, I don't think I'm going to make it in today.'

'OK,' he said hesitantly. 'Is everything all right?'

'It's just that . . . can you talk?'

'Wait a minute.'

There were some muffled noises on the end of the line, then John said, 'It's OK now,' and waited.

'It's not that I'm ill exactly, John. It's just that I feel absolutely exhausted by recent events. That business about Murray has really upset me. I hardly slept a wink last night or the night before.'

'I know,' he said sympathetically. 'It's pretty awful news. And finding out about me must've been a shock as well.'

'It was, but a nice one,' said Kath and she imagined John's easy smile on the end of the phone.

546

'Thanks for saying that, Kath,' he said and then said, more businesslike, 'Look, don't worry about the hotel. I can manage. Just try and relax and get some rest.'

'I will. I should be in tomorrow all being well.'

Kath put the phone down, glad that she'd told John about Murray. He'd been very concerned and understanding and it was a very convincing cover. For her extreme distress was caused, not by father's infidelity, nor by the news about Murray — terrible though they both were — but by Bridget.

Or rather by Bridget and Mike Mulholland and what they'd done. She couldn't help but picture them together, making love, and when she did she was filled with revulsion and jealousy.

How could Bridget have been unfaithful to big, good-natured Ned who loved her and the children with a passion? A good husband who provided for his family well, didn't drink excessively or give Bridget any cause for concern. His only vice, according to Bridget, was playing too many rounds of golf on a Saturday afternoon.

Was he just too good, too boring? Had she been looking for some sort of excitement that Ned couldn't provide? Whatever her reasons, Bridget had plummeted in her sister's estimation. She could not forgive her for what she'd done.

But worse than cheating on Ned was the fact that a baby was on the way — Mike's child, according to Bridget. Briefly, Kath wondered how Bridget could be sure the child was Mike's. Could it be that her sister and Ned weren't sleeping together? But, in that case, there was no way Bridget could pass the child off as Ned's.

Not that she should try. Hadn't they seen at first hand the damage that such a course of action would cause? One lie couldn't be cancelled out with another. She had promised Bridget that she wouldn't tell anyone, but she'd be damned if she'd stand aside and allow the wool to be pulled over Ned's gullible eyes!

Kath stormed into the lounge, walked round the sofa three times and returned to the kitchen where she sank into a hard-backed chair, deflated. She would have to talk to Bridget soon. There were far too many questions left unanswered. Whatever happened, this pregnancy would tear the family apart.

Unless, as Bridget suggested, she had an abortion. It would get rid of the baby and Ned need never know a thing. Kath covered her face with her hands. She believed abortion to be wrong and she thought, until now, that Bridget did too. Brendan might have been a lapsed Catholic but it was one of the values that he'd drummed into his children. But what else could Bridget do? If she and Mike had no future, perhaps it was the best plan.

Kath thought of Mike and shook her head. Clearly her judgement of men was utterly flawed. She found it hard to believe that Mike had slept with a married woman. It was hard enough accepting that he had a girlfriend. And now this.

She knew that he did not love her and yet . . . yet she had still hoped that one day he might. And in spite of what he'd done, she realised that she loved him still.

But she would purge herself of that love, rip it from her heart and destroy it, she thought angrily. She placed her hand on her breast over her heart. After this there was no way she could ever look at Mike Mulholland in the same light again. She would give up the farmhouse immediately — she wanted nothing to do with him.

And this, perhaps, was the hardest part of all. For, though she was concerned and distressed for those she loved, she mourned the passing of hope and of the dream that had been Mike. A man she'd set on a pedestal, just like her father and Carl, only to find he was a weak, immoral creep, who preyed on vulnerable women like Bridget.

When she heard an insistent rap on the door she sat, not breathing, and waited for whoever it was to go away. The tap, tap, tap continued, louder this time, and she stood up. It might be Bridget.

She ran through to the hall. There were no windows surrounding the solid wooden door and no security peephole to spy on the person outside. If she tried to sneak a peek through the downstairs window they would see her. She pulled her dressing-gown tightly round her and opened the door.

When she saw Mike standing on her doorstep, she could barely contain her rage.

'What do you want?' she said curtly and he frowned.

'Didn't you get my messages? I left three on Saturday.'

'I did,' she simmered through clenched teeth. 'And?'

'What?' she snapped.

'Don't you think it would be polite to let my mother know whether or not you were coming for lunch on Sunday? She ended up cooking for you in case you showed up, which of course you didn't.'

'I'm sorry about that,' mumbled Kath. 'I didn't mean to put Gladys out.'

She opened her mouth and closed it again. She had promised Bridget that she wouldn't tell anyone. Did that include Mike?

'I'm giving you notice on the farmhouse, Mike. I'll pay you what I owe you, of course, but I'm moving out immediately. Today.'

The angry look fell from his face immediately to be replaced by one of dismay.

'But why?' he stumbled. 'I thought you were happy here.'

'I can't stay here any longer,' she said with as much dignity she could muster, 'and I think you know why.'

'Kath, what are you talking about?'

The bubble of anger inside her suddenly burst.

'Don't you stand there pretending you don't know!' she screamed. 'Don't you stand there like that as though you've done nothing wrong. How could you, Mike? How could you?'

Violently she pushed the door in his face but, with lightning speed, he jammed his trainer-clad foot in the gap between the frame and the door — and it bounced open again. She stormed into the lounge where she threw herself onto the sofa, buried her face in a pillow and burst into tears.

'Jesus H Christ!' he shouted, standing in the middle of the small room, and she looked up at him through her tears. He was shaking all over and the tendons on his neck stood out like metal wires. 'Will you tell me what the hell you're talking about?'

'How can you stand there and act like nothing's wrong? How can you?' she cried, her sobs more restrained now. 'After what you've done to Bridget!'

Mike shook his head. He took two steps forward and stretched out his hand towards her. She swiped it away and it was like hitting the branch of a tree, hard and unyielding.

'Don't you come near me,' she hissed. 'Don't you dare come near me!'

There was a short silence that crackled with tension, and he said in a deep, firm voice, 'Kath. What have I done to Bridget?'

'Pah!' she cried. 'As if you don't know!'

'There must be some sort of misunderstanding — ' he began but she didn't let him finish.

'I loved you! Even though I knew you couldn't love me back!' She was thinking of Anne. 'I still loved you, Mike.' She sobbed quietly into the tear-stained cushion.

'You do?' he said and his eyes opened wide in surprise. 'Oh, Kath,' he said, his voice softening, and he took another step forward.

'Get away from me!'

'But you said — '

'I said I *loved* you, Mike. How can I love you now after what you've done? I can never forgive you!'

'For what, for Christ's sake? For *what*?'

'For sleeping with Bridget and getting her pregnant!'

The colour drained entirely from Mike's face and he said, very quietly, 'Who told you this?'

'Bridget, of course.'

All of a sudden, his head started to tremble uncontrollably, all the colour rushed back into his face at once and suddenly it was bright red. He slammed a tightly closed right fist into the palm of his left hand and cried, 'I'll fucking kill her! I'll fucking kill her!'

'You didn't think she'd tell me, did you?' said Kath triumphantly.

He unfurled his fist and all the anger leached from his body. 'And you believed her, Kath,' he said, shaking his head, 'you believed her.'

'Of course I did,' she said, as an uncomfortable feeling took hold. 'She's my sister.'

'Right,' he said, in a drill sergeant's voice, 'get your clothes on.'

'Why?' she said, feeling suddenly afraid.

'Because we're going to see Bridget.'

Mesmerised by his anger and confused by what she had just heard, Kath did as she was told. Upstairs, she threw on jeans and a T-shirt, slipped her feet into a pair of flip-flops and stopped for a few seconds to run a brush through her hair. Mike was not acting like a man who had just been found out — he was acting like a man who had just found something out. Was it possible Bridget had not been entirely truthful with her?

He was waiting at the bottom of the stairs, jangling a set of car keys in his hand. As soon as he saw her, he opened the front door — she stepped outside and he slammed the door shut behind him.

'Where is she?' he demanded.

'At home, I guess. During the holidays she doesn't work on Mondays.'

'Right. The car's down at the house. Come on,' he said and set off at breakneck feet, his muscular legs moving like pistons. Kath, in her soft-soled footwear, hobbled over the dry rough stones as fast as she could but he soon left her behind. When she reached the car, the passenger door was hanging open, Mike was already in the driver's seat and the engine whined and growled like a restrained bull.

Kath hopped in the car and, as soon as she had closed the door, it swung into reverse sending up a cloud of dry, brown dust. Thrown forwards by the violent motion, she only saved herself from injury by bracing her hands on the dashboard. 'Wait a minute!' she cried out. 'I haven't got my seatbelt on.'

The car paused and Mike glanced down impatiently at the belt in her lap. She fastened the buckle and once again the car leapt into action. It tore down the bumpy road past the hotel, and Kath had to hold onto the door handle to prevent herself from being thrown from side to side.

At the junction at the bottom of the road, Mike turned onto the coast road and put his foot on the accelerator. His lips were clamped into a thin line, both hands were fixed on the steering wheel so tightly that his knuckles were white and his eyes stared straight ahead.

'You're going to get us both killed,' she ventured and his grip on the steering wheel relaxed a little. The car slowed to a safe speed and Kath said, 'Didn't she tell you about the baby?'

'There is no baby, Kath. At least not mine.'

'But Bridget said — ' began Kath and then she shut up. If what he said was true and there was no baby, was the rest of what Bridget said a lie?

'She said you slept together,' said Kath and this time it was she who stared straight ahead, not daring to look at his face.

'I never laid a finger on your sister,' he said, ramming the car into fifth gear. 'Not since we dated years ago.'

'If that's the case,' said Kath, horrified while at the same time so wanting it to be true, 'then why did Bridget say it?'

'I have no idea. I don't know what's going on in her twisted mind. But we're about to find out.'

Kath fell silent then and stared unseeing out the window. Her heart pounded in her chest and her mouth was dry. She was so aware of Mike's presence beside her, her whole body tingled with fear and longing. She prayed that he was telling the truth. And yet she couldn't believe that

Bridget would invent such terrible lies.

'Now, she lives out towards Kilwaughter, doesn't she?' said Mike, as they reached the outskirts of Ballyfergus. 'You're going to have to give me directions from here.'

It was shortly before ten o'clock when they pulled up outside Bridget and Ned's converted steading. They got out of the car and Kath looked for Ned's car. It wasn't there. The sun was already hot in the sky and she could hear the sound of children's laughter coming from the side of the house. She remembered that Ned had just bought a giant trampoline for the garden.

'Let's go in the back door,' she said, her stomach churning with nerves, 'so that the children don't see us. I don't think they heard the car.'

She put her hand on the door handle, pushed the door open and stepped inside. Mike followed her. The kitchen was empty but the table was strewn with the remains of breakfast. Kath heard the sound of footsteps in the hall and suddenly Bridget appeared in the doorway carrying a bundle of clothes in her arms. She was dressed in brown trousers and a cream blouse and her face was made up.

As soon as she saw them she dropped the clothes on the floor and put her hands up to her mouth. Then, suddenly recovering, she bent down, scooped up the clothes and said, 'I was just going to put these in the wash.'

She walked towards the utility room but was stopped by Mike's stern voice.

'Bridget!' he began.

But Kath put her hand up in the air and said, 'Wait a minute, Mike.' Then, turning to her sister, she asked, 'Where's Ned?'

'Work.'

'And the children?'

'They're all out in the garden on that wretched trampoline,' said Bridget, forcing a thin smile. 'They can't get enough of it.'

Kath stared at Bridget and the smile fell as quickly from her face as it had appeared.

'Bridget McVey,' said Mike and both women looked at him, 'I want you to tell me what you told your sister.'

'I told you not to tell anyone, Kath,' snapped Bridget, her eyes wild with fear.

'Bridget,' said Kath, and her legs felt so weak she could hardly stand. She held onto the end of the breakfast bar for support.

'Did you tell Kath that I slept with you and got you pregnant?' demanded Mike.

Bridget did not answer but stood for a long time simply staring from Mike to Kath and back again.

'Bridget, please,' said Kath when she could find the strength to speak.

Suddenly Bridget started to cry.

'Bridget,' said Kath gently, going over to her sister and taking the clothes out of her arms. She helped her onto a barstool and said, 'The things that you told me, were they all lies?'

Bridget nodded and a flood of relief washed over Kath. She looked at Mike and he was standing with his hands over his face and his legs slightly apart. His shoulders were shaking and

556

Kath thought he must be crying but when he pulled his hands away he was dry-eyed. And very, very angry looking.

'You never slept with him?' probed Kath, turning her attention back to Bridget.

'No,' said Bridget, her voice hardly audible.

'And there is no baby?' said Kath, intent on ferreting out the truth.

Bridget sniffed and looked into Kath's face. 'Yes, there is. But it's not Mike's.'

'Whose is it?'

'My husband's.'

Kath stood up straight and looked hard into her sister's face. 'How could you, Bridget? How could you say such terrible things about Mike?'

Bridget shook her head without speaking.

Mike said, 'I'm so angry with you, Bridget. I can never forgive you for this. Kath, I'll wait for you in the car.'

Kath wanted to run out after him straightaway but she looked down at the snivelling figure in front of her and knew that she must get to the bottom of this first.

She climbed onto a barstool beside her sister and said, 'Why did you do it, Bridget?'

Bridget raised her tear-streaked face and said, 'Because I was jealous of you.'

'Jealous of what?' said Kath in bewilderment, thinking that her life so far had been an utter failure. She might have a fledgling success in the hotel, but she was up to her eyes in debt and facing the prospect of a lonely old age. Bridget, on the other hand, had what Kath would've given her right arm for — a loving husband and family as well as another baby on the way.

'Everything,' said Bridget flatly. 'The way you look. Your cleverness. The way Mum and Dad, Dad especially, preferred you. You know that favourite memory you have of sitting on his knee in the office, getting fed his secret stash of sweets?'

'Yes,' said Kath hesitantly, not sure where this was leading.

'How come I don't have that memory, Kath? How come?'

Kath shook her head, alarmed at Bridget's increasing aggression.

'I'll tell you why!' Bridget said, spitting out the words like the seeds of a watermelon. 'I never got made a fuss of like you. I never got bought party dresses — '

'That was just the once,' said Kath in astonishment, but Bridget went on as though she hadn't spoken.

' — and told how beautiful I was. I was always the ugly one.'

Kath stared at her sister, wondering where all this bitterness came from. Was it really true that she'd been spoilt to the detriment of her siblings? Had she been blind to the truth all these years?

'I don't believe you, Bridget,' she said. 'We were all treated equally.'

'By Mum, maybe, but not by Dad,' said Bridget, calm now. 'You were always his favourite.'

Suddenly Kath remembered her father telling her not to tell the others when he gave her a treat. She'd assumed that Bridget and David were likewise treated to moments of secret spoiling.

'Well, if I was,' said Kath, suppressing the feelings of guilt, 'it's hardly my fault.'

Bridget inclined her head slightly in tacit agreement.

'And what about David?' said Kath. 'Does he feel the same way about me as you?'

'He doesn't appear to. Even as a child, it never seemed to bother him the way it bothered me.'

'Are you sure you're not imagining it?'

'No, I'm not imaging it, Kath. It happened.'

'But what has all this got to do with those terrible lies about Mike?'

'I watched you. I saw the way you looked at each other. I knew it was only a matter of time before you had him too.'

'I don't follow — '

'I loved him, you see. I wanted us to get married but he didn't want me. And when I saw the way things were heading I couldn't bear it. Why should you have him too? On top of everything else.'

'You did this to stop Mike and me getting together?' said Kath, her head reeling with shock and hurt. 'Bridget, you're sick in the head. What if your plan had worked and I'd never mentioned it to Mike? I would never have found out the truth. How could you have lived with yourself?'

'I know it's hard to understand,' said Bridget lamely. 'But that's how I felt. And I said those things on the spur of the moment — it wasn't as if I had planned it or thought it out. I'm sorry.'

Kath had come back to Ireland to be amongst her family — people she, foolishly, thought she knew and could trust. But first of all she found out that her father was a philanderer and now, even worse, that her sister hated her.

'Sorry for what?' she said as her pain turned to anger. 'Sorry for being a liar or sorry for hating me?'

'I don't hate you,' said Bridget feebly. 'I always wanted to be like you.'

'You are nothing like me, Bridget. I could never do what you have done. It is — unforgivable.'

'You're not going to tell anyone, are you?'

Kath stood up and looked down at her in contempt. 'It's not my place to do that. It's yours and I think you should start with Ned. Don't you think it's about time he knew he's going to be a father?'

'Yes. I suppose so,' said Bridget heavily.

'You don't sound very keen. Do you think he won't want it?'

'No, Ned will be delighted. It's me that doesn't want it.'

'Why not?' said Kath, puzzled more than ever by Bridget.

'You don't know what it's like being a full-time mum. I was so enjoying being out at work and having a life outside the home. And a baby will put a stop to all that.'

'Not necessarily. Bridget, do you love Ned?'

'Yes.'

'Then I think that you and he have got a lot of things to sort out, don't you? And I think you owe Mike an apology.'

'Yes, I suppose so,' mumbled Bridget.

'Do you know what, Bridget?' said Kath, still angry with her sister. 'There's one person you haven't considered in all this. What about the baby? Doesn't he or she have rights? How could you talk about abortion? And what about Ned? It's his baby too.

'I just don't understand you. You're sitting here in this gorgeous house with three perfect children and a lovely husband and you just can't see how lucky you are, can you? What do you think I would give to have what you have?'

Kath heard light footsteps in the hall and they both looked up.

'Auntie Kath!' cried Charmaine bounding into the room, and Kath couldn't even raise a smile for her little niece. 'Come and see our new trampoline. It's really cool.'

'No, darling, not today,' said Kath with a heavy heart and she moved towards the door. 'I have to go now,' she said and stepped outside, leaving a confused Charmaine staring at her dishevelled mother.

She climbed in the car beside Mike and he drove off without either of them saying a word.

Despite her shock and anger at Bridget, all Kath could think about now was the fact that she had told Mike she loved him. What had she been thinking of? He already had a girlfriend.

After a few minutes had passed, Mike asked, 'Well, what did she have to say for herself?'

'She did it because she's jealous of me,' said Kath, rubbing her hand across her greasy brow

561

and remembering suddenly that she hadn't washed that morning or put on any make-up. She must look a complete mess. 'And because she's in love with you, Mike. Or she used to be. I'm not sure which. She said that she didn't want me to 'get you', as she put it, and that was her way of stopping any relationship from getting off the ground.'

'A bit extreme, don't you think?'

'But effective,' said Kath wearily, exhausted by the confrontation with Bridget. 'I think she needs to get counselling or something. She's very mixed up. I'm sorry I believed her, Mike. I should've believed in you.'

He shrugged as though it was of no consequence now. 'Like you said, she's your sister. If one of my sisters told me something, I'd believe them too.'

They drove in silence then the rest of the way home and Kath kept sneaking glances at Mike. But his face was unreadable as he concentrated on the road ahead. She squirmed with embarrassment. He was probably mortified at her declaration of love — she'd just have to act as though it never happened, to save both of them any further awkwardness.

He pulled up outside the farmhouse, turned off the engine and twisted in his seat to look at her, his right arm resting on the steering wheel. His face and arms were tanned from days spent in the summer sun. With the contrast of his swarthy brown skin against the white T-shirt and his dark, piercing eyes — which were now locked on Kath's — he looked sexily Mediterranean rather than Irish.

'Kath,' he said, breaking the spell, 'are you OK?'

She glanced out the window at the flat fields surrounding the farmhouse. They were on a kind of plateau sandwiched top and bottom by steep barren land. These fields were full of lush green grass that would soon be cut and stored for winter feed. She remembered as a child looking for grasshoppers in the tall grass with Bridget until Mr Mulholland saw them and chased them off.

'Yeah, I'm fine. Or I will be once I've got over the shock of Bridget doing that. I just never in a million years imagined that my sister was capable of such deception. I thought I knew her but she's a stranger to me. I don't know that I can ever forgive her.'

'Whatever she's done, Kath, she's still your sister. Don't fall out with her because of me.'

'Did you ever love her?' she asked and looked at him. When he frowned she noticed the way his thick black brows jutted out over his eyes.

'No. I was fond of Bridget but I never loved her. That's why we broke up. I knew she was getting far too serious about me and I couldn't return her feelings.'

'She obviously never got over it.'

'Listen. Let's not talk about her,' said Mike and he shifted in his seat.

'OK.'

'You said back in the house, Kath, that you loved me.'

'Mmm,' she squeaked in response and felt her

face burn, like she'd spent too long in the sun.

'Look at me, Kath,' he said, his voice all raspy.

Kath raised her eyes to meet his and their eyes locked once more. She focused on his black pupils and everything in the periphery blurred, like an out-of-focus photograph.

'Do you still feel that way?' he asked.

She opened her mouth to speak but no words would come. She nodded her head.

'Oh, Kath,' he said in a husky voice, 'I've waited so long for this moment. I thought that you would never love me.'

And he leaned towards her and placed his lips very gently on hers. They were soft and hot and she took them greedily. She moved towards him as far as she could across the handbrake until his arm was around her waist and hers around his broad shoulders.

'I love you,' he whispered and he pulled her roughly to him, pressing her chest against his. His scent was heady — a combination of aftershave and musky, fresh sweat.

After what seemed like a very long time they pulled apart and he smiled at her, the anxiety from earlier all gone from his face. He looked handsome and carefree and joyous.

Kath slid back into her seat. 'But what about Anne?' she said tentatively.

'Anne?' said Mike, and his face creased up in confusion. 'What's Anne got to do with anything?'

'Your girlfriend, Mike.'

'My girlfriend? I don't have a girlfriend!'

'Anne is not your girlfriend? The Anne I met

at your house, the one that came with you to Emmy and Steve's party?'

'She's not my girlfriend, Kath. She's far too young for me,' he said, as though she had offended him by the very idea. 'What on earth made you think that?'

'But I saw you together a few times. And Bridget said . . . ' Her voice trailed off as she remembered with sudden clarity the conversation she'd had with Bridget at the reception for the opening of the hotel. Bridget hadn't said that Anne was Mike's girlfriend but she hadn't corrected Kath when she had made that mistake.

'Oh, Kath! Is that why you went all cool towards me? I wondered what had got into you when you declined my dinner invitation. I couldn't work out what I'd done wrong. Was that all about Anne?'

Kath nodded. 'What was I to think?' she said, feeling foolish. It was true that she had never witnessed any intimacy between them.

'You daft eejit!' said Mike and Kath couldn't help but smile. 'She's the daughter of a very good friend of mine, Ronnie Montgomery, who I used to play rugby with. He broke his neck in a match and was left paralysed from the neck down. He moved back up to Belfast to be near his parents after his marriage broke up. It was such a shame. His daughter stayed in Ballyfergus with her mother.'

'I'm so sorry, Mike. I had no idea. Poor Anne!'

'It happened a very long time ago. I promised him that I would look out for Anne. She broke up with her boyfriend a few months back and

565

was pretty depressed. That's when I took her under my wing for a bit, trying to be a surrogate dad, I suppose. She's over the break-up now, though. How could you think me and her . . . ? She's just a kid, Kath.'

'But what about the inscription on the book you lent me?' said Kath, thinking that it didn't sound like it came from the hand of a child.

Mike's brow furrowed in confusion once more.

'The book of poetry, Mike. She'd written something about hoping you found some comfort from the poems. She said that she loved you.'

'Oh, that Anne!' exclaimed Mike. 'That's Anne Cameron, an old friend of mine. She's married to my best mate, Ian, from uni. We've been friends for years.'

Kath blushed with embarrassment, feeling utterly foolish.

'I've been a complete idiot, haven't I?' she said and he answered her question with another long kiss.

When at last he pulled away he gently smoothed her hair off her forehead and said, 'I thought that you were going to go back with Carl, you know.'

'No, that was never going to happen. The thing that swung it was the fight you two had over me. Carl told me that you split his lip in an unprovoked attack. I saw his face — you must've given him one hell of a punch.'

'He told you that I started it!' said Mike, his eyes growing wide with incredulity. 'He was the one that attacked me first. He grabbed me by the collar and damned near ripped it right off my shirt. I think he deserved what he got. But I must confess I'd been itching to sock him one ever since I set eyes on him. I hated him for what he'd done to you. What a prat!'

So Carl had even lied about that, thought Kath. Had he ever told her the truth about anything?

'When I heard about that incident,' she said, 'I thought that you must care about me. And that gave me hope even though I thought that you already had a girlfriend.'

'Well, thank God we've finally got all these misunderstandings sorted out, Kath O'Connor. Because, you know what, I really don't think I can live without you any longer.'

Kath's head spun with happiness. She was in love and she wasn't going to let anything, even the treachery of a very silly sister, spoil the best moment of her life.

38

Kath's words had hit Bridget like a slap in the face and bounced around inside her head for the rest of the day and all the next night. The more she thought about it, the more she realised Kath was right. She was so busy yearning for what her sister had, and feeling hard done by, that she couldn't appreciate what she did have.

When she'd walked into the kitchen and found Mike and Kath waiting for her, Bridget's first thought was the fear of Ned discovering what she'd done. She suddenly realised that she might lose him and possibly the children too, because of her foolishness. Ned was easygoing and genial but he was also a man of great principle — he would be deeply hurt by her not telling him about the pregnancy. And he would never forgive her for the rest of it. He wouldn't believe her if she said she loved him and not Mike Mulholland.

Because she wasn't in love with Mike. She was in love with the idea of love itself — the obsessive, all-consuming, incapacitating love she'd had for Mike and which he couldn't return. When he'd finished with her that love became frozen in time, undiminished by the passing of years and held up by Bridget as the romantic ideal. It had no relevance to real love, the type that survives the birth of children, financial ups and downs, the daily grind of domestic life and growing old together. In other words the sort of gentle, enduring, forgiving love that she shared with Ned.

There were flaws in their relationship of course, as there were in every marriage. She had a tendency to play the martyr, grumbling about her lot but never actually making a stand. If Ned did play too much golf or she felt he didn't help around the home, it was time she acted like a grown-up and had a sensible adult conversation about it with him — like when she took a stand about working outside the home. Not her usual sulking and giving him the silent treatment. And if her marriage lacked passion, there were things they could do to spice it up. She simply hadn't tried.

But it was not too late to put things right. Thank God her lies had been discovered before any real damage had been done — apart from her relationship with Kath. She realised that she no longer cared what Mike Mulholland thought of her.

The first thing she had to do was tell Ned about the baby and put her foot down about how the McVey household was going to accommodate the new arrival. Her days of being the general dogsbody were over and all of them, including the children, were going to have to pull their weight.

Kath was a trickier problem. Bridget was desperate for her forgiveness but, from the way Kath had looked at her, she guessed it would not be easily forthcoming. She realised what a fool she'd been. She had never considered that Kath might envy her and yet that was what Kath had said, hadn't she? 'What wouldn't I give to have what you have,' she'd said — or words to that effect. The fact that Kath envied Bridget her life suddenly made it so much more desirable to Bridget herself.

That night, when the children were all asleep, Ned was lying in bed reading a golfing magazine. Bridget came out of the en-suite bathroom, dressed in a silk robe, and stood in front of the dressing-table taking off her jewellery.

'Have you seen John Routledge, then?' said Ned, without glancing up. He turned the page of the magazine.

'No.' Bridget took off one of her large diamond studs, a present from Ned on her thirtieth birthday, and placed it in the jewellery box. 'Not since work last Thursday.'

'How do you feel about it — about having him as a half-brother?'

'It doesn't bother me in the least. I'm actually quite glad that it's all out in the open now. It proves that Dad wasn't the big hero the rest of the family seemed to think he was.'

'You really didn't like your dad much, did you?'

'I didn't like some of the things he did,' she said, placing the other earring beside its partner and staring at her reflection in the mirror.

She saw an overweight woman of unremarkable looks with lank brown hair. From her mother she had inherited her slightly large nose and from her father the puffy bags under the eyes that no amount of expensive eyecream, or

570

well-applied make-up, could entirely disguise. They became even more pronounced with each passing year — she would have to resort to plastic surgery if they got any worse.

'I just don't think he liked me very much,' she said.

'I'm sure that's not true, Bridget,' said Ned, this time lowering the journal onto the bedcover.

Bridget took off her rings and heavy gold bracelet. 'I don't think he was as impartial as he should've been,' she said carefully, still facing the mirror. 'I don't think, for example, that he cared for me as much as he did for Kath.'

'Oh, darling,' said Ned, 'I don't believe that for one minute. How could anyone not adore you?'

Bridget blushed with embarrassment, knowing she was not worthy of Ned's love. 'I'll tell you what though,' she said, wondering what she had done to make this clever, kind man love her, 'I was far more upset by the news about Murray.'

'Yes,' said Ned gravely. 'That was very disturbing. I really feel for David. I can't imagine what he must be going through right now. Imagine finding out that a child you raised as your own wasn't yours?'

Remembering her own recent fabrications, Bridget refrained from criticising Viv. Who was she to judge, after what she'd done?

'David is just devastated,' she said, turning now to face Ned. 'Thank God he's got Simone to look after him and the baby to focus on, or I really would be concerned that he might do something silly.'

571

Ned nodded gravely.

Bridget took off her gown and hung it on a hook behind the door, standing on tiptoes to reach it. She was wearing a short pink silk nightdress with spaghetti straps. She never wore pyjamas — they made her look like an elephant.

When she turned round again Ned was looking at her admiringly. Self-consciously she walked quickly to her side of the bed and slipped under the covers. She lay on her back, pulled the covers up to her chin and stared at the ceiling. Her heart pounded so hard she could almost hear it.

'Ned,' she said. 'How would you feel about another baby?'

He leaned up on his elbow and looked down into her face. 'Do you want to try?' he said eagerly and then his expression darkened. 'But wait a minute. A few months ago you said you didn't want one. What's happened to change your mind?'

'Let's just say events have taken an unexpected turn.'

'Come again?'

'I'm pregnant,' she said.

Immediately a big happy smile spread across Ned's face and he placed his hand on the bedcovers, over her stomach. He kissed her on the nose and said, 'I'm absolutely delighted. Imagine another wee tiddler running around! Won't it be great?'

'Yes, it will. But some things are going to have to change.'

'Like what?' said Ned, his eyes narrowing and the smile fading a little.

'I'm really enjoying my job, Ned, and I don't want to give it up. I know it's only part-time and it doesn't earn much, but it's getting me out there in the real world, meeting people and doing something I enjoy.'

'I understand that,' said Ned, nodding and pursing his lips sagely.

'I know I'll have to take maternity leave but I'd really like to go back to work as soon as possible, say after six or nine months, just for a couple of mornings a week.'

'By the time you pay for childcare it'll hardly be worth it.'

'Maybe not financially. But it'll be worth it for my sanity, Ned. Believe me, I'm not really cut out to be an at-home full-time mum. I thought I was and I've tried it, but I need something more. I'll be a better mother and a happier person for it.'

'So what did you mean when you said that some things would have to change?'

'I meant at home,' said Bridget and she held her breath.

'In what way?'

'I need more help round the house. I can't be standing until one and two in the morning doing the ironing, for example. Now, whether we pay someone to come in and help, or whether you and the children pull your weight a bit more, I don't really care. But I can't continue taking responsibility for the entire family on my shoulders.'

'But I thought you were managing OK,' said Ned.

'I was, just about, but it's been a struggle. And with a new baby, well, basically the old order has got to change.'

Ned thought long and hard for a few moments and then said, 'Do you know what, Bridget, I think you might be right. I've noticed that the children aren't terribly independent. And I think that we've made them that way, doing everything for them. Alex should be capable of making a simple meal, but he doesn't even know how to boil an egg. And Laura's incapable of making her bed or putting clothes in the laundry basket.'

'That's my fault, isn't it?' said Bridget, feeling like she was a crap mother.

'No, no, it's not and I didn't mean it that way,' said Ned hastily. 'We're both to blame. I don't set a very good example, do I?'

Bridget smiled for the first time since her altercation with Kath. 'No,' she said laughing. 'Sometimes you're worse than the kids.'

'No, I'm not!'

'Yes, you are. When did you last change an empty loo roll?'

'Mmm, you have a point there.'

'And I'd like you to take more of an active interest in the children's homework and after-school activities. Sometimes I feel it's all down to me.'

'OK, I can do that.'

'So what do you think we should do?' said Bridget, even though she had a very clear idea of how they should proceed.

'How about we start with a rota for simple chores like emptying the bins, setting the table for dinner, clearing up after meals — that sort of thing?' said Ned, surprising her. 'And then we can take it from there as the kids — as we all — get used to doing more around the house.'

'Oh, Ned,' said Bridget, almost crying with relief, 'that sounds just perfect to me.'

'Right then! The new regime starts tomorrow. But you have to accept that things won't be done to your standards, Bridget. Especially when the children do things. You'll have to learn to live with that.'

'I will. I promise I will,' said Bridget, and silent tears ran out of the corners of her eyes. 'Cross my heart and hope to die, I won't say a word.'

⋆　⋆　⋆

Going to work on Monday morning was hard — Bridget was dreading it. She wished she had had the courage to go round to Kath's yesterday and seek her forgiveness, but she also sensed that any approach would have been rebuffed. Kath had been so angry that Bridget guessed she needed time to simmer down.

And right enough Kath treated Bridget with a faux-genial reserve that was disturbing both for its forced brightness and subtle chilliness.

'Good morning,' chirped Kath with a smile on her face that looked like it had been pasted there with glue. Her eyes were cold as ice.

The office was neither the time nor the place to have the conversation that Bridget so needed to have with Kath, so she tried to concentrate on her work — compiling a computer list of prospects for the festive season. But her stomach churned with anxiety and she could not concentrate. The air was thick with tension and any conversation from Kath was strictly limited to business.

Bridget was quite sure Moira must have noticed Kath's cool manner towards her, but Moira, tactful as always, carried on as though nothing was amiss.

By mid-morning Bridget's shoulders were aching from pent-up tension and the physical act of sitting hunched in front of the computer screen. She was relieved when it was time for morning break. Normally she took her break at her desk, chatting to Moira and Kath over a coffee, but today she had another important task to do.

She sought out John and asked him to take a turn about the garden with her. It had rained in the night and the sky was still grey so they stuck to the gravel paths that dissected the lawns. Tommy was kneeling on a plastic bag on the grass by the pergola — he glanced up briefly and waved when they entered the garden.

'Tell me about your relationship with Dad,' said Bridget and she listened while John told her the story of his life. Bridget was struck by the love and respect he displayed for Brendan and she felt guilty for not sharing those sentiments with the same intensity. He had, after all, far more reason to be angry with Brendan than she had.

'But weren't you angry when you found out?' she said, as they crunched along the pebble pathway.

'Oh, yes, I was very upset,' he said, matching her slow pace, with his hands shoved into his trouser pockets. 'But after my dad — Dennis Routledge, I mean — died, we became quite close.'

'But you had every reason to hate him. After what he did to your mum and refusing to make your relationship public.'

'Brendan kept me secret to protect my mother from scandal.'

'And to protect himself,' said Bridget dryly. 'My mother would've left him, I'm sure, if it had gone public.'

'Well, we don't know what might have been, Bridget,' he said wisely. 'We just have to deal with the here and now.'

'You're very forgiving, John.' Bridget stopped and looked into his face. 'I wish I could be more like you.'

'Well, I've found that harbouring resentment is a pointless exercise. It serves no purpose only to make you bitter and unhappy.'

'You're right, John. You're absolutely right,' said Bridget as a plan took hold in her mind. She put her hand on John's upper arm and said, 'How about you come to dinner sometime soon and meet the kids properly? I want to introduce them to their Uncle John.'

'I'd love that more than anything,' said John with a grateful smile and, linking arms, together they returned to the hotel.

As the rest of the morning came to a painfully slow close, Bridget created the illusion of business without achieving anything at all. She sneaked glances at a grim-faced Kath, who caught her looking once and glared back unsmiling. Bridget blushed and looked quickly away.

She couldn't continue to come to work under these conditions. They would have to have to talk soon.

When, at last, it was time to go home Bridget switched off the computer, put her bag over her shoulder and said, 'Well, that's me off then. Bye, everyone.'

Moira looked up briefly from her work and said goodbye. As she passed Kath's desk, Bridget said, 'Will you be at home tonight?'

'I might.'

'Well, if it's OK with you I'll call around eight,' said Bridget and, without waiting for an answer, she left the room.

That night at just past eight o'clock she knocked nervously on the farmhouse door and it was answered immediately by Kath. She was wearing a pair of grey sweat-pants and a coral-coloured strappy vest top layered over a white vest.

Kath said, 'You'd better come in,' and left Bridget to follow her into the house and close the door behind her.

Bridget took off her linen jacket and hung it over the newel post at the bottom of the staircase. It felt strange being in the house that she'd visited so often when she and Mike were dating. That time felt like a lifetime ago.

She went into the lounge where Kath was standing in front of the empty fireplace with her arms folded, glaring at her with glassy eyes, her head cocked slightly to one side.

Bridget sighed and sat down on the sofa. 'Come and sit with me,' she said, patting the seat beside her.

'I'm OK here,' said Kath flatly.

'Please don't be angry with me, Kath.' Bridget nervously fingered the pendant hanging from a silver chain around her neck.

'How can I not be angry with you, Bridget?' said Kath, her chest rising and falling rapidly. 'Put yourself in my shoes. How do you think you would feel?'

'All I can say is that I'm sorry, Kath. I'm so very sorry.'

'The lie's not the worst of it. Though it was completely bloody terrible. It's knowing that you despise me so much you actually dreamt up a scheme like that to hurt me.'

'I didn't plan it!' cried Bridget. 'I told you how it was! It just came out of my mouth before I even had time to think about it. And I don't despise you.'

'What about afterwards then? You could have retracted it.'

Bridget looked at the floor, unable to meet her sister's gaze any longer. Her cheeks burned with shame. 'I told you why I did it,' she mumbled. 'And I don't know what I was thinking of. I must've been partly deranged. What happened between Mike and me is over and done with. It's in the past now. I think I was under a lot of stress worrying about the baby and how I would cope. Ned's no help at home. Though,' she added hastily, 'I know that's no excuse for what I did.'

'Have you told Ned yet?' demanded Kath.

'Yes,' said Bridget, meeting her sister's icy gaze again. 'We've talked about things and I think everything's going to be OK. He says that he and the kids are going to help more around the house and I'm going to keep working.' She paused and blinked back the tears. 'That's if you'll have me back.'

'What did you come here for?' said Kath, her eyes narrowing into slits.

Bridget swallowed and said, 'To ask for your forgiveness. I can't bear it if you hate me.'

Kath unfolded her arms and sat down suddenly on the edge of the chair by the window. She rested her elbows on her knees and joined her hands together as if in prayer. She stared at the faded rug on the floor.

'I came back here to get away from Carl and his lies, to start a new life amongst people I thought I could trust,' she said, the anger gone from her voice. 'I never thought my own sister would lie to me and hurt me like this.' She lifted her eyes to look at Bridget and they were full of tears. 'I had fallen in love with Mike,' she went on, her voice choked. 'And you knew that, didn't you?'

Bridget looked at the floor, engulfed by shame at the pain she had inflicted. 'I'd do anything to take back what I did Kath,' she whispered. 'Please believe me.'

'I still love you, Bridget. You're my sister.'

Bridget felt the relief rush through her body.

'But I'm still very angry. I think I'm going to find it very hard to trust you again.'

'What,' said Bridget gently, and she tried to calm her irregular breathing, 'can I do to make you believe in me again?'

Kath said, sadly, 'I don't know. But I think you should get counselling for a start. For the way you envy me and the issues you have with Dad. You seem to think that you were hard done by and I don't know if that was really the case. I think your perception's a bit skewed.' She sighed and went on, 'Even if it was true, you have to come to terms with it, Bridget — none of us can change the past. And maybe you haven't got over Dad's death yet — I know I haven't. All I know is that if this is how you react when you're under pressure, who's to say you won't crack again?'

Perhaps Kath was right, thought Bridget. Maybe it would help to talk to someone detached and objective about her deepest thoughts and fears, things she couldn't discuss with Ned, her family or her friends. She wasn't entirely convinced that Kath was correct — she *had* been her father's favourite but Kath couldn't see it.

Still, if she learnt to let go of the past, thought Bridget, then maybe she could rid herself of the envy that dictated the nature of her entire relationship with Kath. They could form a new and better one, based on honesty, love and mutual respect rather than a relationship rooted in the past.

'OK. I'll do it. I want us to be friends, Kath. I want us to be proper sisters.'

'So do I.'

The two women stood up simultaneously and embraced each other briefly, then pulled apart.

'It's going to take time, you know that, don't you?' said Kath.

'I know,' said Bridget, grateful for the thawing in Kath's demeanour. 'But we'll get there. I know we will.'

Outside the front door, Bridget turned suddenly and said, 'What about you and Mike?'

Kath smiled the sort of smile you see on the faces of women in love — all coy and embarrassed looking. 'It looks like it might work out.'

Bridget smiled and said, 'That's great.' She thought momentarily of Mike. 'But what if Mike never forgives me, Kath?'

'He will. It's just going to take time, Bridget. For all of us.'

* * *

Simone had gone into Ballyfergus to do the weekly shopping that she hadn't managed to do on Friday because she'd been working overtime. David would have done it but he always came home with the wrong things, spent too much and forgot essential items. Simone preferred to do it herself.

David and Murray stayed behind in the cottage, the first time they'd been together alone since David had told Viv what he knew. He shuddered to think of that bitter, rancorous telephone conversation a few weeks previously. He had vented his anger freely, calling her a slut and a whore, a liar and a thief. He wasn't proud of himself — and it had done absolutely nothing to assuage his all-consuming grief.

And now he knew the time had come — indeed he could put it off no longer — when he must tell Murray the truth. He had spent many long hours trying to find the simple words to explain this shattering concept to a child of five.

In spite of his resolution that things would go on as normal, it had been two weeks since David had last seen Murray. He hadn't felt able to face him for nearly a month after the results of the test. Sullenly, Viv had agreed to this weekend stay, most likely because she had other plans and she wasn't likely to turn down the offer of a free babysitter.

David took Murray for a walk in the forest, waiting for the right moment to tell the boy what he had to hear and hoping that he would, somehow, find inspiration from nature.

It was a breezy day at the end of August and the late summer sun shone warm through the leaves, dappling the forest floor and their faces. The branches creaked with the weight of their lush foliage as though tired of carrying the burden. Soon they would begin to shed their leaves and autumn would be here.

Murray ran ahead, ignoring David's pleas to stick to the path and not to pick the unripe nuts off the hazel trees. But David did not chastise him. He no longer tried to discipline him the way he used to. It wasn't that he didn't care — it was simply that he felt Murray would face enough hardship in life, without David being on his back all the time. The friction that had once characterised their relationship was gone.

Back in the cottage, David made ham sandwiches for lunch. He sat at the table and watched Murray munch on a sandwich, unable to eat himself. He wondered who the child's father was and found himself searching Murray's face for a prominent feature that might give a clue to his real parentage. There was, of course, the hair — the double crown — but he couldn't think of anyone of their acquaintance who shared Murray's 'swirlies'.

'Why are you looking at me like that, Dad?'

'Like what?' said David, picking up the sandwich in front of him and taking a bite. It felt like sawdust in his mouth.

'I dunno,' said Murray with a shrug of his slight shoulders and a shy smile.

Murray was usually at his calmest and most attentive after he'd eaten. David watched the sandwich disappear into his mouth as though it was an hourglass counting away the minutes. His mouth was dry and the hairs on the back of his neck stood up with fear. He watched Murray chew and swallow the last bite of food.

'Can I leave the table now?' said Murray, forgetting to say please.

'Not just yet,' said David, and he moistened his lips with his tongue. 'I want to talk to you.' His hands started to tremble and he hid them under the table. 'There's something that I have to tell you, Murray. Something that I wish I didn't have to and that I wish wasn't true.'

Murray shifted in his seat and looked bored. David realised he was losing him.

'Murray,' he said. 'I'm not your Dad.'

Murray frowned crossly and folded his arms. 'But that's what Mummy said. She said that you don't want to be my daddy any more.'

'Oh, Murray,' said David and he felt like he'd just been punched under the ribs, 'it's not a question of not wanting to. I'm just not.'

'But you are, Dad.'

'No. I know you call me 'Dad' and you think I'm your dad, but I'm not your real dad.'

Murray's eyebrows creased into a frown and he pouted his lips.

'Murray . . . do you understand what it means to be a real dad?'

'I know how babies are made,' said Murray proudly.

'That's good.'

'The mummy and daddy put their sperm together and that makes babies.'

Under other circumstances David would have laughed. Instead he smiled gently and said, 'That's right, Murray. Well, close enough anyway. You know the time when Mummy made you in her tummy?'

Murray nodded.

'She didn't use my sperm, she used someone else's.'

Murray stared at David, looking bewildered.

'So you see, because Mummy didn't use my

sperm to make you, you can't be my son. That means I'm not your dad.' He paused, praying that the child understood.

'How come mummy used the wrong sperm?'

'She just did. She . . . eh . . . she sort of made a mistake. No, that's not quite right. Maybe that's something I'll have to explain to you when you're a bit older and you can understand it properly,' said David, realising that his explanation was inadequate. But how could you explain such things to a child?

There was a pause then, while David waited for a reaction, and Murray said, 'Who is my daddy then?'

'I don't know. You'll have to ask your mum that.'

'Is it Brian?'

'Who's Brian?'

'Mummy's friend.'

David paused and then said carefully, 'Does Mummy see Brian a lot?'

'Every day,' said Murray and laughed. 'He sleeps in Mummy's bed.'

'I see,' said David slowly.

'I don't like Brian very much. He says I shouldn't come here any more.' Murray's head drooped slightly towards his chest. 'Can I go and play with my Tamagotchi now?'

'Yes. In a minute, Murray,' said David and he paused, barely able to speak. He hated Viv. He hated himself for having to do this. 'I want you to know that I wish with all my heart that you were my son. And you can come here as long as your mummy allows you to. I love you.'

Murray slid off the chair without making eye

586

contact and soon David could hear the shrill pips and bleeps of the Tamagotchi coming from the other room. David did not go after him.

He had said what he had been compelled to say. What he could not stop himself from saying. But he found no peace or comfort in the telling. His relationship with Murray, he suddenly realised, was altered forever.

He would buy Murray gifts and continue to be good to him, but he feared that Viv would only agree to visits as long as it suited her. He looked into the future and saw how contact with Murray would dwindle and then, one day, perhaps stop altogether.

If and when Viv married this Brian or someone else, she would not want David hanging around as a reminder of her past. She would want a fresh start. And perhaps that was what was best for Murray too. Maybe one day he would meet his real dad, a father who would love him. But, in spite of the rather happy ending to the story of Brendan and John Routledge, David knew this to be unlikely. He also knew that he could not pretend that his feelings towards Murray were unchanged.

He still loved him but not as fiercely, not as possessively, as before. He could not pretend to be what he wasn't. He hung his head and wished with all his heart that he was a better man.

He tried to focus on all the good things in his life: Simone, the new baby, his family and John Routledge, the brother he never had. Because, if he thought about Murray for much longer, he was certain that his heart would break.

39

Kath and Mike sat shoulder to shoulder on the hard concrete slipway at Ballygally beach, on a tartan rug. The sun had disappeared behind the hills over an hour ago and now dusk was beginning to fall. The deserted beach was peppered with black rocks, large and small, and it seemed to Kath much smaller and stonier than she remembered as a child, when an excursion here had provided an entire day's entertainment. Behind them, in the low stone-walled car park, Mike's Land Rover was one of the few cars remaining and the post office, the only shop in the village, had closed hours ago.

The tide was coming in — the blue-black water nibbled at the sand, colourless in the failing light, as it crept stealthily up the beach. To their left was the old stone boathouse, which Kath had often fantasised about turning into a summerhouse so that she could live, and play, on the beach all summer long. It had been converted into an artist's studio — a fitting transformation in a landscape so beloved of painters, both amateur and professional.

A little further along the road, the lighted windows and turrets of the fairy-tale Ballygally Castle Hotel glowed warm and welcoming in the twilight. With only a few miles between this hotel and the Sallagh Braes, Kath had worried that there might not be room for two successful hotels on this section of the coast. But her fears had proved unfounded — the response of local people to the reopened Sallagh Braes had been extremely positive and the hotel was now exceeding Kath's original business forecasts. She'd stopped worrying about it — it was going to be a success.

The Ballygally Castle Hotel dated back to 1625 and was the only lived-in seventeenth-century building in Northern Ireland. Local people said it was haunted and Kath still half-believed the rumours, which used to terrify her as a child, of a woman in white seen only in one of the turret rooms. She shivered and pulled her grey cropped cardigan, loose-knit like a spider's web, and just as holey, round her frame.

'Do you remember when Lough Brothers used to have a café here?' said Kath.

'God, yeah! Those chips were the best thing in the world after a day spent on the beach.'

'And the whippy ice-creams! I used to think one of those with a Flake in it was sheer heaven.'

Mike nodded and smiled. 'And now it's just a post office and a little shop. Seems a shame.'

'People don't come here so much, not the way they used to. Bridget rarely brings the children, you know,' said Kath. She pulled her knees up, encircling her legs with her arms, and rested her chin on them. 'You could count on one hand the number of times they've been down here this summer. She says they get bored. Can you imagine?'

'Kids nowadays all want to be playing on their computers, Gameboys and God knows what else. I think we were better at making our own entertainment.'

Kath pondered this for a moment, wondering what sort of a dad Mike would make. A good one, she thought — she hoped he would have the chance to try.

'How are you and Bridget getting on these days?' said Mike, disturbing her thoughts.

'OK,' said Kath slowly, experiencing the little stab of hurt — or was it disappointment? — that she still got when Bridget's name was mentioned. 'I'm still a bit wary of her, though. I don't completely trust her yet — maybe I never will. Though she seems a lot happier within herself. I think she and Ned had a lot of issues to sort out but they seem to be addressing them.' She paused and then said, 'And what about you, Mike. Have you forgiven her?'

Mike picked up a small stone and launched it expertly at the sea — it bounced twice on the surface of the inky water and disappeared.

'I don't hold any grudge,' he said and Kath felt a little of her anxiety unravel. 'To tell you the truth, I just think she's a wee bit unstable. She was very intense when we were dating — to be honest it scared me a bit. But she's not a malicious person by nature, sure she's not?'

'No, if anything she's the opposite. Generous and kind to a fault.'

'So I think that what happened was just some sort of aberration. A one-off. She was very contrite about it when she came to apologise to me. I actually felt sorry for her.'

'Good. I'm glad you think like that, Mike,

because it's important to me that you and Bridget get along. It would make me feel very uncomfortable if there were friction between you two.'

'There isn't,' said Mike firmly. 'She didn't stop us getting together, did she? So, thankfully, no harm was done.'

'No,' said Kath dreamily and she leaned her head against Mike's shoulder. 'Although I wish I could say the same about Murray and David. I think the damage caused is irreparable.'

'So what's happening there? Does David still see him?'

'Well, he saw Murray a few times after the test result, but now Viv's got this boyfriend — a rough sort of character by all accounts — and he's trying to stop Murray from seeing David.'

'What's it got to do with him? Is he the father?'

'Apparently not. I think he just doesn't like the idea of David being around. And Viv's so pathetic she just does what this Brian says. And of course David has no rights as far as Murray is concerned even though, in practice, he's been his dad for nearly six year ... seven, actually, counting the pregnancy ... and kept up maintenance payments even after he and Viv split. Well, that may in fact give him some rights but he would have to go to court to establish them and that would create too much rancour.'

'I'm sorry, Kath. It's a terrible mess.'

'It is. I really feel for David and I feel even more for little Murray. I left a present round at Viv's for his birthday next week and she didn't even invite me in. She brought Murray to the door to say hello but that was about it. It's so — so hurtful. I can only imagine the damage it's doing to Murray.'

'They say children are pretty resilient.'

'I hope so, Mike. Because that wee boy's got a lot to cope with.'

There was a silence then and Kath let out a long sigh. 'To tell you the truth, Mike, I'm worn out worrying about my family. Let's not talk about them any more.'

'OK,' he said and they both fell silent.

'Do you remember when we were teenagers and everyone used to come down here in the summer and hang out?' said Kath, after a few moments. 'You couldn't get into the car park for all the boy racers and the girls strutting their stuff.'

'Yeah, I used to watch you.'

'You did not! You're only saying that.'

'No, it's true Kath. I fancied you even then.'

'You never let on.'

'I knew you wouldn't look at me.'

Kath thought back to Mike's unfortunate hairstyle, bad skin and crushing shyness, which he seemed to have shed with maturity. He was right — back then she wouldn't have given him a second glance.

'It was that hair,' she said and nudged him with her elbow. 'You looked like one of the Beatles gone wrong!'

'Oh God,' said Mike with a grin, 'don't remind me.' He leaned in towards her and gave her a gentle shove.

They sat on in silence for a few moments longer, staring out into the darkness, and then Kath said, 'I guess we'd better be getting back. My bum's gone to sleep.'

'Let's sit a little longer,' said Mike and he touched the back of her hand lightly. 'You're cold! Here put this round you.' He took off his jacket — a casual, linen-mix affair — and draped it across her shoulders. It was warm from the heat of his body. Something heavy weighed down the right-hand side pocket.

'Now you'll get cold,' she said.

'I don't feel it,' he replied and his teeth shone white in the gathering gloom. He rested his elbows on his knees, his legs splayed apart and said quietly, 'I loved you even then.'

The only sound was the lapping of the water on the beach and the slipway, and the soft rush of the retreating waves. A car passed on the road above, roaring like a juggernaut through the stillness.

'Kath,' said Mike when it was quiet again, 'I know that we've only been dating properly for a few weeks . . . '

He paused and Kath waited. She felt giddy, as though she'd just come off a fairground ride. Was he about to say what she had hoped to hear for so long? He turned sideways to face her, leaning now on his right hand which was spread-eagled on the cold concrete. His face was illuminated by the orange glow of the streetlamps on the road above.

'Will you marry me?' he said and Kath felt the tension inside her explode.

'Of course I will!' she cried and threw her arms around him. They fell backwards onto the hard ground, their bodies entwined. She pressed her lips to his and they kissed hungrily.

He cradled the back of her head with his strong hand, holding her as though she was something precious and fragile. Kath stroked his broad back and shoulders, taking pleasure in the solidness of his body and the contours of the muscles underneath her fingers. She longed to be at home right now, making love.

At last they pulled apart, looked at each other and laughed.

Mike said, 'That's killing my back!'

'Mine too!'

They sat up and grinned at each other. Mike's face was creased with smiles and Kath felt as though she would burst with happiness. She felt wet tears on her cheeks.

'Don't,' he said and he wiped them away gently with work-roughened fingers.

'I'm just so happy.'

He smiled and said, 'So am I.' Then, after a short pause, 'I not going to buy you an engagement ring, Kath.'

'Oh!' she said, suddenly disappointed. 'It — it doesn't matter,' she added hastily, realising that this was not true. She told herself not to be so silly, so shamelessly romantic. What did a circle of gold matter when they had each other? When Mike loved her? But somehow it did.

'I got you something that I think you'll like much better,' he said.

Kath couldn't think of anything she wanted

right now more than an engagement ring — public proof of Mike's love for her and their commitment to each other.

He leaned over and grabbed his jacket, which had slid from Kath's shoulders onto the rug. He put his hand in one of the pockets and pulled something out. Kath heard the jangle of keys and her first thought was that they were car keys. Had he bought her a car as an engagement gift instead of a ring? Her heart sank a little. If Mike thought that her heart's desire lay in a new car then maybe they weren't so compatible after all . . .

'Open your hand, love,' he said gently and she obeyed without taking her eyes off his. In the dimming light she could not see them clearly, but the expression on his face was deadly serious.

He held her right hand in his left one and pressed a set of cold keys into her palm. He folded her fingers over them and, suddenly, she realised that there were too many for a set of car keys and, furthermore, some of them were too big. They felt more like a set of house keys. Had he bought them a house already without consulting her? Her heartbeat quickened.

'What have you done, Mike?' she said, full of apprehension.

He rubbed his chin with his thumb, looked down at her hand and said without smiling, 'Look at them.'

Slowly, Kath unfurled her fingers and stared. She saw a familiar red-enamelled key fob in the shape of a heart. She started to tremble uncontrollably but it had nothing to do with the cold.

'It can't be,' she said softly, certain that it was just a coincidence that the fob was the same as the one that used to hang from her mother's keys.

And yet, when she looked more closely, the keys were similar to those for Highfield House. Two long aged ones, two short shinier brass ones for a Yale lock. Just exactly like the keys for Highfield.

She started to cry.

'Are you angry with me?' he said.

She looked up and, through her tears, she saw him bite his bottom lip. She shook her head, unable to speak.

'I thought it was what you would want, Kath. Was I wrong?'

Again she shook her head, swallowed and said, 'No, no, you weren't wrong. Far from it. This is — it's the best present in the world! Better than an engagement ring by a million miles.' She smiled and held the keys, encircled in both hands, to her chest. 'But I don't understand,' she said, puzzlement now beginning to replace the euphoria. 'How did you get the house?'

'I bought it at the auction. I did it through an agent so you wouldn't find out it was me.'

'But why? That was months ago — long before we got together. Long before we fell in love.'

'But I told you I always loved you, didn't I, Kath? And I knew how much the house meant to you and your family, and how it broke your heart when it had to be sold. I knew that one day I would ask you to marry me and I couldn't stand by and watch it be sold to someone else.'

'But why did you keep it a secret for so long?'

'I didn't know if you were going to go back to Carl and then you gave me the cold shoulder over Anne. Though of course I didn't know at the time that was what it was all about. I thought that you didn't care for me.'

'I'm sorry about that,' said Kath, and then she frowned. 'But what would you have done with the house if I'd said no, Mike?'

He shrugged his shoulders. 'I don't know. I hadn't thought that far ahead. I just couldn't imagine a life without you, Kath.'

'Oh, Mike,' she said and sighed, her heart aching with happiness at this reckless romantic gesture. 'This is the most loving thing that anyone has ever done for me. You have made me the happiest woman in the world.'

Then she leaned forward on her knees and kissed him tenderly on the lips.

'And I love you for it,' she said.

★ ★ ★

It was a cold, windswept Monday morning in late January, exactly a year to the day that Brendan O'Connor took his own life. Up on the Braes, away from the warming influence of the sea, the remains of last night's snowfall were still visible, like daubs of white paint applied by a child on the landscape. And the sky, blue-grey with heavy clouds, threatened more snow.

Kath pulled her scarf tightly round her neck

and shivered in the nipping wind. She looked around at the little family gathered in a circle on the wet grass to pay their respects to the man who, for all his faults, they had loved.

There was Bridget standing by Ned, her swollen stomach protruding beneath a long black wool coat. And beside her, the children, warmly wrapped up against the foul weather, looking glum-faced.

The past few months had seen a gradual improvement in Kath's relationship with Bridget. They made a point of going out together, just the two of them, once a month and the effort had paid off. Kath had come to know her sister, not as the self-assured, assertive person she presented to the world, but as an essentially shy, rather nice woman lacking in self-confidence.

The counselling sessions seemed to be helping her overcome the crippling insecurity that she had suffered from childhood. And Kath liked her a whole lot better for it.

Bridget caught Kath looking at her and they smiled at each other — poignant smiles, but ones full of hope and forgiveness.

Next there was Simone, standing beside David, plump and happy-looking in spite of the bags under her eyes caused by lack of sleep. She held onto the handle of a pram chassis onto which was clipped a grey-and-blue checked car seat. She never took her eyes off the treasured bundle inside it, so well wrapped up in pink clothes and blankets and shielded by the rain-cover that her new baby daughter was invisible. Kath smiled and hoped that she too, one day soon, would have a child of her own to fret and fuss over.

David was just as bad as Simone, glancing anxiously at his new daughter every few seconds, his brow creased, no doubt worrying if it was too cold for her to be outside. But his anxious concern was a good sign, Kath thought. She hoped it would help him to come to terms with the grief of losing Murray — a loss as real, and just as painful, as bereavement.

On his arm, sandwiched between him and John Routledge, was Fiona, standing erect and ladylike in black suede boots, a sensible black felt hat and matching coat. John leaned towards her, said something and she smiled, placing her gloved hand momentarily on his forearm.

Kath was full of admiration for her mother — she had survived the death of her husband, the loss of her home, her husband's infidelity and finding out the truth about Murray. And, against all Kath's expectations, she had welcomed John, her stepson, into the family with kindness and graciousness. She was truly an inspiring woman.

And then there was Mike, standing at Kath's side where he would be all the rest of her days. She looked into his face, almost level with hers because of her high-heeled black leather boots, and he squeezed her hand. He had restored in her the trust that Carl had so brutally ripped out.

For many long months she had thought that she would never trust a man again. But Mike was no ordinary man. And who would've thought that the happiness she had sought so far away in Boston was to be found much, much closer to home . . .

David read out the words of the *Our Father* in a voice that stumbled only once. Then he lifted up a small hammer with a black rubber handle and hammered a small brass plaque onto the tree.

Kath felt spots of icy rain on her face.

Fiona, referring to her newest grandchild, said, 'Angela's been out in the cold long enough. Let's go in for lunch.' She went up to the tree, touched it briefly and said, 'Goodbye, Brendan.' Then she mouthed a few silent words, turned and walked away.

The others followed suit, each privately saying their goodbyes to Brendan. Even the children participated, though Kath could see that it took Laura and Alex all their self-control not to break down in tears. Charmaine cried freely and Ned led her away with his arms around her shoulders.

At last just Kath and Mike were left.

'You go on in,' she said. 'I'll be along in a minute.'

'OK,' he said and she loved the way he respected her need to be alone for a few moments. He kissed her lightly on the nose and followed the others back to the hotel, his shoulders hunched against the cold.

Kath removed her glove and placed her bare hand on the rough bark of the tree. Inscribed on the shiny plaque, in black writing, were the words: '*In memory of Brendan O'Connor, a beloved husband, father, grandpa and friend. Always loved and never forgotten. 30 January 2005.'*

She looked up through the stark black branches of the tree at the grey, swollen sky.

'I love you, Dad. And you don't need to worry. Because, do you know what?'

She paused as though listening for an answer on the wind.

'We're all going to be just fine.'

THE END

We do hope that you have enjoyed reading this large print book.

Did you know that all of our titles are available for purchase?

We publish a wide range of high quality large print books including:
Romances, Mysteries, Classics
General Fiction
Non Fiction and Westerns

Special interest titles available in large print are:
The Little Oxford Dictionary
Music Book
Song Book
Hymn Book
Service Book

Also available from us courtesy of Oxford University Press:
Young Readers' Dictionary
(large print edition)
Young Readers' Thesaurus
(large print edition)

For further information or a free brochure, please contact us at:
Ulverscroft Large Print Books Ltd.,
The Green, Bradgate Road, Anstey,
Leicester, LE7 7FU, England.
Tel: (00 44) 0116 236 4325
Fax: (00 44) 0116 234 0205

SECOND CHANCES

Erin Kaye

Roisin Shaw hasn't forgiven the smug Donal Mullan for what he did to her sister Ann-Marie, and she's determined to make him pay for it . . . But Donal's perfect marriage to Michelle, daughter of the wealthy McCormicks, isn't all it appears. He's facing the most difficult decision of his life. What will he do? . . . Pauline McCormick has had enough of her philandering husband, Noel. When she meets the handsome sculptor, Padraig Flynn, sparks fly and Noel gets a wake-up call. But does it come too late to save his marriage? . . . Hearts and marriages are broken, but everyone deserves a second chance. Who will find the happiness they've been searching for?

CHOICES

Erin Kaye

When Sheila gave birth to Claire she was just sixteen years of age. Persuaded by her family to give the baby up for adoption, this choice would affect her life — and the lives of those she loved — forever. Two decades later, Sheila and her older sister Eileen face heartache. Eileen's cancer has returned and Sheila can no longer live with the decision she made all those years ago. She wants her daughter back. But life is never that straightforward and Sheila's desperate yearning threatens to shatter family relationships. With her entire family in crisis, Sheila takes reckless measures to heal the wounds of the past.

MOTHERS AND DAUGHTERS

Erin Kaye

Catherine Meehan was born into a respectable working-class Roman Catholic family in Ballyfergus on the coast of Antrim. She is determined to flee the poverty, bigotry and antagonism that shaped her early years . . . Jayne Alexander is infused with the privileges that go with being part of a well-to-do Protestant family. Despite her self-assurance, she has a need for love and yearns for approval . . . From 1959 to 1984, the lives of the Meehan and Alexander families become inextricably linked, in moments of great passion and hatred, as deeply held loyalties are threatened.

ONE SUMMER

Rachel Billington

K, an English painter, has returned from Chile to attend the wedding of a girl he once loved to the point of obsession. But the wedding has been postponed. He drives to an hotel — a place he'd visited many years before — opens a bottle of champagne and, with it, a door to the past. When K first saw Claudia fourteen years earlier, he fell instantly and dangerously in love. He was already married and Claudia, a schoolgirl, was twenty-four years younger than him; their love proved to be ultimately destructive and tragic. Now K returns to find Claudia facing a very different future. But the past cannot easily be banished. As they are inexorably drawn towards each other, long-unanswered questions surface.

LIKE NOWHERE ELSE

Denyse Woods

When Vivien Quish arrives in the mystical city of Sana'a, her hope is to redeem her ruined dream of being a great traveller. The last thing she expects is to become embroiled in a passionate affair, but she finds herself falling for anthropologist Christian Linklater. However, Vivien is sure that they can have no future together. In the heat of the Yemeni desert, Vivien's love affairs — with a man and with a country — are challenged to their limits and she must rediscover the spirit she once had as a young woman. But on the eve of the Iraq war, Christian is in danger of being a victim of the clash between east and west, and she is finally forced to stop playing it safe.

SPARKLES

Louise Bagshawe

The opulent world of the Massot family,
wealthy owners of one of the last great
jewellery firms in Paris, was plunged into
confusion seven years ago when Pierre
Massot, its charismatic head, disappeared.
Now, his widow Sophie has decided that the
family and the firm must move on to survive.
But her enemies have other ideas, and a trail
of scandal waits to be uncovered which could
rip the Massots' world to shreds. What really
happened to Pierre, and what is the family
secret he tried to conceal? The answers lie in
the past, entangled in a maze of deception
and naked ambition. And the secrets of the
past shape the future — in a way no one
could ever have guessed.